THE GARNEAU BLOCK

THE GARNEAU
BLOCK

todd
babiak

McCLELLAND & STEWART

Library and Archives Canada Cataloguing in Publication

Babiak, Todd, 1972-
The Garneau block / Todd Babiak.

ISBN 13: 978-0-7710-0988-4
ISBN 10: 0-7710-0988-7

I. Title.

PS8553.A.2435G37 2006   C813'54   C2006-902554-1

We acknowledge the financial support of the Government of Canada through the
Book Publishing Industry Development Program and that of the Government of
Ontario through the Ontario Media Development Corporation's Ontario Book
Initiative. We further acknowledge the support of the Canada Council for the Arts
and the Ontario Arts Council for our publishing program.

Typeset in Garamond by M&S, Toronto
Printed and bound in Canada

This book is printed on acid-free paper that is 100% recycled,
ancient-forest friendly (100% post-consumer recycled).

McClelland & Stewart Ltd.
75 Sherbourne Street
Toronto, Ontario
M5A 2P9
www.mcclelland.com

1   2   3   4   5   10   09   08   07   06

For Gina and Avia

THE GARNEAU BLOCK

1

the coldest morning in recent memory

Madison Weiss woke to the smell of scorched dust and nearly wept. Though she had lived in Edmonton her whole life, and knew well that with September came the first blast of the furnace, Madison felt the city – at least the five houses on her block – deserved a year off. Summer had ended poorly, by anyone's estimation, and lying in her garage-sale bed, in the suite her father had built in the basement of 12 Garneau, Madison could see no romance in autumn.

The previous night, reading a new collection of nineteenth-century haikus, Madison had forgotten to close her curtain. Now the heatless sun splashed on the upper half of her bed, informing the engines of worry in her brain that a new day had begun. She would have preferred to construct a fort of darkness with her pillows, but she had to be at work in a few hours and the dizziness had arrived.

In the tiny half-bath, as she finished throwing up, Madison remembered:

> First autumn morning
> The mirror I stare into
> Shows my father's face.

And she threw up some more.

The secret to a comfortable pregnancy and an agreeable postpartum experience is regular exercise. Madison had learned this from Dr. Stevens, a former classmate at Old Scona. Of course, the fact that one of her teenage peers was a doctor, with an Audi and a husband and her own two-storey clinker-brick house overlooking the river valley, was reason enough to search the clinics of Edmonton for an aged gentleman with a British accent, loose jowls, and cold hands. But Madison trusted her doctor, Dr. Stevens, and by way of consolation she did have fat ankles and dry hair.

Madison put on her tights and shiny yellow running jacket. Now that the explosion of hormones in her body had begun its slow work on the size of her behind, Madison appreciated the utility of the rear flap that extended nearly to her knees. She ate a banana in the dimly lit kitchenette and watched a spider stitch its web outside the small window with a view of 10 Garneau's mustard-coloured vinyl siding. Mid-banana, she wondered about her baby's father, where he might be at this moment. Trois-Rivières? Prison?

At the door, Madison paused. The furnace had warned her that it would be the coldest morning in recent memory, so she took a moment to prepare herself. Madison closed her eyes and pretended it was February. In February a morning like this would be a miracle.

She stepped out into the September-February morning, breathed in the crisp air, and hurried back inside. Television beckoned. Surely there was something on besides bland cartoons and that program where they talk about Jesus and ask for your credit card information.

Soon, Madison would be thirty. She knew, from literature and television shows, that this was no way for a thirty-year-old single mother to behave. So she burst out the door again and down the cobblestone path to the sidewalk. Madison did not linger next to 10 Garneau, with its grey flowerbeds and small jungles of dandelion and chickweed. Potato-chip bags and Styrofoam coffee cups had blown into the yard, and were now trapped under the apple and plum trees Benjamin Perlitz had planted. Benjamin Perlitz, once the most patient and committed gardener in the neighbourhood. A two-week-old strip of yellow police tape, coated with dust, hung in the shrubbery. Madison glanced up at the second-floor window, into the darkness and silence of the room where he died, and turned away.

Leaves had already begun to change. Soon the North Saskatchewan River valley would be a brilliant orange and yellow, and her morning jog would smell of decomposition and moist soil. The air was clean and the long shadows cast by neighbourhood trees were like old friends.

Madison turned to press against the mountain ash tree in front of her parents' house for a calf stretch, and discovered a sheet of fresh white paper duct-taped to the bark. Since the night Benjamin Perlitz was shot and his wife and daughter disappeared into the secret grief of the city, Madison and her neighbours had become less likely to be surprised. But this was something. In all her years living under the regulatory shadow of the university, where it was strictly forbidden to affix advertisements, notices, and flyers on historically significant trees and lampposts, she had never seen such mutiny.

Laser-printed in capital letters, in a classic font: LET'S FIX IT.

Underneath, a date and time and the address for a downtown office tower. Madison knew instantly what Let's Fix It referred to, and understood she was implicated in the "us" of the apostrophe s.

Across the street, the philosophy professor, Raymond Terletsky, ripped a sheet off the tree in front of his house, 11 Garneau.

"What is this?"

The professor crossed the street, waving the sheet like a flag. He was dressed unfortunately, in a turquoise sweater that didn't quite cover the pink of his stomach. He was a tall man, with a slouch. His snug black pants, like all of his pants, displayed too much sock. Madison averted her eyes from Raymond Terletsky's ensemble and saw that identical sheets of paper were duct-taped to every tree and lamppost on the Garneau Block.

"What is this?" said Raymond. "Is this new? 'Let's Fix It'?"

"They weren't up last night when I came home from work." Madison turned to study the sheets in silence with the professor.

He stood a little too close for her taste. The professor's woody-fruity cologne was so powerful it threatened to give her a nosebleed. Raymond Terletsky smiled. "Someone is going to receive one hell of a fine for this." He turned and raised his voice, though no one seemed to be about. "*One hell* of a fine." Birdsong erupted, during which the professor waited for a response. Then he slapped the sheet of white paper with the back of his hand. "What does it mean, do you think?"

Pressing once more against the mountain ash, Madison released her left hand from the bark to point at the second-floor window of 10 Garneau.

"Well, obviously," said Raymond. "But what does it *mean*?"

2

philosophy of death

*L*et's Fix It.

This was just the sort of romantic naïveté Professor Raymond Terletsky despised, even if it originated in a place of warmth and decency. A man, their neighbour, was dead. So? Twenty-five hundred years of philosophical history had proven, beyond a doubt, that human beings were incapable of accepting and understanding death, let alone fixing it.

Walking past the eco-house on the east end of campus, wherein the environmental fanatics recycled their own poop into T-shirts or somesuch, Raymond reached into his briefcase and pulled out a notepad. The notepad, a birthday gift from his wife, featured a merry bit of African cave art on the cover. By now, it should have been filled with insights and aphorisms. But, apart from a couple of phone numbers and a grocery list, the soft yellow pages remained blank. Raymond stopped walking and pulled a pencil out of his briefcase.

The blank page lulled him into a sort of trance. Trees at the top of the river valley gave off a pleasant aroma, and a team of cyclists was passing. The thought of Madison Weiss, her voice and round cheeks, her legs in those black tights, inspired a shiver of lust. If only she hadn't been wearing that jacket with the long flap in the rear, he might have admired her behind, too. Perhaps he would see her again tonight at the opening of this season's theatrical soap opera, without the vexing yellow jacket.

Raymond wrote: *The neighbour was bad. Two weeks ago, the police shot the neighbour. He breathes no more. His shadow is long.*

Then he sketched a jack pine with a giant squirrel on one of the branches, making love to another giant squirrel. Or a bear, depending on interpretation. Raymond closed the notepad, slipped it back into his distressed leather briefcase, surely one of the best briefcases in Western Canadian academe, and continued along. There weren't many cars on Saskatchewan Drive yet, shortly after seven in the morning. At this hour he liked to pretend that instead of these walk-ups and parking lots and eco-houses there were a few hundred teepees in the valley. The river water so clean you could drink from it, or at least bathe your steed. No bridges or power plants or running paths or pitch-and-putt courses. Just sweet wilderness, the contrary of philosophy departments.

Inside the Humanities Centre, Raymond took the stairs to the second floor and considered the elevator. His office was on the fourth, which meant two more flights. The elevator was slow and smelled, mysteriously, of boiled cabbage. But it wouldn't bother his knees or cause his lungs to burn or his heart to hammer in his ears; the elevator wouldn't remind him, quite so poignantly, that he was an old man now – six years from sixty.

The previous evening, Raymond had told his wife, Shirley, that he was off to Save On Foods. They were out of kosher dill pickles and he wanted nothing more than a kosher dill pickle as he brawled with Heidegger. "Okay, darling," Shirley had said, without looking up from her *Alberta Views* magazine. Raymond loathed *Alberta Views* because its editors had rejected his latest essay on the philosophy of death in the context of Pope John Paul II, calling it "not right for our readers."

What readers? Shirley Wong? Raymond knew his wife and knew her heart, and she had *adored* his essay on the philosophy of death in the context of Pope John Paul II. The massive gathering in Vatican Square had been a giant call for help. "Help," said the Catholic people. "We're scared to die!"

In the new darkness of September, Raymond had driven across the river and east, under the ornamental arch and into the as-yet-ungentrified regions of Chinatown. It had been a relatively warm and clear night, and the women in their tight jeans, little leather jackets, and poofed-up hair had been out in great numbers. They waved to him from the sidewalk. Three times he flirted with the idea of shifting his foot to the brake pedal, but he didn't stop. He turned left and started back in the direction of Grant MacEwan College, Save On Foods, and Bubbie's Pickles.

It had been Raymond's fourth trip to Chinatown, and each visit had been the same. He wanted to speak with one of the women, to undertake a vigorous intellectual and sexual quest, to accompany her to Denver or The Hague or Whitehorse. As he passed through another heavy door onto the fourth floor of the Humanities Centre, Raymond vowed – like the great Montaigne – to reveal himself to himself. "Help," he had said the previous evening, "I'm scared to die."

Raymond walked down the hallway, past the office of Claudia Santino, the new thirty-seven-year-old chair of the philosophy department. Of course she was in. "Raymond. You're here early."

"Oh, I'm always here this early. Unless of course I'm doing some reading or marking or writing in my home office. I have a home office, you see. Perhaps I should leave the number with you, in case you ever need to get hold of me. If you ever need help or whatever. Not that you need help. But . . ."

Claudia stood up out of her chair and adjusted her heavy black-framed glasses. "Thank you, Raymond, for the offer. Just leave the number with the secretaries." And with that, Claudia Santino closed her door.

The hiring committee had been so smitten with postmodern Claudia, her master's degree from Harvard and her four languages, her post-graduate work at the Sorbonne, that they had neglected to see what Raymond so plainly saw: she hated men. At least she hated men like Raymond, obvious intellectual threats from the more classical, more rigorous side of criticism. If she lasted more than a couple of years in Edmonton, Claudia Santino would destroy the fine reputation of the department he loved. She was nothing more than a precocious child wearing grown-up spectacles. A child that practically *slammed* the door in his face.

In his office, looking out at the valley and at the sandstone Legislative Building on the opposite bank, Raymond took the folded sheet of paper from his back pocket, the sheet that had been affixed to the trembling aspen in his front yard. Somehow, in the process, he cut his pinky finger, which left him only one option: to kick his waste basket.

Let's Fix It.

Raymond sucked the salty blood from his pinky and marked the date on his calendar.

3

sparkle vacations

Madison's first customer of the morning was a mouth breather. A mouth breather with sideburns and a head cold. Like most clients, he had already looked up his all-inclusive package trip to Cancún on the Internet, and wanted Sparkle Vacations to beat the price. Madison found the identical booking and lopped five dollars off. The man, whose name was Les, took the seventh tissue from Madison's desk without asking, and blew his nose. Then he placed the soiled tissue, with the others, next to Madison's tiny black Buddha.

"So that'll be $1,240 each, for you and your wife."

Les shook his head. "You said you'd beat the price. Sign on your window says you beat any price."

"You were quoted $1,245 on-line, sir."

"Five bucks? You're saving me a fin?" This time, Les didn't bother with a tissue. He addressed his nose with two hairy fingers. "That don't seem like any real savings to me. How about you make 'er an even twelve?"

Madison graduated with a master's degree in comparative literature in 2000, and sent hundreds of resumés to businesses and government departments in Edmonton and Calgary. She could write. She could think. She had received the Edith Mummler Humanities Prize for her thesis on the future of the haiku, for Christ's sake.

After eight months of searching and mailing and phoning and faxing, Madison received exactly one reply, from the Public Affairs Bureau of the Alberta government. Yes writing, yes thinking, yes Mummler, terrific, but why didn't she sign up for the PR diploma program at Grant MacEwan College, where she might learn some actual skills?

The service industry, she discovered, was only too pleased to have her. On account of Edmonton's labour shortage, Madison had her choice of hotels, restaurants, shoe stores, American big-box shopping outfits, and, it turned out, travel agencies. Madison's parents had written her a cheque at graduation so she might purchase several tasteful downtown outfits for her new professional life. To honour these outfits, Madison chose the closest thing to a tasteful downtown job she could find, even though it was located five and a half blocks south of the Garneau Block on Whyte Avenue and paid less than an assistant manager position at Wendy's. *Sparkle Vacations: get away today.* Five years later, the outfits were out of style and she was too scared to tell her boss, Tammy "Sparkle" Davidson, let alone her mother and father, that she was almost three months pregnant.

Madison had just finished printing Les's itinerary when her parents, David and Abby Weiss, walked into Sparkle Vacations with Garith, her father's Chinese Crested dog. Upset that Madison wouldn't "make 'er an even twelve," Les had gone silent but for his sniffling, mouth breathing, and sighing. He snatched his itinerary from Madison's hand and looked down at Garith – deep brown and completely hairless aside from cream-coloured tufts on his ankles and the top of his head. Garith returned the stare, cocked his head, and released a rare, high-pitched yip.

"What is that thing?" said Les to David Weiss, retired high-school math teacher, former champion amateur wrestler, and president of the Strathcona Progressive Conservative Riding Association. As if to prove something, Garith shook his head and bounced, and the bells on his collar chimed. Les bent down. "Is that a dog or –?"

No doubt sensitive to his daughter's position at Sparkle Vacations, David didn't deliver his stump speech designed for fat men in windbreakers who insulted Garith. Instead, he pointed at the line of moist, crumpled tissues on his daughter's desk. "Is that your rubbish or –?"

It took Les a moment to figure out what David was referring to. So David raised his eyebrows and cleared his throat until Les picked up the tissues and scuttled out of Sparkle Vacations. Madison called Garith up onto her lap. The dog shivered and licked the air while her parents sat down. David rested for a moment then sprung up. "Blech. That seat is warm."

Abby Weiss dangled one of the Let's Fix It sheets. "Did you see all these?"

"I did."

"Rather a waste of paper, I'd say. It isn't even recycled stock. But the sentiment is wonderful." For most of her career, Abby Weiss had taught grade one. It had instilled a gently pedantic tone in her out-of-classroom speaking voice. "Why *should* we sit around and allow ourselves to be emotionally tortured by what happened in that awful house?"

"It's bunk," said David. He was flipping through the thick brochures displayed along the back wall, advertising southern getaways. "Probably a pyramid scheme. Honduras. They speak Spanish there, right?"

"Yes, Dad."

"Back to Hawaii for us this year."

Abby waved the paper in the air again. "This isn't a pyramid scheme, David. It's what we need, as a community. That family's tragedy will destroy us if we let it."

"Garith needs moisturizer, Dad. His skin's a bit dry."

"Honduras. It sounds druggy, doesn't it?"

"We owe it to Jeanne and Katie Perlitz to take this seriously." Abby swiped the brochure from her husband's hand, replaced it on the shelf, and pointed at the chair.

"But the seat's warm from that slob."

"So sit in the other one."

Her parents sat. Abby straightened her posture. "I think we should go to this meeting. As a family. I think we all agree the air isn't right since Jeanne and little Katie left. We can either do nothing about that and let the block fade into a sad and scary place where a man was shot, like some street in an American town that used to build Buicks, a place where ghosts toss buckets of blood around while good families are trying to enjoy dinner. Or. Or we can fix it. For God's sake, we're human beings. We're Albertans. We're full of can-do spirit!"

Madison exchanged a glance with her father, a glance that had acquired subtlety and significance since her teen years. As much as they both loved and respected Abby, as much as they appreciated the sincere, boundless, crusading warmth in her heart, Madison and David found her hilarious.

4

the price of coffee in paris

A Cadillac Escalade pulled up, its alloy wheels gleaming in the morning sunlight. Tammy "Sparkle" Davidson hurried around her SUV and walked into the agency, thanking someone enthusiastically on her little silver cellular phone. In a black denim ensemble and red scarf, Tammy waved at the air in front of her as though she were a queen visiting the colonies, swarmed by mosquitoes, bad architecture, and bad smells. "It'll be a delight, an absolute delight."

Madison stood with her parents near the door, unsure whether to release them. A few months earlier, the proprietor of Sparkle Vacations had read a self-help book that contained several rules of etiquette designed to cultivate powerful friends and allies. From time to time, Tammy asked about David's position as president of the Strathcona PC Riding Association. Did he know many of the provincial cabinet ministers, or even the premier? Could he get her invited to some events that might be advantageous to her, both as a small businesswoman and as a gorgeous single woman in her mid-forties looking for – how do you say – a not-too-ugly, not-too-stupid, not-too-boring man with a lot of pre-boom oil stock?

Tammy finished her call, looked at them, and screamed. "Oh my goodness, the Weisses. And their little sweetie!" Tammy pulled up her black denim skirt and bent down daintily. "Come here, girl. Come to mommy."

Garith looked up at David, with a blend of confusion and horror. The dog didn't move until David said, "Go on, boy," and gave him a gentle nudge with his sneaker.

For the next few minutes, the hairless dog squirmed while Tammy mauled him and baby-talked him and called him a girl. There was a conquered look in his eyes, the look of a gazelle just as a cheetah takes it down. Madison knew what her mother would say before she said it. "Do you have children, Tammy?"

Tammy froze just long enough for Garith to escape her clutches. She inhaled and shook her head. "No. No, I don't, Abigail."

The social error hung in the air like a cloud of unclaimed flatulence. Madison lifted her arms. "Wasn't it cold this morning? Brrr."

No one responded. Garith jumped at David's shins.

"Um." Madison cleared her throat. "I'm going to the soaps at the Varscona tonight, in case anyone wants to join me. It's opening night."

Seemingly revived by the opportunity to talk about herself again, Tammy rolled her eyes. "That was my sister-in-law on the phone. She has these tickets to some sort of fundraiser at the Winspear tonight, with classical music? I had to pretend to be excited. The mayor'll be there, I guess."

Madison snapped her fingers. "Dad, Tammy was wondering if she could join you one night for an association meeting."

"Yes! Yes! Could I?"

David picked up Garith, in case Tammy's enthusiasm inspired another outburst. "We're always looking for fresh voices and ideas."

"I'm the freshest, David." Tammy whipped a business card out of a small dispenser in her purse.

For the next while, David talked about the merits of joining the PC party. Why fight it, really? No political organization is perfect, of course, but by supporting the Liberals or the New Democrats, what are you doing? Further dooming the City of Edmonton, that's what. Further empowering Calgary and the rural caucus.

"Nonsense, David," said Abby. "That's the sort of talk that leads to tyranny, and we've had plenty enough of it in this province."

"Tyranny, she says! Tyranny!" David took a few steps in Tammy's direction, so they formed a political triangle. "No wonder the left is so flabby."

Madison felt the way she always felt when her parents argued about politics. Light-headed, dreamy. She approached the Europe brochures relegated to the secondary shelf and felt the acid-charcoal taste of panic swish through her mouth: she had not been to Paris. Now that she was pregnant, Madison knew she would never get there. The agency paid her ten dollars an hour and Tammy didn't allow junkets. Madison didn't have a car and rent was free, but she still couldn't save any money. In Paris, a cup of coffee is ten dollars.

In university, Madison had felt superior to all her grubby backpacker girlfriends who had taken a year off during their English degrees to ride the EuroRail, smoke Dutch marijuana, and have sex with Spaniards. But look where responsibility and hard work and serious scholarship on the haiku had led Madison Weiss. She would be thirty soon, an untravelled and unilingual spinster.

Abby bemoaned the exploitation of the word "progressive," and flapped the white sheet of printer paper. Madison walked around a chair and snatched it from her hand. *Let's Fix It.*

The gesture interrupted the argument. Tammy shrugged. "I don't know much about politics. I just want to, you know, be a part of it all."

"Perfect," said David.

Abby sighed. She lifted her finger to make a point, then she dropped her hand, lowered her shoulders, and sighed again. "I need to do yoga tonight."

"We can do that yoga DVD together, before bed." David leaned over and kissed his wife on the cheek. Garith shivered between them. "I'll even wear tights."

Tammy and the Weisses said their goodbyes. Garith endured a brief cuddle and a "smoochie woochie." Mid-cuddle, Tammy's cellular phone began ringing again – to the tune of "Summer Lovin'" from the *Grease* soundtrack.

At the door, Madison returned the sheet to Abby. "I checked on-line again. There aren't any new listings for a Jeanne Perlitz anywhere in Canada or the States."

"Jeanne will call when she wants to talk. I can't imagine it's easy to digest your husband's death, especially given the unfortunate circumstances of Benjamin's final hour."

"Unfortunate circumstances?" said David. "He went nuts and took her hostage."

Abby sighed. "We just aren't trained to deal with that kind of trauma, at least in central neighbourhoods." Abby grimaced and looked down at the Let's Fix It sheet, then closed her eyes. "I really feel Jeanne and Katie are fine. I wouldn't be surprised if Jeanne sneaked into the block last night and put these up herself."

David stole the sheet from his wife and folded it into his pocket. "Let's not think too hard about pyramid schemes and time shares. When you girls go, leave your chequebooks at home. And don't eat the coffee cake. Don't even touch it."

"You girls?"

"I'm not going."

Abby licked her lips, nodded to her daughter, and opened the door for her husband and Garith. Through the glass door, Madison witnessed the early stages of her father's re-education.

5

that warm thing

Jonas Pond stood near the gazebo in McIntyre Park, among the squeegee punks and lost, drunken teenagers, and considered the lineup across the avenue in front of Varscona Theatre. Who were these people, really? And what did they want from him?

A giant pickup truck passed the park, obscuring his view of the lineup. The two young men inside, wearing sunglasses and baseball hats, bobbed their heads to the thumping bass of a gangster rap song. On the back window, a giant Ford decal. If Jonas weighed another fifty pounds, and if he weren't worried about going to prison, he would flag down the giant truck, pull the young men from inside, slap them upside their heads, and ask for some good explanations. Why the giant truck? Why the gangster fantasy? Did you idiots *pay extra* to advertise for Ford? Jonas would punish them for their yob-hood, and then he would play good cop. *So, fellas, have you ever considered experimenting with a man?*

"Hey, Jonas!" Two young women in oversized Value Village clothes and colourful sneakers approached him.

"Hello." He tilted his head and did that warm thing with his voice, that thing he did whenever a large organization hired him to host an awards ceremony or funding announcement. *I am a friend of the people.* He didn't know these women, mid-twenties and puffy and shy, consumers of Monty Python and Sylvia Plath.

But they knew him. "How are you lovely girls this evening?"

"Awesome," said one.

"Awesome," said the other, not quite as loudly.

"That's really awesome," said Jonas.

The first woman, in an enormous polyester ski sweater from the 1970s, nodded and looked around. "Cool. Cool."

Jonas wondered about this exchange, what these women had in mind when they approached him. Did they feel obliged, simply because they recognized him? He waited for them to speak, but they didn't speak. They shuffled their shoes and bobbed their heads to the gangster rap, as the large truck was still waiting at the red light on Calgary Trail. The situation passed from uncomfortable into grotesque. Why were they still here? What did they *want*? Finally, when it became obvious that the women were never going to walk away without his help, Jonas asked if they were going to the show.

"We never miss the soaps. Ever."

The quieter, more deferential girl sniffed and stood on her tiptoes for an instant. "We totally love you?"

"Yeah, you're the funniest one for sure."

Not far from the gazebo and the squeegee punks, who appeared to be drinking vermouth straight from the bottle, a small flock of magpies pecked at a squirrel carcass. Jonas sympathized with the squirrel. Perhaps he would work the squirrel into his character's introductory monologue tonight. "Well, I totally love you guys, too. Totally."

Then the young women hugged Jonas. The more confident woman in the polyester sweater said, "So, are you gonna be funny tonight?"

"Nope."

The woman in the sweater pointed as she and her friend walked away. "You're so funny!"

Near the back of the line, where the young women were headed, Jonas spotted Raymond and Shirley from the block. He remembered the signs on all the trees that morning, and guessed that either Abby Weiss or Shirley Wong had put them up. He could already taste the hummus and pita, the deli olives of community activism.

The squeegee punks with their ripped-up denim, black leather, and haphazardly pierced faces grew in number. Cigarette smoke drifted toward Jonas. A tightrope walker was setting up a mini-circus between a park bench and the gazebo, and his balancing stick had crowded the punks toward Jonas, so close he could smell their booze breath amid the smoke. They laughed and pushed each other, speaking as though they had entered a cussing bee. Jonas saw they were a bunch of middle-class kids from the new subdivisions playing anarchy and revolution in the theatre district; tattoos, cigarettes, and vermouth weren't cheap.

He started across the avenue and squeezed through the lineup. People stepped back as they recognized him. They smiled and said hello, nervously, and he did that warm thing with his voice again. Of all his roles in the theatre, his work in the weekly improvised soap opera had made his career. This only disturbed Jonas in the summer and over the Christmas holidays, when the soaps weren't running. And when one of the bald, pockmarked head cases from theatre school got a decent review for something at Stratford. And whenever a local moron just out of university, with twelve minutes of stage experience, landed a pilot in Los Angeles. And on Thursday nights. And Saturday mornings. And each time a rapper became a movie star. And when he travelled outside Edmonton, into the painful world of anonymity.

Near the front of the line, he found Madison and pulled her to the side. "Girlfriend."

"Jonas." They kissed each other's cheeks, *à la* French people. "So what's this season about? The suspense is like a rash."

"I daren't tell. I was going to call you today. Did your mom put up those stupid signs?"

"No. But, boy, is she excited about them."

"Who do you think it was?"

"Abby thinks it was Jeanne."

Jonas laughed. "Jeanne is in Mexico right now, spending Ben's insurance money on papaya licuados and Vichy showers."

"I don't think so."

"Madison, come on."

"They were my friends."

"I'm your friend. They were the people you talked weather and traffic and *Survivor* with when you were pulling weeds. It's awful but we can't let it affect us."

"How can it not affect me? They lived next door."

"Homeless people die around you every day, Maddy. In the next three seconds, another five thousand Africans will die of AIDS. Oops, there go another five thousand. Another. Another. Another."

"You were asleep, Jonas. I saw."

"Don't make shit up."

"Well, I heard. I heard. And I think we *should* be affected by violence in our community. Especially our little neighbourhood, where . . ." Madison paused for a moment, squinted, and pushed Jonas. "You invented that five thousand people every three seconds."

"A vile accusation."

Madison snorted and smiled. For a moment she seemed her regular, pre-pregnant, pre-shooting self. Still, there was a worrying carelessness in the way she had clipped her hair up. Depressed or not, Madison was usually vigilant about the hair. Jonas put his arm around Madison and kissed her on the cheek. "I think you need a good, strong drink after the show."

"I'm not allowed."

"You need a good, strong cup of herbal tea after the show."

"What kind of herbal tea? The medicinal stuff can give a baby brain damage and cause early contractions."

"Just meet me at the bar."

6

Tacumseh and his daughter

Shirley Wong held Raymond's hand tightly as the lights went down. They had been regulars at the soaps now for three years, even though Raymond didn't always enjoy confining himself to a room full of smug twenty-somethings every Monday after teaching two survey courses to smug twenty-somethings. As he eased toward retirement, he found young people increasingly lazy and obnoxious. They referenced movies, not books. They wore flannel pajama pants and dirty fleece jackets to class. They said "like" and "um" and "you know" constantly. Instead of asking about Kant's categorical imperative during office hours they harassed Raymond about the subtle differences between a B+ and an A– in the context of their atrociously written essays.

The musicians on the side of the stage broke into the soap opera theme song. Raymond sighed.

"Sweetheart, are you glum?" said Shirley, into his ear.

He kissed his wife's hand. "Just pensive."

"Why did you read ghastly Heidegger during dinner? Not reading Heidegger is what Monday nights are all about."

"Shhh."

The performers began walking out on stage, one by one, to introduce themselves. Every night of the soaps began this way, with the major characters delivering an improvised monologue. According to the photocopied program notes, the new season was set during the fur trade. There was a British governor type, who claimed in his monologue that he sought to deflower each of the savage virgins of the river valley. Next came a sexy native princess, wearing almost nothing, her warrior suitors wearing even less, a Jewish whisky trader, and a few voyageurs speaking snarly French. Shirley and Raymond's Garneau Block neighbour and crowd favourite Jonas Pond came last, as the noble chief Lacumseh. During his brief introductory appearance on stage, Lacumseh sucked most of his laughs out of insulting the coureurs de bois.

Madison Weiss was sitting directly in front of Raymond. She was another regular at the soaps, and she almost always came alone. The show began in earnest, with the director calling out the first scene – Lacumseh meeting with his sexy princess daughter to discuss birth control. Raymond waited until the audience was fully engrossed. When it was clear Shirley was not paying attention to him he leaned forward and tried to smell Madison's shiny red hair and the soft skin at the back of her neck. The lights flashed, so he eased back. Raymond admired the texture of Madison's laugh – the demure squeak at the climax and the falling rumble into silence.

On stage, Lacumseh called his princess daughter a nihilist for refusing to believe in Manitou, the god of all that is good. The daughter sulked in the Cree equivalent of a black turtle-neck and beret, and smoked her peace pipe in an affected manner. Raymond knew several people in his department, including the chair, would be shocked and offended by these portrayals: in 2005, First Nations peoples were not on the list of approved subjects for mockery. Personally, he was offended by the troupe's shallow treatment of nihilism.

Nihilism, for Raymond, was a rigorous philosophical concept. Once you got past yourself and your being-in-the-world, once you fully grasped nothingness, nihilism overcame nihilism. Once you understood there was no self and no soul outside the one you know intrinsically, the one who eats and drinks and excretes in the mundane world, you could return to the mundane world and see its magic. Once you accepted that everyone in the theatre, the performers and the audience, and all their dreams, would be rotten and forgotten in a hundred years, the world was a sudden carnival. Public opinion no longer affected you. Trends and fashions became irrelevant, or they became everything. Hallelujah, you would die. The blood pumping beneath the surfaces of your old skin was the entire universe.

"Isn't this hilarious?" Shirley whispered.

Now the competing warriors were drinking firewater with the jolly whisky trader and a blindfolded voyageur whose eyes had been eaten out by bears. The warriors wanted to discover a way to impress the indifferent princess, so the blind voyageur suggested a semi-nude wrestling match: "It is the foremost desire of every princess." Since the rules of improvisation require the dramatization of every suggestion, the warriors began removing their leather clothing.

The audience howled as the lights went down. Madison clapped and said, "Aw, jeez."

What would it take, Raymond thought, for Madison Weiss or even her mother to say "Aw, jeez" about something he had done? Raymond applauded with the crowd as the lights came back up. The sweaty young men had dropped to the black stage floor in the darkness, and now they were fighting. Raymond could practically see the whirring of the improvisers' brains as the battle transformed from amateur to professional wrestling. Lacumseh and his daughter were in birch thrones, sitting before the combatants. How old was Jonas Pond now? He must be in his mid-forties, yet he remained here, frolicking with these children. A man with his talent and nimble intelligence might have done anything, yet here he was, a professional actor in Edmonton. Living in one half of a rented duplex.

Raymond vowed to speak with Jonas about his hopes and dreams, such as they were, and to correct his naïve definition of nihilism. Nihilism was so much more than an affectation. He wondered if Jonas would attend the Let's Fix It meeting downtown next week.

The scene ended as expected, with the beautiful princess bored by the display of masculinity. Yet the audience exploded in applause at the end of it, as though they had just witnessed a work of unqualified genius. This is what we do in Edmonton, thought Raymond. This is why Jonas Pond didn't move to New York.

Shirley had taken Raymond's hand again, so when it came time to clap she slapped his wrist. In the darkness between scenes she leaned over and kissed him on the cheek. Then, just before the lights came up again, Raymond seized the opportunity to lean down and smell the back of Madison's neck.

It smelled sweetly of nothing.

7

his name was carlos

In the corner of The Next Act pub, three men in baseball caps and rugby jerseys smoked on the sly. They cupped their hands over their cigarettes, and the smoke sneaked up between their fingers. Jonas interrupted his theorizing about the Let's Fix It signs to flag down the server.

"Those three assholes back there are smoking."

The server took a deep breath, closed her eyes for a moment, and exhaled slowly. "Jonas, please. Don't do this to me."

"I'll call bylaw enforcement tomorrow morning if I must. What if a pregnant woman came in here? What about your own fragile lungs, and the cancer that runs in your family?"

"How did you know cancer runs in my family?"

Jonas pointed to his temple. Then he made a phone out of his hand.

"You're a dirty narc."

Jonas lifted his nearly empty pint glass and smiled. "And another one of these?"

"I'm gonna spit in it," said the server, and started over to the men in the corner.

Madison pushed her glass of club soda and cranberry juice around the table. "Remember, it's still a secret that I'm pregnant."

"I didn't say anything specific about you."

"You haven't told anyone?"

"No and I never would. Not until you're ready or it becomes obvious, fat-wise, and I can't bear to hear people gossiping about how you've let yourself go."

In the darkness of her basement bedroom, during episodes of insomnia, Madison often found herself thinking about Jonas. He drank too much beer and he was about three times more sarcastic than he had to be, but she felt he would make a terrific father. Plus, he was smart and handsome, and sported visible stomach muscles. Out of selfishness, Madison found herself wishing Jonas could set his homosexuality aside for seventeen or eighteen years so they could raise her child together. Once or twice a week, with the bedroom curtain open, the moonlight hitting his body, they could . . . no.

Jonas had been wondering aloud about 10 Garneau, whether Mr. or Mrs. Let's Fix It was a literalist. Did the mystery person intend to erase Benjamin Perlitz from history? To repair the bullet holes and bloodstains, and make the house pretty again for Jeanne and Katie to move back in? If so, the mystery person was a jackass. The men in ball caps extinguished and surrendered their cigarettes. Jonas mimed applause and returned to his thought. He had started backstage with half a bottle of champagne, so a slur was easing into his voice. "In a couple of months, someone new will be in 10 Garneau. Your mom and Shirley can make dips, throw a welcome barbecue, a bottle of red and a bottle of white, some microbrew, the Barenaked Ladies on the hi-fi . . ."

"Jonas, it's not that easy."

"I'm not going to any meeting. No way. I'm ideologically opposed." He lifted his glass, to remind the server. The server squinted with mock-malevolence. Jonas winked at her. "Our waitress covets me."

"We all do, Jonas."

"I know, I know. Yet I'm so old."

"You're not."

"For the last twenty years, I've been waiting for this special thing to happen to me. Do you know what that thing is?"

"Yes, Jonas."

"I have been waiting patiently and tragically for Lorne Michaels to fly up here and whisk me to New York."

Madison played an invisible violin.

Jonas slapped at the instrument. "All these cute young Edmonton boys have made it down there in the last few years, *inferior* performers. But I've been good about it. Haven't I been good about it, supportive and gracious?"

Madison had been through this many times before. For people like Jonas, to live in Edmonton was to live in a state of perpetual failure. His successful friends in Vancouver and Toronto begged him to leave, to live in a place where the same-sex marriage debate hadn't been so mean. And what about the trucks? All the big, shiny, pointless trucks? "Absolutely supportive and gracious," said Madison.

The server arrived with his third pint of Honey Brown ale, and Jonas thanked her and called her gorgeous. "Swoon," she said, and swooned.

Jonas tinked his glass with Madison's, and took a great slurp of beer. "I think, after I'm done this, we should go on a little expedition."

"Tonight?"

"Yes, tonight."

"What sort of expedition?"

"You'll see, sister."

A young man, about Madison's age, approached the table and cleared his throat. He wore khakis and a white T-shirt with a West Coast Choppers logo. On his right arm, just below the hem of the shirtsleeve, a Canadian flag tattoo. Madison expected him to ask for directions to the nearest Bruce Willis film festival.

"Hi. Um, I just wanted to, uh, say . . ."

Jonas hopped up out of his chair. "Spit it out!"

Frightened, the young man took a step back. "I, uh, I think you're real good."

"Real good, eh?"

The young man swallowed, and nodded. "I just wanted to say that."

"Well, thanks. That's very kind of you."

They stood about five feet apart. Madison recognized this as the usual distance between boxers, before they stepped in to wallop one another. The young man was handsome enough, in his way. But next to Jonas's canary-yellow shirt and tight Diesel jeans, the stranger looked like a soccer referee.

"My name's Carlos," he said, and extended his hand for a shake.

"Oh, it is not!"

Carlos took another step back and turned his head slightly, like a confused cat. "But. It is my name."

The oddly tense handshake made Madison feel like a voyeur. Jonas slapped him on the tattoo. "Carlos. I've seen you before."

"Whenever I'm not working I come to your plays, and the soaps."

"Want to join us for a drink?"

Carlos looked down at Madison and smiled. "Uh, no. Thanks. I have to split. Bye." And with that, he snaked around the tables and exited onto the sidewalk.

"That was bizarre." Jonas sat down, and took a sip of beer. "Wouldn't you say?"

"Quite bizarre."

"Sorry, I'm drunk and forgetful. What were we talking about before Carlos came around?"

"An expedition."

"Yes!" Jonas attempted to finish his beer in one giant gulp. Near the bottom, he took a break to burp and breathe and say, "Whoa, that really burned." He dabbed the corners of his mouth with a napkin. "Are you ready?"

8

fear and scotch whisky

Jonas and Madison began the expedition at the Commercial Hotel liquor store. While Jonas went inside to spend his meagre theatrical earnings for the night on a bottle of twelve-year-old Scotch – the craving had hit him "like a tongue in the ear" – Madison waited on the sidewalk. She watched the bikers and the university students mingle inside Blues on Whyte and felt the bass line in her stomach. Mozart was good for developing babies. How about "Sweet Home Chicago"?

The father was Québécois, she knew that much. One day in the middle of June, a different sort of craving had hit Jonas. Rocky Mountains! They borrowed David's Yukon Denali and started out on the Yellowhead Highway. Jonas had never tried camping and he seemed quite eager, but as soon as they reached the site he grew fearful of grizzly bears, mosquitoes, bush people, and needing to pee in the middle of the night. So they booked a room at the Amethyst Lodge in Jasper.

That evening, in the Downstream bar, they met a group of five unshaven Québécois. Jonas fell for their accents but, unfortunately, they were all straight and none of them was given to experimentation. One of the Québécois, who said his name was Steve, taught Madison how to play the Deer Hunter video game. When they were both drunk, Madison noticed that Steve's friends smiled every time they called him Steve. It occurred to her that Steve was not, traditionally, a French name.

Minutes after she agreed to go back to his hotel room, so she could try the Québécois delicacy Map-o-Spread, Madison was quite certain that one of these friends called him Jean-François. Or was it Jean-Luc? Jean-Marc? Looking back, she had been disappointed to learn that Map-o-Spread was sugary goo with artificial maple flavouring. And that Steve didn't believe in deodorant. And, finally, that he had impregnated her sometime between 3:00 and 3:05 in the morning.

Jonas emerged from the Commercial Hotel liquor store with a beige tube labelled The Balvenie. "Next to the liquor store, all these sad old people are playing video lottery terminals. You wanna see?"

"I'm good, Jonas, thanks."

They started east down Whyte Avenue. Even on Monday night it was a zoo of young drunks screaming at one another. Harleys and four-cylinder cars with modified mufflers popped and roared past young women, and the young women ignored them. Madison remembered a word from high school biology that defined this behaviour in the context of birds and baboons: displaying.

Jonas pulled the Scotch bottle out of the tube, admired its shape aloud, and dropped it back inside.

When the bars and nightclubs gave way to restaurants, clothing stores, and purveyors of French bread, they ventured north and walked up the dimly lit residential streets so Jonas could drink Scotch without getting a ticket. Lost in vague memories of her baby's father and feeling guilty that she hadn't been listening to any classical music in the last three months, Madison ignored Jonas. Somehow he had veered from video lottery terminals to the plight of Aboriginals. Inhabiting the great chief Lacumseh on stage had made him thoughtful.

"It's the great social tragedy of our era," he said, with a rolling slur. "What are we supposed to do?"

Madison knew what her father would say, so she said something like it. "There isn't enough money in the world to pay everyone whose parents or grandparents or great-great-grandparents have been wronged. We can only facilitate."

"That doesn't mean anything."

The dark living rooms of Strathcona flashed with blue television light. It felt later than midnight to Madison, who was losing her taste for an expedition. One of these days she would pass into her second trimester and she would stop feeling so tired and nauseous. Laundry detergent and roasted garlic would stop smelling like raw sewage.

"Jonas, what sort of expedition is this? It seems we're going home."

"Don't attack the dignity of the expedition."

"I'm pretty tired. If this expedition ends in my bed, I'll be very pleased."

When they reached the block, Madison was overcome with fatigue. She hoped Jonas had drowned his expeditionary energy with The Balvenie. She followed him past his duplex and past her parents' house next door, and stopped with him before the shadowed misery of 10 Garneau. Street lamps illuminated the logo'd trash on the front lawn, evidence of the university students who had walked through the block that morning on their way to school. Madison stopped on the sidewalk and opened her mouth to repeat her preference for going to sleep when Jonas stepped into the yard.

"Where are you going?"

"Let's move."

Madison hadn't been on the property for two weeks, since the police and fire trucks and media vans had been parked out front. It was like walking under a ladder or crossing the path of a black cat or committing to atheism: maybe supernatural forces didn't exist but maybe, just maybe, they did. She remained on the sidewalk.

With the bottle of Scotch in one hand and the beige tube in the other, Jonas crept along the side of the house like a ninja with an inner-ear infection. He stopped at a basement window and turned around. "Come on, Maddy!"

"I don't think so."

"What are you afraid of?"

Well, everything.

9

madison and jonas partake of an expedition

When Benjamin and Jeanne Perlitz bought the half-burned brick bungalow at 10 Garneau in late winter 2000, large machinery arrived almost immediately. Madison's parents had been relieved to learn a new family was moving into and renovating the house which had been a rental property before the electrical fire. The Garneau Block remained the cheapest and blandest crescent in the otherwise upscale historic neighbourhood, but the burned husk and the random piles of trash sitting in the yard for two years had dragged the other four houses into the realm of residential decay.

Relief transformed to alarm at the end of March when the large machinery began tearing the house down. Soon afterward, a crew arrived to start building another one. What were those items in the trailer? Those *couldn't be* strips of mustard-coloured vinyl siding. One morning in April, David Weiss wandered over and asked for the architect in charge of the project.

Four men in hard hats laughed at him. Architect! That was a lulu.

David got a petition together and took it to city council as treasurer of the Garneau Community League. He also subtly tossed in the fact that he was president of the Strathcona PC Riding Association. City council listened and understood, but there was really nothing they could do. Since the ninety-year-old house on the site had been damaged by fire, Benjamin and Jeanne Perlitz could build whatever they liked as long as it was up to code. Yes, Mr. Weiss, even a mustard monstrosity, a "retarded cardboard schoolbus of a house" that looked like it belonged in the deepest, most treeless subdivisions of northeast Calgary.

Shirley Wong and Abby Weiss organized a neighbourhood barbecue for the Perlitzes when they moved in that autumn, and everyone put down their hamburgers and applauded when they learned Jeanne was pregnant. A young family was just what the Garneau Block needed. Benjamin was a senior bureaucrat with the provincial government and Jeanne was a junior-high physical-education teacher. He was a birdwatcher and she competed in triathlons. They liked cross-country skiing and Thai cuisine, and they immediately took out a membership in the community league. Sure, the house was an uninspired mess, but wary of being snobs, the neighbours – even David Weiss – decided to look past appearances at the new interior of 10 Garneau.

Five autumns later, Madison and Jonas stood in the back-yard among the weedy flowerbeds and empty bird feeders. Jonas took a drink of Scotch and stumbled.

"This is the expedition? Standing in the backyard and drinking booze?"

"We're in stage one of the mission. For stage two, we need to be inside."

Madison began walking across the lawn to the gate in the properties' shared cedar fence and toward her bed. There was no point arguing with Jonas tonight. He had a thirst on and clearly wasn't interested in logic or reason.

"Come back, Maddy. Let's reconnoitre."

The latch on the gate didn't work. Had it ever worked? Madison prepared to hop over into her parents' yard, when she heard the familiar squeak of 10 Garneau's back screen door. She turned around. "Jonas, stop it. This is dumb."

"Dumb like a *fox*," he said, and pulled out his wallet.

Madison leaned against the fence. The moon was bright enough to see that Jonas was having trouble with his wallet. Like a baby with formula and a teddy bear, he seemed unwilling to set the Scotch bottle and tube on the concrete deck pad. He whispered cuss words to himself, and swayed against the white door.

"Hey, do you have a credit card? In the movies, all you need is a credit card to open doors. And it turns out I don't have one. I thought I still had a card from Canadian Tire, but I guess I cut it up on account of my, you know, inability to pay credit card bills. Plus, there's nothing I want from Canadian Tire. Maybe a blender, I don't know. I was there with a set builder when I got the card a couple of years ago, zombie-ing through the lamp section – ugly lamps. This cute guy with a clipboard asks if I want a free gift. Did I ever! So I went ahead and –"

"Jonas, please. I'm tired and pregnant."

"Shut up. I know you have a credit card. I've seen it. Get over here and reconnoitre with me."

Madison sighed and walked back across the grass. Now that she was on the property, at night, she wondered why she had felt so spooked. And spooked was the word. Despite her best attempts she had never been able to believe properly in God, so why should she believe in bad luck or creepy vibes or living history or . . .

"Do you think the ghost of Benjamin Perlitz prowls the house?"

"I don't believe in ghosts."

"Really?" Jonas burped. "I do. I saw one when I was a kid, in Stavely."

"You did not. What's a Stavely?"

"My uncle has a farm there, and I used to leave the concrete jungle of Beverly every summer for a long visit." Jonas handed the Scotch bottle and tube to Madison, and she placed them on the deck. "Once I slopped the pigs. Me. Can you imagine? Anyway, I saw a ghost of a woman in the barn. She seemed ticked off."

Madison looked through the small window of the heavy white door. There was just enough moonlight to see bits of the kitchen – the stainless-steel stove and fridge, the matching toaster – and past the kitchen to the laminate floors of the living room. On the counter, three cans of Diet Coke and a donut box. How could the police eat donuts in here, with all the blood upstairs? Didn't human blood smell like *human blood*?

"So can you?"

"Can I what?"

"Imagine me slopping pigs?"

"I wasn't trying."

Jonas shrugged. "Come on, get going. Try."

There he was, in overalls and big rubber boots, singing "A Spoonful of Sugar" and dumping brown goo into a pig trough. "Done."

"Good. Now, card me."

"This expedition has been a real gas but let's go to bed."

"Card me."

Madison pulled her wallet out and removed the dread VISA. In three days, the minimum payment was due. Jonas took the card and held it in the light. "Are you sure you want to do this?"

"No, Jonas. I never wanted to do this."

"Do you think there's still blood in there?"

"I don't know. Yes?"

Jonas nodded sagely, and slipped the card in the tiny groove between the door and the jamb. As soon as he hit something solid, an alarm whooped inside. Jonas screamed, tossed the VISA card in the air, knocked Madison down, and sprinted through the yard. Madison, with some satisfaction, heard him wipe out in the gravel back alley, cuss, and stumble back to his feet. "Scatter!" he hollered, as he sprinted into his own yard two houses away.

On her hands and knees, Madison found her VISA in a terra cotta pot. She collected the bottle of Scotch and the tube, and walked to the gate. When the latch still didn't work, she kicked it open. By the time she had closed her basement suite door and locked it behind her, Madison could already hear the sirens.

10

the rabbit warren

At least once every day, Shirley Wong wondered what the city, her life, and hockey would have been like if Gretzky hadn't left. It seemed on August 9, 1988, a great barrier crumbled on the south side of Edmonton, allowing the American retail and fast food chains to transform the marketplace and the character of her city's heart. Now look at the booming detritus. What distinguished the outskirts of Edmonton from the outskirts of American and proto-American cities like Denver, Minneapolis, and Calgary?

Usually, Shirley considered Gretzky at 9:55 in the morning Monday to Saturday, and at 11:55 a.m. on Sunday. This was when she walked the four corners of her Whyte Avenue store, the Rabbit Warren, to make sure everything was in place and no dust was visible.

The southeast corner of the window display housed a tiny Gretzky sculpture by the great artist and philosopher Raymond Terletsky, her husband. The proportions were all wrong and the orange paint had bled before it dried, but that was the beauty of the piece. All the flaws and sorrows and calamities and ruined dreams of the city were alive in this little sculpture of Gretzky in his Oilers uniform. It had been sitting in the southeast corner of the Rabbit Warren window since she opened the store in late 1989; every year she adjusted its price for inflation. Now it was going for $235.

Shirley unlocked the front door and considered the change in morning light. Soon autumn, real autumn, would be here and mornings would become cold and dark. Not that she despised winter, or even disliked it. This time of year reminded her of being a little girl, in and out of sleep early in the mornings as her father prepared for work in the adjacent bathroom: the sound of his razor, the smell of his aftershave, running water, his car warming up outside. Soft hallway lamplight sneaking under her closed bedroom door.

The Divine Decadence woman with the striped tights and enormous black boots gave her a wave from across the street. Shirley stepped outside.

"Beautiful day," said the Divine Decadence woman.

A couple of cars and a bread truck stopped at the lights. "Cool and crisp and sunny," said Shirley. "Just how I like a Tuesday to be."

"Pardon?"

The bread truck was a diesel. Shirley was going to wait until it passed to repeat herself, but she was in her Rabbit Warren T-shirt and it *was* cold at this hour. The Divine Decadence woman wasn't burning to know what Shirley thought about this particular Tuesday, so: "Beautiful! Yes!"

She went inside and laid out the newspaper. No one wanted to buy perfumed candles, soap, cards, vases, and other tchotchkes this early in the morning, so the first hour at the store was always hers to read a newspaper or two and, inevitably, stare into space and think about the strange, new, vacant feeling at the bottom of her tummy.

Unless, of course, Abby Weiss knocked on the glass door.

"It's open."

David was with her. So was Garith. Abby opened the door. "You want anything from Starbucks, Shirl? David's going."

"No, thank you. Hi, David. Hello, Garith."

David leaned down and picked up Garith. He hid his mouth behind the hairless dog and said, in a Chinese accent, "Hello, Shirley Wong. Sell much potpourri lately?"

"Out," said Abby, to her husband and his dog. "And if you're going to sit around and argue with that homeless man, get my caramel mochaccino first."

"Bye bye," said David, still with his mouth hidden behind the dog's rear end.

Abby stopped briefly at a rack of thin candles and glass holders. She fondled the items. "Ooh, are these new? I just love them." Then she leaned on the other side of the cash counter and said, "Did you hear the sirens last night?"

"I did. What was it?"

"Someone tried to break into 10 Garneau."

"Why?"

"Satanic rituals, I heard. Apparently you go inside a place where someone has recently died in a violent manner or what have you, and then you burn crosses on the wall and listen to heavy metal music and have sex. It's good luck for a Satanist."

"Who told you that?"

"David was speaking to someone this morning."

"Who?"

Abby swivelled on her toes and stood in front of some locally woven baskets. "I don't know. The mayor or someone."

"Why would the mayor know anything about that?"

"They're all plugged in, these Conservatives."

"The mayor's a Conservative?"

Abby flipped through some art deco posters advertising Banff, Jasper, and Lake Louise. "I wish we could go back in time. Wasn't it so much better then, Shirl? Wasn't the air so much cleaner, people smarter?"

"My parents were exploited. My grandparents paid a head tax."

"All the forests. All the virgin land. The noble First Nations peoples, fashioning pemmican."

Shirley shook the newspaper and wished Abby could go back in time sixty or 160 years and leave her alone.

"You know, you should diversify your media." Abby picked up and examined one of the Lake Louise posters. "If you rely only on the corporate propaganda, you won't get the truth."

Shirley sighed. "What truth?"

"Hey, does anyone know who put up those flyers yet?"

"I heard it was you and I heard it was me. So, no. Maybe it's an invitation to a Satanic sex ritual."

"You think? I wouldn't mind giving it a shake." Abby cleared a strip of hair that had fallen in front of her face and placed it behind her ear. As much as Shirley loved her old friend, she coveted the softness of Abby's still-brown hair and it came between them like an ugly secret. "So darling, what are you doing tonight?"

"There's a pre-season Oilers game."

"Hockey, hockey, hockey," said Abby.

"Satan, Satan, Satan," said Shirley.

"At the university there's a fundraiser and workshop to oppose logging and coal mining on the eastern slope of the Rockies. I'm talking slide show, some music, a silent auction, activist seminars, organic wine. If you change your mind about hockey."

For the past few years, Shirley had sensed a distinct hollowness in hockey. Would the salary cap restore passion and soul to the game? Would there be enough left over for her? "All right."

"All right what?"

"I'll come to the whatever-it-is tonight."

Abby placed her hands together in yogic prayer, closed her eyes, and exhaled through her nose. Shirley sensed she had made an error.

11

life after oil

David Weiss had intended to walk straight into Starbucks and order two caramel mochaccinos. He wanted to be prompt so Abby wouldn't change her mind.

For years, Abby had refused to buy hot beverages at chain stores because they never sold fair trade organic coffee and because they squeezed locally owned cafés out of business. One afternoon during the Fringe Festival David had bought his wife a caramel mochaccino at Starbucks. She reluctantly took a sip, and something in her was transformed. The taste of a superior product had finally overpowered her absurd guilt and frankly dangerous notion of liberal duty.

At that moment, during a sunny dusk waiting in line for a play in the Masonic Hall, with a nearby clown smoking a cigarette, David loved Abby so much he would have married her all over again. In the weeks since then, she would only drink

Starbucks if David made the purchase. And it always had to be a specialty coffee unavailable at the Sugarbowl, their local.

David and Garith were waiting to cross Calgary Trail when Barry Strongman stepped out of Second Cup. "Hey, I was just using the crapper. What is *up*, Garith?"

Barry Strongman plopped in his usual chair outside Second Cup, with his street magazines and his coffee. He called Garith up on his lap and Garith obeyed. So did David, in his way, sitting in the opposite chair.

"Were you going somewheres or –? Don't wanna interrupt. But you are retired."

"I am, I am."

Barry lifted one of the magazines. "New issue, still toasty from the press. You ready to be educated?"

"I guess so." David sighed and took five dollars out of his wallet. Whenever he read the street magazine, it annoyed him. The articles were almost always poorly written rants about the Klein government, blaming hard-working public servants for the writers' own personal shortcomings. "Did you contribute anything for this issue?"

"Page sixteen. Do you and the little lady shave Garith so he looks like this?"

"No. It's natural. The Chinese Crested dog was originally bred for –"

"That is effed-up, man." Then Barry did one of David's least favourite things in the world, more loathsome than the New Democratic Party. Barry said to Garith, in a cartoon voice, "Who's the effed-up puppy? Who's the ugliest dog in Alberta?"

For a moment, David allowed the farce. Then, when Garith mistook Barry's insults for praise and began licking the hobo's mouth, it became too much. He reached over and took Garith back. "That's cruel."

"Allowing good people to die on Alberta streets every winter is okay, fine, not your problem, their own damn fault, but talking crazy to an animal that doesn't understand English is cruel? I said it before and I'll say it again: you got comical views, David."

A tiny capsule of adrenaline burst inside David Weiss. He could pretend he didn't love arguing with Barry Strongman, but he loved arguing with Barry Strongman. Here he was, the nephew of a chief, living on less than thirty dollars a day. Sleeping on the streets, in front of bank machines and in shelters. Why didn't he get a regular job? Was he incapacitated in any serious way? Nope. Barry didn't want a regular job, he didn't want to live on the reservation, and that was that.

David flipped through the latest edition of the street magazine until he found Barry's article, an essay about peak oil. "Oh, come on, Barry."

"Your cushy western middle-class life is coming to an end, David. The oil is running out. And when the oil goes, so does our rich city."

"Just like the year 2000, when the capitalist system was going to collapse over a computer glitch. Baloney."

"Just read the article and try not to be scared. I dare you to try, David."

A group of five punks in dreadlocks and studded leather jackets approached with a golden retriever that looked hungry and desperately in need of a bath. Did she even have her shots? Garith stirred, eager to inspect the dog's bottom. The punks smelled sugary, of last night's booze. The leader wiped his nose and asked if David could spare change for a coffee. He was just about to tell them to cut their hair, wash their faces, and get proper jobs so they could take care of their dog when Barry handed over a toonie.

"Keep on keepin' on," said Barry.

The leader winked. "Thanks, brother."

David wanted to stand up and slap the punks. What was *wrong* with young people these days? The only looming crisis, as far as David was concerned, was a social one. When the light changed and the kids were halfway across Calgary Trail, he shook his head at Barry. "I know you've got your issues, being a mistreated Indian and all, but don't enable those nasty kids."

"I'm a mistreated *Aboriginal* to you."

"Wee-aww, wee-aww, pull over." David formed a mock loudspeaker around his mouth. "Language police."

Barry made like he was going to splash his coffee at David, and both men sat back in their chairs to watch the pedestrian traffic on the avenue: video-game programmers and cooks and sellers of marijuana paraphernalia preparing for another day of commerce.

The sun appeared, then hid behind a cloud, then appeared again. David pulled the Let's Fix It notice out of his jacket pocket and slid it over the silver, uneven table. "What do you make of this?"

A couple of Harleys passed while Barry examined the sheet. David plugged his ears. Albertans didn't need any more government interference in their lives, but there ought to be some restrictions on noise. He took out his notepad and jotted down "Harley noise" as a resolution to be debated at next Tuesday's PC Association meeting.

"This is amazing." Barry nodded at the sheet of paper.

"It's about the shooting next door. Where Benjamin —"

"Maybe sure, but it's really about the city, the province, the country, the continent. This is about effin' George W. Bush. It's about the humans, David, don't you get it?" Barry waved the sheet. "Can I have this?"

"There's thirty of them on my block."

Barry stuffed the paper into his duffel bag, with the street magazines. "This changes everything."

The street paper salesman started to his corner. David opened the magazine to Barry's essay, began to read, and felt anxious. He hugged Garith, who shivered in the cool morning air. It wasn't the prospect of declining oil supplies, of course. David just strongly felt the lack of a caramel mochaccino, and he knew his wife did too.

12

understanding godlessness

The weekly meeting of the philosophy department was held in an expansive room on the fourth floor of the Humanities

Building, overlooking the jogging trails on Saskatchewan Drive and the river beyond. Thirty years ago, these meetings were populated by forty-five men, all of them wearing suits and smoking cigarettes. They never scheduled classes on meeting days, so nearly everyone sipped Scotch out of coffee cups. As Raymond recalled these meetings, and his youth, he closed his eyes in wonder. How handsome he had been, how droll, and envied by his aging mentors.

In 2005, professors drank coffee, vegetable juice, or bottled water. Nearly half of the attendees wore jeans, shorts, or sweatpants. The men still outnumbered the women but not for long; nearly all the young assistant and associate professors were female. The few men hired into the department were either gay or foreign. Once the tenured brontosauruses like Raymond Terletsky retired, the dominion of the white male would end, finally, and women could rule as the great pagan gods intended.

A Running Room group, in matching white T-shirts, passed on the Drive below. In the bright late-morning sun, their black shorts and tights gleamed. Some were chubby, others not so chubby, and a few were in spectacular shape. Mothers, Raymond assumed, working off those pregnancy pounds. He wished, variously, that he was running behind the women and that he was alone in the meeting room with a pair of binoculars. How far could he run without stopping or suffering a massive stroke? When was the last time he had actually gone for a jog? Either 1967 or '68.

"Raymond?"

"Yes."

Half the room erupted in laughter. Obviously, Claudia had been calling his name for some time. "Am I interrupting? Were you figuring out a new application for *Tractatus Logico-philosophicus*?"

More laughter. Even though he stopped seriously studying Wittgenstein in the early 1980s, Raymond's opponents in the department still brought up the now-unfashionable subject of his dissertation. "I was looking at some joggers, actually, critiquing their bums."

The other half of the room, a collection of Raymond's beleaguered and sickly peers in old blazers, fleece jackets, and Birkenstocks, broke out in laughter. Then a few of them trundled into coughing fits.

"It says here you now have only five students registered for your Death in Philosophy seminar."

Claudia lifted her black thousand-dollar spectacles and looked at her watch. "If you lose one more this week, we're going to have to cancel the class."

"Oh, come on."

"We can split one of the surveys, and you can —"

"This is harassment. I'm not teaching two greatest hits courses this semester, Claudia. I'm sorry."

"Harassment." The chair of the department smiled and nodded. Her posture was impeccable, her control of the room complete. Raymond's peers, his teammates, one or two or five years from retirement, were already broken. The men who weren't still coughing slumped in their chairs and inspected the weave in their sleeves or the lines in the palms of their hands. Claudia Santino was beautiful and intelligent and, when she wanted to be, quite cutting. Unbeatable. She lifted her chin, took a breath in through her thin nose, and nodded. "We'll discuss this in private."

If Claudia did cancel his Death in Philosophy seminar, Raymond would press for extra time to work on his new idea for an article. There had been a record number of violent deaths in the Edmonton area in 2005, the most recent one across the street from his house. The Let's Fix It signs were clearly a cry for understanding in a Godless universe. How do individuals or even communities seek to comprehend tragedy when religious answers no longer resonate in their hearts? The paper could ripple out from Edmonton to the avian flu scourge in Asia and the phenomenon of suicide terrorism.

According to social and political trends, these were difficult times for unbelievers in North America. In popular culture, the atheists had gone underground. Yet Raymond felt – no, he knew – that millions of North Americans still sought philosophical answers to traditionally spiritual questions. Even if only five students showed up to his seminar on Thursday night, he still had faith in atheism. Just because something was old didn't mean it was powerless.

Claudia asked if there were any more questions or contributions. Of course, Raymond had a few obscene suggestions for Claudia and her acolytes, but articulating them wouldn't quite fall under the protection of academic freedom.

Both Claudia and Raymond stayed seated quietly while the philosophy professors filed out. Two of his withered associates were brave enough to drop a hand on his shoulder as they passed into the hallway. Claudia stood up. The chair of the philosophy department closed the door and smiled with artificial geniality. "Coffee?"

"I shouldn't."

She returned to her seat and folded her hands on the table. Long fingers, ringless. A pianist's fingers. Raymond glanced out the window again, searching for joggers, but there was only a man pushing a baby carriage while speaking on a cellular phone. The only sound in the room now was water travelling through distant pipes, until he looked back at her.

"Are you a very troubled man, Raymond?"

13

not a rotary meeting

Shirley Wong sat in a giant chanting circle in the yellow Universiade Pavilion – better known as the Butterdome – clapping. Next to her, Abby sang along.

> We got power
> We got faith
> We got John Kenneth . . . Galbraith

A bearded and shirtless man played guitar and two others slapped drums. In front of them, twenty or thirty people danced like Hollywood witches. Thinking this activist fair would be semi-formal, like a theatre opening or box seats at an Oilers game, Shirley had put on a black dress and tan cardigan.

More and more people were jumping up to dance, including Abby. She stood in front of Shirley in her tie-dye T-shirt and loose jeans, her hands out. "Come on, Shirl. Let's shake our things."

"I'm good, thanks."

"Suit yourself." Abby slipped off her sandals and joined the dancers in front of the musicians. She swayed her hips and moved her arms as though she were groping to find a door handle in a dark and turbulent airplane.

Shirley stopped clapping and got up to explore the booths and small seminar groups along the edges of the Butterdome. The incense and patchouli could not overwhelm the rubber smell from the floor of the athletic complex, an odour that reminded Shirley of the turmoil attending her children's winter track meets.

Greenpeace, Amnesty International, Canadian Parks and Wilderness Society, and the David Suzuki Foundation had professional kiosks, with pamphlets and public relations specialists. Other local groups sold hemp products and recycled goods. In the back, fenced off, was a licensed area with organic beer and wine.

In the corner farthest from the entrance, a young man in dreadlocks stood before fifty or sixty people with a microphone attached to his *Utne Reader* T-shirt. He was giving a PowerPoint presentation about the latest, most radical methods to stop logging. On the white screen behind him, photos from Clayoquot Sound and northern California. The young man advocated treehouses, chaining strategies, playing dead in front of the machinery.

"Are we gonna write letters to the editor?"

"Yes!" said the crowd, in unison.

"Are we gonna *live* the change we want?"

"Yes!"

"Are we gonna play dead?"

"Yes!"

That was the formal end of his presentation. The crowd clapped and he lifted his hands. "Now comes the hard part," he said. "At booth twenty, I have chapbooks and CDs and sandalwood soap and T-shirts for sale . . ."

Shirley walked close enough to the chanting circle to see that Abby was still waving around for the door handle. So she checked her wallet and was delighted to discover two crisp twenty-dollar bills.

At the organic beer and wine garden, Shirley bought a glass of Chardonnay and wandered around looking for a seat. All of the tables and most of the chairs were taken. Finally, after walking through the area three times, a woman and her male companion waved.

"Would you like to join us?"

"Thank you," said Shirley, and sat.

The couple introduced themselves – Chris and Nancy Cook. They each had a glass of beer and a bag full of pamphlets, hygiene products, and carob snacks. They pointed out their thirteen-year-old son, Noam Chomsky Cook, who sat with his Game Boy just outside the fence. When Shirley said she owned the Rabbit Warren, they complimented her on the store.

"Though you could certainly have more fair trade products," said Chris. "Don't you think?"

Shirley had endured criticism like this from Abby. Rather than explain the retail business to the Cooks, she nodded and took a sip of organic Chardonnay.

The activist fair was no less hollow than professional hockey, no less hollow than anything she could buy or sell or experience on a night like tonight. Trapped in the vinaigrette aftertaste of the wine, Shirley wished she had just stayed home with Raymond, in the bloody echo of the house across the street. An echo that likely inspired her recent and unprecedented bout of skepticism. Doubt. Gloom.

"Not that we're asking you to change," said Nancy. "Goodness knows."

After another sip of Chardonnay, with her nose plugged, Shirley cleared her throat. "Almost everything in my store is from Canada and the United States. I try to focus on local artists."

"Oh," said Nancy.

"*Almost.*" Chris leaned back in his chair and touched his goatee. "What does 'almost' mean?"

"Not that we're, you know," said Nancy.

Chris began telling Shirley about their recent trip to Peru, wherein he understood for the first time that life here in the northern half of the world is what the Latin Americans call *una broma* – a joke. He used the words bourgeoisie and imperialism in one sentence. The music and singing from the chanting circle halted, and a great roar of applause began. Shirley was just about to tell Chris and Nancy Cook to eat their German sandals when Noam Chomsky appeared at the fence. "Can we go home now?"

"What's your highest score, buddy?" Chris raised his voice toward jollity but didn't actually look at his son.

"I got 1,449."

"As soon as you get over 1,500, then we'll go."

Noam Chomsky stood staring at his parents for a long moment, and then returned to his spot on the rubber floor of the Butterdome. Beyond him, the chanting circle had broken up. Shirley could see Abby wandering around, with her hand above her eyes as though she were blocking out the sun.

Risking a gastrointestinal revolt, Shirley plugged her nose again and finished her glass of wine. "It was a real treat."

"The pleasure was ours," said Chris.

"Absolutely," said Nancy.

The Cooks didn't stand up to shake Shirley's hand, so she didn't bother leaning down to shake theirs. This experience at the activist fair, in sum, had been the opposite of a Rotary meeting.

Shirley exited the organic beer and wine garden and passed over Noam Chomsky Cook, who looked down at a blank screen. Noam Chomsky was only pretending to play his Game Boy. In the distance, Abby spotted Shirley and started jogging toward her.

Instead of meeting Abby halfway, Shirley bent down and put her hand on Noam Chomsky's head. "It gets better."

Noam Chomsky placed his Game Boy on the rubber floor. "When?"

14

a white van arrives

In their investigations, no detectives or CSIS agents had battered down Madison's basement suite door. No one had even left a voicemail message. The police cars hadn't stayed long Monday night, so she assumed the attempted break-in at 10 Garneau had been blamed on teenage miscreants or frat boys. Poor teenage miscreants and frat boys: how much of their nasty reputations did they truly deserve?

All week the crisp mornings had given way to warm afternoons and evenings with light, fragrant winds, the sorts of September afternoons and evenings that inspired false hope in Edmontonians. How could snow dare destroy this?

On Thursday, her day off, Madison agreed to help her mother clear a final growth of weeds from the flowerbeds in their front yard. Though they had talked constantly for almost two hours, Madison had absorbed precisely nothing of her mother's current opinions on global warming, same-sex marriage, marijuana deregulation, and the tenor of a new and inevitable Alberta, controlled by a fiscally conservative yet socially liberal and enlightened urban elite.

"I love talking politics with you, love it." Abby trimmed three rose bushes, tossing the dead or unnecessary bits in a pile of dandelion carcasses. "You don't interrupt me. You never laugh sarcastically or call me a pinko. Your father is my husband and my best friend but sometimes I'd just like to take a strap of leather and . . ."

The soil was so warm and moist, Madison wanted to crawl into it with the earthworms and huddle for six months. When she emerged, strong and rested and wise with her baby, she would be healed. No more anxiety or laziness or regret or confusion.

Madison knew it was immoral and foolish to squander these hours with her mother, who was nearly sixty and would not live forever. Already some parents of her childhood friends had succumbed to cancer; Madison went to three or four funerals every year. In 2002, Jonas lost his grandfather, mother, and cat. Crawling out of his sorrow, what had Jonas suggested? Jonas, who didn't carry a teaspoon of mush in his heart? Listen to them. Phone them back when they call. Go for breakfast. Watch bad movies on Sunday nights. Tell them you love them.

Recalling this advice made Madison's daughterly transgressions seem doubly sinister. As she ignored her mother, she chewed on the consequences of ignoring her mother. A good person would make a memory out of this afternoon in the yard. Instead, Madison stuck her hands deeper into the soil, and twisted them, and made fists.

". . . and what kind of person even *thinks* about buying a Hummer? It's a crime against humanity. And guess what your father thinks? He thinks they're cool. Cool! As though his Yukon Denali isn't big and pointless enough. To him I say, once global warming melts the Arctic and the oceans go cold and start another ice age, well, what then? What about Madison, or your grandchildren if – we hope and hope – we have grandchildren? What are *they* going to do when Alberta is rendered uninhabitable?"

"We'll move to Belize."

"Madison Weiss! How could you say such a thing."

The women were ten feet apart in the yard, separated by a tray with ice water in a sealed pitcher. Madison crawled over and poured herself a glass, and watched Abby clip and trim, the purple veins snaking through her legs and the slight tremble in her hands. "I love you, Mom."

Abby Weiss stood up with a foot-long rose-bush branch in one hand and a pair of hedge trimmers in the other. She looked as if she had been slapped with a glove. Her straw hat was crooked and her 1993 Folk Fest T-shirt had ridden up, revealing her fifty-eight-year-old abs. "Did you just say you love me?"

"I did."

"But you never . . ."

"I just did."

"Well, frick." Abby's eyes glistened and she dropped the hedge trimmers and the rose-bush branch and baby-walked to Madison. They hugged on the warm front lawn, with the laughter and provocations and tinking glasses of nearby restaurant patios audible about them. "That made my day, sweetheart. It really did."

Madison squirrelled out of her mother's grasp. "Get back to your roses."

"Gladly." Abby wiped her tears with the Folk Fest shirt. "Gladly."

Her mother returned to the rose bushes and Madison hunched over the annuals bed again, digging deep into the soil with a decommissioned screwdriver. It was her job to battle the seemingly endless white roots of dandelions. She reached to the bottom of a particularly nasty one and heard a large vehicle apply its brakes. On her knees, she saw one white van and then another in front of 10 Garneau. Without a word, both Madison and Abby dropped their tools and hurried to the sidewalk.

A small team of men and women in matching blue uniforms resembling hospital scrubs emerged from the vans with a variety of indoor and outdoor implements of improvement: buckets, sponges, mops, bleaches, rakes and shovels, garbage bags and touch-up paints in appropriate colours.

Abby approached two deeply tanned men who stayed outside while the rest of the team went in the front door. Stunned and feeling oddly violated, the way she had felt on Monday night when Jonas slipped her VISA card into the door jamb, Madison hung back on the sidewalk.

"Lovely to see you," said Abby.

The two men looked at one another.

"What are you people doing here?"

Now that Madison had grown used to the idea that Jeanne and Katie were in Mexico or Calgary, that Benjamin Perlitz had died in a pool of his own blood in the master bedroom upstairs, she was beginning to accept 10 Garneau as it was. Madison realized, on the sidewalk, as a cloud of tiny bugs formed over her head, that she had been taking a sort of secret pleasure in the tragedy; the sort of pleasure she once took in muscle injuries after cross-country ski races.

The whole city had been implicated in the death of Benjamin Perlitz, just as it had been implicated in the murdered policemen, the thirteen-year-old girl found dead on the golf course, the Somali cab driver stabbed and stuffed into his own trunk, the pregnant wife beaten to death and abandoned in a ditch. The whole country and culture had been implicated. Yet this particular horror wasn't just local. It was next door. Jeanne Perlitz was her gardening friend. Once, when she had locked herself out of the house, Jeanne had come into Madison's basement suite and they'd watched a cooking show together. Madison had babysat Katie several times, while Jeanne and Benjamin went to the theatre, the opera, the ski hill in Whitemud Creek.

This was Madison's special horror. It bestowed certain rights upon her. The right to feel victimized, to sulk dramatically, to surf the Internet for something more substantial than crib prices. How could these people in stiff blue cotton uniforms bleach, rake, mop, and shovel it away?

15

the block party

Soon, the sidewalk in front of 10 Garneau was congested with the curious. Shirley Wong and Abby Weiss insisted on filling a cooler with German beer and Costco pop. David Weiss suggested pizza and Raymond Terletsky agreed it was a brilliant idea, as long as pepperoni and mushrooms were involved.

It took several minutes for Jonas Pond to appear, his short brown hair twirled by the pillow. He stood next to Madison and yanked her ponytail. "Toot toot. So is there an exorcism going down or what?"

"It's four in the afternoon. Did you just wake up?"

"Don't judge me, woman."

"Did you just wake up?"

"I had a rehearsal last night, absolutely gruelling, for a two-hander about – you guessed it – coming out of the closet. What we really have to do is ban stupid people from getting theatre degrees. In fact, let's set up checkpoints at all roads leading into Old Strathcona and downtown. That way . . ."

"They're in the house."

"Who are?"

"Cleaners."

"What house? This house?"

"You know what, Jonas, maybe you should grab another fourteen or fifteen hours of shut-eye."

"Are those men Bolivian? The ones picking up the garbage?"

"I have no idea, but they only speak Spanish. Abby tried to get some info from them, but all they can do in English is apologize."

"Well, at least they're adapting to Canadian culture." Jonas shook his arms, rolled his shoulders, and initiated a mouth-stretching exercise: "Pah-Teek-Hah. Pah-Teek-Hah. Joowish. Joowish. Kansas City Rollers. Boooomtown." Then he started up the grass to speak to the workers.

"What's he doing?" said David Weiss, who sat in a lawn-chair with Garith on his lap. He had just returned from playing eighteen holes at the Mayfair with a party donor. "Does he know those guys?"

"He's practising his Spanish."

"That seems inappropriate."

Madison shrugged.

"Sit down, have a beer. It really strips some of the macabre out of this."

"I don't want a beer, Dad."

"Hey, you love beer. Come on. Tell your old man a story."

Madison watched the women moving rhythmically behind the upstairs window. It took two of them to mop the wood floors. On the night it happened, she hadn't been able to see Benjamin up there with the gun. It was too dark, and the tactical unit kept everyone back. Residents of the Garneau Block weren't allowed to be in their houses, so they huddled behind roadblocks with the media and local bystanders, drinking Sugarbowl coffee and trying to hear what Benjamin was screaming out the window.

The last Fringe play of the festival had been earlier that evening, and afterward she and Jonas had sat in the Casa RadioActive tent drinking with a table full of actors. Since she had been nursing a cranberry juice, the competition for speaking time and attention between the drunken performers had been almost too much to take, so she daydreamed about her baby. Names she might give him or her, and whether or not she could afford one of those running strollers with the big mountain-bike tires.

When Jonas lost the ability to deliver a coherent sentence that Sunday night, she helped him up and they started home.

Four blocks away, with the flashing lights visible behind the Garneau Theatre, it was obvious something had gone wrong. Madison's first worry was that her parents were dead. A break-in, a fire, a violent left-wing reprisal against David Weiss.

They reached the roadblocks as fast as Madison could drag the stumbling, mumbling Jonas, and the policewoman guided them to a safe place to wait out the ordeal. Madison was pleased to see her parents and Jonas was pleased to see a soft patch of grass. Luckily, one of the ambulances had several extra woollen blankets. Madison covered him up.

So what did they know? They knew that Benjamin, who Jeanne had kicked out, was back in the house. They knew he was drunk and raving and that he had a gun. What was he thinking? Well, no answers there.

Now, more than two weeks later, Jonas concluded his exploratory interview with the Latin American men working in the front yard by shaking their hands and kissing their cheeks. He reported back to Madison with a cringe.

"What did they say? Who hired them?"

"Their accent is strong, their vocabulary is quite advanced, and they talk really fast. I'm only in level two Spanish."

"But you spoke to them. In Spanish."

"I did, I did. But I opened with *buenas tardes* so flawlessly they must've figured I was bilingual. After the first bit I just nodded and said *si, si.*"

"So you don't know who hired them?"

Jonas attempted to flatten the pillow swirls in his hair. "I didn't catch anything like that. But I think they're looking forward to Christmas time, and they enjoy living here in

Canada." He turned around, southward, and raised his hand to block the sun. "Hey. Hey, hello to you!"

On the opposite sidewalk, in a suit and carrying a stiff black briefcase, stood the young Indian man from across the street. The young Indian man from across the street looked around to make sure Jonas was speaking to him. Then he waved and started up the red stone walk leading to 13 Garneau.

"Now that is a good-looking gent."

Madison nodded.

"Have you ever heard him speak? Or seen him with anyone?"

Madison shook her head.

"Do you think he's a member of India's secret service?"

"No, Jonas."

"Let's ask him right now if he wants to go on a date with you. Unless, of course, there's a language barrier."

Jonas began pulling Madison's arm. She resisted, and eventually kicked him. "Absolutely not."

"Did you see that briefcase? That means he's employed. You have to ask him out."

"Why, because I'm such a sweet catch? I'm sure he's looking for a pregnant travel agent who lives in her parents' basement."

"Sometimes you're just miserable, Madison, and I have to say it affects your degree of attractiveness."

"You go talk to him. You can practise another pretend foreign language."

Jonas started to push Madison across the street. She was just about to get a hand free and slap his heavily moisturized face when Garith barked. The cleaners inside 10 Garneau were coming out.

16

massage therapy

Raymond Terletsky didn't understand what they had all expected to learn from the cleaning crew that had been inside 10 Garneau. Surely they knew blood was nearly impossible to remove from hardwood, especially after settling in for two weeks. Had they hoped to extract some deep human truth or even Jeanne's new address from Sandi, the only person among the cleaners who spoke fluent English?

The neighbours seemed particularly disappointed when Sandi raised one eyebrow and answered their concerns with a query of her own:

"Yeah, any you guys got a smoke I could bum?"

Sitting on the sidewalk in lawnchairs, drinking two Heineken and talking about peak oil with David Weiss, had been somewhat comical, especially when David started quoting from the street paper. But after the cleaners drove off, when Raymond's wife and neighbours decided to have a final drink at the Sugarbowl and, according to Jonas Pond, "decompress," Raymond decided to go his own way, and his way was clear.

He needed a massage.

The masseuse was a former student, a divorcée from Kamloops who tried a year of philosophy courses in 2001 to see if they might make her life more meaningful. Apparently, knowing a thing or two about the trial and death of Socrates, *cogito, ergo sum,* and the central argument in Mill's *On Liberty* merely strengthened her determination not to think so hard. She decided there was no shame in daydreaming about Cozumel while she pressed her palms into flesh.

Charlene the masseuse lived in a two-bedroom suite in Windsor Park Plaza, with a partial view of old Corbett Hall. Before he knew she was available, Raymond made his way westward and called her on his cellular phone.

"I don't know, Dr. Terletsky. Thursday's my TV night."

"How about I pay double."

"Why would you do that?"

"I just will. Say yes."

Charlene sighed. "Yes."

In the elevator, Raymond grew nervous. He always grew nervous in the few minutes before seeing Charlene. Though she was not beautiful or even pretty, Charlene had a focused stare and a disarming way of speaking that he knowingly mistook for flirtation. The door was open when he arrived, and Charlene had already changed into the loose, nursey white shirt and pants she wore when she worked.

Instead of saying hello, Charlene bit her bottom lip when he came through the door. "I was thinking."

"About what?"

"How am I supposed to fill out your receipt if you're paying me double? I bet your health plan only covers about sixty bucks an hour."

"The rest is a tip."

"You're gonna give me a sixty-dollar tip?"

"Yes. I am."

Charlene crossed her arms, tilted her head, and left him to change.

The massage room was Charlene's second bedroom, so the sliding closet doors were mirrors. Before he covered himself with the towel, Raymond considered his naked body in reflection. To live authentically, says Heidegger, we must learn to confront death. We must welcome it here, alone before the mirror, in the jam-and-jelly scent of our aging skin. We must appreciate that despite our broad consciousness, despite our instinctual special-ness, we were born to die.

Heidegger's secular update of Kierkegaard's leap of faith produces a deep and irrevocable transformation in anyone who manages to make it. In front of the mirror, relatively certain he had made the leap, Raymond comprehended the totality of existence. Then he grabbed the loose flesh around his waist and wished beyond wishing that he could just slice it off with a butcher knife.

Charlene knocked. "Ready?"

"Ready."

The shades were down and the lights were low, the minia-ture fountain tinkled and *The Goldberg Variations* played on the tiny stereo in the corner. Charlene didn't speak as she worked, which made Raymond think naughtier thoughts than he might have if she'd chatted about her parents or her fear of squirrels. With her slippery fingers digging into his back and then – sweet daisy – his front, Raymond had to work like an Egyptian slave to maintain decorum.

Then, remembering Heidegger, he relaxed. He was born to die. This was an opportunity for adventure, and he really didn't have that much time left. If he wasted this, he would waste everything.

"Charlene."

She said nothing.

"Charlene."

"Shhh. No talking. It ruins the healing."

"How much extra would it be, I mean just theoretically, if someone wanted more than a massage?"

Charlene's fingers halted. She cleared her throat, walked to the light switch, turned it on and exited the room. On her way out, she slammed the door.

Raymond suspected this adventure was over.

Dressed again, and with some time to absorb and appreciate his humiliation, he checked the window. Charlene was on the eleventh floor, far too high to jump. So Raymond sighed, and opened the door.

"Charlene, I was just . . ."

"Out."

"I was conducting an experiment."

"Zero tolerance policy. Out."

Raymond opened his mouth twice more, but Charlene interrupted him sternly. She picked up her cordless phone and dialled three numbers. Nine-one-one? He hurried out of her apartment, down the hallway, and into the elevator. Four men in T-shirts and baseball caps were in the car, and they didn't stop talking when Raymond entered. It seemed the young men were on their way to Whyte Avenue, where they hoped to meet like-minded women, bring them back to Windsor Park Plaza, and do what comes naturally to drunk people between the ages of eighteen and twenty-one.

Perhaps Shirley and his neighbours were still at the Sugarbowl. Perhaps he could catch them there, take his wife's hand and apologize in silence, secretly beg forgiveness. For the first time since 1967 – or was it 1968? – Raymond ran.

17

bison with fancy bacon and blueberry sauce

Downtown sidewalks were crowded with noon-hour joggers and their opposites, the grey-faced cigarette people banned from office complexes. Young men and women in shorts and wrinkled T-shirts wandered down the promenade of lofts, not long ago a ghost town of deserted warehouses. Pimply high-school dropouts in giant pants and crooked baseball caps stood in front of the old Bay building, now home to a television and radio station, and swayed to the dull rhythms pumped out of little speakers on Jasper Avenue.

It was Friday and summer had returned in earnest. Edmontonians smiled and laughed into their cellular phones, adjusted their sunglasses, flipped through newspapers, sipped coffee on patios. The everywhere construction workers, putting up yet another condominium, told each other blue jokes and stared at passing women.

David Weiss wanted to kick every one of the idle workmen, with their hard hats covered in union stickers. *If you love communism so much, why don't you go to China, or Quebec? Get to work! The dominion of Alberta isn't going to build itself.*

Every Friday, he dressed in a black suit and took lunch with three other riding association presidents. Instead of paying six or nine dollars to park in an underground garage downtown for a couple of hours, David nearly always left his Yukon Denali in a Save On Foods lot and walked twelve blocks to the restaurant.

The previous evening had been difficult for his wife and daughter. Abby and Madison had hoped to discover the whereabouts of the remaining Perlitzes, Jeanne and Katie. But the cleaning crew that had been in 10 Garneau consisted of inarticulate dim-bulbs, working for someone else who may or may not have known anything.

Of course, the resonance of his family's disappointment explained David's failure to phone in a lunch reservation the day before. He didn't like to flaunt his power, but David had called the Hardware Grill as soon as it opened that morning and mentioned, casually, that he needed a table to discuss PC policy. The premier would likely join them this afternoon.

David arrived at the Hardware Grill and the manager was summoned. He shook David's hand and called him Mr. Weiss and asked if there was anything he could do to make the premier's experience an enjoyable one. There was a line of sweat along the manager's hairline, and a faint twitch in the skin beneath his right eye. David realized it would be immoral to break the news to the poor man now.

"We'll let you know. For the moment, just the table and a wine list."

"Right away, Mr. Weiss."

David felt he had made the best possible choice in restaurants. The air conditioning was at a civilized level, and the baroque chamber music inspired him to sit with excellent posture. Somewhere, he knew, a chef was wrapping fancy bacon around a hunk of bison and drizzling blueberry sauce over it.

David had spent his working life as a high-school math teacher, with a high-school math teacher's salary and pension, so the Hardware Grill and its pleasures should have been at least two notches above him. How barren and middling would his retirement be today, David wondered, if he hadn't joined the party? Why, at this very moment he would be slouching over a plate of grilled tofu at the Roots Organic Market with his wife and Maddy.

This is what vexed him about Edmonton: the city's tragic habit of voting against its interests, of settling for grilled tofu when it could have bison with fancy bacon and blueberry sauce. Calgary had a better airport and more head offices than Edmonton simply because its citizens voted as a Conservative block. In the nine years since he joined the party, David Weiss had come to see himself as a walking and talking Calgary. If he hadn't joined, he would be a plain old Edmonton – needlessly complicated, unsure, artsy, and angry.

David waved when his colleagues entered the restaurant. That morning, he had tipped them off about the premier ruse.

He watched the manager of the Hardware Grill bow before them, and hoped his friends wouldn't spoil the man's day with the truth quite yet.

All week, David had been eager to meet with his fellow riding association presidents. Though he would never admit it, David had grown somewhat concerned about the notion of oil running out. His research on the Internet had only inspired further anxiety, as Barry's warnings and conspiracies were only heightened and expanded on American web sites. Since reading the street magazine, he had stared at the ceiling each night in the darkness, listening to his wife's gentle breathing and thinking about a world without oil.

David wanted his colleagues, especially Grant, a former executive with Suncor, to tell him this peak oil stuff was left-wing hocus pocus. The middle-class Canadian lifestyle was invincible. It would last forever.

Right?

They shook hands and sat around the table. David's three colleagues each motioned to the empty chairs. Grant leaned forward. "You didn't tell the manager yet?"

"I didn't have the heart."

The four men turned to the manager, who smiled and nodded enthusiastically from across the room. Grant offered a thumbs-up and turned back to the table. "It's sort of sick, what we're doing here."

"Who's going to tell him?" said David.

Grant and the others laughed. It was obviously David's job to tell the manager, as he had fashioned the lie. The server passed and Grant ordered a bottle of Australian Cabernet.

David borrowed a cellular phone from Al, president of the Mill Creek riding association, the only one among them to have a winner in the legislature.

Then, for a minute or so, David had a pretend conversation with the premier's chief of staff. "What?" he said, into the silent phone. "An emergency involving cattle? Well, yes, we understand completely. Godspeed, godspeed."

18

jonas has a stalker

Friday afternoon, only two customers came into Sparkle Vacations. They were first-year university students, girls, wondering about flying home to Kingston and Montreal during the Christmas break. Madison saw them every year, the shy kids in residence who haven't made any pals by the end of the second week of classes. Missing the smell of their own beds, their parents' cooking, and boyfriends who had stayed behind.

Then, by December, all that is forgotten. They don't want to leave their new beds or their new boyfriends.

Madison browsed a few local classified Internet sites – men looking for women – but it only discouraged her. So she clicked around looking for "Perlitz" in white page listings across Mexico and flipped through the new winter travel brochures. As soon as the days turned as cold as the nights, business would increase dramatically at Sparkle Vacations and Madison would have to know her southern destinations as though she had actually been somewhere more exotic than Knott's Berry Farm.

Most travel agents go on free trips paid for by a variety of resort and hotel chains to introduce them to their properties. However, Tammy "Sparkle" Davidson didn't allow it. At a Chamber of Commerce luncheon, just before Madison was hired, Tammy had a long conversation with the then-editor of the newspaper. The conversation touched on various subjects not limited to their mutual love of sailboats as ideas more than actual things, what with all the waves and ropes and dependency on wind. The then-editor told her that his journalists were regularly invited on free trips, junkets, organized and bankrolled by Hollywood studios and the tourism departments of cities around the world. Of course, it was immoral to take such trips; one's objectivity would be compromised.

Tammy found the then-editor of the newspaper quite charming. They went out on a couple of theatre dates together and spent a sunny afternoon at the Folk Festival before they both realized, over a plate of chicken bhoona in Gallagher Park, that a relationship between them was more interesting as an idea than an actual thing. But she bought and retained the compromised objectivity argument, even if it made very little sense in the context of travel agencies.

When the door beeped a third time, just before six, Madison exited the Guadalajara white pages directory. She had made a list of seven possible Perlitzes in the state of Jalisco, and even though she didn't have anything more productive to do,

Madison didn't want to argue with Tammy about wasting company time and resources.

It wasn't Tammy but Jonas, in one of his blue rehearsal sweatsuits, looking as though he were on the verge of an asthma attack. He sat across from her with his eyes open wide.

"What?"

Jonas raised one eyebrow. "Do you really want to know or are you just humouring me? I know I talk too much."

"Shut up and tell me."

"I have a stalker! Finally, after all these years being astonishing, I have a stalker. Is there any coffee?" He hopped up and sprinted to the customer service counter. There was coffee but it was several hours old, and he seemed to sense it. "When did you make this stuff?"

"Ten."

"Gross, Madison." Jonas turned to her and shook his head. "That is so disgusting." Then he poured himself a cup and dropped in six lumps of sugar.

"Who is this stalker?"

"It's Carlos. Our friend Carlos."

"I don't have a friend Carlos." The acrid smell of the old coffee stirred up with half a cup of sugar brought forth a familiar trickle of nausea. Madison pushed back her chair and prepared to pick up the nearby garbage can, in case the trickle became a wave. "Is that your Spanish teacher?"

"Carlos! Carlos!" Jonas took a long drink of his coffee. "Yum, it's like iced coffee, but hot. From the Next Act that night? The nervous guy."

"The frat boy?"

"My stalker is a frat boy. What do you think I should do?"

Madison picked up the garbage can and walked to the door. She opened it and smelled the exhaust of late-rush-hour Whyte Avenue. It was much better than the syrup Jonas was drinking. Once, in high school, to impress a hockey player, she had guzzled a mickey of Kahlua. It was best not to remember this incident, so Madison thought of bears riding bicycles.

"If you throw up, preggy, then I'll throw up. We'll both be throwing up for hours, in an endless cycle of convulsions. So please, please try not to."

"That's why I opened the door."

"You don't even care about my stalker."

"Just let me be nauseous for a minute here."

Jonas got up and examined the travel wallets and passport carriers for sale on the spinning trolley. "He isn't much of a covert operative, our Carlos. My rehearsals are at the Roxy, and he was loitering across the street in front of a quick cash place. The first thing I do, whenever I walk on to 124th Street, is dish an evil eye to those quick cash places. Usurers. Dirty usurers! And there was Carlos, crouched next to a Sunfire. At first I didn't know who it was. I recognized him, but from where? The gym?"

It was past six and the nausea had faded, so Madison closed and locked the door. "Then you remembered him."

"Then I remembered."

"Are you sure it wasn't a coincidence? Maybe he needed some quick cash. Maybe that was his Sunfire."

"Would you please let me tell the story?"

"Sorry." Madison turned off her computer and leaned against the poster of Athens.

"I walked to the bus stop and waited for a long time before I turned around. I knew Carlos was still there because my intuition is extraordinarily strong."

"Of course it is."

"Was that sarcastic?"

Madison felt another trickle of nausea. "I don't even know."

"I waited and waited and then I *sprung*. I turned and there he was, by that little fence around Albert's Pancakes."

"Wow."

"Jim howdy wow. So I yelled at him. 'Carlos!' I said."

"What did he do?"

Jonas demonstrated. "He made eye contact with me for a sec, did a little stutter step, and ran across the street. He just kept running and running, until I couldn't see him."

"Maybe he's touched. In the head, like."

"Maybe, but he's my stalker. You can't deny that. So are you ready?"

"For what?"

"Ethiopian cuisine, home to change into something tight and shiny, then *boom boom boom*. We're going to the Roost."

"I'm not going to the Roost."

"Oh, yes, you are." Jonas jumped up on Madison's desk. "*Boom boom boom*."

19

the young indian man from across the street

Jonas had read about the Ethiopian place in the newspaper, but obviously he hadn't read carefully. Instead of utensils, you pick up and eat Ethiopian food with sour, rolled-up bread. To Madison's delight, Jonas treated this like a practical joke. He folded his arms and pouted while Madison sopped up a lamb and spinach dish with the tasty bread.

"Just eat, Jonas. No one has to know."

"Listen, I saw you lick your fingers and put them right back in the platter. If I wanted to share your nasty hormone-laced saliva, I'd just French kiss you. No, don't worry about me. I'll just get something at the A&W on the walk home."

It was impossible to ignore Jonas in this state. The server came by. "Is everything good?"

"*Fine*," said Jonas.

Madison laughed. "Could you bring Mr. Poopypants a fork, please?"

The server explained the tradition of eating this sort of food with your hands, and mentioned that it is perfectly hygienic as long as all hands are clean. After the speech, Madison thanked her and asked, again, if Mr. Poopypants could have a fork.

"No, don't even bother, *thanks*." Jonas sat up straight in his chair and lifted his chin like a new member of the royal family. "Mrs. Door Handle Toucher, Mrs. Didn't Wash Her Hands Before She Started Eating has already contaminated the whole bit."

"Um," said the server.

On the way home, Jonas stopped at A&W to purchase a bag of Chubby Chicken and fries. They didn't talk much as they walked, and Madison hoped the Ethiopian cuisine debacle had weakened his interest in dancing at the Roost. Jonas finished his dinner-in-a-bag as they reached the parking lot behind the Garneau Theatre. He rubbed his now-greasy hands together and began to cackle.

"What?"

"I have a scheme."

"What sort?"

Jonas remained silent and menacing, so Madison took him by the arms and shook him. "What? What?"

"Before we change into our club clothes and embark on an emotional and possibly romantic journey, I'm going to invite the young Indian man from across the street to come out with us."

"Oh, no, you're not."

"How long have we lived across the street from the young Indian man from across the street?"

"Just no. Please."

"You owe me, after the Ethiopian food thing."

Madison pushed him as they entered the Garneau Block. "No, you owe *me*. You acted like an ass in there, and embarrassed everyone."

"It almost sounds like you don't want to go dancing tonight."

"I never did want to go dancing, Jonas."

Madison hated the silent treatment but it was preferable to a night of thumping disco. So she decided not to apologize or allow herself to be manipulated by any wounded expressions. But instead of marching through his front door and slamming it behind him, Jonas started across the street to 13 Garneau.

"What are you doing?"

Jonas sauntered up the walkway, past a small rock garden with two choke cherry trees, a small paper birch, and a spruce. The house was a white wooden two-storey with red trim and a small terrace. From time to time Madison would watch the young Indian man from across the street through his front picture window, sipping a glass of wine or a single bottle of Dutch beer in the evening while reading a novel. She wondered if he was lonesome or if he just preferred things this way. No one had ever seen another being enter or exit 13 Garneau, but that didn't mean he wasn't caring for sick parents or grand-parents inside.

Every morning the young Indian man from across the street left at the same time, 7:15, in one of his fine suits, carrying a black leather briefcase. He walked toward the university, presumably to take the LRT across the river. No one at the university, even in the business faculty, dressed as well as the young Indian man from across the street. Madison guessed he was a lawyer.

Jonas stood on the young Indian man from across the street's front terrace. Already he had rung the doorbell twice. He pressed the button a third time, knocked, and waited thirty seconds. Jonas turned and addressed Madison. "You are *so* lucky."

The young Indian man from across the street appeared in the picture window. He watched Jonas walking away from his house, and looked up at Madison. The young Indian man from across the street shrugged. It was a "should I bother with this?" sort of shrug.

Madison shook her head. No.

Jonas had not stopped talking. "And you were going to be a freak because I *know* how you are about new people."

The young Indian man from across the street smiled and waved goodnight. At that moment, to her surprise, Madison was stricken by the desire to dance.

20

dancing with herself

Madison hoped they could stand in line on the concrete steps of the Roost for a while, with the people. The two men in front of her were talking about the cleverness of Conservative politics. One, who looked like an accountant, said, "It's the only way to get poor people in rural Alberta to vote against the welfare state. They make it seem like you and me and the Canadian figure skating team are on our way out there, in our pink Smart Cars, to get married in the Baptist Church and have anal sex in the town hall bathroom."

His partner fashioned his cardigan into a veil, and they walked along the step as though down an aisle.

Madison wanted to hear more but Jonas was already at the top of the stairs, and the front of the line, with one hand on the doorman's arm and the other waving her up. In certain Edmonton communities, Jonas was famous. The gay community was one of them.

There were two dance floors at the Roost. That night, the main floor featured thumping college rock anthems from the 1980s. Madison checked her coat and by the time she was finished, Jonas was already under the flashing lights with a gin and soda in his hand. It was wrong to drink and dance at the same time, and Jonas knew how she felt about this. But Madison joined him anyway, to the tired old sissy laser rock of "Tainted Love."

Why couldn't Madison be like Jonas and everyone else on the dance floor? Why couldn't she stop worrying about everything? She knew there were probably pills she could take; she knew the secret to gaining pleasure from an overplayed song was to shut off her critical faculties, to stop being herself, to stop feeling that someone just like her might see her on the dance floor and think, "Guh. Loser."

She wondered if anyone in the club actually liked "Tainted Love." Surely, it was just a memory trigger. Jonas and everyone else screaming the lyrics, raising their arms and lowering their heads triumphantly, bumping into each other with their eyes closed, were twenty-one again. Young and clever and beautiful again.

Like marijuana, homosexuality had lost its outlaw reputation. When Madison first danced at the Roost, in the wake of another notorious Edmonton gay club, Flashback, the room still hummed with the naughty energy of the 1980s. No one could be gay at a day job, so everyone had to be extra gay at night. Men dressed up as women, or at least wore makeup and black nail polish. Women took their shirts off and danced until they were shiny with sweat. They kissed with tongue, and more. There were those guys who wore nothing but chaps, and girls in bicycle shorts and pasties.

Now the Roost was just an older and smarter version of kiddy clubs, without the fistfights. Madison and Jonas were dressed like everyone else, in jeans and the most flattering T-shirts in their closets. As "Tainted Love" ended and "Love Song" by The Cure began with a howl of nostalgic joy, Madison spotted the only real wildcat in the club: a cowboy who looked like he'd just walked off the ranch. Jonas saw him at the same time, and said, "Giddy-up." He handed his drink to Madison, and approached the cowboy.

And that was the last Madison would see of Jonas in the Roost.

She put his drink on the bar and walked upstairs, where there was more room on the dance floor. Up here, the DJ played somewhat dated techno music. Madison found a corner, away from the small hordes of curious straight boys in Molson shirts and baseball caps, and watched herself dance in the mirror. She felt this would be her last night on a nightclub dance floor, ever. She wanted to remember what she looked like before she turned thirty and had a child, before her youth ended officially. The bass went straight to her stomach, and she imagined her baby swimming to the beat.

Several songs later, with a layer of sweat forming on the back of her neck, Madison left the dance floor to splash some water on her face and buy a glass of cranberry and club soda. Before she hit the washroom door, she saw Jeanne Perlitz pass on the other side of a pillar.

Madison turned and slammed into a man in an airline pilot's suit who had apparently taken a bath in Issey Miyake for Men. He spilled some beer on himself and said, "Excuse *me*!" If she had not been pursuing Jeanne Perlitz, Madison would have helped him sop the beer out of his sleeve. But there was no time.

"Sorry," she said, and ran to the top of the stairs. Madison looked down, and saw the top of Jeanne Perlitz's head in the crowd at the bottom. She pushed her way through heavy streams of people going up and down the stairs.

Madison weaved around the pool tables, toward the coat check. She ran past the lineup and out on to the street. Two women were hugging and crying, and some people were on the sidewalk across the street, smoking, but there was no Jeanne Perlitz.

Back inside, she retrieved her jacket and described Jeanne Perlitz to the coat check man.

"Blonde and pretty and sort of forty? That sounds like just about every woman to me." The coat check man leaned on the counter between them. "Just get back in there and find yourself another one, sweetie. Put a band-aid on that heart and get right back in the game."

Madison waited for a cab and bounced to keep warm. A large white SUV rumbled slowly up the street. The rear passenger window opened and a young man in a baseball cap yelled,

"Lezout!" As his friends howled with laughter, he threw a McDonald's cup out the window and it exploded on the pavement in front of Madison. Strawberry milkshake covered her sneakers and the cuffs of her jeans. She looked down at the pink mess for a few minutes, until a cab appeared.

21

louis chopin of armstrong crescent

Toward the end of the Monday Introductory Philosophy class, Raymond Terletsky questioned his motives. Earlier that morning, he had received an e-mail from Claudia Santino; the department had decided not to cancel his Death in Philosophy seminar. In a gushing fit of animation and fellow-feeling, he sent a message to his five seminar students. If any of them was interested, he wanted to take a class field trip to the World Waterpark at West Edmonton Mall tomorrow. They would meet in the lobby at ten in the morning.

An hour after sending the message, as his survey students debated whether or not a modified version of Plato's Republic would be better than Canada's constitutional monarchy, he stared at the back wall of the classroom and wondered: Did he truly see any philosophical value in sliding down the Sky Screamer? Or had his guilt over the unpleasant episode with Charlene the massage therapist already faded, leaving only an impish desire to see his female seminar students in bikinis?

"But the guys we elect are crap," one of the survey students said, while chewing gum. "At least a philosopher king would be smart."

A nearby woman with purple hair snuffled at the words guys and kings. "Yeah, but what if *she* went mental? What if *she* woke up mental one morning and decided to bomb China? Then we'd all end up dead. Thanks, philosopher *queen*."

Raymond glanced at his watch as the debate continued. He worried, briefly, for the collective intellectual power of this generation. Then he questioned his motives again. Nay, his sanity. It wasn't healthy to drive past hookers on his way to buy pickles. It wasn't healthy to fantasize about Claudia Santino and to make subtle suggestions to his massage therapist, not when he had a beautiful and utterly supportive wife. As the class ended and the students filed out into the bright hallways, Raymond considered Purple Hair's warning. What *about* waking up mental one day?

Back in his office, he flipped through the yellow pages until he found a list of psychologists. Most of them were downtown, a short LRT ride away, so he chose one at random: K. L. Fisketjon and Associates. The woman who answered the phone was jolly. "You know, we had a cancellation this afternoon at one. Are you free?"

Raymond was free.

"Your name and address?"

In the next few seconds, a variety of events took place inside Raymond's skull. He didn't understand the process, which is why the fields of philosophy and psychology exist. But he was startled by his answer. "Louis Chopin."

"Okay, Mr. Chopin. Your address?"

"Thirteen . . . Armstrong Crescent."

"Wow," said the scheduling secretary. "Your name and address, together, are a jazz singer. And Chopin, too. You sure sound famous."

"Everyone seems to notice that."

Raymond took lunch, a donair, in Hub Mall. As the sweet yogurt sauce dripped out of the aluminum foil and down his wrist, he watched the women pass. So many of them on their cellular phones, having inane conversations. Presumably with thug boyfriends. If they only knew how well a certain fifty-four-year-old philosophy professor could treat them, how carefully.

In Hub, he made an effort to look down at the newspaper instead of at young women. As usual, he read every word in the obituary pages. From a philosophy of death point of view, the contemporary funeral ritual was fascinating. The last paper Raymond had published, in a journal out of Malta, had been about the hierarchy of funerals.

Family and friends gather so they can be introspective together in the glow of the body, so they can use the body as a means of communication and a social trophy. It is a special day for the family and friends of the corpse, whose names are in the obituary section of the newspaper. They are principal mourners, surrounded by peripheral acquaintances. Pretenders. Even in their exalted position, principals will stand over the dead body and wonder about their dry cleaning, remember a gag from the rerun of *Seinfeld* that had been on television as they changed into their black suits that morning.

Eloquent and typically self-concerned members of the principal group will offer to say a few words in tribute to the corpse, tell some lighthearted anecdote about that time the corpse spilled coffee on the dog. Members of the audience will laugh before the corpse and afterward, over a table of date squares and caffeinated refreshments, they will compliment the speaker for delivering an entertaining eulogy.

Raymond had bought several hundred copies of the Maltese journal to send to colleagues across North America and Europe. Only two sent notes of congratulation, and they were largely personal. About his two children, how they must be grown up by now.

At a quarter to one, Raymond started down into the LRT station. The chance of receiving a fine was more remote than being slapped across the face by the schizophrenic woman playing the ukelele, but Raymond bought a ticket. At five to one, in front of the Western Canadian Bank tower, Raymond decided he didn't need a psychologist after all. He feared it would be an uncomfortable and expensive experience. The jovial secretary would attempt to locate Louis Chopin of Armstrong Crescent, and she would fail.

Raymond continued to the City Centre Mall, where he browsed the clothing and accessories at Urban. This is where the wealthiest and most fashionable of his students shopped. Complicated music played out of the public address system. A man with a black Mohawk, wearing ripped jeans and a blazer that looked as though it had been vandalized by spray paint artists, asked if he was shopping for himself or his son.

"My son," said Raymond. "Of course."

22

spaceship sounds

One of these days, before she actually gave birth, Madison would have to tell David and Abby about their impending grandparenthood. The thought struck her as she waited in the rain at a long, long red light on her way to the clinic. Keeping the pregnancy from her parents made her feel like a mischievous teenager, a shoplifter. A lonesome shoplifter.

Madison had borrowed her father's Yukon Denali for the afternoon. Perched above the rest of traffic in the puffball of imaginary convenience, she usually ducked whenever she saw someone she knew. But as Madison pictured her child in the backseat, protected by all this weight and leather, she saw how the automobile companies created demand. Bring on a meteor strike or a jihad or a dinosaur attack or World War III, she thought. Junior and I can bivvy in.

The cellular phone on its cradle began to ring. Its tone, to her dismay, was "Born to Be Wild." Assuming it was one of her father's friends hoping to meet up and be exceedingly right-wing sometime soon, Madison ignored it. Then the phone rang again. And again.

She pulled into a gas station. "Hello, David Weiss's phone."

"Why weren't you picking up?" Her father cleared his throat. "I've been calling."

"You need me to grab something for you, Dad?"

"Nah. How's the old girl running?"

"The Yukon? Fine, I guess." Madison turned off the engine. "Do you need groceries?"

"Not really."

"So why did you call? I left the house five minutes ago."

"Can't a father call his daughter just to talk once in a while?"

"We ate breakfast together. And I don't like talking on the phone and driving. It's dangerous and I look like a goof."

David Weiss sighed. "The old girl runs like a dream though, doesn't she?"

"Not my dream. And stop calling it an old girl. It's a 2003."

"Oh, don't get all David Suzuki on me. Buy your own hybrid, you want one so damn much. They aren't cheap, you know. And what if it blows up, with that big weird battery? It's not like we're gonna *run out of oil* around here, right? Right? You haven't heard that, have you?"

"I'm gonna go, okay Dad?"

"Don't worry about filling her up. I'll take care of that."

"Thanks."

"Love you."

"Love you too, Dad."

"Love you. Bye. Love you, sweetie. Say bye to Maddy, Garith. Woof woof. I ruh you. I ruh you ro ruch."

In the waiting room at the clinic, Madison chose from among five 2002 *Maclean's* magazines and looked at the words in an article about Leonard Cohen's son without actually reading.

She doubted the machine would hear the baby's heart over the insistent hammering of her own. Reaching twelve weeks in her pregnancy meant it was actually going to happen. Soon, too soon, Madison would be a mother. A mother. The thought sent a jolt through her so potent that she pressed a thumb through Adam Cohen's neck.

When the nurse called her name, Madison surveyed the room. Maybe someone else wanted to go first? Large woman with a beard in the Old Navy shirt? Terrified teenager with her parents? Anyone?

In the examination room, Madison looked at the illustrated chart. According to the full-colour drawing, at this stage in her pregnancy the baby resembled a naked mole rat. There was a knock and without waiting for a response Dr. Stevens opened the door.

On Canada Day, Madison had run into Dr. Stevens at a bar downtown. There, out of her white doctor coat, Dr. Stevens was known as Cecile. They hugged and reminisced about that party Madison had hosted in grade eleven while her parents were in Italy. Burned carpet downstairs, that couple no one recognized having sex in the bathroom – with the door open. Where you living now? Yep, same basement.

At the clinic, there was no Cecile. Dr. Stevens said hello, asked if Madison was still throwing up regularly, and told her to lie down. Madison pulled her shirt up and pushed her skirt down while Dr. Stevens put clear goo on the Doppler.

"Any questions for me?"

Abby had suffered uterine rupture when Madison was born. Both of them had almost died in labour. At her last visit, Dr. Stevens had assured Madison that it wasn't a concern. "If I was at risk for uterine rupture, how would I know?"

"Shhh, just a second." Dr. Stevens was hunting around with her machine. "Hear that? That's gas." Then, a whooshing spaceship sound came out of the speakers. "There it is. Can you hear that?"

"What is it?"

"The heartbeat."

Without giving it much thought, Madison started crying. The whooshing spaceship sound faded.

Dr. Stevens smiled and pulled the machine off Madison's stomach.

"Wait." Madison sobbed. "Can I hear some more?"

"Once you start crying, it's really hard to hear. But next month it'll be easier."

"With uterine rupture . . ."

"Please don't worry about that." Dr. Stevens wiped the goo off Madison's stomach, sat in an old metal chair and crossed her legs. "It's a freak thing. And we're far better equipped to handle emergencies like that now. Worrying about it is way more dangerous than the risk of having a rupture."

Madison wiped her eyes. "So how's your husband?"

"Oh, he's great." Dr. Stevens shook her head and laughed as she started into an amusing story about her man and his friends going on a fishing trip in August. None of them had ever fished, of course, being a bunch of spoiled rich kids. The rain, a bear, no toilets.

Madison had wanted to be a spoiled rich kid so badly, and she hoped her own child would be spoiled and rich someday. As Dr. Stevens spoke, Madison decided to concentrate on the dryness of the woman's light brown hair. It was so dry, and her ankles were so puffy. Gloriously, there was a pimple on Dr. Stevens's forehead and another one on her chin.

In the clinic parking lot, the rain was fierce and cool. Madison walked slowly and deliberately as the big drops splashed down on her face. As she stepped into her father's Yukon, completely soaked, "Born to Be Wild" began to play. "David Weiss's phone."

"Your dad gave me the number. He also let me talk to Garith. You know what Garith said?"

"It's two in the afternoon on a Monday, Jonas. What are you doing up?"

"Planning a reconnaissance mission. You in or what?"

"I'm feeling sorry for myself, and the last time you planned an adventure you got drunk and pushed me down and the cops came. Leave me alone."

"Borrow the tank or your mom's Civic and take it to the soaps tonight. Recon!"

And with that, Jonas hung up.

23

leduc, leduc

Lacumseh and his braves planned an attack on Fort Edmonton in the opening segment of the soap. The natives wanted to move from bloody colonialism to merely depressing post-colonialism, and felt they couldn't wait 180 years for the poorly dressed palefaces in arts faculties to help them along. Only half the audience in the Varscona Theatre thought this was funny. Behind Madison, Raymond Terletsky clapped and said, "Yes, yes, too much. Way too much!"

When Madison turned around, Shirley Wong just shrugged.

In the end, the attack was thwarted by sex. The country wife of the Chief Factor had fallen in love with Lacumseh. She convinced him it would be a boneheaded idea to attack the fort because a bigger army would come down the river and kill everyone. Most importantly, if Lacumseh started a war, the country wife vowed not to come to his teepee anymore.

Somehow, everything ended with a Viennese waltz competition.

After the show, as planned, Madison spied on Carlos. She followed him across Calgary Trail to the Next Act, where he sat in a corner booth by himself. Still in his Lacumseh costume, Jonas met Madison on the sidewalk. Inside, Carlos checked his watch a few times. He ordered one beer and drank it quickly. Then, without warning, he left the bar.

Jonas and Madison ducked behind a Dumpster. Madison ran down the avenue and fetched the Yukon. She pulled up in front of Jonas, who gestured wildly. He jumped into the SUV. "He's in a black Mustang, headed south. Floor it!"

It was late on a Monday night, and Calgary Trail was deserted. They caught up to Carlos at a set of street lights near a Superstore.

"Stay a few car lengths behind him, so he doesn't get wise."

"All right, Starsky."

The Mustang passed the big-box circus of South Edmonton Common, anchored by the gigantic blue-and-yellow IKEA, and sped up. "Faster." Jonas bounced in his seat. "We're gonna lose him."

Madison sped up, even though she was already twenty kilometres over the speed limit. "What are you going to do when you find out where he lives?"

"Stalk him right back. I mean, he's going to all this trouble. Maybe he's psychotic but maybe he's the exquisite man I've been looking for to settle down with, raise a brood."

"Raise a brood?"

"Go to church on Sundays, join a community league. Get a garden going, put a block parent sign up in my window. Get into a book club and start watching *Dr. Phil*."

Madison tried to imagine Jonas doing all these things, and to her surprise it worked. "Why don't *we* get married and you can help me raise my brood. It'll be a marriage of convenience, with the odd neck massage, like in Hollywood."

Jonas swallowed and looked down at his hands for a moment. As soon as the words were out of her mouth, Madison realized she had said them in a tone that was entirely too sincere. She wanted to drive the Yukon off the highway and into a bluff of spruce trees. They passed the Nisku industrial park and the airport in silence.

"By which I mean to say I hate you," she said, finally.

This was atmosphere tonic. Jonas smiled. "No, it is I who hate you, you awful bitch, and I intend to hate your child with equal . . ." The Mustang began to slow down for the turnoff into Leduc. Jonas reached over and grabbed Madison by the arm. "Leduc! Leduc!"

The Mustang drove past the McDonald's and the Safeway and the car dealership, through the main intersection in Leduc. Madison followed Carlos until he reached an intersection on the south end of the park surrounding the Civic Centre. The Mustang turned right.

Near the Leduc Golf and Country Club, the Mustang turned into a crescent of large houses facing a reservoir. There were Buicks about.

"We've driven into the seventies," said Jonas.

"Your stalker is rich." Madison turned off the lights.

Carlos pulled into a driveway and the garage door opened, revealing a space filled with snowmobiles, red all-terrain vehicles, and an extensive collection of tools. Parked next to the Mustang was a large truck with four tires in the back: duallies. Carlos took a sports bag from the trunk of the Mustang and dropped it on the garage floor as the automatic door closed behind him.

"All that's missing is a poster of Heather Locklear in a pink bikini." Jonas sat back in his seat and shook his head.

"Maybe he's house-sitting."

"Our boy's practically a Texan."

They sat in the Yukon for several minutes, watching the lights go on and off. Eventually, Jonas opened the door and stepped out. He sneaked up to the house and peered into the front window. A flock of something, perhaps bats, whispered through the trees and over the Yukon. Madison searched the radio until she found the French classical station on FM. This was the sort of music they sold at mothers' fairs, brain music for babies, so Madison turned it up.

As Jonas slouched to the Yukon, along the sidewalk, "Born to Be Wild" began to play on the cellular phone, interrupting the purity of Isaac Stern doing Schubert. Madison picked it up and imagined, once again, Jonas as a father. Then, fatherlessness in general.

Instead of saying hello she smacked herself in the head with the phone, turned it off, and tossed the warm bundle of silver on to Garith's backseat bed.

24

an authentic conversation

Four out of five Death in Philosophy students arrived for the field trip at West Edmonton Mall's World Waterpark. When Professor Raymond Terletsky arrived at the lobby, one of the men – Matt – was playing Ms. Pac-Man on a wristwatch. The other three – Jess, Dannika, and Paul – watched the action.

"It kicks ass, Dr. T," said Dannika, a tall, black-haired graduate student from the political science department. She was taking Death in Philosophy as an option. "This baby's from the *eighties.*"

Raymond crowded close to Dannika and feigned interest in the wristwatch game, controlled by a tiny joystick. Dannika wore a thin, baby-blue button-up sweater that highlighted her collarbone. Around her neck, a gold Saint Christopher pendant. While Dannika watched Ms. Pac-Man, Raymond took the opportunity to peek down at her breasts. Unfortunately, her backpack pulled the shirt up, obscuring the view.

"I got this thing on eBay." Matt, who wore his hair in a ponytail, shook his head in disbelief. "Sweet deal, too."

"Cool," said Raymond, and immediately regretted it. He was walloped with the certainty that the word *cool* stopped being cool 'round about the time *Happy Days* went off the air. Since his son and daughter had moved to Calgary and Seattle, he wasn't regularly exposed to fashionable jargon. Not like Madame Chairperson Claudia Santino, hired because the committee felt she was "edgy" and "plugged in."

Indeed, Raymond was so smooth and unplugged he didn't understand what eBay was, exactly, or how it worked. Was it an Internet antique dealer of some kind? Why *eBay*? He felt obliged to add something, to offer a piece of analytical context for Ms. Pac-Man and Matt's high-tech mode of acquisition. However, once he had mentally committed to saying something, he had nothing. So he added, "Really cool."

The game ended as these games always seemed to end, with Matt's avatar in ruin. "So, Dr. T," said Matt. "What are we doing here?"

Raymond proceeded to the counter with five hundred dollars in petty cash, and explained. They were going to participate in two of the indoor waterpark's most popular attractions, the Tropical Typhoon and the Bungee jump, in order to better understand the pricey games we play with death. He quoted

Kirilov, a character in Dostoevsky's *The Devils*, who says everyone who desires supreme freedom must kill himself.

"Yet Camus said the refusal to commit suicide gives meaning
to life," said Dannika.

Raymond stopped and faced his four students. Matt, the
lazy skateboarder; Paul, the silent veteran of the first Gulf War;
Jess, the future lawyer with perfect posture; and Dannika, a
polished gem of prairie Polishness. "Exactly, Dannika. That's
exactly what I want to get out of this field trip."

"I just want to see you three fellas in bathing suits," she said,
without allowing a moment to pass. Her three peers laughed,
and so did Raymond.

What a coincidence.

In the men's change room, Paul stripped immediately. He
scratched at a Tasmanian Devil tattoo on his right arm, pulled
some lint out of his coarse orange belly hair, grunted and walked
into the bathroom to stand in front of a urinal. Raymond and
Matt, who allowed themselves to be naked for all of 1.5 seconds,
shared a knowing glance. Now that was supreme freedom.

Matt had the age advantage but each of the three men was
at least thirty pounds away from the statue of David. When
they met the women on the mock beach, Raymond sucked in
his belly. So did Matt. Paul wiped the snot away from under his
nose and uttered a rare comment: "Humid in here."

Of the five, only Dannika had remembered a notebook and
a waterproof pen. Raymond was pleased to see that unlike
uptight, one-piece Jess, Dannika had also remembered to wear
a white bikini. Since they had all just taken showers and the air

in the waterpark was a few degrees cooler than comfortable, they decided to begin in the hot tub.

Raymond got in first, and hurried underwater so he could relax his belly. To his delight, Dannika got in next. It was only then that Raymond understood the strangeness of this field trip, the first he had ever organized. Without the seminar room, the wooden chairs and peeling plastic table, the stained blackboard, nothing bound him to these people. They were near-naked strangers in a hot tub, obliged to speak to one another.

Instead of presenting their thoughts on entrepreneurs who used death to charge exorbitant fees for the illusion of risk, they talked about novels. Then movies. Then horror movies. Then, finally, Raymond had an idea.

"Paul, you must have thought a lot about the meaning of death. During the war."

"It was pretty remote out there, sir. We did killing, but it was more like Matt's wristwatch than anything you might see on the TV."

"You weren't afraid of getting shot? Or shooting someone?"

Paul lifted himself out of the water and sat on the ledge. "I was more afraid of catching something. And I did catch something."

"What did you catch?"

"I'm not at liberty to say, sir. I signed a nondisclosure agreement?"

Matt hopped up. "I'll meet you guys back here. I'm gonna slide a couple times, get pumped."

"Me too," said Jess.

Even though he wasn't submerged, Paul reached into his trunks and scratched himself. The subject of the military had inspired him. "Folks in the forces these days aren't ready to die. That isn't what it's about, sir. Ma'am. You know, boys in Rio de Janeiro fight to the death in the middle of the street, surrounded by crowds. With knives, bats. One-on-one. Just for honour. Now, from the point of view of our lives here in Canada, sir, ma'am, I think we find that sort of thing real foreign."

Raymond nodded in pretend-thoughtfulness. He wanted to say something about street fighting but Dannika had turned to face Paul, and one of her velvety knees was touching Raymond's thigh.

There seemed to be no accidental reason for this physical contact. The hot tub was almost empty, and the ambient blend of pop music, screaming schoolchildren, and rushing water in the wave pool wasn't overpowering. It was clear to Raymond that Dannika had crowded into him like this because she wanted to send a message.

An erotic message.

"I used to be into death in a big way," Dannika said, moving even closer to Raymond. "All black clothes, matte-white face, silver jewellery, Sisters of Mercy, the whole vampire thing."

Paul scratched his left nipple and grunted but Raymond wasn't really listening to Dannika. He was certain that a silent and more authentic conversation was going on between them.

25

a little progressive in that conservative

David Weiss paused for five seconds and smiled. This was the secret to conflict resolution, creating and controlling the tone of the conversation. In his teaching days, David had calmed hundreds of hormonal monsters using this method.

Tonight, his adversary was a harmless dullard called Andrew. The young man stood behind the Metterra Hotel counter with posture that contrasted with the slick surroundings. Poor skin, poor diction, poor manners, brown hair sticking straight up with frosted tips.

"Andrew, there are hundreds of hotels in Edmonton and thousands of conference rooms."

"Yes, Mr. Weiss, I understand that and we appreciate the fact that you've chosen the Metterra. But our new policy states no dogs. No dogs means no dogs. I don't know what else to say."

"May I speak with your manager?"

"He's on dinner break. I'm the assistant manager."

David bent down and lifted Garith on to the counter. The dog shook his head, tinking his bell. "Chinese Cresteds don't shed. They're hypoallergenic. He hardly makes a peep. In the three years since I house-trained him, has he ever had an accident?"

"An accident?"

"A poop or a pee, Andrew. An accident. Well, let me tell you, Andrew, no. This dog is accident-free."

Andrew cleared his throat and leaned forward so he could take a closer look at Garith. The dog wagged his tail and pulled his lips back, performing his smile trick. Andrew reached forward, tentatively, and ran his hand along Garith's smooth brown back. "I've never seen an animal like this."

"This dog is more intelligent than your average high-school graduate today, Andrew. He deserves to be treated with respect."

"But –"

"But nothing, really. We walked here tonight, so I can't leave him in the vehicle. Which would be a sin against decency even if I could do it. And it doesn't seem fair that you should make this decision now, a half-hour before my meeting, with no warning whatsoever. How many meetings have we had here with Garith, with nary a whisper of disapproval from the management? This city shall bring itself to ruin with all these petty regulations designed to bolster the egos of dull bureaucrats. Yes?"

"But –"

"But nothing, Andrew."

David paused for another five seconds, took Garith in his arms, and walked upstairs to the boardroom on the mezzanine level. For a moment, he remained aware of Andrew. The assistant manager walked around the counter and followed David up the stairs for a few steps. Then Andrew sighed, whispered "Whatever," to himself, and returned to his perch behind the computer screens.

Everything was ready in the boardroom. On a credenza against the wall, a large Thermos of coffee with various whiteners and sweeteners. Next to the Thermos, a selection of soft drinks and a box filled with muffins, donuts, and squares.

David sat at the head of the table with Garith on his lap. To warm himself up, he ate a muffin and read the minutes from the final spring meeting aloud to Garith. The Strathcona PC Riding Association had raised several motions, including a "no idling" automobile initiative and a resolution supporting a strengthened fine arts curriculum in high schools. These were the sorts of concerns that eroded support for the opposition in central urban ridings. Gosh, the pinkos will think, maybe there *is* a little progressive in that conservative.

The first to arrive was the newest member, Tammy "Sparkle" Davidson, who had just purchased her PC card. She sat in the chair nearest David and opened a bottle of water. "I'm so nervous," she said. "This all seems so important."

David squinted, a strategy he learned at Toastmasters long ago. "You *should* be nervous, Tammy. Nothing in your life is more important than active citizenry. Congratulations."

The Terrys, a couple from Gillingham, England, arrived next. Terry and Terry Ashton were two of the most devoted members of the Strathcona PC Riding Association, helping with barbecues and softball games in the summer and the family sleigh ride every December. But as far as David could see, they were shameless liberals. All the Terrys ever did was introduce motions about spending the budget surplus. Tax cuts? Not for the Terrys.

Next came Cheese, who stood at the snack table with a coffee. Before he said a word, Cheese – a grown man who insisted on being called Cheese – ate a blueberry-bran muffin and a date square. He was bald and wore a motorcycle jacket. His only reason for joining the Strathcona PC Riding Association was to fight for marijuana legalization and to denounce the federal government in "Taxawa." Most meetings, Cheese argued against the Terrys until David was able to broker a compromise.

This was everyone, it seemed. Just before the meeting started, Tammy "Sparkle" Davidson walked around the room shaking hands. Then, after relations seemed cozy and Cheese was finished snacking, Tammy sat down and said, "I'm hoping to meet some real power brokers here."

Woman Terry put up her hand. "Are we to call you Tammy then, or Sparkle?"

"Either way!"

"Well, Sparkle it is then."

"I love your accent. Is it Australian?"

"No."

"I love it, Terry. I really do."

David stood to lead the Strathcona Progressive Conservative Riding Association through a rendition of "O Canada" when the door opened. Barry Strongman walked in, smelling of campfire. "Sorry I'm late," he said. "I'm the new guy."

"Dear doctor," said Man Terry.

Barry removed his poncho, jean jacket, and toque, and sat next to Tammy, who plugged her nose with her muffin napkin. He pulled a sheet of white paper out of his bag, held it up for David to see, and slapped it on the table.

"I'm pumped, David, fellow Conservatives. I'm inspired. Let's Fix It."

26

the newest member of the party

Once or twice a year, David Weiss had a nightmare. Since he spent a remarkably small amount of time amassing worries and fears, his nightmares were random instances of humiliation and forgotten responsibilities.

It is 1975 and Abby is giving birth in the Royal Alexandra Hospital, on the verge of dying from a ruptured uterus, and David is playing cards and drinking Cuba Libres with strangers in a smoky hotel bar on Fort Road. David is late for school on his first day as a teacher. He is in the middle of making a speech to like-minded men in suits and every time he opens his mouth, a cuss word comes out. He sleeps through his mother's funeral. A meteor is crashing through the atmosphere, on its way to Old Strathcona, and he's stuck in the middle of Whyte Avenue, naked.

Since he was not well-practised in the art of managing fear, David stood in the conference room on the second floor of the Metterra Hotel and stared silently at Barry Strongman for close to a minute. David understood it was his duty, as riding president and as Barry Strongman's acquaintance, to respond to the intrusion. Yet something – the blueberry muffin, the coffee, the plaque in his arteries left over from twenty-two years of cigarettes and saturated fat – prevented him from acting.

"Do you know this man, David?" There was a hint of pleasure in Woman Terry's voice.

"Well, of course he does." Barry gathered a bagel and an orange juice from the credenza. "David's one of my best customers and best friends. He's my boy." He plopped back down beside Tammy "Sparkle" Davidson and elbowed her gently. "How you doin', sweet pea? My name is Barry Strongman and I'm the nephew of the chief."

The fog of fear began to lift from David, and he regained the power of speech. "What?"

"What what?" Barry chewed.

"What are you doing here?"

"Oh, right. My credentials. I wasn't sure how all this worked." Barry pulled a card out of his front pocket. "Here's my membership number. They were real understanding about things at head office, even though I'm currently without a permanent dwelling."

"You can't just barge in on a meeting like this, Barry. Unannounced."

"Lady on the phone said I could."

Tammy "Sparkle" Davidson squinted as though something about Barry Strongman stung her eyes. She wheeled away from him. On the other side of her, Cheese seemed unusually jocular. Man Terry's mouth hung open, as though he were preparing to nibble at corn on the cob. His wife flared her nostrils.

At that moment, David wanted to be in a hot-air balloon floating over the river valley. He wanted to be stuck in traffic on Quesnel Bridge in the middle of January. David wanted to be sick with avian flu, back teaching high-school algebra, eating tofu burgers with Reiki practitioners or attending an Amnesty International convention with Abby in Newfoundland. Anywhere but in the second-floor conference room of the Metterra Hotel, responsible for Barry Strongman.

The newest member of the Strathcona PC Riding Association lifted the Let's Fix It sheet high enough for everyone to see. "I trust everyone's read this effer. It's mind-blowing."

"Barry, I don't think you want to be here."

"I know what you're saying, David. I know." Barry called Garith up on his lap, and Garith began licking the homeless man's neck. "But there comes a time in every man's life when he's got to join the system, sick as it is, and try to fix it – to *fix it* – from within. You know what I'm saying?" Barry leaned over the table, extended his hand toward the Terrys. "I'm Barry Strongman. It's a pleasure."

The Terrys introduced themselves, as did Cheese.

Tammy "Sparkle" Davidson raised her left index finger. "I'm confused."

At this point, the monthly meeting of the Strathcona PC Riding Association could go in one of two directions: David could work to normalize the meeting by making excuses for Barry's appearance and behaviour or he could attempt to remove his debating partner. It was the face of Woman Terry that steeled him in the direction of toughness, the smile in her eyes. David knew Woman Terry wanted to be president and that she enjoyed this breach, this chaos, this display of weakness. It was laudable to work with the homeless, to make public statements about the homeless, to sponsor legislation that might improve the plight of the homeless. However, a PC Riding Association president was not supposed to be a "boy" to the homeless.

"Maybe we can talk about the Association, Barry, before you begin attending meetings."

"Sure we can talk. Whenever you like. That's what I'm here for, David, to make a contribution. For too long I've been idle, screaming from the fringes."

David took a deep breath. He would not lose control of the room. As he exhaled, he caught a glimpse of Woman Terry's half-smile.

"I'm asking you to leave, Barry."

"What do you mean?"

"Please, Barry. Just leave."

For ten seconds that felt like ten minutes, Barry Strongman stared into the eyes of David Weiss. Then Barry slid the Let's Fix It sheet across the table to Woman Terry, and began gathering his poncho, jacket, toque, and scarf. He bent down and kissed Garith. As Barry passed David at the front of the room he paused. "I didn't know you were this sort of man."

Woman Terry followed Barry Strongman out of the room. Man Terry nodded at the seat Barry had vacated. "Who is he?"

"He smelled like burning tires," said Tammy.

David cleared his throat. "Sorry for the interruption. Now, three, two, one, *O Canada* . . ."

David knew the words so well he didn't have to think about the national anthem. But he wanted to think about the national anthem, deeply, because thinking about the way he had just treated Barry Strongman made him feel unpleasant.

Why did everyone have to be so difficult, and different? There were people who agreed with David: wonderful, superior people in positions of power. But out here, among the rabble, they were rarer than burrowing owls.

It was obvious, if one sat and considered them, that each of David's values and principles was wholly reasonable. One doesn't just show up unshaven and smelling of burned pork – tires was unfair – at a PC Riding Association meeting.

By the end of "O Canada," as Woman Terry re-entered the room, David had convinced himself that Barry Strongman, not David Weiss, should be cross with himself. The Let's Fix It sheet was on the table before him, covered in stains and marked with barely legible notes in red pen. The date, circled three times, was tomorrow.

Tomorrow night.

27

another national tragedy

On Wednesday morning, Madison woke at six with hunger pains. In the last few days, her potent appetite for carbohydrates had pushed the nausea aside, but she wasn't sure which she preferred. It was still dark and her newspaper hadn't arrived yet, so Madison took her giant bowl of muesli and frozen blueberries in front of the television. Though it had been over two months since she struck caffeine from her life, she deeply missed the hopeful smell of fresh coffee, the hot cup in her hands, the shock of clarity that came with her first sip.

Madison was rarely up this early, so she almost never saw the morning news from studios in New York City. On all three American stations, the hosts spent most of their time on celebrity concerns, upcoming movies, self-help books, and handy recipes, with only a whisper of actual news. Information breaks on the channel with the most attractive male host – balding-a-licious Matt Lauer – focused on missing children, runaway brides, bad weather in Georgia, and some important senator's gall bladder operation.

Madison knew missing children, bad weather, and runaway brides weren't important concerns, but in her fuzzy, coffee-less haze, she was powerless to turn the channel. It was junk, all of it, buttressed with expensive sets and fake importance that made her feel part of the American experience. But here in Canada, Madison didn't have the luxury of feeling superior.

On the night Benjamin Perlitz returned to 10 Garneau with a rifle and the divorce papers Jeanne had sent, the television and print media outlets interviewed Madison. They interviewed everyone but Jonas, who snored near some shrubbery.

The story of the hostage drama that appeared on television that night, and in the newspaper the next day, went like this: Benjamin was a full-time bureaucrat and a part-time day trader. When technology stocks crashed, he lost a pile of money. He took out a second mortgage on 10 Garneau and continued to gamble.

And lose.

By the end of 2004, everyone in the neighbourhood had noticed the changes in Benjamin Perlitz. He looked and smelled

desperate and ill, occasionally wandering into the Weiss backyard or curling up drunk on the sidewalk. Just before Christmas,
his superiors in the government realized he was gambling on-
line when he should have been working, and laid him off.

In January of 2005, to the delight of everyone on the block,
Benjamin left. Even Jeanne was relieved, though she feared
raising her daughter alone. Katie, when Madison babysat, said
her daddy was "getting fixed." There were rumours in the
springtime, circulated by Madison's mother, that Jeanne was
having an affair. This made perfect sense to Madison, as Jeanne
was blonde and smart and almost six feet tall.

At some point in the summer, Jeanne sought a divorce
from Benjamin Perlitz and that, really, was the whole story.
Until he brought a rifle to 10 Garneau on the last night of the
Fringe Festival.

The news channels had presented several versions of
Benjamin's recent biography, which was expanded upon in
the newspaper. It seemed artificially dramatic on television,
with the piano music in the background, but Madison
learned a lot about Benjamin's interests in golf, water skiing,
snowboarding, and deer hunting. Quick shots of the tactical
team sneaking through the front and back yards of 10 Garneau
and the house next door, Madison's parents' house, were on all
the national stations.

When the single shot echoed through the block, everyone
stopped talking. No one knew if Benjamin had shot Jeanne or
Katie, or if one of the snipers had shot him. The answer came less
than a minute later, as Jeanne appeared in the window and, in an
exhausted voice, announced that her husband was bleeding.

The sun came up and startled Madison out of her early morning doze in front of the American news. She wanted to go back to bed but she hadn't been out for a run in more than a week, and guilt was more powerful than fatigue.

Outside, in the flinty dawn air, Madison stretched her calves. As she did, a woman in shorts approached on her bicycle. At first, Madison thought the woman was on her way east, out of the university area, but she dropped her bike on the lawn at 10 Garneau. The canvas bag on the back of her bike said "Carol's Courier Service." She pulled out a pile of letters and proceeded up the walkway.

"No one lives there anymore."

The courier, presumably Carol, dropped the letter into the mailbox and stomped across the lawn. "Not my business." She dropped an envelope into each of the five mailboxes of the Garneau Block, retrieved her bicycle, and started back in the direction of the university.

Madison walked across her parents' front lawn and removed the envelope from their box. It was from the university, addressed to "Occupant." She opened the letter and read it, twice, and decided she wouldn't be going for a run that morning. Even though David and Abby Weiss didn't usually get out of bed until 8:30, Madison was determined to wake them. She didn't have a key with her so she began knocking, and yelling, and kicking the door.

28

temper

The morning sun filled the kitchen where David Weiss paced, from the refrigerator to the patio door, for over an hour. He was in the midst of calling every one of his influential friends in the PC party on the speakerphone. Nearly all of them pleaded helplessness. His final friend, the past executive director and a fellow Freemason, said, "David, listen. If we're going to be a party that's against government interference, how do we go about interfering?"

Madison and Abby, leaning on the wooden chopping island, jumped back as David picked up a Mandarin orange and spiked it on the ceramic floor. Garith, who had been at his master's feet, yipped and hopped and sprinted away. "That's bullshit! We interfere all the time! Who do you think you're talking to?"

After holding her breath for a few moments, Madison led Abby and Garith out the patio door and on to deck chairs. At first, her mother seemed frightened. Then, as a gentle breeze began to blow through the backyard, tinkling the chimes, Abby chuckled. "Those barbarians are great allies when they want something from you, a few extra hours to help ruin the environment or discriminate against homosexuals. But now that David's in trouble, they're abandoning him."

Madison didn't know what to say to her mother. Since waking her parents and presenting them with the letter, she hadn't said much. There didn't seem to be any room for optimism.

The letter indicated that in the coming weeks a property evaluator would call for appointments. The appraiser would determine the current market value of the five houses in the Garneau Block, and the university would offer a ten-per-cent bonus. Thanks to the University Land Acquisition Act of 1928, this was non-negotiable.

"It'll work out, Mom."

"How?"

This was exactly why Madison hadn't said anything. All she could do was recite empty and meaningless clichés. In the real world, nothing ever worked out. "Well, you know, Dad didn't join the party for his own personal gain. He . . ."

Abby chuckled again, in a particularly un-elementary schoolteacher sort of way. "Oh, my sweet naïve girl."

The dog, having recovered from his scare in the kitchen, attacked a plush pig in the middle of the yard. Instead of talking about the university buying their house, bulldozing it, and transforming the Garneau Block into a nanotech or health sciences something or other, Madison and Abby watched Garith stalk and chew the pig. A brief gust of wind felled two or three apples from the tree, and Garith left his pink companion to sniff and growl at the fruit.

A helicopter flew overhead, on its way to the hospital. Now here was something Madison could say to make her parents feel better about losing their house: at least they didn't have spinal injuries or massive head trauma. She was just about to bring this up when David opened the patio door and walked out onto the deck.

"Sorry I lost my temper in there."

Abby crossed her legs and her arms, and looked away. Madison reached out, took her father's hand, and squeezed.

A chorus of distant lawnmowers filled the air, along with tinking silverware and laughter of the restaurant patios one block north.

David sighed, sat on the stairs, and told Garith to "Bring it here!" Garith picked up the pig and dropped it in front of David. He tossed it across the yard, into the side of the garage, and Garith bounded after it. "Do you two think everything happens for a reason?"

"Not the way you mean," said Madison.

Her mother laughed her poisonous laugh again.

"I stood in there, after the last phone call, and wondered if the Big Guy isn't trying to tell us something."

"Ralph Klein?" said Abby, crossing her legs the opposite way.

"The other Big Guy. I'm thinking maybe He wants us to move to Calgary."

"What?"

"Maybe we can afford a condo in Calgary and a little plot of land somewhere warm. A place with uncontaminated water and stable politics. English spoken. That way, if the oil runs out and the northern world descends into murderous chaos, we can still grow tomatoes and papaya."

Abby walked into the house. She locked the patio door behind her and pulled down the blinds.

"I don't think Mom likes that idea, Dad."

"The university's wanted this land for years. Thanks to Ben Perlitz, property values and morale are down. They know we're weak."

"Maybe if you got a lawyer."

Slowly, a slouch worked its way into David's shoulders. "We're retired, pumpkin. We can't afford a lawyer."

"Are you going to the Let's Fix It meeting tonight?"

"What's the point? If we're not going to live here, we'll just be Fixing It for the university. And I say a *curse* on the university. I hope Ben's ghost whips a demonic possession on their large intestines and they all get dysentery." In his shorts, black dress socks and unreasonably tight United Way T-shirt, David went out into the yard and began wrestling with Garith. He flopped on the grass and held the dog over him. "Maddy, would you be upset if your mom and Garith and I moved to Cowtown?"

Madison felt a rumble in her stomach. The baby demanded more muesli.

29

death and the tropical typhoon, revisited

Dr. Raymond Terletsky wore his only suit to the morning meeting, with a white shirt and a plain black tie. Claudia Santino and the sleepy-eyed Dean of Arts, a South African man called Kesterman, had already met with Dannika and two witnesses from the Waterpark, Paul and Jess from Death in Philosophy.

On Tuesday afternoon, after two hours of shameless flirting, Raymond had been waiting in line behind Dannika to slide down the Tropical Typhoon. On his way up the stairs, he had studied Dannika's behind. It was round without being chunky, though a few patches of endearing cellulite peeked out from either side of her white bikini bottoms.

As Raymond studied Dannika's backside, he had outlined Montaigne's views on death, and how these views might relate to North American society's current fascination with so-called extreme sports and activities. Let us rid death of its strangeness, he said, quoting the Frenchman. Let us come to know death, befriend it. Let us have nothing in our minds as often as death. At every moment let us picture it in our imagination, in all aspects. It is uncertain where death awaits us; let us await it everywhere. Premeditation of death is premeditation of freedom. He who has learned how to die has unlearned how to be a slave.

"Or she," Dannika had said, at the top of the stairs.

Raymond smiled. "Or she."

The other students disappeared in that moment, along with his fatigue from climbing the stairs and the noisy teenage fact of the World Waterpark. Dannika smiled back at him, a warm and sweet and pure smile, and Raymond nearly lost all muscle power in his legs. She turned from him, toward the entrance of the Tropical Typhoon, and he did what any man in his situation would do.

Raymond slapped her little bum.

Seventeen hours later, Raymond waited to be called into Dean Kesterman's office. At home that morning, before she left for work, Shirley had been typically wonderful. There had been a letter in their mailbox, from the university, declaring a hostile buy-out. Shirley wanted to fight it. She wanted to study the Land Acquisition Act of 1928, find the holes in the document. To Shirley, it was a horrifyingly inappropriate move considering the recent death of Benjamin Perlitz. Cynical and manipulative. Raymond had just watched her, as he might watch a curling match on television.

Dean Kesterman walked into the waiting area with his hand outstretched. "Raymond."

"Dean. I'm so sorry about this awful misunderstanding." Raymond hoped the Dean would stay with him in the waiting area outside his office for a moment, so they might discuss this like gentlemen. But the Dean didn't respond to the apology, or linger after their handshake. He adjusted his eyeglasses and led Raymond immediately into the largest office in the Humanities Building.

Claudia stood up from her seat at the small conference table. "Raymond," she said. "Thanks for coming."

"No, thank *you*. I was so pleased to be invited."

Neither Claudia nor Dean Kesterman found this amusing, so Raymond laughed to encourage them. It didn't work. The Dean walked around to his chair, looked down at a couple of closed file folders before him, and sat. "Please," he said, and motioned for Raymond to do the same.

There was, at that moment, a tightening sensation in Raymond's chest. He hoped, before the proceedings got underway, that he might suffer a mild stroke or heart attack. Sympathy, in that case, would trump punishment. The tightening passed with a burp, so Raymond said, "Pardon me," and sat in the stiff chair.

"You know why we're here," said Claudia, as she opened the red file folder. "My office received a complaint yesterday afternoon, from a pay phone at West Edmonton Mall. We followed up on that complaint, meeting with the complainant and two witnesses earlier this morning."

Complainant, thought Raymond. What sort of word was that for a philosophy professor to use? Obviously, her veins were filled with weevils and black ice.

The Dean took it from there. "These are serious accusations, corroborated by two witnesses, Raymond. But we'd like to hear what you have to say for yourself."

"What did Dannika say?"

Claudia looked at the Dean for permission, lifted her chin, and said, "Quite simply, Raymond, that you slapped her in a private place. While she wore a bathing suit. The fact that you took your Death in Philosophy class to the World Waterpark without permission, using five hundred dollars of departmental petty cash, is grounds for disciplinary action, but sexual harassment takes us into a whole new league."

The Dean tilted his head in thoughtful confusion, as though he were regarding a piece of abstract art. "Did you do it?"

Raymond had considered pleading academic freedom, claiming the slap was a bit of social science. In the office, however, this defence seemed dangerous. "Yes," he said.

"But why?"

"I thought it was our little thing." Raymond felt the muscles in his neck and shoulders soften.

Claudia shook her head and removed her eyeglasses. "Your little thing? Do you understand how demeaning it is, to slap a student on the backside?"

For ten or twelve seconds, Raymond held his breath and flexed every muscle in his body, hoping for an aneurysm. Nothing. He turned to his right, to the river valley out the Dean's window, bathed in glorious autumn sunshine. No clouds today and only a slight breeze. The institution that was about to sack him had also announced it was going to annex the Garneau Block and render him homeless. Unemployed, and with housing prices this high, he imagined the noisy beige condominium of his immediate future. "Are you going to tell my wife?"

For the first time since he arrived in the office, both Claudia Santino and Dean Kesterman smiled. They covered their mouths. The Dean actually snorted. A minute later, as Raymond walked to the Dean's north-facing window, Claudia outlined the terms of his dismissal.

30

the next hit at sundance

Jonas had a concern. The writer, director, and producer of *Haberdasher*, a feature film set in Detroit, sighed and put his hands on his waist. "What now?"

With respect, Jonas outlined the concern. His character, the wise older brother of a doomed gangster, was supposed to be an accountant. Jonas couldn't imagine an accountant, even an accountant who grew up *in the hood* saying, "Yo, dawg, your lifestyle is wack. You gots to be on dat Ghandi tip."

"Dude," said the writer, director, and producer, a twenty-four-year-old named William, "I'm paying union rates here. I'm paying you to realize my vision. Are you gonna realize my vision or what?"

William, Jonas, and several other actors and crew members were in a quiet southeastern playground. The surroundings were more suburban Idaho than Detroit, with a Tim Hortons and Blockbuster Video strip mall on the other side of an abandoned soccer field dotted with lost Safeway bags, but Jonas had opted to keep quiet about this. He and the gentleman playing his doomed younger brother were sitting on swings and having, according to the script, a *mano-a-mano*.

At the end of the day, Jonas would make $280 for this mano-a-mano. And from what he had seen in the script, no one would ever see this movie outside William's family and circle of close friends in a rented theatre. Unless, of course, someone uploaded it onto the Internet as a joke.

"Yes, William, I apologize. I am here to realize your vision. I'm just wondering if a white accountant in his early forties would say dawg and wack and dat. Do gangsters in Detroit even say that stuff?"

The writer, director, and producer squeezed his chin and looked around at the rest of the people in the playground. Most of them glanced down to avoid William's gaze. With his chin-squeezing hand, he summoned Jonas. "Walk with me."

It was a bright day, just after noon. Even if Jonas delivered his lines as they appeared in the script, the shot would be burned out by the sun. The way William had said *walk with me* made it clear that he saw himself as the star of *Haberdasher*. And the star of contemporary human existence.

No one wanted to be an actor anymore. In the era of reality television and pop star movie crossovers, craft was irrelevant; everyone wanted to be famous, as though it were a legitimate career goal. This was the fourth local film Jonas had worked on this year. Each had been bankrolled by some kid's parents, each had included gunplay, and each was set in an American city to improve its potential in Hollywood.

Jonas followed his employer into the adjacent area of slides and swinging bridges. "Umkay, Jonas. Are you the writer and director of this movie?"

"No."

"Did you put up the cash?"

"No."

"Have you graduated from a recognized radio and television arts program?"

"No, William, I haven't."

"Then why are you trying to be the writer and director of *Haberdasher*? You're here for one day, in one scene."

Jonas wanted to reach down, pick up a handful of urine-encrusted sand, and stuff it into William's underbite. Yet as much as he despised William and everything he represented, it wasn't the boy's fault. Walt Disney, sitcoms, teen novels, the school system, and William's parents were to blame for telling him he could be whatever he wanted to be as long as he followed his dreams.

William's parents should not have supported his passion for film. They should not have called him special and smart when he was a teenager. If they were honest people, with integrity, William's parents would have encouraged him – nay, forced him – into a career in the navy.

"You're right about that, William. I apologize for my behaviour. This morning, I received a rather disturbing letter in the mail. It seems I'm going to be evicted."

William removed his beret and looked up at a cloud that had obscured the sun. "We all got our problems, buddy, but we're making magic here."

"Right, right."

"So are you ready to get back on that swing? To make this happen for us? In a few months, in our hospitality suite at Sundance, we'll look back on this moment and laugh."

"Ha ha." Jonas slapped William on the back. "I suppose we will."

On his way back to the swing set, Jonas had trouble getting back into character. His landlord in Vancouver would receive the letter he had forwarded that morning, and before long Jonas would have to find a new place. A new place in Edmonton, the anticipation of which tasted quite a lot like that handful of urine-encrusted sand.

In truth, he wanted the same things William wanted: respect, success, millions of dollars, a proper tuxedo and an apartment in New York, perhaps some cocaine from time to time. But that was impossible now. A twenty-four-year-old moron with an underbite had a better chance of getting that apartment in New York than a theatrical genius.

"Action," said William.

The gangster talked about their dead mother, who had perished from a marijuana overdose. Jonas didn't have an encyclopedic knowledge of street drugs, but he didn't think this was physically possible. Of course, he wasn't going to bring it up. Earlier that morning, when Jonas asked why a film without any clothing manufacturers is called *Haberdasher*, William told him he "didn't understand creativity."

As the gangster delivered the remainder of his lines, Jonas scanned the playground for Carlos. He supposed even stalkers had days off. Or maybe he'd begin stalking this afternoon or evening. Maybe Carlos would follow him to the Let's Fix It meeting downtown, and enjoy some of Abby's hummus.

"Yo, dawg." Jonas made what he took to be a gang sign from the 1980s, and turned to his doomed brother. "Your lifestyle is wack. You gots to be on dat Ghandi tip."

31

convincing david

Shirley Wong and Abby Weiss stood on the sidewalk in front of 12 Garneau with bowls of baba ghanouj and hummus, respectively, while Madison begged her father to attend the meeting.

"There's nothing to fix." He sat in front of the television in a Bush-Cheney 2004 T-shirt. On the television, *Wheel of Fortune*. "Gin rummy. The phrase is gin rummy."

Madison looked at the screen. Her father was right about gin rummy. "The future of this block is important to me, Dad. I grew up here. We have to fight for it."

"I called everyone. No one can do anything."

"They're Tories. They never do anything for gay liberal Edmonton."

David Weiss sighed. "That's a myth. A dirty, lazy myth. Take it back."

"If you agree to come, I'll take it back."

"Bah." David waved her away and went to stand in front of the bookshelf in the living room, filled with Abby's favourite novels in hardcover. He pulled out *Love in the Time of Cholera*, shook his head, and then slid it back into place. "I'm disillusioned, Maddy."

"Because your friends blew you off?"

David grunted. "Last night I kicked Barry out of an association meeting. I can't stop thinking maybe it was the wrong thing to do."

"Barry the street paper guy?"

"Yes."

Madison shifted the bag of pita and cut vegetables into her right hand and looked out the window at her mother and Shirley. Abby lifted her bowl of hummus.

"I don't know, send him flowers. Come on, Dad."

"Send flowers to a homeless man?"

Madison saw that by making ridiculous suggestions she wasn't going to steer the conversation, naturally, to the importance of the Let's Fix It meeting. "Please just come. We need you there. We need your intelligence, Dad, and your experience with gatherings of a social and political nature."

"Bah."

"I'll give you fourteen dollars."

"Madison, come on. Just leave me to mourn in peace."

"I'm pregnant."

David dropped the remote control on the hardwood floor, and the battery slot popped open. Two AAAs rolled under the coffee table. "No, you aren't."

"Yes, I am."

"But you don't have a boyfriend."

Madison took a deep breath. "For about five minutes in the summertime I had a boyfriend in Jasper."

"Who is this five-minute boyfriend?"

"His name might be Steve but I suspect it's Jean-something. He's from Quebec."

"First the National Energy Program, then the special status nonsense, and now this. May they freeze in the dark!"

"Dad." Madison opened her arms for a hug.

"What is *with* those people? Distinct society, my ass." David hugged his daughter and kissed her in the ear. "Well, this is wonderful." He took a step back, held her out before him, and wiped the burgeoning tear from his left eye. "I mean, is it wonderful? You're happy? You're going to . . . ?"

"Yes, I'm keeping it."

"How far along are you?"

"Just entered my thirteenth week."

David shook his head. "What a dope I am. I thought you were just getting a little pudgy, not doing enough sit-ups."

"And that's why you have to come to the meeting. Pregnant women shouldn't be subjected to stress and uncertainty. I need my daddy to protect me."

For a moment, it seemed David was going to argue the point. Then he relaxed and walked down the hall toward his bedroom. "Just let me put on some decent clothes." While he changed, he mumbled about "the damn Pepsis" and called out, "Hey, does your mom know?"

"Just you and Jonas so far, and my doctor."

"So I know before your mother?"

"Yep."

David came out of the bedroom in a pair of blue chinos, sandals, and a Hawaiian shirt. "How sweet it is!"

When Madison and her father emerged from the house, Shirley and Abby put their matching bowls of baba ghanouj and hummus on the sidewalk so they could clap. "Hurry," said Abby, "we were supposed to meet everyone at the Sugarbowl five minutes ago."

David took the pita and vegetables from Madison, as though the bag were burdening her. He put his arm around his wife. "Where's Raymond?"

"I don't know. Maybe he got held up at the U."

"He's coming though, right?"

Shirley raised her eyebrows. "This morning he was acting strangely, and I know he's deep into research on Victorian death rituals."

"Whoa." David kissed Abby on the cheek twice. "I can't believe someone pays him to do that."

They walked through the parking lot behind the theatre. Jonas was sitting on the Sugarbowl patio with a glass of red wine. When he saw them he said, "Finally. I had to fight some sorority girls to save these seats. Seriously fist-fight them. Where's Raymond?"

Everyone shrugged in unison. As Shirley, Abby, David, and Madison took their seats, Jonas snapped his fingers at the server.

"Mademoiselle. We're in something of a hurry."

The server didn't react to Jonas. Instead she smiled, said hello, and took their orders. When Madison ordered a soda with a spot of cranberry juice in it, David squeezed her hand. "That's my girl," he said.

Jonas took the plastic wrap off the hummus and sniffed. "So I was thinking maybe we should stop by the young Indian man's place and see if he wants to join us."

"He doesn't talk," said David. "I've tried. He's either a deaf mute or he doesn't know English. It'll just be humiliating for him."

Abby sat up straight. "We should stop anyway. I bet he's lonely. That's a perfectly lovely idea, Jonas. This is his neighbourhood, too."

"Whatever you think, hon," said David. "But he doesn't talk."

"Remember when we tried the Welcome Wagon routine on him?" said Shirley. "He could barely say thanks for the fruit basket."

Jonas finished his first glass of wine. "He was just stunned by your beauty. Who could blame him?"

"You only say that because it's true." Shirley slapped Jonas on the arm.

Raymond Terletsky approached with a box in his hands.

"Oh, there's my professor." Shirley pushed her chair back and started out to meet her husband. She turned back to her neighbours and smiled. "Looking cute and rumpled."

32

cute and rumpled

In the past, whenever he had mused upon personal apoca-lypse, Raymond Terletsky imagined physical torment. Severe gastrointestinal problems in public, migraines, an invasion of cockroaches and termites. Yet there had been an unexpected, dreamlike quality to the worst day of Raymond Terletsky's life. Neither his bowels nor his head was troubling him, and so far no insects had crawled out of his mouth or anus. He hadn't even walked through a spider web.

That afternoon, after Claudia Santino and Dean Kesterman had sacked him, Raymond opened a bottle of champagne and sat in his office. It was Veuve Clicquot, a gift from one of his colleagues upon the "Hierarchy of Funerals" publication in the *Maltese Journal of non-Continental Philosophy*. Since he didn't have a glass handy, Raymond sat in his office and drank the champagne straight from the bottle.

It is dispiriting to spend five hours drinking champagne and thinking up a good lie to tell your wife. It is especially dispiriting when, at the end of those five hours, you have nothing to tell her but the truth. Shirley Wong was a wise and insightful woman. She knew it was extremely difficult to fire a tenured professor.

An instance of physical violence was the only possible alternative, but Shirley would not have believed it. Raymond couldn't picture himself striking a student or another professor, so selling the story to his wife would have been impossible. If he told her the reason for his dismissal yet pleaded innocent, she would support him all the way to the Supreme Court of Canada. However, in the end, the university would win the case. Raymond would lose Shirley and the legal fees would swallow up everything they owned. Their children would be shamed.

So on the way to the Sugarbowl, with a box full of his most cherished books, Raymond practised the truth. At least the university was buying their house, which would carry them financially until he found another job.

Perhaps the Maltese were hiring.

Shirley met him in front of an old two-storey house in the midst of renovation. There was dust in the air, from the process of refinishing hardwood: generations of foot sweat. Shirley laughed and waved it away. "It feels like we're in the middle of a desert storm."

"It does," he said. "It really does."

"What's in the box?"

Raymond lowered it so his wife could see inside. Shirley Wong was five-foot-two and he was six-foot-three, which had made for some comical wedding photographs. There were five or six first editions in the box, historically significant works in Latin that needed repair, and several copies of the *Maltese Journal of non-Continental Philosophy*.

"Why are you taking these home?"

Raymond had practised. It was best to be simple and direct about it. He didn't want to stutter his way into an explanation, and telegraph his guilt, so he looked her in the eye.

"Hey." Shirley smiled. "Are you drunk?"

"They fired me."

The smile faded and then returned in a more authentic way. "Go on, you."

"Claudia Santino and the Dean fired me today. This morning."

Shirley sniffed and took the box from her husband. She put it down on the grass next to them, and embraced her husband in the hardwood dust. It took Raymond close to a full minute to realize he was crying. "I made a big mistake, Shirley. I deserved it."

"The bastards. What happened?"

"They're only giving me two weeks. No severance, nothing."

"Do you want to go home, talk about it?"

In their usual manner of hugging, Raymond was bent forward so they resembled an arch. It seemed, at that moment, that he was the short one and Shirley was the tall one. She stroked his head. Over her shoulder, Raymond saw their neighbours at the Sugarbowl with a bottle of red wine. They all looked away or at their glasses. Even in the desert storm they had seen him shaking and rubbing his eyes. And when he tried to stop himself it only got worse. He sobbed and held his breath, hoping that might help. But it didn't help.

"Raymond? Can you tell me what this is about?"

A few students walked, rollerbladed, and bicycled past them. Eventually, Raymond found clarity and a measure of control. He wiped his face with the bottom of his untucked white shirt. "Wow. Sorry."

Shirley laughed too. "That's very healthy, you know."

"I'm a new man."

"We can skip this meeting."

"No, I want to go." Raymond picked up his box of books and led Shirley to the Sugarbowl patio. "I'll tell you all about it later."

As they drew nearer, Shirley announced, "Raymond feels strongly about Fixing It. Very, very strongly."

Abby applauded. "Hooray for you, Raymond. Let's Fix It. But first, put that box down and take a fortifying drink of wine. It's Shiraz, if that's okay."

Raymond sat next to Shirley and took her hand. A cloud of discomfort had settled over the table, despite Abby's efforts to blow it away. Jonas snapped his fingers and ordered the server to bring another wine glass. There wasn't time for a new bottle, as they had to be downtown for the meeting in thirty minutes. But after Jonas filled Raymond's glass, there was enough left to top up everyone else's.

"To the future of the Garneau Block," said Jonas.

They touched their glasses together and took sips and sat back in their chairs. Then they smiled politely at one another, and nodded, and watched the students and professors and Kung Fu practitioners and home renovators pass and mingle in the avenue. Finally, when the collective anguish seemed unbearable, and Raymond was on the verge of crying again, David brought up the weather. He had heard it was supposed to rain overnight or in the morning.

"That'll smell nice," said Madison.

"We could sure use the rain," said Abby.

Shirley nodded. "And the farmers."

"Just watch, the basement'll flood," said Raymond.

Jonas stood up. "Oh, finish your drinks and let's get on the LRT before we all kill ourselves."

33

light rail transit

The Australians who lived in the other half of Jonas Pond's duplex were away studying monkeys in southern Nigeria, so the young Indian man from across the street was the only other missing resident of the Garneau Block. Abby suggested that even though he was eerily quiet and perhaps dangerous when provoked, Let's Fix It was a call to him as well. Maybe the young Indian man from across the street wanted to join them on the LRT.

No one was keen to knock at 13 Garneau, so David Weiss volunteered. He hoped the young Indian man from across the street would answer the door in flowing white robes, splattered in sacrificial blood and holding the severed head of a kitten or a swan, to sate his neighbours' desperate appetite for mystery.

David volunteered to knock because he would be a grandfather soon. Nothing about the university annexation or Barry Strongman or Raymond Terletsky's emotional breakdown or even the end of oil could prick the balloon of pride that had formed in his chest. Pride and wisdom. Proper grandfathers showed the way by calm example, and knocking on the young Indian man's door when everyone else seemed nervous about it was his first opportunity.

The young Indian man from across the street did not concern David. At least not now. Of course, in the aftermath of 9/11, David lay awake a few nights wondering about the quiet occupant of 13 Garneau. Who wouldn't have? As Jacques Chirac had said, *Nous sommes tous américains* now, and George W. Bush was asking his countrymen to report suspicious activity.

Eventually, as politics and economics and episodes of *The Apprentice* had come to drown out the multiple anxieties of imminent terrorism, David stopped worrying. Some folks were just peculiar and shy. There was a decent chance the young

Indian man from across the street didn't talk to Osama or anyone else over a satellite phone.

David jogged up the red stone walkway as the professor dropped his box of books off next door. Jonas and Abby remained on the sidewalk, chattering.

"The young Indian man is really cute in his suits, though, isn't he?" said Jonas. "I just want to take him home and seal him up in a jam jar."

"There's very little in this world more attractive than a trim man in a dark blue suit," said Abby. "A fireman's outfit, maybe, or a unitard."

"Yahtzee, Mrs. W.," said Jonas. "Yahtzee."

David sighed and knocked. Long ago he had learned to tolerate the homosexual tendencies of his daughter's best friend, but sometimes he wished Jonas would just shut it off for an hour or two. David knocked again, and rang the doorbell. Then he turned to his neighbours on the sidewalk. "He's probably already on his way, driving a vehicle like civilized people do."

This was a shot at his wife's ridiculous suggestion that they take public transportation. There were only six of them, and the Yukon Denali seated eight comfortably. Why pay to ride the smelly train with a bunch of young offenders in sweatsuits? On weekday evenings, downtown parking was only two dollars. And that way, they could have taken Garith.

As they walked across campus to the station underneath Hub Mall, David put his arm around Madison. A few paces behind, he could hear Raymond bawling again. It was an embarrassing and distasteful display, so he attempted to drown the professor out with a father-daughter heart-to-heart.

"So," he said. "You going to go with cloth diapers you think? Or Huggies or whatnot?"

"I haven't thought about it, Dad."

Mindful of her mother just ahead, discussing the upcoming theatre season with Jonas, Madison spoke quietly. David wanted to honour his daughter's discretion, so he matched her volume. "Do you think it's a boy or a girl?"

"I don't know."

"What are you hoping?"

Madison bit her bottom lip and furrowed her eyebrows, a look of concentration she had mastered before kindergarten. Thinking of her at that age, three or four, ponytails and scabbed knees, could have turned him into a bawling idiot like the professor. Here was his little girl, on the verge of starting her own family. It wasn't an ideal situation, of course, thanks to the typically boorish behaviour of the Quebecker, but she would have help. Lots of help.

"I guess I'm hoping for a girl," she said.

To David, it only seemed natural to want a boy. If Abby hadn't suffered debilitating complications during Madison's birth, they would have tried for a boy and named him Jake. "If it's a boy, I think you should name him Jake."

"Can we talk about it later? I'm scared Mom's going to hear, and if I don't tell her myself, in that mother-daughter way, she'll be crushed. You know how Mom likes things."

"Do I ever."

David imagined the confession. It would have to be in the dining room, over dinner, with Tchaikovsky or Cuban something-or-other playing on the hi-fi. Madison would have to

announce, coyly, that she had news, and Abby would have
to turn down the music and prepare herself by sitting up straight.
Then she would insist on guessing. She would guess a new job,
then a new boyfriend. After her two unsuccessful guesses,
Madison would make the announcement and the screaming and
hugging and kissing and hysterical planning would commence.

They entered the LRT station and started down the stairs to
purchase their tickets. David took the bowl of hummus from his
wife and whispered "waste of money," just loud enough for her
to hear. Whereafter he endured a swift kick in the shin. Then,
downstairs on the platform, as they waited for a car to arrive, a
couple of drunken hillbillies in jean jackets wrestled and bumped
into an elderly woman reading a novel. As David started over to
give them a stern lecture, the hillbillies shocked him by picking
up the woman's book and apologizing like gentlemen.

David leaned against the emergency phone and counted.
That made three surprises in one night.

34

six guesses

Back when he started acting, Jonas was prone to diarrhea and
even fainting before a show. Almost nothing unnerved him now.
Yet in one week, he had found himself shaken by Carlos the
suburban theatregoer and, oddly, by the Let's Fix It meeting.

Inside Commerce Place, between the art gallery and the men's spa, Jonas turned and stopped his neighbours. No one had said a word since they exited the train, not even Abby Weiss, and the tension was beginning to cause sour gurgles in his stomach. "What's going on here?"

No one answered. The neighbours looked at one another and then back at Jonas. Madison shrugged. "We're going to the Let's Fix It meeting. How many glasses of wine did you drink, Jonas?"

"I know what's going on. What I mean is, *what's going on*? We're acting like we're about to be executed."

Abby lifted her hummus, said, "Um, hello?" and turned to Shirley, who lifted her bowl of baba ghanouj.

"We're all thankful for the dips, ladies. No, it's the tension I can't stand. I feel like going back home or turning straight into the nearest bar. Are we a community or what? Are we doing something positive here?"

David stepped forward and stood next to Jonas. He shook the bag of pitas and cut vegetables. "I think I know what Jonas is getting at. We have to go into this thinking like a team, a winning team."

"I'm going to need some serious pharmaceuticals to feel like a winner," said Raymond Terletsky.

Jonas had an urge to slap the weepy professor. But not slapping your neighbours, he remembered, is the very essence of community. Instead, Jonas whistled and waved everyone into the rotunda. Under the skylight, in the centre of the building's *chi*, Jonas had his neighbours form a circle. He stood in the middle. Just when he was about to make his announcement, Madison whispered, "Kumbaya, my Lord, kumbaya."

The neighbours laughed, and Jonas pointed at her. "Don't upstage me, woman."

"Sorry."

"This is all I can do. This is all I got."

"Sorry. Really."

A few moments of dramatic silence passed. Then, Jonas said, "We're going to have a contest."

Abby clapped around her bowl of hummus. "Goody, goody!"

"Everyone has to guess what the Let's Fix It meeting is going to be about, and whoever's closest to the real thing wins a bottle of wine. And not just Wolf Blass either. We'll all throw in ten bucks and buy something nice."

It took a moment of shuffling and sighing, but they eventually agreed. The professor managed a diabolical smile. "Who guesses first?"

Abby raised her hand. "I know what it is. The people who own the High Level Diner are going to set up a charity for Katie Perlitz's post-secondary education."

"No way," said her husband. "This is for time shares in Kelowna. Either that or it's an invitation into a pyramid scheme. I smelled this one ages ago, compadres. Within the hour, we're gonna be sitting across from closers with bad cologne."

Jonas swivelled. "Shirley, what do you think?"

"I don't have a guess."

"Come on. You have to guess."

She took a step closer to her husband. "Maybe it's Jeanne Perlitz herself, wanting to speak to us all."

Everyone rumbled with appreciation and approval. "Ooh, you're going to win," said Abby.

Raymond cleared his throat and said, "I'm hoping to walk through a portal. Either a time machine or a door into another dimension. The seventh or eighth. Or maybe we're going to have a séance."

"What dimension are we in now, professor?" said David Weiss.

"Third. Third or fourth. I don't know. We're in the TV dimension."

Jonas pointed to Madison.

"I've thought a lot about it since the signs went up but I can't figure out what it could be." Madison stepped out of the circle toward the optical store, and then came back. "What if this is standard for neighbourhoods where something awful happens? What if there's a nice lady, a rich fairy-godmother type from Old Glenora, who throws parties for people who live next to murder-suicides and drive-by shootings and kidnappings and rapes? Maybe there's going to be yoga and grief counselling."

"My hummus *is* grief counselling," said Abby.

Jonas looked at his watch. "We're five minutes late. Perfect." He walked out of the circle and started toward the rotunda and the escalators, and his neighbours followed. It was his turn to guess, and he wanted them to ask for it.

At the top of the escalator, between the McDonald's and the Sunterra Market, Jonas paused. No one asked. Through the doors and into Manulife Place, no one asked. To the right of Holt Renfrew and into the Manulife mezzanine no one asked. In the corridor of elevators no one asked.

"Hello?" he said, finally. "There's one more guess, people."

Abby squeezed Jonas's arm. "What do you think Let's Fix It is all about?"

"An orgy. I think we're heading into a bacchanalian festival of liquor and flesh, whereby we will forget Benjamin Perlitz ever happened." Jonas pressed the up button. "For one night. And it's going to work wonders for us all."

As Jonas intended, a few moments of shoe-looking ensued. They remained silent in the elevator, possibly considering each other naked, which filled Jonas with creative pleasure. More than happy or sad, he enjoyed making his audience feel uncomfortable. Their nervousness replaced his own.

The elevator door opened and Edith Piaf began to sing "Hymne à l'amour." A woman in a pinstriped navy-blue suit, with her blonde hair pulled back tightly, stood before them with a clipboard folded across her chest. Jonas opened his mouth wide enough for a sparrow to fly in as he beheld the tallest and most beautiful stewardess in the world.

"Welcome to the thirty-eighth floor," she said.

35

the thirty-eighth floor

Madison's Uncle Sid was a criminal lawyer in Toronto. Every three years until her late teens, Madison's father would insist they fly east for a couple of weeks to stay with Uncle Sid and his family in their Edwardian mansion in Forest Hill. There were two servants, one to cook and one to clean and garden. There was a well-dressed aunt and two cousins, a boy and a girl, who had unimpeachable grammar and always seemed to be taking tennis or Italian or fencing lessons.

As long as Madison didn't think about Uncle Sid's house and family and cottage in Muskoka, growing up as the daughter of two schoolteachers in Edmonton seemed perfectly acceptable. But in the aftermath of every trip, on her way back home, surrounded in the airplane by people who looked and smelled and talked like Albertans, Madison felt like smashing her Walkman. It wasn't fair that Uncle Sid was rich and her dad wasn't, that her cousin Anita had a sailboat and she didn't even have a decent bicycle.

Madison would interrupt the inflight movie to ask her parents, "Why can't we live in Toronto?" It wasn't because she enjoyed her cousins, who were stiff and remote. She just wanted to live in a city of ravines and mansions and well-dressed people who drove German sedans and spoke in full sentences.

As she grew older, Madison learned there were several other neighbourhoods in Toronto, and that Forest Hill wasn't representative of the city at large. In her twenties, oil prices went up and Edmonton filled with German sedans and well-dressed people who spoke in full sentences. At that time, Madison learned to appreciate the wealthy, even the Edmonton wealthy, for what they were: extraterrestrials.

The thirty-eighth floor of Manulife Place was the most impressive piece of real estate Madison had ever seen, including the Edwardian mansion in Forest Hill. The floor was modern and classic all at once, with stainless steel playing off deep, reddish woods. In every other high-rise office complex she had been in, the walls were thin and the furniture was cheap. Nothing about the thirty-eighth floor was cheap. There were paintings and photographs on the outer walls, with a series of glass partitions creating mini-rooms throughout the floor. Some rooms housed nothing. Others, sculptures and desks. The music played out of tiny speakers hidden in the ceiling.

Residents of the Garneau Block followed the six-foot woman, stumbling and bumping into one another. The view south and west, of the river valley and the pink setting sun, caused vertigo.

Since they exited the elevator and began their long walk through the maze of windows, Madison hadn't seen a corporate logo. She tapped her father. "Dad, what is this place?"

"Heaven."

"No, really. Is this one of your political friends?"

"I sure hope so. If it's an angry Liberal I'm in big trouble."

The woman opened large wooden doors that led into a boardroom – one of the few concealed corners of the thirty-eighth floor. Two men in tuxedos, one behind a bar and the other tending a miniature buffet table, stood smiling with their hands folded before them. "Please, make yourselves comfortable," said the tall woman in the navy pinstriped suit. "Your host will be with you shortly."

She closed the doors behind them. A new romantic French song played through the stereo system. Madison walked to the southwest corner window and looked out over the vastness of Edmonton, the western hills leading to Jasper and Jean-something.

"Well, I guess hummus and baba ghanouj don't really cut it, do they?" said Abby.

Shirley didn't respond.

Two of the walls in the rectangular room were wooden. So was the long table and surrounding chairs. Behind what must have been the head chair was a small nameplate. The logo Madison had been looking for, to explain this place. It said, "Anonymous."

Jonas had already secured himself a crab cake. Now he was at the bar. "So, sailor boy, how about an old-fashioned, what say?"

"Yes, sir. Brandy, bourbon, or Canadian whisky, sir?"

"Bourbon."

The bar man set to work. Jonas turned to Madison and winked. He was a social chameleon. Even without a tuxedo, Jonas seemed to be wearing a tuxedo. The bar man garnished the drink with a twist of lemon, and Jonas bowed and accepted it. He took a sip and said, "Marvellous," a word Madison had never heard him use.

A small line formed in front of the bar man. Jonas walked to Madison with his drink, saying hello to Raymond and David as though they belonged to the same gentleman's club.

"So, Pond, old liege," Madison said, in her best rich-girl voice. "How are your watermelon futures performing?"

"Very well indeed, sister, and your polo ponies?"

Madison pointed out the tiny Anonymous sign and together they watched everyone else get their drinks.

Everyone but Raymond, who sat at the table and held his chin up with both hands. Shirley slipped a glass of white wine in front of the sad professor and he said, in a wounded whisper, "Thank you, my love."

Soon, the residents of the Garneau Block were sitting at the long table with appetizer plates and drinks before them. Jonas was quietly singing along to "Non, je ne regrette rien," complete with rolled Rs, but everyone else was quiet. What was it about a place like this that inspired silence? Madison wondered. It would have seemed coarse or impolite to talk about weather or that new Chris Rock sitcom or health concerns. The thirty-eighth floor demanded more from them.

As the sun set, soft overhead lights gradually eased into brightness. Jonas went up for another old-fashioned, this time with extra bitters, while the man at the food carriage took his leave. After the bartender finished with Jonas's drink, he left too.

No one spoke or even sipped. Now that the serving men had departed, it was obvious their host would enter the room at any moment. Without the aid of alcohol, Madison was giddy with nervous anticipation. She hoped her son or daughter – who had eyelids already! – wouldn't be subjected to acidic conditions or become more likely to inherit anxiety attacks every time Madison felt this way. She so often felt this way.

The door began to open. David stood up as though he were preparing to salute a general, and Abby clapped. Raymond and Shirley swivelled their chairs and Jonas lifted his drink.

Madison closed her eyes.

36

the young indian man from across the street

The young Indian man from across the street thanked everyone for coming. With a slight accent, he asked if the snacks and drinks had been to their liking, and if they had any trouble finding Manulife Place.

When no one answered, he commanded his neighbours to get up at any time during the meeting to get more food or to fill up their glasses. "I want this to be an informal gathering," he said, standing in front of the closed wooden doors in his black suit. "I want this, if at all possible, to be fun."

David Weiss remained standing. So far, he hadn't saluted the young Indian man from across the street. Madison worried for a moment that her father had been stricken with a heart ailment, as most of the blood had drained out of his face. She was relieved when he lifted his finger to point. "You."

"Yes. Me." The young Indian man from across the street moved into the centre of the room, directly in front of the Anonymous sign on the wall. "Please, Mr. Weiss. Sit down."

"Yes, darling," said Abby. "You're making everyone nervous."

David sat and stared at his hands.

"My name is Rajinder Chana and I am twenty-seven years old. I have lived at 13 Garneau since 1998." He walked to the bar and continued. "You may be wondering why I have never spoken to any of you, and I am afraid I do not have a good answer for that. For a few years after my parents died I rarely spoke to anyone and these habits become difficult to break. They enter your personality like footprints in wet concrete."

With a quivering hand, Rajinder Chana removed a glass from the cabinet behind the bar and poured some red wine. He took a sip. "I apologize. I practised and imagined this moment, and it never involved an urgent need for alcohol." He took another sip and looked at Jonas. "Not that I disapprove of drinking. It is healthy, to have a little wine every day. Is it not?"

"You bet it is, Rajinder," said Jonas. "And if you really want this to be informal and fun, you better sit down too. I can't speak for anyone else, but you're freaking me out."

"Right." Rajinder sat. "Before we begin talking about Fixing It, does anyone have any questions?"

"I have a million questions, Rajinder," said Abby. "But let me just say I love the way you've decorated this floor. It's gorgeous."

"And the music," said Jonas. "Edith Piaf's on my top-five list."

"Thank you both. I am interested in both interior design and French culture."

David Weiss raised his hand. "What is this place?"

"My office."

"The entire thirty-eighth floor of Manulife Place?"

"Yes."

"But it's mostly just art and whatnot."

"I also have a screening room and exercise facilities on the opposite side. There are several studios, for my artists-in-residence. I am currently supporting a painter, an interpretive dancer, and a novelist."

"What do you do, Rajinder?"

"Well, I guess you could say I am a patron of the arts."

"Yes, but what do you *do*?"

Rajinder turned and looked at Madison. He smiled and Madison smiled, and her face went hot. "Dad, he just told you what he does."

"This makes no sense," said David. "I need another drink."

Rajinder stood up.

"No, sit. I'll get it myself." David started to the bar. "All I meant is I don't understand how you can make money being a patron of the arts. Maybe Abby and I are doing it all wrong, but being patrons of the arts causes no end of credit card debt."

"Worth every penny," said Abby. "Isn't it, Rajinder?"

Madison saw that Rajinder wanted to be careful not to isolate or insult her father. Instead of saying, "Amen!" or "Yes, indeed!" Rajinder simply nodded at Abby. In the chairs nearest Rajinder, Shirley and Raymond sat close. Madison had never seen them like this. First, Raymond crying, and now Shirley squeezing his hand and rubbing the back of his neck and saying, "Shhhh," as though he were an infant.

"Is this about death?" said Raymond, with a drunken tilt on *death*.

Rajinder paused and then nodded. "It is partly about death, I would say. But you should not be asking me. This is a joint project. I hoped we could meet to discuss ways to rejuvenate and strengthen our block. The Perlitz tragedy has interrupted my life in ways I could not have foreseen. Psychologically, I mean. Perhaps you understand."

Everyone nodded.

"The university annexation proposal, I have known about it since July. Since then, with the help of a lawyer friend, I have researched ways to fight it, apart from the usual petitions and hearings. But I am getting in front of myself."

"Ahead of myself. That's the phrase."

"Thank you, Mr. Pond."

"Jonas."

"Thank you, Jonas."

"Are there any other questions about me, before we begin?" Rajinder took another sip of wine. "I know a little bit about all of you, I suppose, through observation and some Internet research. You all know each other quite well."

David put his hand up again. "Okay, so maybe I'm thick. But you still haven't really answered my question. Your office is the penthouse of Manulife Place?"

"A long-term lease. It was a bizarre opportunity, a trough in the real estate market."

"And you're a patron of the arts. Great news. You're a hero and a saint. But I'm wondering what you do for money."

Madison shook her head. "Dad, you can't ask that."

"I can't?"

"No." She turned to Rajinder. "Don't answer. It's none of his business."

Rajinder tilted his head. "I am willing to answer. Would you like to hear the story, Ms. Weiss?"

"It's poor manners, on my dad's part. Call me Madison."

"If it were not poor manners, would you like to hear my story?"

She turned and squinted at her father, who shrugged. Then she looked back at Rajinder. Madison enjoyed looking at Rajinder. "Yes."

"Then I will tell it."

37

the story of rajinder chana, part one

Before he began the story of how he came to be a rich man, Rajinder Chana implored his neighbours to fill their plates with brie and asparagus crêpes, duck confit, fresh melon wrapped in prosciutto, miniature beef Wellingtons, and crab cakes. He took large spoonfuls of hummus and baba ghanouj, and complimented Abby Weiss and Shirley Wong.

"Garlic is godly," he said.

Then Rajinder topped up everyone's glass but for Madison and Jonas. Madison took a can of club soda and Jonas insisted on making his own old-fashioned. As Rajinder hurried through the boardroom, serving his neighbours, Madison tried not to stare at him. Even when Rajinder smiled, his big eyes appeared sad to her. Though she knew it would always keep her from complete happiness, Madison preferred sad men.

"Where should I begin?" said Rajinder. "I should not like to bore you."

"I couldn't imagine being bored here," said Abby.

Everyone else shook their heads. No, they couldn't imagine it either. "Well," said Rajinder, "I am flattered. But believe me, I am a boring man at heart. Until the night of Benjamin Perlitz's death, I do not think I would have been capable of this."

"Of what?" said David.

"Of hosting a gathering."

Jonas lifted his glass. "Let's call it a party from now on. A toast to Raj, for throwing us a fish fry."

The table was quite wide, so everyone had to stand up and reach in order to touch glasses. "To Rajinder," they said.

"No, to you, to you," said Rajinder.

"This is a rare thing we got here." Jonas remained standing while his neighbours settled back into their leather chairs. "This is a real community thing, to get together like this."

David pounded the table. "Exactly. And we have to fight to preserve it, or we'll end up spread all over the city and into Calgary. A diaspora. We'll be the Garneau Block diaspora."

"You're picking up what I'm laying down, my friend." Jonas pointed at David and they backed away from their chairs and met for an impromptu hug. "I am laying it down and you are *picking it up.*"

"I'm sorry for that time I called you a filthy sodomite, Jonas."

Jonas slapped David's back and squeezed hard for a moment before they separated. "Those were the early nineties. A lot of people were still in the dark about, you know, being civilized human beings."

Instantly, like a cloud blocking the sun, the mood in the room changed from one of love and drunken frivolity into confusion and embarrassment. No one looked at Jonas and David as the men returned to their chairs. Yes, they were a community, a winning team. But Jonas Pond and David Weiss hugging? Madison knew both men would regret it in the morning.

She turned to Rajinder and smiled. Eventually, everyone turned to Rajinder. He nodded, took a deep breath, and removed the handkerchief from his pocket. With it, he dabbed his forehead.

"I was born and spent my early years in the city of Kapurthala, in the Punjab, close enough to smell the Kanjli wetlands. When I was nine, my parents moved to London, England, where my uncle owned and operated a McDonald's restaurant. Three years later, my father wanted to seize a business opportunity in Edmonton. So we arrived here in February of 1991 and opened a Subway sandwich shop in the west end."

"Can you eat beef?" said David, with a forkful of Wellington.

Madison shook her head. "Dad, please."

"Cows are sacred in India, Maddy. I was just wondering."

"I have chosen not to have religion, Mr. Weiss. So I can eat whatever I like."

"Good on ya, Raj," said Jonas, who seemed to have recovered from the aftertaste of the hug.

Shirley Wong lifted her drink. "Please continue, Rajinder."

"Thank you, Ms. Wong. I promise not to tell the long version of this story. My parents, for the first five years of their lives in Edmonton, did not take vacations. My mother worked during the day and my father worked at night, so they rarely saw one another. In 1996, they hired a manager. And for the first time since their arrival here, in the summer after my initial year of university, we took a family vacation into the Rocky Mountains."

Rajinder smiled nervously and took a sip of wine. Then he took another sip. Just when it seemed he was about to continue the story, he paused for a third sip. "I am sorry."

"You can skip this part if you like, darling," said Abby.

"No, thank you. I am just unaccustomed to telling it. On the highway between Lake Louise and Jasper, a drunk driver turned into us and hit our Toyota directly. My parents were killed and I was in the hospital for a month with several broken bones and a ruptured spleen."

"Your parents were insured?"

"David!" Abby pointed to her temple. "Sorry, Rajinder."

"Heavily insured, yes."

"But not *this* heavily."

"Not another word, David. Not. Another. Word."

"After my recovery I moved into an apartment in Oliver. I decided not to continue my studies. Instead, I endeavoured to learn about this part of the world. I drove about, and read books, and visited the historic sights and stayed in small-town hotels. I ate a lot of meatloaf and Reuben sandwiches. But this did not make me happy. Nothing made me happy."

"Modern life is a conspiracy against happiness," said Raymond, whose eyes were red and sore from crying. "Death and disappointment and –"

"Hush." The gentleness in Shirley's voice had given way to irritation. "Continue, Rajinder, please."

38

the story of rajinder chana, part two

The thirty-eighth floor's sound system went quiet. The residents of the Garneau Block, who had grown accustomed to the haunted Edith Piaf, looked up at the tiny speakers embedded in the hardwood ceiling. Rajinder Chana looked up with them, and waited. Spare piano music and the static of a spinning LP introduced the confident and shaky voice of Charles Aznavour singing "Sa jeunesse."

"Why do you like French music so much, Rajinder?" said Abby Weiss. "Do you have a French girlfriend?"

"I do not have a girlfriend at present. And I cannot explain why I like French music so much. Or French movies or French novels or French food."

David pointed at Rajinder. "French culture is phoney, my Indian compadre. The government pays for it all and censors foreign music, books, and movies. It's practically Soviet."

No one responded to David. Instead, they listened to Charles Aznavour. Madison didn't care how the majesty of Charles Aznavour and "Sa jeunesse" came about. The important thing was it existed. "Perhaps I'm talking too much?" said Rajinder.

No, no no. They all said no.

"Where was I?"

Raymond raised his hand. With a note of fellow-feeling in his voice, he said, "You were orphaned and very unhappy."

"One afternoon in January of 1997, driving south on Highway 2, I stopped in at a restaurant with a teapot on top. What is this place called, the strip of unimaginative restaurants and service stations in Red Deer?"

"Gasoline Alley," said Madison.

"Yes. In this teapot restaurant on Gasoline Alley a man and a woman sat in the booth next to me. The gentleman was having a cellular phone conversation, and since I was bored I listened. He had a mass of papers in front of him. I felt badly for the woman, because her companion seemed to be rather discourteously ignoring her. They were both agitated. As I began eating my soup, the gentleman ended his call. He said, 'We did not get it.'"

"They didn't get what?" said Jonas.

"Funding. Investment. I continued to eavesdrop and learned the man and woman – they were not married – were attempting to expand their oil and gas exploration company. They needed close to a million dollars and they had been soliciting funds from a potential partner, a venture capitalist in Calgary. I listened to them as I ate my soup, and when I finished my soup I asked if I could join them at their table."

Now completely plastered, Jonas flattened his arm on the table and laid his ear on it. "You had a million bucks?"

"Now you are ahead of me."

Jonas winked at Madison. "You hear what he said? Rajinder said the words I taught him."

"I will make it a short story. I invested 80 per cent of my money in their oil and gas exploration company, so they could expand into promising new territory."

"Weren't you afraid it was a scam?" said David.

"I was young and naïve. I did not understand a thing about the oil business. It just sounded right."

Abby shook her head and addressed her neighbours in a general way. "It's always about oil."

"So what happened?" said David.

"I bought thirty-three per cent of the company for one million dollars. The expansion proved more promising than they could have imagined. As we have seen, oil prices have risen considerably. And in February of this year, a large corporation from Texas battled with the Chinese government for the right price and bought us out."

Jonas laughed. "For how much, Raj?"

"Enough so that I will be a full-time patron of the arts for the rest of my life. Now, shall we move on to more important concerns?"

"Let's Fix It," said Madison.

"Yes."

"So how are we going to Fix It?"

"Exactly," said Rajinder.

Madison was confused. She turned to her parents and Jonas, and back to Rajinder. "Didn't you ask us here so you could reveal your plan?"

"I have no plan, Madison. I invited you here so we could divine and discuss a plan."

This last phrase from Rajinder was like the first kernel of popped corn in an empty pot. It reminded Madison of the effect in grade seven when a substitute teacher announced the class would be watching a movie. David accused everyone of dragging him out for no reason. Jonas cackled sarcastically. Shirley asked Jonas for a piece of gum and Raymond stumbled to the bar, where he proceeded to drink Crown Royal rye whisky straight from the bottle.

Rajinder cleared his throat and turned to Madison again. "Perhaps I should have hired a public relations professional, to help manage expectations."

"No, you did a great job," said Madison. She spoke softly, under the noise. "It's obvious you put a lot of effort into this. I think we were all hoping for an easy answer, someone to save us."

"I do have some ideas, a general framework. Should I shout?"

"No, they'll calm down eventually. You know what liquor can do to people."

As Madison predicted, the residents of the Garneau Block did calm down. It happened suddenly, when Raymond threw the now-empty whisky bottle against the wooden wall. The bottle didn't break but the red wood chipped and the noise was sharp enough to silence the room.

"I got fired today," said Raymond, struggling not to slur. "You want to know why? Because I took my Death in Philosophy class on a field trip to the Waterpark and slapped Dannika on the ass."

"Who's Dannika?" said Shirley.

"Let me finish, sweetheart. I should also tell you that I sort of asked my massage therapist for sexual favours the other night, to no avail. Oh, and I should also tell you that I've driven past the prostitutes on 95th Street not once or twice but *thrice* in the past few weeks. And since I'm up here, doing this, let me add that I've had lurid fantasies about you and about you, too." Raymond winked at Abby and Madison. "There, now I've said it. Let's fix *that*."

For some time, Raymond swayed at the bar. Through the ceiling speakers, Charles Aznavour sang "Il faut savoir." Instead of considering what her neighbour had just said, Madison attempted to translate the song with her high-school French. The lyrics seemed sad even though the music had an appealing bossa nova quality.

Discomfort filled the conference room like the scent of burned garbage. To ease it, Madison wanted to scream, laugh, or sing along with Charles Aznavour. Raymond bumped into the table, bent down and kissed Shirley Wong's hair. He said, "I'm sorry, I love you," and started out of the room. Rajinder's assistant, the tall blonde woman, met him just outside the door.

"Right this way, Dr. Terletsky."

When the assistant returned, one song later, Abby escorted her dazed best friend out of the conference room. On his way after them, David grabbed the hummus and baba ghanouj bowls, and thanked Rajinder for a pleasant evening. Madison wondered what would happen next.

A tornado seemed about right.

39

several instances of arrogance

At the Chateau Lacombe, two blocks south of Manulife Place, David called a cab while Abby and Shirley sat on the piano bench outside the lounge. He didn't want to talk about Raymond any longer so he extended his conversation with the dispatcher.

"Can you make sure it's a non-smoking car?"

"All our cars are non-smoking."

"Officially, maybe. But in reality, no. The drivers smoke all the time, and the cars make me feel woozy. I'm an ex-smoker myself."

"Well, if you see a driver smoking in his cab, call him in."

"I'm supposed to rat on the guy?" David turned and watched his wife and her best friend, and felt warm with marital satisfaction. For the rest of his life, whenever he felt tempted by wicked desires, he would remember this night. It had already been decided, on the short walk to the Chateau Lacombe, that Raymond would have to find somewhere else to sleep.

"Sir?"

"Yes."

The dispatcher had been speaking to David about the science of ratting on cab drivers. He had been ignoring her. "Contravening the bylaw carries a significant fine, and punitive action."

"How long will it take?"

"The fine and punitive action?"

"The cab. Our cab."

"Five to fifteen."

"Thanks."

David hung up the phone and approached a pot of Alberta wildflowers in the lobby. Not far away, he could hear both Shirley and Abby gently crying on the piano bench. It was clear he would be paying for the cab. A greasy cab, when they might have been in the private comfort of the Yukon. He sniffed the wildflowers, and without thinking too much about it, said, "Mmm."

The doorman, standing nearby in a suit, nodded and smiled. "They're fake."

"Oh, I know. I was just pretending they were real."

"Of course you were, sir."

"What's that supposed to mean?"

"Nothing at all. I simply agreed with you."

David had heard enough from this generation of self-assured, entitled, artificially polite young men tonight. "You enjoy mocking your customers?"

"Not at all, sir." The doorman adjusted his white gloves. "Are you a guest of the hotel?"

David noted the doorman's nametag. "Your name's Ronald, is it?"

"Ronald. Yes sir."

"Well, Ronald, I have half a mind to speak to your manager about your arrogant behaviour."

"Sir, I don't mean to be arrogant."

"Arrogant people rarely know how arrogant they truly are."

"Yes sir. Thank you, sir."

At the piano bench, the women dried their eyes with the shred of silk Abby used to clean her glasses. David wandered over to them.

"Cab's on its way."

Abby thanked him.

Shirley touched a low E on the keyboard. "This is so odd. I don't know what to say. I've been feeling off lately, since the night of the shooting. It's as if my life has been leading to this."

"No, sweetheart, not to this." Abby put her arm around Shirley. "It's leading in a wonderful new direction. This is just a pothole."

"Yeah," said David. "And it's not like he cheated on you. He just . . ."

Abby looked up with the most fearsome glance in her arsenal of glances. "Go away and call another cab or something."

David turned around to see the doorman watching him. Since he didn't want the doorman to see him chastised by his wife, David walked to the window with a natural gait. No, said the gait, I'm walking to the window because I *want* to gaze up 101st Street. He pulled the cellular phone off his belt and called home for messages. There were no messages. So he pretended to talk to Preston Manning for a few minutes.

From the lobby of the Chateau Lacombe, David could see the thirty-eighth floor of Manulife Place. The lights were on. Maybe Madison and Jonas were still up there, finishing off the crab cakes.

Rajinder Chana, with his fancy posture and money and youth. And, behind all those manners, a good dollop of arrogance. That icy assistant of his. The presumptuous signs, the "lawyer friend," the naïve meetings with the university, the catered mini cocktail party that the host himself was too posh to participate in. If Rajinder Chana weren't drunk with his own self-regard, he might have sought out an experienced advocate. Didn't he know who David was?

Experience had taught David the only way to fix anything in this world was to cultivate important relationships and trade favours artfully, nudgingly. Maybe a sit-down with a few simpatico cabinet ministers was in order, a coffee with the mayor, a couple of pointed letters to the editor. If only Rajinder had asked, instead of charging forward with a doomed meeting that would only lead to useless petitions.

The cab pulled up. David informed the women, and led them toward the doors. "Goodnight, sir," said the doorman.

David veered toward him and spoke slowly and quietly, like Rajinder. "Young man, I occupy a very important position."

"Congratulations, sir."

Between the two sets of doors, the heater made David feel sleepy. He took out his wallet, so he wouldn't have to reach for it when they pulled into the Garneau Block. It was best, in a cab, not to move around much. It stirred up invisible microbes, foreign dandruff.

The women got in the back seat together. David opened the front door and sat next to the driver. It was like diving into a soup of cigarette smoke. "I asked the dispatcher for a non-smoking car."

In front of David, on the glove box, was a cigarette with a red line through it. The driver flicked at the sticker.

"Yes, I see, but you've been smoking."

"No."

David told the driver where to take them, and noted his name. He would bring civility back to human relations, in his small way, by ratting the driver out.

On the High Level Bridge, looking west at the water, as the women whispered at one another in the back seat, David had a premonition. There were two spare bedrooms upstairs and the professor knew it. Dr. Raymond Terletsky would have nowhere else to go.

40

the river is deep

In 1960, Raymond Terletsky's grandmother had a brain aneurysm on the toilet and died. Lost with grief, her husband sold his ranch and purchased six plots of converted swamp where Ellerslie once met south Edmonton.

Raymond's grandfather found several houses built during the First World War that were about to be ripped down for a grocery store on the north side of the river, and placed one of these houses on each of his six plots. He planted spruce, aspen, plum, and apple trees, and got the right price on concrete. Once the neighbourhood was complete, Raymond's grandfather lived alone in the smallest bungalow and sold the remaining homes to his five children and their spouses for almost nothing.

This is where Raymond passed into adulthood, among parents and sisters, his uncles and aunts, his cousins – and everyone's favourite, the dark-skinned patriarch. The old man played the violin, danced, built bicycles out of salvaged parts, and unconsciously slipped into Eastern European languages when he drank vodka.

Five years after they settled into their house in Edmonton, on Halloween night, Raymond's grandfather got drunk, spoke Polish, gave candy to kids, walked into the wooden shed behind his bungalow, and committed suicide with a rifle.

Raymond considered his grandfather's death as he walked home drunk on the east side of the High Level Bridge. The noise had been loud enough to bring five fathers running, and everyone who was still awake at 10:20 p.m. had stood in a storm of adult tears and screams and long, confused silences. Even though he never saw the scene in the little wooden shed, Raymond had created the memory. He knew what it looked like and smelled like, the secret power of the thing.

Halfway across the bridge Raymond stopped and looked over the rail into the dark water fifty metres below. There were swirls and eddies in the North Saskatchewan River; now and then a tree would float by. Raymond knew the river was cold and deep, and that the mysterious sturgeon swam along its bottom.

Three men tumbled from the bridge while building it in 1912 and 1913, but what had killed them? The fear of death while falling? The impact on the river surface? The rocks on the bottom? Ravenous sturgeon?

With a drunk man's precision, Raymond climbed to the outside of the black rail. His feet tingled and a layer of clammy sweat flashed over his body. Instead of looking down into the roaring soul of the city, Raymond stared at the old power plant and at the lights of million-dollar houses nestled around the valley. Regular people doing regular people things: reading books, watching movies, making love.

The confession on the thirty-eighth floor of Manulife Place hadn't been liberating. He hadn't felt unburdened afterwards. Halfway across the bridge Raymond understood he may have cut himself off from regular people things for the rest of his life.

"Hey, fella." There was a woman behind Raymond. He could hear her sniffling. "Whatcha doin'?"

"Go away. I'm thinking."

"You're not gonna jump, are you? That's illegal."

Raymond could not see the woman, but he didn't like the nasal quality in her voice. He worried he might catch her cold. "I'm not going to jump. I'm just thinking."

"What about?"

"Football. Go away."

"The Eskies?"

"I'll give you money if you promise to leave me alone. How does a crisp twenty-dollar bill sound?"

The woman leaned out over the water so she could get a look at Raymond. She was a moon-faced forty-year-old with a crooked toque and a bubble of visible snot under her left nostril. "It's dumb to kill yourself, man. All your friends'll be –"

"I don't have any friends."

"Bull."

"Earlier this evening, I made myself into a pariah."

"What's a pariah?"

"How about this: how about thirty-five dollars?"

The wind was light. For a minute Raymond and the woman looked to the east, where the river curved. "I just thought about the worst stuff," she said.

"Pardon?"

"I just stood here and pretended everything was the worst it could be for me. Ten times awful, with shit on it, the way you feel I guess. But I still think it's dumb to jump. You might as well stay around until you get cancer or a stroke or whatever, even just to watch TV. Think about all the TV you won't see. It's September and all the new shows are just starting. And then there's hell to think about. You'll go to hell for sure."

"There is no hell."

"Bull."

"Just dark. Nothingness."

"So you don't believe in God?"

"No."

"Oh man, that is *dumb*."

"Take my whole wallet, please. Just reach down and slip it out of the right pocket of my suit jacket. I went to the bank machine yesterday so there'll be about seventy dollars in there. Use my credit card. Buy some Adam Sandler movies."

"Yeah, but my DVD player's busted."

"Get it repaired."

"For seventy bucks? You can almost get a new DVD player for that."

Raymond sighed. His arms were locked on the rail behind

him, but they were beginning to fall asleep. It was uncomfortable to stand like this, with his feet hooked on the outer bar. If he were going to jump he had to jump now, or soon. But he didn't want to jump and sail through the air in a final moment of majesty while this sniffling stranger with the crooked toque and onion breath watched. He wanted his death to have mythic power.

That was what had been missing from his life all these years. His career, his city, this bonehead province.

Mythic power.

"Excuse me," Raymond said. He started to shift so he would turn away from the water, but it was an awkward transition. If he let go with an arm and took the weight off one foot, he could slip. And if he slipped he would be gone. Not flying with slow-motion black-and-white movie majesty but flopping and spinning straight down.

"You need help?"

As it turned out, Raymond did need help.

41

name that father of confederation

Jonas directed Rajinder and Madison to a corner table in the Hotel Macdonald's Confederation Lounge, surrounded by tapestries and people speaking Russian. "This is where I come to play rich and carefree." He pretended to smoke a cigar. "Isn't the lighting in here perfectly, romantically, heartbreakingly dim?"

"It is a lovely spot, Jonas." Rajinder held the chair for Madison and then sat down.

The server arrived immediately, said good evening, and left menus on the table. Jonas raised his eyebrows a couple of times. "Are you paying, Raj?"

Rajinder smiled and slid the wine list across the table. "Of course."

"Come to papa."

While Jonas scanned the wine list, Madison sat back in her chair and tried not to look at Rajinder. They were sitting under the giant *Fathers of Confederation* painting, which offered her the opportunity to play a round of Name That Father of Confederation. She feared it would be a short game – John A. Macdonald, Charles Tupper, the assassinated Thomas D'Arcy McGee . . . And it was.

Rajinder didn't seem to share her bashfulness about staring. Madison felt his eyes burning into her cheekbones, and the fathers of Confederation hadn't done much to slow her heartbeat. Somehow she had to respond. Weather? Hockey? The struggle in Iraq? Instead, she blurted, "Yeah, I'm a travel agent but don't judge me because I *do* have a master's degree in comparative literature. Not that being a travel agent is anything to apologize for. Sure, I live in my parents' basement, but I'm not, you know, a complete failure."

Rajinder blinked.

"So, Raj," said Jonas. "I can order whatever I want?"

"Within reason, yes." Rajinder looked away from Madison.

"I have never been able to taste the 250 dollars in 250-dollar wine, but perhaps it is a deficiency in my palate."

Jonas waved at the server, who had just popped the cork on a bottle of champagne for the Russians. As the server approached, Jonas turned to Madison and Rajinder. "Dig this accent."

"You're ready?" the server leaned forward with his hands behind his back.

"We'll have the Joseph Drouhin Clos Vougeot Grand Cru."

"The Burgundy?"

"Yes."

"Good choice, sir. Will that be all?"

Jonas nodded. "For now, my good man." When the server was gone, he turned to Rajinder and pressed his hands together in prayer. "So. Will you be my best friend?"

"Jonas, stop that." Madison leaned forward and cuffed him lightly on the ear. "I'm sorry for his behaviour, Rajinder. And for mine and everyone's behaviour tonight. We all acted like it was a trailer-park keg party, without the dignity."

Rajinder nodded. "I must admit. It was not as I had imagined."

"What is, my brother? What is?" Jonas moved his chair away from Madison so he would be closer to Rajinder. "But I have to ask you something. You have, like, many millions of dollars, right?"

"Well . . ."

Madison made a fist and shook it.

"Some Texans bought up your company. You have all this cash. Why don't you live in New York or London or – since you're a Francophile – Paris? Of all the cities in the world, why *Edmonton*?"

"Only an Edmontonian would ask such a thing."

"That isn't exactly true, Raj. My friends in Vancouver and Toronto ask me all the time why a gay man would choose to live in Alberta. All the time."

"They are ignorant. They do not understand."

"You've lived in London. You've been to Paris and New York. So why –"

"There is an inferiority complex in your DNA," said Rajinder, as the server returned with the wine. The server removed the cork and poured a bit for Jonas to sniff and swirl and taste while Rajinder continued speaking. "You have the foundation of Canadian inferiority reinforced with Edmonton inferiority, a species of inferiority that insinuated itself after Wayne Gretzky moved to Los Angeles. Yes?"

Jonas lowered his head. "The parties. The cocaine. Like a potato-chip bag in the wind."

"Soda and cranberry, please." Madison wanted to try the wine, badly, but she turned her glass over so the server would leave it empty.

Rajinder smiled at her. "You don't drink?"

"Not really, no."

"That is wise."

"Yeah."

Jonas took a second sip of wine and closed his eyes. "Oh, this is the balls. Isn't it?"

"Yes," said Rajinder. "The balls."

"Anyway, all the redneckery and big trucks and Harley

Davidson T-shirts when you could live in the Marais. I'll never understand it."

Rajinder smiled at his wine. "European cities are relatively monocultural, and the vehicles are getting larger, not smaller. There are equivalents in Paris for all our local shortcomings, and a global entertainment machine that is beginning to erode what we find charming about older countries. It's cold in the wintertime in Paris and London, too. People are frustrating and complicated and . . ."

"Stupid."

". . . wherever they live." Rajinder turned to Madison. "Why do Edmontonians grow West Coast plants in their back-yards instead of native species?"

"Edmonton suffers from an anywhere-but-here disease. It's a great city, but it's not a *city*."

"But it is, Madison, you see?"

She didn't see.

"Edmonton is a real city as soon as we, as Edmontonians, believe it is real."

"We're a communal Pinocchio," said Jonas.

The server brought Madison's soda and cranberry, so she lifted her glass. "To believing."

Rajinder and Jonas leaned in. "To believing."

The Russians had gone quiet. Madison turned and saw the Russians were looking at them. Had they been speaking too loudly? She talked more quietly. "Rajinder, what is Anonymous? It was on the wall in your conference room."

"I am Anonymous."

Jonas pointed. "That's *you*?"

"I don't get it," said Madison.

"The era of government support for the arts in Canada, especially around here, is waning. Health care is too dear."

"Farmers and suburbanites think arts funding is a homo plot." Jonas swirled the wine in his glass. "And those people actually vote."

"I fund the arts, Madison, but I don't want to be seen as a replacement for broader public support. I don't want to be in the newspaper either. So: anonymous."

Jonas snorted. "But you could be famous. They'd make documentaries about you."

"Who would?"

"They would."

"That is not my measure of success, Jonas."

"It's mine. Oh, it's so mine." Jonas slugged his wine. "Did I already ask if we could be best friends?"

"Twice in the conference room after the others left, three times on the walk to the hotel, and once a few minutes ago."

"Think about it, Raj."

"I will, thank you."

Without any warning, an acutely foolish desire bloomed in Madison's chest. As Jonas continued to press Rajinder for a best-friend commitment, Madison wanted to make a similar proclamation. Instead of building toward an afternoon ice-cream date with Rajinder, instead of asking him about growing up in India or his thoughts on landscaping, code words for *I want you like I want a gulp of 250-dollar wine*, Madison wanted to say, out loud, I want you like I want a gulp of 250-dollar wine.

42

cowards that jump

Professor Raymond Terletsky wanted to be free of the woman who had dragged him, by the neck, over the rail and onto the pedestrian path of the High Level Bridge. But she had insisted on escorting him home.

"Your name is Helen?"

"Yes, Helen."

Raymond pulled the beige handkerchief out of his pocket and passed it to Helen so she would stop sniffling. Nearly falling off the bridge had sped up his hangover by several hours, and the seeming omnipresence of Helen's snot was making him feel queasy. "This is for you."

They reached the top of the small hill on the south side of the bridge and stopped at the red light. Helen waved the hand-kerchief. "What's it for?"

"To blow your nose."

"I'll get it all gross."

"You can have the handkerchief. It's my gift to you. Just please blow your nose, Helen."

The green walk symbol appeared and they started toward Garneau. Candlelight shone up on the faces of attractive couples and parties of four inside the High Level Diner, eating salmon and tiny steamed gourds. A gust of wind came up out of the valley and dislodged several leaves from a nearby aspen tree. Helen stopped in the wind and blew her nose for a while. As she did, Raymond leaned against a bicycle rack and hoped that somewhere, perhaps Egypt, a genius was inventing that time machine he wanted.

"I should tell you, Helen, what you did tonight was temporary."

Finished with the handkerchief, Helen stuffed it into the pocket of her ski jacket. "What d'ya mean?"

"I mean I don't have a choice in the matter. When a man only has the past, when his future is a most certain disaster, he has to be honest with himself. Ask the bus driver to stop and get off."

"Dr. Terletsky, I don't even have my grade twelve, but I think I'm way smarter than you."

"All recent evidence suggests you're right about that."

Raymond led Helen through the parking lot across the street from the diner and into the Garneau Block. They passed through the tall mountain ash trees and shrubbery that hid the alley from the block, and Helen stopped. She turned to Raymond and back to the five houses in the crescent. "Hey. This is the place where that guy got shot." Helen pointed at 10 Garneau. "That's the house. It was on the TV. He held his wife and daughter hostage for a while, right?"

Raymond nodded.

"I remember watching and thinking, geez, what a scumbag. Then when they shot him . . . what was his name?"

"Benjamin Perlitz."

"Then when they shot him I figured, hey, come on. Did you really have to kill the guy?"

A silence ensued.

"Benjamin Perlitz. Why do people do stuff like that?"

Raymond thought for a moment and said, "Because they have nothing left. Their hearts are broken. I guess Benjamin Perlitz didn't have the guts to jump off the High Level Bridge either."

"That's not guts, Dr. Terletsky."

Since he was on the verge of sleeping on his feet, and since the muscles in the front of his neck hurt when he talked, Raymond conceded the point. He stepped toward his home across the street from 10 Garneau and said, "This one's mine."

Helen followed him, and moved in close as they passed in front of the Perlitz house. "You can feel the blood in the air, can't you?"

"Well, actually . . ." Raymond started, but he was interrupted by the sound of his front door opening. Shirley Wong stood on the front porch, with a velour housecoat wrapped around the dress she had worn to the Let's Fix It meeting. Raymond waved at her. "Hi, honey."

"A new friend already? That didn't take long."

Helen smiled. "You must be Shirley. When we were still on the bridge he told me about you. I'm Helen Radowitz and I saved his life."

"You aren't sleeping here, Raymond."

"It's my house."

"You aren't sleeping here."

"The couch?"

Helen took a couple of steps away from Raymond. "Now I get it," she said.

"You don't get anything, Helen." He turned back to Shirley. "Technically, I didn't cheat on you."

By the time Raymond had finished the word *cheat*, Shirley had already slammed the door.

"That's why you were gonna jump."

"Yes." Raymond began considering the cheapest hotels in Old Strathcona when another door opened behind them.

David Weiss called out. "Professor!"

"Hello, David."

"Abby's making up the spare bed for you, but I don't think she'll be keen on your companion."

Raymond and Helen started across the street, with Helen taking a wide route around 10 Garneau. "I'm Helen Radowitz and I saved his life."

"Thank you, David. I know Abby probably isn't all that thrilled with me."

"No one is all that thrilled with you. But friends are friends."

Helen shook her head. "You see, Dr. Terletsky? You have friends."

"I guess I do. Thanks very much, David. I'll make this up to you."

"Just don't bawl all night if you can help it."

"Can Helen wait inside while we call her a cab?"

"Oh, I don't need a cab."

"Helen, I insist."

"It'd be fifteen bucks. Just give me the fifteen bucks and I'll walk."

"Are you sure?"

"I'm sure."

Raymond took out his wallet and gave Helen a twenty-dollar bill. She gave him a quick hug and started out of the block. The cool wind messed his hair. Slowly he walked across the Weisses' lawn, with a glance back at his house. Shirley Wong stood in the picture window. Raymond lifted his arm to wave at his wife, and she walked out of the living room and turned off the light.

43

the queen of the night

For a few months during university, Madison had dated a vegan. One night they rented a documentary about veal production, wherein baby cows are taken from their mothers two days after their birth and shut into crates. Madison was already tired of the vegan by the time they rented the documentary – he had a ponytail and he was curiously indifferent to matters of the flesh – so she sided with the farmers.

Ten years later, Madison sat in her parents' dining room and chewed the same piece of veal cutlet for five minutes while Abby clapped her hands. Abby was going to be a grandmother. Finally a grandmother. "It's a girl, I just know it. Do you feel that too, darling? You must. You absolutely must."

Madison could not respond. It was the calf, mooing on its way to slaughter amid the mother cow's great bellows of mourning.

"Darling?"

"Sorry." Madison lifted her IKEA napkin and spit the well-chewed hunk of veal into it. "I'm not . . . I don't know."

"You're not feeling it?"

"I'm not feeling it."

Abby turned to David. "That's because she's still early along. Right?"

"You bet." David sipped his beer and ran his hand through the tuft of white hair on Garith's head. The disruptive quality of Madison's news had allowed this breach in protocol. Most nights, Abby didn't allow Garith to be on David's lap during dinner.

Madison exhaled, and both Garith and David took note. "Not hungry, kid?"

"Nope."

Abby laughed. "You can be so hungry it feels like your stomach is eating itself. Then you get some food in front of you and you can't touch it. Am I right? Am I right?"

"Yes, Mom."

A loud flourish arose from the spare bedroom, and died again. Abby sighed. "That poor, mixed-up man."

David motioned toward the spare room with his thumb. "The ol' professor's been listening to *The Magic Flute* on repeat."

"He says he wants to get back in touch with reason, truth, and virtue." Abby took a bite of veal. "Oh, honey, that's marvellous. You cooked it perfectly."

David put his head on Abby's shoulder for a moment. "Thanks, sweets."

"What else does he want again, David?"

"He wants something called mythic power."

Madison walked into the living room. She flopped on the couch, hungry and not-hungry. Her new feelings for Rajinder Chana, stirred by the strange spectacle of her parents in love, the swimming baby inside her, and the Queen of the Night aria in the spare bedroom, made her feel cloistered. She closed her eyes and imagined herself bursting out of the house and into the neighbourhood, the city, the province, the country, the western hemisphere.

Wishes and dry heaves blown against all the fences in the world.

Garith hopped off David's lap and scurried across the hardwood floor to Madison. He jumped up on her chest and licked her face.

"There's only one bedroom downstairs, David," said Abby. "That just won't do."

"What do you mean it won't do?"

"I mean, since Madison's partner abandoned her . . ."

"He wasn't my partner!"

"What shall I call him?"

"Jean-something."

"Sons of bitches." David sliced the air with his knife. "Filthy separatists."

Abby paused for a moment. "Since Jean-something abandoned her, we're going to act as grandparents and as a father."

"Please, Mom. Never say that again."

"But Maddy, you're underemployed and alone. Even if the university *doesn't* plow over the block, the basement suite only gets sunlight for an hour or two a day. The little darling will end up with rickets."

David pushed his chair back and took the three plates into the kitchen. "I'll load the dishwasher."

For years, Abby had been telling Madison there is no good time to have children. Just have a kid, and adjust. Now that she was pregnant, Madison saw that the adjustments were going to be more annoying and more expensive with each new aspect of her mother's involvement.

She lifted Garith up off her chest and started to the door.

"You're not going downstairs already?"

"No, I just need a bit of air. I'll take the dog out."

Abby met her in front of the door for a hug. "Isn't this spectacular?"

"It sure is, Mom."

"From now on, only organic food for you. You'll need a daily dose of Omega-3 fatty acids. Are you taking multi-vitamins? And we'll have to buy you one of those pregnant yoga DVDs. Yoga and Pilates, maybe some salsa dancing. We can do it together, up here. Oh, and you can have the Civic. I'll get myself a Toyota Prius. How long have I wanted a hybrid?"

"Mom –"

"Look at your big boobs. They look wonderful. What a dope I am, for not noticing sooner." Abby squeezed her daughter's breasts and lifted her shirt. She bent down and shoved an ear into her daughter's stomach. Abby listened and then spoke. "Hello in there! You little inchworm. I could take a fork and *eat you up*. Hellooo."

Without a word, Madison wriggled away from Abby's grasp and slipped on a pair of her father's rubber boots. She opened the big door and Garith began to yip and hop in anticipation.

"Take my down vest. Don't get a chill."

Madison took the down vest and hurried out the screen door. The dog bounded across the front porch and down the steps, delighting in his freedom. Behind Madison and Garith, standing in the doorway, Abby waved.

"I'm the proudest mother in Alberta!"

Madison hurried away from the Weiss household, past 10 Garneau toward the university. As usual, the students in the walk-ups were drinking Pilsner and Hard Lemonade on their balconies. They listened to rap music and insulted one another's private parts. Garith pranced down the sidewalk, and in and out of bushes and hedgerows. The threat of rain buzzed in the air.

After a short walk along Saskatchewan Drive, Madison returned to the block. The lights were on in 13 Garneau, but Rajinder Chana was not visible. Garith bounced around on the front lawn of 10 Garneau, which had grown to a ticklish length.

Madison walked toward the sound of a woman singing, "Ah ha ha ha ha ha ha ha ha huh," repetitively. The spare room window was open so *The Magic Flute* leaked out into the block. Madison didn't mean to spy but she could see the professor, by dim orange lamplight, kneeling over a large book as if in prayer.

44

self-concern

Three teenage sisters wandered through the Rabbit Warren, arguing quietly over the right gift for their mother. Shirley Wong looked up from the front page of the sports section to watch them. The youngest girl was nervous, washing her hands without water and making too many suggestions – lavender bath salts? Moses doll? Smelly candles? Finally the oldest sister, wearing jeans so low-cut that the veins along her pelvic bones were visible, whispered, "Shut it, shut it. Oh and *please* shut it."

Shirley stepped out from behind the counter and smiled at the sisters. "Can I help you in any way?"

"No," said the oldest. "We're just looking."

"For a friend? A relative?"

The youngest sister, her dry hand-washing less deliberate now, stepped away from the other two and said, "Our mom."

"Is it her birthday?"

The youngest turned to the other two, who looked away. One of them sighed and mumbled something. "Well," said the youngest girl, perhaps thirteen, "she's sick and we just want to get her something. We thought flowers but they'll just die and we didn't want to, like . . ."

For a moment, Shirley watched the quiet interplay between the sisters. She understood their mother didn't have a cold or the flu.

"Well," said Shirley, to the youngest. "I have a few things your mother might like."

The other two reluctantly joined Shirley and their little sister in front of a display in the back of the store. Instead of selling something, Shirley wanted to take the girls into her arms and squeeze the worry out of them.

"A woman I know carves these from solid blocks of wood." Shirley ran her fingers along the smooth backs of several small sculptures. "She only speaks Chinese even though she's lived in Edmonton for thirty years."

"They're pretty," said the youngest girl.

Among them was a butterfly, a crab, and a crane. Shirley took each off the shelf but the oldest daughter seemed most interested in the cicada. She reached for the sculpture and cradled it. After a moment, Shirley said, "The cicada represents immortality."

"Immortality?" said the youngest.

"Yes," said the oldest, to cut off the conversation. She turned it over and looked at the price. "It's nice, thank you, but kind of expensive for us."

"How much do we have?" said the youngest.

The oldest sighed and they congregated at the counter to pool their money. Between them, they had $37.86. The cicada, before tax, was $45. Shirley's cost was $35 so she took the money and wrapped the little wooden sculpture. The youngest and oldest smelled candles while the middle sister leaned forward on the counter. "Our mom has bowel cancer."

Shirley whispered so the oldest sister wouldn't hear. "I'm terribly sorry."

"We've known for a while that she'd get really sick but now she is and it's, um . . ."

Shirley stopped wrapping for a moment and put a hand on the girl's wrist. "Your mom is very lucky to have such lovely and thoughtful daughters."

The middle sister bit down hard and looked at the floor.

"How old are you?"

"Fifteen."

"What grade is that?"

"Ten."

Shirley finished wrapping the cicada and passed it across the counter to the middle sister, who said thank you and hurried out the store. The other two girls turned to Shirley, thanked her, and followed their sister on to Whyte Avenue. When they realized the middle sister was crying, they put their arms around her and guided her around the corner. Shirley watched them go, and sat behind the counter again.

Since Raymond confessed that he was a sexual deviant, Shirley hadn't been feeling too sprightly. But it was immoral to be so self-concerned when mothers were dying of bowel cancer. She thought of Katie Perlitz, who had watched her own father bleed to death.

Shirley forced herself to smile, and then laugh: she imagined Raymond, her donkey of a husband, asking his masseuse if she might, you know, perhaps, in a perfect world, er, well, harrumph. The yearning to beat him over the head with a spatula came and went like hunger pains. Someday soon, she would speak to him about why he had not been satisfied with her. It would be a dreadfully humiliating conversation and she hoped, somehow, it would be unnecessary. For now, to avoid thinking about this conversation, there was merchandise to order, a store to keep tidy, and two newspapers under the counter.

Deep in the sports section was a small story about a new team in the Alberta Junior Hockey League, the Edmonton Jesters. Their season was just about to begin and three of the players, from small towns in the north and south, needed to be billeted. At the bottom of the article was a phone number. Before Shirley had much time to think about it, she was speaking to the wife of the team's general manager.

"You sure you're interested in that sorta thing?" said the woman. "Seventeen year-olds can be . . ."

"Maybe you could bring them by for a coffee?"

"Coffee." The woman coughed. "Since the story was in the paper, we've had a few calls. One boy's already found a place. How many bedrooms you got?"

"Two downstairs. My kids lived down there, when they were home."

"I can bring the boys by tomorrow night, Mrs. Wong, if you're free."

"Ms."

45

best friends unto the end of time

Rajinder Chana hooked his iPod to a couple of speakers and placed them at the corner of the front porch. "What would you like to hear?"

"Something sophisticated, my good man, and in English please." Jonas sipped his beer. Since he had became Rajinder's new best friend, Jonas had graduated from Pilsner to Grolsch. Inspired by Rajinder's tendency to wear suits for virtually every occasion, even to drink beer on the porch of an evening, Jonas had also taken to shirts and ties.

Earlier in the kitchen, while eating leftover snacks from the Let's Fix It meeting, Jonas had spied a tube or two of decent Scotch in Rajinder's cupboard, which had cheered him. "The sun is going down, so keep that in mind. We'd also like the music to complement the sounds of lawnmowers and the professor crying in the Weisses' spare bedroom."

"Is he really crying?" Rajinder sounded worried.

"I don't know."

A moody art-rock song began playing from the small speakers. "Is this all right?"

"Sure, Raj."

"This band is from Edmonton." Rajinder unbuttoned his suit jacket. To Jonas it sounded as though the singer were being whipped with something. Rajinder nodded his head in time with the bass. "I have seen them in nightclubs downtown. They do this thing with meat. It is all quite avant-garde."

"I don't think avant-garde's possible."

Rajinder opened his beer and sat back in his chair. Soon it would be dark and the air would cool. "Would you like me to tell you a secret, Jonas?"

"Secrets are my favourite."

Rajinder nodded toward the darkness of 10 Garneau across the street. "I know where Jeanne and Katie Perlitz are now."

Jonas sat up. "Really? Madison'll wet herself."

"Perhaps you are unfamiliar with the nature of secrets."

At that moment, the basement suite door of 12 Garneau opened. Madison waved and began crossing the street.

"She reminds me of a movie star." Rajinder stood up and waved.

"Which one?"

"A plain yet beautiful movie star, with a sincere smile."

Jonas turned to Rajinder, whose posture was painfully straight. Almost imperceptibly, he wet his lips and adjusted his tie.

"You be careful, pal," said Jonas. "She's a viper, that one."

"A viper." Rajinder laughed, and smiled as Madison started up the red walk. "Thank you for coming, Madison."

"Thanks for the invitation." She stood at the bottom of the stairs. "Hey, Jonas."

Jonas wished she would go away for a couple of weeks while he solidified his new best-friend status with Rajinder. He realized Madison had certain gifts that, given the nature of Rajinder's sexual orientation, could offset his charms. But all in all, Jonas was confident his wit and warmth were more winning than her sincere smile and silky red hair. "Maddy."

"Please, sit down." Rajinder pulled a chair out from behind the patio table, which was decorated with a mosaic of stained glass. "What shall I get you? Wine or beer? A cocktail? Or if you are still refraining from alcohol, a soft drink?"

Madison asked for a soft drink and Rajinder hurried inside. She sat and smiled at Jonas. "What's this music?"

"Some S&M thing. Rajinder's really into S&M."

"Oh, he is not."

"He also mentioned he hates babies and haikus."

"Jonas, stop it."

He took a long drink of beer. "Stop what? What?"

"I'm not going to take Rajinder from you. I know you want him to be your new best friend."

"That isn't true. I'm hurt that you should say that. You're my best friend unto the end of time."

Madison shook her head. Rajinder opened the door with his elbow and walked out with a small red cooler filled with ice, beer, and an assortment of pop and juice boxes. In the other arm he carried a platter of devilled eggs. Madison helped with the cooler, placing it next to the patio furniture.

"Did you make these?" said Jonas, while Rajinder pulled the plastic off the devilled eggs.

"After work today, yes. I followed a recipe from the Internet. It is nothing special."

Jonas realized that Rajinder had been holding out on him. The devilled eggs were in the fridge all along, and Rajinder had waited until the divine Madison showed up before he unveiled them.

All was lost.

"Should I leave you two alone?"

"What?" Madison looked at Jonas as though he had punched her in the stomach.

"I just thought . . ."

"No, Jonas. You shouldn't leave us alone."

Rajinder walked around the table and nodded. "I cannot speak for Madison, but I enjoy your company very much. Do you feel slighted because I kept the devilled eggs hidden until Madison arrived?"

Having his feelings aired like this made Jonas feel somewhat petty. "No, of course not. I was just being provocative for no good reason. Earlier today I smoked crystal meth with some kids in the alley and it's messing with my bean."

Rajinder opened his mouth. "You did?"

"Stop being so *serious*, you two. We're young and clever, and we live in a country with universal health care. Let's party."

"Let us party, then." Rajinder walked around and took a new beer out for Jonas. "And Madison? What is your poison?"

"Did I spot some cranberry cocktail in there?"

"Indeed you did."

The three new best friends sat on the porch, listening to the tortured prairie pop music while the sun began to set. Jonas was about to begin a conversation that might steer toward Madison's unfortunate pregnancy when the front door of 12 Garneau opened. David Weiss emerged with Garith.

Rajinder waved. "Mr. Weiss, sir. Hello."

"Howdy, Rajinder."

"If you and Garith would like to join us for a beverage, please feel more than welcome."

David said he wouldn't mind if he did, but he had to take Garith for a jog around the block first. Would it be okay if he invited Abby?

Jonas sighed and popped a devilled egg into his mouth. And another.

46

cultural designations

Jonas and Rajinder and Madison hung a line of blue Christmas lights along the back of the porch, to counter anxieties about looming homelessness with what Rajinder called "an atmosphere of gaiety." When darkness fell, everyone but Raymond Terletsky had gathered at 13 Garneau. With the faint sound of slow accordion in the background, Jacques Brel chatted about being alone yet in love.

The lights in place, Rajinder and Madison walked out on to the sidewalk to look from afar. "It is imperfect," said Rajinder.

In what she took to be a brave move, a signal, Madison slapped Rajinder's arm with the back of her hand. "All the best things are."

Since there were only five chairs, Rajinder sat on a large rock in his front yard. Madison had preferred it earlier in the evening when they had been sitting next to one another, looking out on the avenue. An avenue that already seemed lost.

No promising news or developments had come since the Let's Fix It meeting. On the contrary, the newspaper had not even published David's letter to the editor. It had been far too long and possibly libellous.

"Has your lawyer friend looked into a historical designation, Rajinder?" said David.

Abby shook her head. "Only two of the houses are original and Emily Murphy didn't live in either of them."

In his reclined deck chair, David shrugged gently and patted Garith, who was asleep in a blanket on his chest. "It was only an idea."

"A good idea, Mr. Weiss, thank you. Unfortunately, neither petitions nor lobbying will achieve our goals. I was planning to offer a generous donation to the Arts faculty but I am afraid that would offer us no guarantees. It might only delay the inevitable."

Abby went to open a bottle of Okanagan white wine. "Can't we try to do it without money? You might not know this, Rajinder, but since I retired from the teaching profession I've become a political activist."

"Here we go," said David.

"Clam up, honey. We certainly can't rely on your Tory friends."

David looked down. "That's between me and my party."

"I have *real* friends who can teach us how to protest in a serious way. These are deeply unpleasant yet committed people." Abby pulled the cork and shook it in the air. "I'm talking chains. I'm talking black blocs. I'm talking Raging Grannies. To the barricades!"

A long silence ensued. Madison didn't look at her father, as she feared they would both crack up. Abby poured wine into her glass and Shirley's glass, and sat back.

"I haven't heard any better ideas," she said. "At least mine's creative."

Rajinder smiled. "Mrs. Weiss, thank you for your enthusiasm and your contribution. It may be our only recourse, to enlist the services of your deeply unpleasant friends."

"Just say the word, Rajinder."

"But the notion of creativity does lead us to one more option, somewhat similar to the historical designation."

Rajinder was interrupted by an orchestral fanfare from across the street. Raymond Terletsky, it seemed, was listening to opera again at top volume. Abby reached over Madison to put her hand on Shirley's shoulder and squeeze.

"What the hell is he doing?" said Shirley.

"Recharging his psychological and philosophical batteries," said David. "At least that's what he said this afternoon. The good news is he took a shower today. Sorry, Rajinder. Back to your idea."

"It is not an idea. It is an option. Instead of an historical title, we can attempt to get a cultural designation."

No one responded for a moment. Madison wondered how that could be possible. There were no Fringe venues nearby, and even though bands and DJs performed at the Sugarbowl, you could hardly hear it from the Garneau Block. Then she snapped her fingers. "All we have to do is make Jonas a celebrity."

"I *am* a celebrity."

"A celebrity in the United States. Those are the only celebrities that matter."

"Why don't you just punch me in the nuts, Maddy. I'd prefer that."

Abby clapped. "Yes, yes. His house would be a monument, like Bob Dylan's childhood home. We drove by it once. Where was that again?"

"Hibbing, Minnesota," said David.

Jonas got up and started into Rajinder's house. In the doorway he turned and said, "I'm not famous. I'll never be famous. And if any of you actually cared about me, you'd know I grew up in Beverly. Beverly, not Garneau." He closed the door behind him.

Madison looked out into the yard at Rajinder, and signalled toward the house with her eyes. Rajinder said, "Of course," so Madison followed Jonas inside.

This was her first time in Rajinder's house, which was not so different from her parents'. The crown moulding was newer and prettier, and the paint was fresher. Rajinder had art on his walls, and framed yellow pages with Indian script, instead of plaques and photographs of the premier and other Conservative politicians competing with matted Greenpeace and Amnesty International posters.

She found the bathroom, and guessed the glow underneath the door meant Jonas was inside. "Knock knock."

"Leave me alone, Maddy."

"Please come out."

"You made light of my failures."

"Jonas, you aren't a failure. You're my hero. Who comes to all your shows?"

"Carlos."

"Who else?"

After a moment, Jonas said, in a small voice, "You."

"I think you *should* be a Hollywood celebrity. You're way funnier and talented than so many current ones, and more handsome, too."

"Well, I've always known that. In my heart of hearts. But thinking it won't make it so."

"Jonas, you're the greatest actor of your generation."

The door flung open. "Do you really figure?"

"I do. I'm your biggest fan."

Jonas hugged Madison. Then he stepped away. "Can I put my hand on your little pot belly?"

Madison lifted her shirt. "If it'll make you feel better."

"Let's name him Jonas," said Jonas, with his hand on her belly. "Don't you think it's a majestic name?"

Back on the front porch, Shirley had vanished. Raymond Terletsky was crossing the street toward 13 Garneau.

47

mythic power

Raymond Terletsky stopped in the darkness of Rajinder's walkway and watched his wife sprint home. "Shirley," he said. "My love. Please."

Though she had been stunned by the professor's creepiness at the Let's Fix It meeting, Madison felt sorry for him. If she were to publicly declare all her nasty dreams and fantasies she wouldn't be all that popular either. Shirley entered 11 Garneau and slammed her door, so Madison waved. "Come on up, Raymond."

He slouched in his sloppy jeans and T-shirt. "Are you sure?"

"Please," said Rajinder. "We have wine and beer and cocktails, and a variety of soft drinks in a cooler."

Raymond paused for a moment to tuck his T-shirt into his jeans, highlighting his paunch, and started up the red walk. "I'll stay away from the liquor but a root beer might be nice. Those blue lights surely are pleasant."

"We just put them up." Rajinder stood up from his rock. "To create an atmosphere of gaiety."

All evening, Madison had been waiting for Jonas to respond to the word gaiety but he stayed silent. Instead of dropping a witticism, he just winked. Raymond sat in Shirley's chair.

Rajinder cleared his throat. "I was just telling your neighbours, Dr. Terletsky, that one way to save the Garneau Block is to get a cultural designation from the city."

"How do we do that?"

"That's just it," said David. "We don't know. So far we've established that if Jonas here stars in the next Indiana Jones movie, we got nothing to worry about."

Madison put her hand on Jonas's knee, to make sure he stayed put.

"I've been sitting in a small bedroom across the street for two days straight, listening to the greatest musical genius in human history." Raymond opened his can of root beer and took a drink. "I also read *King Lear*, twice."

"That's great, Raymond," said Abby. "Bravo."

"After spending my whole career on death, I'd like to focus for a while on life. All the great life-affirming themes come through death, you understand. For example, did you know Mozart was sick and depressed and tumbling toward his last days when he composed *The Magic Flute*?"

In the past, listening to Raymond, Madison had always felt lucky to have avoided his classes. But on Rajinder's porch, in the blue light, with Jacques Brel in the background, he gave off a nervous yet curiously appealing energy. For the first time in her life, she was actually interested in something the professor was saying.

"Western philosophy," he continued, "my specialty, ignores thunderstorms and sunshine, winter and summer, the natural world and instinct and care. The smell of lilac. The dignity of a rainy day. Quiet and nothingness. *Art*, my friends."

"Amen, Raymond," said Jonas.

"I have wasted my life in shadows."

"Testify!"

The professor began pacing the front porch. Disturbed, Garith hopped off David's lap and began following Raymond. "We have to accept death and incorporate it positively into our lives. Embrace it. Life is death and death is life. Tragedy is comedy. Do you understand what I'm saying?"

"Not a lick of it," said David.

Raymond sat down again. "I've realized what's been missing from my life. My dry, false, secret and cold and craven life. Fifty-four years I've wasted. Wasted!"

"What is missing?" said Rajinder.

"Mythic power. A deep and abiding self-awareness, a sense of grandeur, a way to transcend my routines, my flaws, my interest in what people wear to the Academy Awards. And it's not just me. It's the block, the city, the province, and the country. Mythic power is missing from our lives. An abundant celebration of life through death, like *The Magic Flute* or *King Lear*. Something big and brave and messy. Here." Raymond pounded his chest. "Here." He pointed to each of his neighbours' hearts. "And here and here and here." After a moment of heavy breathing, he opened his arms to the neighbourhood. "Here. And most importantly, my friends, *there*." Raymond squinted and tilted his root beer can triumphantly toward 10 Garneau.

Jonas walked over to Raymond and hugged him. "I'm all sweaty, just from listening to you."

Abby applauded, and Madison and Rajinder joined in. David called Garith back up on his lap and shook his head. "I still don't understand what you're on about."

"Well, I don't either, David. Not yet." Raymond tapped his temple with the can of root beer. "But the idea is in motion, the great big idea."

"I think this is what I meant by Fixing It," said Rajinder. "I did not know this is what I meant. But this is what I meant."

Raymond walked down the steps. He continued to the street in front of 10 Garneau. Rajinder turned to follow him. Abby and Jonas and Madison started down the stairs, and after a series of annoyed mumbles, so did David.

The neighbours stood together in front of the dark house. "I don't have a job at the moment, so I can spend some time on this," said Raymond.

Rajinder nodded. "On Monday I will find out what the city means by cultural designation."

"I think a buffalo or two should be involved." Raymond took a step back and made a viewfinder out of his hands. "The northern lights, snow and stucco, and somehow the noble buffalo."

Without a word, David and Garith started to their front door.

Abby yawned, looked at her watch and followed her husband and his dog. "I'm really excited about this, whatever it is. Keep me posted."

Raymond and Jonas returned to the porch, discussing the mythic potential of buffalo. Would it be too *rural*? Under the soft yellow street lights, Madison looked at Rajinder and smiled. They followed their neighbours back to the porch and she shivered.

"Would you like a sweater, Madison?"

"That would be great."

Rajinder stopped her, looked down at her baby-blue sneakers and then up into her eyes. After three breaths and a faint stumble he said, "In addition, would you allow me to take you to dinner some evening? Anywhere you like, excepting sushi. It does not agree with me. Please, please do not feel obliged to say yes. I enjoy my time alone. In fact, forget I asked. It was ridiculously presumptuous of me to assume you would be . . ."

"I'd be delighted, Rajinder." They continued along, and Rajinder placed his hand on her lower back. A tingle rushed through her body, and she felt unpregnant for almost ten seconds.

48

shirley wong acquires billets

The hockey billets were named Craig Buckner and Blair Kravchuk, but everyone called them Steamer and Patch. They moved in on the first Monday of October, just as the crisp leaves and crabapples began to clutter Shirley Wong's backyard. As she gave the boys a tour of their bedrooms in the basement, she attempted to refer to them as Craig and Blair, but they were adamant about being Steamer and Patch.

"Really, Mrs. Wong," said Steamer, the blond Mormon boy from Cardston with big blue eyes. "No one calls us anything else, except our parents."

"I'm Patch," said Patch, the slow-talking giant from Lac La Biche. "I'm just Patch, you know what I'm saying?"

Chopping onions and garlic upstairs, while Patch unpacked and yelled at Steamer about how much he was hating this final year of high school, Shirley wondered if she had done the right thing.

There was so much extra room in the house, and after thirty years of marriage she had found the silence of the last few weeks to be disturbing. Yet Steamer and Patch lacked the rhetorical skill and eager curiosity of her children, whose travels through the house she had really been hoping to replace.

For years, she had watched hockey with three high-school friends. Two had recently moved to acreages and the third had sworn off the game during the NHL strike. So the hockey talk with Steamer and Patch would be sublime. But she couldn't imagine sitting in the living room with Steamer and Patch after dinner, watching *Biography* on A&E. She couldn't imagine referring to them by their preferred nicknames without feeling like a disc jockey on the classic rock station.

Steamer, she had learned, after some embarrassed laughter, was called Steamer for his tendency to take bowel movements in locker rooms just before games. Patch liked to squeal the tires of his truck as he accelerated from a resting position. In Lac La Biche, and apparently elsewhere, this was called "laying a patch."

Neither boy had heard anything about the tragedy at 10 Garneau. It seemed neither boy had ever read a newspaper or watched *The National*. When she told them what had happened across the street, Patch seemed to be thinking about something else. His truck, for instance.

Steamer had been puzzled. How could someone gamble all his money away? How could a woman just kick her husband out of his own house? Why had the law not intervened earlier? For Steamer, the events at 10 Garneau simply reinforced his feeling that life in the city was altogether wrong.

For their first dinner together, Shirley prepared a large tray of lasagna with Caesar salad and garlic bread. She put a bottle of red wine on the table and tuned the stereo to the modern rock station. Shirley was about to call the boys for dinner when Patch bounded up the stairs in his jean jacket. He smelled of cheap, musky cologne.

"I'm headin' out, Mrs. Wong."

"Ms."

"Huh?"

"Aren't you hungry, Patch? I'm just finishing dinner."

Patch stepped into his cowboy boots. "Me and some of the guys are gonna hit DQ or something later, after a couple beers on Whyte. We're just goin' out for a couple or whatever."

"Is that allowed? You're just seventeen, aren't you?"

Patch ignored the question and walked, in his slightly bowlegged way, out the back door. His heels were so heavy on the sidewalk leading to the parking pad that she could hear him through the closed kitchen window. The engine of his big red truck roared. To her relief, he didn't lay a patch.

At the top of the stairs, Shirley called down to Steamer that dinner was ready.

"Hot dog!" he said, and hurried up in a pair of sweatpants and a red T-shirt with a scary clown on the front. Underneath the clown it said, "Cardston Children's Festival, 1996."

Shirley sat across from Steamer, who quickly prayed and then clasped his hands in anticipation. He looked shocked at the food, but Shirley came to understand that on account of his uncommonly large eyes Steamer always looked shocked. The boy filled his plate with lasagna and salad and bread, then turned to the stereo and cringed. "Mrs. Wong?"

"Ms."

"Can we listen to something else?"

Shirley hadn't been paying attention to the music, but it featured squealing guitars and angry vocals. "Sure, Steamer."

"I listen to a lot of that stuff around the team and it's just that . . ."

"Classical?"

"How about country? You got that?"

"Some. We have Willie Nelson, I believe. Hank Williams maybe. Patsy Cline."

Steamer excused himself and hurried out of the dining room and downstairs. He came up with a pile of CDs, and put one in. It was pop country music, with lyrics about Jesus. "My parents don't like me listening to this sort of thing too too much but it doesn't hurt."

"No." Shirley shook her head, lying. "It doesn't hurt."

For the next while, Steamer talked about finding a compromise between living the gospel and playing hockey with boys in a state of total apostasy. He pointed to her glass of wine.

"Like, I don't know how you could drink alcohol. It's totally wrong. But I have to accept that, right?"

"Right, Steamer."

Shirley ate a small piece of lasagna and a few forkfuls of salad. Then she sat back and listened to Steamer talk about his religion. A few times, she tried to engage him in a discussion of the Edmonton Jesters – their prospects in the AJHL – but it only led him into a discussion of his teammates and their rampant sinning.

The phone rang and Shirley hopped for it. Her new evening helper at the Rabbit Warren was having a bit of trouble with the Interac machine.

"I'll be right there."

"How about I just re-start it. Maybe . . ."

"I'll be right there!" Shirley hung up the phone. "I'm sorry, Steamer, it's an emergency at my store."

He stood up. "Can I help in any way?"

"No thanks."

"What an awesome dinner. I'll wash up the dishes how about?"

"That would be very good of you, Steamer."

He smiled, raised his eyebrows, and lifted his chin.

In the backyard, unlocking her bike, Shirley began thinking of ways to get rid of Steamer and Patch. Shirley wondered if she had been too hard on Raymond. Maybe they were all twits and beyond judgment. Then *she* felt like a twit for falling under his spell, for trusting him – them – for so long. Were they capable of any better? Lost in this line of reasoning, Shirley discovered she had forgotten the combination of her bike lock. She tried one last time, but the numbers around the dial meant nothing to her. Thinking she was alone, unobserved, Shirley prepared to break into a good cry.

Just to make sure, she looked back at the house. Standing at the sink, Steamer looked out at her with his permanently shocked eyes. Shirley decided to walk to the Rabbit Warren.

49

a dance with mr. goober

In front of the mirror in her tiny bathroom, Madison practised her French. *Je voudrais manger des caillettes provençales ou un boeuf bouguignonne.* Yet she reserved a small percentage of emotional distance. No one could deny this was their first night out together without Jonas or her parents or Garith or the lunatic professor, but Rajinder had not used the word date.

Yet.

Madison didn't want to get her hopes up in case Rajinder, whose social skills bordered on performance art, just wanted to be friends. After all, this was an early dinner on a Monday, a pre-soaps event instead of a romantic Friday night. Then there was the boring weirdo factor: maybe Rajinder was a boring weirdo.

Even so, she drank some non-alcoholic Saskatoon berry wine from the farmers' market, lit sandalwood candles, and filled the basement suite with her most powerful pre-date CD: The Cure's "Mixed Up." Of course, she also wore her number-one pair of panties, the blue-and-white ones with the mosquito on the front.

The tiny bathroom mirror was not full-length so Madison had to stand on a milk crate to check herself out in profile. Her jean jacket and best scarf added a French flair to her ensemble, and helped hide the belly.

Did wanting to go to Paris make her a proper Francophile? Was it a coincidence, *un heureux concours de circonstances*, that they both loved France? It didn't matter, really. What mattered was that for the first time in over two years, Madison was genuinely interested in a male of the species who wasn't a sixteenth-century Japanese poet.

Finished in the bathroom, and with another ten minutes to waste, Madison danced around the basement suite with Mr. Goober, the plush monkey her father had won at a Calaway Park balloon-popping kiosk in 1987.

As Madison danced to The Cure, she told Mr. Goober, in French, that she loved him. She had always loved him. It had been a secret before but now Madison didn't care if the whole world knew. "*Monsieur Goober*," she said, with a tender kiss, "*je t'aime*."

There was a knock on the door, seven minutes early. Madison shrieked and threw the monkey. Mr. Goober crashed into a stone goddess statue on the television, a gift from her mother. Madison shrieked again, this time in stealth. The windows leading into her basement suite were not large, but she was stricken with the certainty that Rajinder had just seen her slow-dancing and smooching with Mr. Goober. She ran into the tiny bathroom to both check her makeup and register her mortification. Then she turned off the stereo, blew out the candles, took a deep and restorative breath, and started up the stairs.

Rajinder stood a few feet from the door in a grey suit and a white shirt opened at the neck. He held a bouquet of freesia. "Jonas told me they were your favourite."

"They *are* my favourite." Madison took the flowers and smelled them, peeking up to scan his face for a clue. No, he hadn't seen the *je t'aime* bit. "Thanks, Rajinder."

"It is probably unwise to carry them with us. Would you like me to wait here for a few minutes while you put them in a vase?"

Madison knew if she went inside she would have to invite him in, but her basement suite was so small and her parents' cast-off furniture was twenty years old and smelled like stale hamburger buns. "Um," she said.

"I have several vases."

"Do you? Because mine are all dirty."

Madison led the way. Loud heavy-metal music seemed to be coming from 11 Garneau, Shirley's house, but Madison assumed it was the Doppler effect – university students a block or two away, destroying their inner ears. The music was annoying but not so loud that it mitigated the silence between her and Rajinder. And since she was not the sort of woman who tolerated silences of this sort, Madison said, to her own amazement, "What do you think about the new conductor of the symphony?"

"He is very dynamic."

"Yes, dynamic."

"Are you a fan of the symphony?"

Madison started up Rajinder's walk. In past relationships, all of them somewhere between unsatisfying and disastrous, she had been something of a liar. If she had felt a lie would make her seem more sophisticated or attractive, she told it. Every time. She was almost thirty, though, and rocketing into single motherhood.

On the porch Madison smelled the freesia again. "Oh sure. But I have to admit I've never really been in the Winspear. It's kind of expensive and, well, I'm poor. A couple of years ago Jonas and I hung around in Hawrelak Park during Symphony Under the Sky and it sure sounded . . . pretty."

Rajinder opened his front door. "Please, leave your shoes on."

"Are you sure?"

"I insist."

Rajinder took the flowers and cut the stems over the sink. He pointed up to a collection of seven vases on a shelf, and asked Madison to choose. She chose a white one, with lime-green polka dots.

"I have spoken to the marketing department about attracting young people to the symphony."

"I am so prepared to be attracted."

"Competing against Hollywood and reality television and sports and video games has proven difficult. With the generation below us, it could be impossible. I am afraid we will witness the near-total erosion of both local art and high art in our lifetimes."

Madison was feeling dense, so instead of responding verbally she produced a thoughtful hum. Rajinder dropped the flowers into the vase and pointed out his kitchen window at the backyard of 11 Garneau. Five hulking young men sat around a fire pit with a case of Pilsner and a ghetto blaster. Madison stepped forward and stood close enough to Rajinder that their hands touched. "I *thought* I heard music next door."

"Ms. Wong has guests."

"Who are they?"

"I had never seen them before yesterday evening. The large man drives a loud red truck."

"Raymond and Shirley's kids were way too fastidious to have friends like that."

Rajinder checked his watch. "Our reservation is in half an hour. Perhaps we can explore this mystery another time."

It was, Madison felt, her gravest misfortune that as he looked up from his watch, Rajinder's gaze lingered on her belly.

50

universal health care

The beige leather seats in Rajinder's Mercedes were cracked and peeling, and there were several large rock chips in the windshield. At first, Madison wanted to ask why he hadn't bought something newer, given his financial freedom, but by the time they reached the strip mall that housed Jack's Grill she had developed tender feelings for the old car; Madison wouldn't have known what to think if he drove a Hummer.

"Strip malls," she said, as they walked across the parking lot to the entrance. "The future of world cuisine."

Rajinder didn't respond to her sarcasm, and she felt slightly shamed.

At the restaurant door, he paused for a moment and they looked at one another. It was a windy fall night. Leaves blew across the parking lot in short gusts and the light of the setting sun went metallic. There was nothing to say and Madison summoned every ounce of her strength to let the quiet to be the quiet. She pushed a stray lock of hair from her face and smiled. A white piece of fluff had attached itself to the lapel of Rajinder's suit so she pulled it off and allowed it to join the progress of the leaves.

The moment became a minute. Madison relaxed and breathed, and focused. She was standing outside the door of a restaurant she could not afford, on a windy but not cold evening, staring at a handsome man who had never made an ironic comment in her company. She looked past the brown of his eyes into the tiny pyramids of colour and shine around his pupils, the biological factness of Rajinder Chana. Who remembers on a date – if this was a date – that we're all just animals making romance out of eating, reproducing, and sleeping?

Madison prepared to be kissed.

Just then, the door flew open and the giant vertical handle whacked Rajinder in the forehead. He stumbled backwards but didn't fall as a couple in mid-conversation barged out. Both the man and woman stood in front of Rajinder, apparently as stunned as Madison. The man apologized and put his arm

around Rajinder for a moment. Rajinder assured them he was
perfectly fine and the couple started away, both of them cringing.

"That door really nailed him," the man said, loud enough
for Madison to hear.

Rajinder stood up straight and dusted himself off, even
though he hadn't come in contact with any dust. He cleared his
throat and wobbled slightly, like a drunk man acting sober. "Are
you ready?"

"Let's make sure you're okay first. That was *loud*."

"Oh I am most definitely okay, Madison. Most definitely."
And with that, Rajinder stepped forward, careened to the left,
and fell to the pavement.

The man who had opened the door sprinted back across the
parking lot to help Rajinder to his feet. Madison wanted to take
him to the University Hospital in the Mercedes but the man
guided Rajinder straight to his pickup truck.

"Just allow me a minute here." Rajinder mumbled, with his
eyes half open. "Rabbit tortellini and grilled organic Sturgeon
Valley pork chop."

The woman opened the passenger door of the pickup
truck and just as Madison and the man began helping him
inside, Rajinder threw up on the seat. Without a word,
Madison and the man turned and propelled Rajinder toward
the Mercedes. The woman, looking as though she too were
about to faint or vomit, took the keys from Rajinder's front
right pocket and ran ahead.

"I am so sorry," said Rajinder. "Thank you."

Madison drove slowly as Rajinder wobbled in the front
seat. The regretful man sat behind him in the back, saying,

repetitively, "You're good, buddy, hang in there, we're almost there, you're doing real good."

At the emergency entrance, the man rushed inside and summoned two men with a wheelchair. They lifted Rajinder out of the car and into the wheelchair, then Madison parked. The woman in the pickup truck stopped next to her. "I'm going to have to find a towel or something," she said. "It smells something awful in there."

By the time Madison began speaking to the admitting nurse, a stern woman with a Jamaican accent, Rajinder was already gone. There was a lot she didn't know about Rajinder. His birthday and his citizenship, his Alberta Health Care number. But she answered the nurse as well as she could, and accepted her final words of consolation. "It just sounds like a concussion, girl. Your boyfriend will be perfectly fine."

"He's not my —" she started, and didn't finish.

51

not staying out late

The hot lights popped on for his opening speech as Lacumseh the Noble Chief, and Jonas scanned the applauding audience. Madison had assured him they would sit in the first few rows on stage left but he only spotted the regulars with their mouths hanging open.

Not only had Madison stolen his new best friend, she was also keeping him away from *weekly proof* that when it came to improvisational genius, Jonas had no equal.

Fine. If that was the way it was going to be, fine. Jonas vowed to be way funnier than usual in Madison's absence.

A fire-breathing dragon of funny.

He looked out upon the audience sternly, and waited in silence until the kids who laughed at everything began laughing at nothing. Jonas lifted his right hand, said, "How," and the kids went wild.

Over the next hour, in a flurry of madness, Jonas scalped two of his cast members and invented a language. After the show, at the Next Act, the scalpees wondered if they were gone from the season completely or if the producer would create a couple new characters. Jonas sipped his beer, which tasted foul tonight.

"Why don't you all just shut up?"

His fellow cast members did shut up. Skilled improvisers, they scanned his face quickly for clues. Was he serious? The woman who played his daughter, the warrior princess, slammed the table with her fist. "Why don't *you* shut up?"

Manitou, the god of all that is good, along with two braves and a whisky trader, started into a pretend-angry dialogue about someone and everyone shutting up. Sick of actors, Jonas stood up out of his booth.

"Some things are real. The pain in my heart, for instance."

Another bout of creative silence, followed by a new round of dialogue about the nature of reality. Isn't it all just dependent on the evolutionary quirks of human perception? Bundles of atoms and quarks, if a heart breaks in the forest? Jonas sighed, grabbed his jacket, and started out of the pub.

"Can I finish your beer?" Manitou, the god of all that is good, called after him.

Jonas insulted the young man's genitalia and continued to the door, where he ran into Carlos.

"Wow, you sure did scalp some folks tonight." Carlos lifted his Tim Hortons coffee. "It was something."

"How can you drink Tim Hortons? You probably put milk in it too, don't you?"

"Double double."

"God." The entrance to the Next Act was barely large enough for two people to stand in. "Why are you here, Carlos? To spy on me?"

"No."

"Do you want to go somewhere?"

"Uh."

"Let's go somewhere. Let's go bowling or to a late movie or – I know – Leduc. Let's go to Leduc."

"That's where I live."

"Yes, I know, Carlos. Where's your Mustang?"

"How do you know I got a 'stang?"

"How do you *think* I know?"

Carlos swallowed and reached up to scratch the back of his neck. "Uh."

"I witnessed your Mustang in action not long ago. My friend Madison and I followed you home one night in her dad's suv."

"No, you didn't."

"I figured since you could stalk me I could stalk you."

Carlos looked up at the posters and handbills on the wall. He took a sip of his coffee and stuck his free left hand into the front pocket of his hoodie. "I wasn't stalking you."

"What were you doing?"

"Looking."

"Oh, looking." Jonas pushed and held the door open. "Less talk more walk."

Jonas followed Carlos out of the Next Act and north on Calgary Trail. It was cool in the wind so he pulled his peacoat closed and tied his scarf. Ahead of him, Carlos slouched in his hoodie and black football jacket – CARLOS on one leather sleeve and RECEIVER on the other – as though he were on his way to prison.

"Hey, Carlos."

He stopped and turned around. "Yeah?"

"You'd make a crap spy."

"I don't know any foreign languages either, and I hate getting dressed up and fistfighting, so."

"So a career in CSIS wasn't in your future anyway."

"I can't stay out late." Carlos handed his coffee to Jonas, pulled a Kleenex out of his pocket and blew his nose. He started crossing the avenue. "I'm hunting pronghorns tomorrow."

"Hunting pronghorns?" Jonas sniffed the creamy coffee, which was its own sort of horror. "What kind of a gayboy are you?"

Carlos stopped walking again. "I'm not gay."

"What do you mean you're not gay?"

"I mean I'm not gay. What, I look gay to you?"

Jonas laughed. "No, actually. You look painfully not gay, with those running shoes and Levi's Superslims and no belt. Oh, and that appalling jacket. But you're gay."

"No, I'm not."

"Then why are you picking me up?"

Carlos took the coffee from Jonas and continued into the parking lot. "Can't two guys be friends without being gay? I just want to be your friend."

At the Mustang, Carlos disarmed the security system and it beeped. Jonas paused to look up at the stars, obscured by the city lights, but they offered neither guidance nor sarcastic comments. He opened the passenger door and got inside. On the console, between the two seats, sat two Red Hot Chili Peppers compact discs. Carlos turned the key and the music blasted. Jonas lowered his head into his hands.

52

sick people

In the waiting room of the University of Alberta Hospital, Madison lifted the pay phone receiver and began dialling her friend Sandra in Vancouver. If Madison left Edmonton now, or soon, and spent her pregnancy on the West Coast, Rajinder would never know. She could give the baby up for adoption, come back to Edmonton and pretend she had been abducted by Al-Gama'a al-Islamiyya.

Rajinder was not boring. He was not secretly ugly, or foul-smelling, or cruel. Their violent first date only endeared him to her further, and it already seemed too late to tell him she was pregnant. Madison hung up before she hit the final digit. Instead of imagining her confession to Rajinder, or the one-bedroom apartment near an industrial park where she would soon live, Madison flipped through a seven-year-old copy of *Details* magazine with Michael Jordan on the front cover.

When she could put it off no longer, Madison took the elevator to the third floor. Everywhere were the smells of creamy protein drinks and steamed spinach, the sound of suction. Rajinder's door was half-open, so she knocked.

"Please come in."

It was dark outside, and the lights in Rajinder's room were dim. She could see both his eyes were faintly blackened. He was propped up in bed, wearing a gown, his hands clasped on his lap. As she approached his bed, Madison wondered why she hadn't bought him something at the gift shop. Anything, a paperback or a granola bar. What sort of black-hearted monstress was she?

"Oh, look at you."

"Madison, this is not my finest moment." Rajinder pushed back the cuticles on his left hand. "If I try to read or turn my head quickly, I feel nauseous."

"Nausea is one of my specialties. I'll get you some ginger to sniff." Madison pulled a chair across the floor. "How did you get a private room?"

"I feel guilty but yes, yes, I paid extra to have it. After the car accident, when I was in this hospital for a long time, I grew to despise sick people. It is a terrible psychological weakness. I recognize that. Excuse me." Without moving his head, Rajinder reached for a bucket to his left. He held it in front of him for a few seconds and placed it back on the table. "False alarm."

Madison slid her chair closer to the bed and touched his arm. He sighed and leaned back.

"I was thinking about Jack's Grill and our reservation."

"Should I call them?"

"Not now. I like that you are in here with me, for the moment."

The television in Rajinder's room was off; sounds from the rest of the hospital were limited to footsteps in the hall and faint voices from the nursing station. Madison started speaking, to kill the dread silence, at the same moment as Rajinder. They both insisted the other should go first, so Rajinder went first.

"I was talking to Jonas the other night, of Jeanne and Katie Perlitz."

"You knew them?"

"Rather foolishly, I lent Benjamin some money at the worst possible time."

Madison wondered why Jeanne had never mentioned Rajinder. "Wow."

"Part of my interest in fixing the neighbourhood, I must admit, comes out of personal feelings about the Perlitzes. If I had not lent Benjamin the money, which merely sustained his gambling habit, perhaps he could have sought help before he —"

"You shouldn't think that way." Madison thought for a moment. "So you were friends with the Perlitzes?"

"I was planning to tell you at dinner tonight, Madison, about my role in this. Jeanne and Katie are safe and doing as well as they can, under the circumstances."

"You know where they are?"

Rajinder reached beside him and positioned the bucket on his lap again. "Summerside."

"Summerside the subdivision? The one by the big box stores, with the fake lake?"

"Jeanne's sister lives in Summerside. She has a different last name, so the reporters did not know where to find her."

"Summerside."

Rajinder heaved but didn't throw up. "I cannot think of a more disastrous or humiliating first date."

"This was a date?" Madison slid her hand down Rajinder's arm, to take his hand. "Really?"

"I had hoped it would be a date," he said, with his eyes squeezed shut.

"Me too. But I wasn't sure if you thought so."

Rajinder gripped the bucket again, and retched a couple of times. Nothing came out. "I want to die, somewhat."

"Should I tell the nurses?"

"Madison, would you be insulted if I asked you to leave me here for the night? They are going to release me in the morning, after observation. When I am throwing up, I must admit, I have a desire to crawl into the bushes and suffer alone. I am pleased you stayed and visited me, and I hope we can try our first date again."

She wanted to know more about Jeanne and Katie, but Madison understood Rajinder's need to be alone. Besides, it was deeply unpleasant to watch and hear him retch. "Next time, if we decide to stand somewhere and look at one another, we'll stay clear of heavy doors."

"That is a capital idea."

Madison paused on her way out. "I could bring back a mini-stereo, some French music. The ginger."

"Thank you for the offer but I will just sleep."

"Maybe I could see Jeanne and Katie sometime."

"I will ask," said Rajinder, quickly, before squeezing the bucket and retching again. "If you will ask the nurses to please knock me out."

53

hunting

On the drive to southeastern Alberta, wearing a fluorescent orange pinafore over a multi-pocketed beige jacket, Jonas learned many things. He learned the pronghorn antelope are found nowhere else but the North American prairie. The pronghorn is not a "true" antelope, a fact that took so much explaining that Jonas began to daydream about how weird thumbs are, when you really think about them.

The fastest North American mammal? The pronghorn. Oh, and if you're looking for one of the prettiest specimens in the world, look no further than the pronghorn buck: when the great beast poses on a hillock to attract a doe during mating season, it's enough to bring tears to a hunter's eyes.

Jonas learned diesel trucks are loud, bow hunting is one of man's most resounding challenges, Guns N' Roses is the greatest band in the history of rock 'n' roll, and there are few things more satisfying of a Tuesday morning than stuffing a plug of chewing tobacco – or, as Carlos called it, "a dip o' chew" – into the space between one's gums and cheek.

After several hours of driving, and chewing and spitting, they arrived at a roadside turnoff in a remote area of hilly grassland south of the Cypress Hills. Carlos hopped out of the truck and, with a hydraulic mechanism, lowered a ramp behind the bed. Then he climbed up on the big red quad, started it, and reversed down the ramp. The bow and arrows were already loaded into a massive black container on the back of the quad, along with some tuna sandwiches and Pilsner.

Carlos threw Jonas a helmet. "Are you ready to go kill something?"

Jonas examined the hard black helmet, decorated with snowmobiling stickers and decided this, right now, was the most surreal drug-free moment of his life. "I've come this far based on one of my personal philosophies: say yes to everything."

"Uh-huh." With his helmet on, Carlos looked like a smiling lollipop.

"But chasing an antelope with bows and arrows? This is a really elaborate joke, yes? A sex thing?"

Carlos laughed. "You don't *chase* a pronghorn. They're way too fast. What we'll do is find a good spot, park the quad, and sneak up on a herd. And since you don't have a licence, you're just gonna watch."

"All I'm saying –"

"But you'll still get half the meat, once it's butchered."

"You're going to *eat* it?"

"Of course, Jonas. It's got a sage taste, 'cause they eat sage. I like to make a nice steak pie out of pronghorn."

Confronted with the reality of hunting, the helmet and jumping beasts and the verb *to butcher*, Jonas suddenly felt weak. A gentle wind blew from the west, and the tall wheatgrass swayed. What sound would the animal make as the bow pierced its neck? Would it roar or whine or wheeze, or would it die silently?

"I'll wait in the truck."

"Come on, man."

"This is wrong."

"Wrong? Do you eat meat?"

"Normal meat, yes. Beef, poultry, pork: the big three."

"How do you think those animals die? In pens. Now that's real suffering. These pronghorns live free and noble lives, and I hunt with a bow out of respect for them. If and when I kill one, I eat it."

"What if you shoot one with an arrow and it doesn't die?"

"Well, we track him until he falls and then I kill him." Carlos opened the black compartment on the quad and pulled out a giant knife.

"Hezbollah!"

"Come on, Jonas. Say yes to everything."

"If I do this, you have to come with me to the Robert Lepage opera in February."

"What's that?"

"Bartók and Schoenberg. It's spooky stuff."

"The spookier the better. Put that helmet on."

Jonas climbed on the quad behind Carlos and reached around his torso, to hold on. If he was squeezing too hard, Carlos didn't complain. At the crest of a hill, overlooking a vast field of mixed grassland, they hit a bump. Jonas lost his grip and grabbed Carlos's left pectoral muscle.

"Welcome to the jungle," said Carlos.

54

fear and wonder

By mid-October, the winds gather chill air over the Rockies and carry the fallen yellow and red leaves into gutters and corners. Filtered through vegetation and soil whipped up by those winds, the moon rises fat and deep orange. Looking out his east-facing window on the thirty-eighth floor of Manulife Place one clear evening, Professor Raymond Terletsky determined the colour was end-of-the-world.

Though he was thrilled to be working full-time for the Save the Garneau Block Foundation, for the equivalent of his professor's salary, Raymond had not spoken to Shirley in three weeks. He longed for the sound of her voice and the warmth of her legs in bed, her night exhalations.

He had missed their autumn rituals. Not once did he cover the tomato plants on frost nights. He didn't help carry the summer clothes and sandals downstairs to the storage room, and he didn't gather the fall and winter outerwear. When he tried to phone his children in Calgary and Seattle, they didn't pick up. He left messages to no avail.

A knock on the office door interrupted his thoughts. It was Rajinder, his employer and saviour. "I'm leaving now, Raymond."

"See you in the morning."

"How are the plans coming?"

Raymond waved Rajinder to the desk, covered in library books and printed Web pages about small museums. "This is the Studio Ghibli Museum, just outside Tokyo." Raymond gathered a few pages of black-and-white photographs, with Japanese characters on the left. "The director, Hayao Miyazaki, opened it to showcase anime and the limitlessness of imagination."

Rajinder held up a photograph of the robot on the roof. "What is this?"

"This is a house of sorts filled with robots, fat cartoon birds, a cat bus, a tiny spiral staircase. It's a distillation of recent Japanese culture and mass delusion. Fantastic and upsetting preoccupations. Fear and wonder."

"I see."

"That's what 10 Garneau should be. If I may be so bold." Raymond walked to the window again, and looked out into the city lights. "Our own anti-museum. I'm talking history, the boomtown culture, gangs and suburbs, oil and immigration, the great river, art and violence, the disturbing nexus of far left and far right politics. Underground energies. Secrets and nightmares and visions. Fear and wonder, Raj. Tomorrow morning I'm having breakfast with a Jungian scholar who's going to teach me all about the collective unconscious of urban Alberta."

One of Rajinder's newest artists-in-residence, a performance poet, began clucking like a chicken in the adjacent office. The clucking increased and soon the poet was jumping and flapping her wings in the hall. "Eat me don't! / Don't eat me! / Me don't eat!"

The poet stopped to make notes and return to her studio, and Rajinder placed the photographs for the Ghibli museum on the desk. "Please speak to this Jungian and write up an initial proposal, one or two pages. We shall organize another meeting to discuss the museum idea."

For dinner, Raymond took his notepad with the African cave art and walked to his favourite restaurant, Hoang Long in Chinatown, where he sat in a tall bamboo chair next to the window and ordered a half-litre of red wine and a small pot of tea.

Raymond listened to conversations around him, in English and French and what he took to be Vietnamese, and he jotted some notes about the Taoists, whose views on death were consistent with their analysis of every unsolvable riddle. Do not worry, Edmonton. Accept death and incorporate it into your life, like autumn winds and shrivelled leaves, the icy hint of winter. Without our winter, we would not long for summer. Without our deaths, we would not appreciate green papaya salad and prawns in coconut curry sauce.

For Tibetans, the transition from life to death allows a

distillation of self, a liberation, a rebirth of soul and personality. At the moment of his death, the authentic Raymond Terletsky would be born. This, *this* was what 10 Garneau had to be: a distillation of Edmonton. An authentic representation of the city, including buffalo and hummingbirds and perhaps green papaya salad.

"Does this mean we have to kill Edmonton before we understand what it truly is?" said Raymond.

Cecilia Hoang, the co-owner of the restaurant, set down his wine and tea. "My son is doing really well in school, and we just opened a new location in the mall. Don't kill Edmonton."

Raymond realized he had been talking aloud. "Do you think there's another way?"

"Some things don't need to be understood, professor."

Raymond crossed out his initial drawing of the museum: the current house turned upside down and reinforced so a second floor window became the front door.

The site of Edmonton's distilled mythic power had to be more, and less, spectacular. After a sip of wine and a sip of tea, the professor ventured to think without understanding.

55

almost guilt

Abby Weiss stood outside Starbucks and tapped her right foot on the Whyte Avenue sidewalk. David was inside buying their mochaccinos. He watched his wife through the window; bursting with defeat, her ideals compromised by taste buds.

On his leash, Garith looked up at Abby and wagged his tail. But Abby would not look down, would not gather him up for a cuddle.

It was cold outside, cold enough to snow, yet Abby had only worn a sweater for their morning walk and refused to come inside. At what point would she give in to the power of Starbucks and the elegance of global capitalism?

He sent her mind messages: *Come into the café. It is warm in the café. Miles Davis is playing the trumpet in that slow and thoughtful way he had before he went screwy. Give in to Starbucks. Give in to Starbucks, so we can sit down.*

When it was clear Abby would not submit to Starbucks, David took the caramel mochaccinos and joined her on the sidewalk. Abby grabbed her cup out of his hand and took a sip in anger. Of course, it was still too hot.

"It burned my tongue."

"Oh, sweetie." David bent down and loved up Garith for a moment while they waited for the light to change.

"Now I won't be able to taste anything all day. Sandpaper tongue!"

Crossing Calgary Trail, David scanned the avenue for Barry Strongman. Since he had kicked Barry out of the riding association meeting, David hadn't seen him selling street magazines.

All Abby knew was that Barry wasn't around these days. David had never confessed what he'd done. Abby saw him looking around and rubbed his back. "Have you looked into it? I mean, you could go to the shelters and ask about him."

"Barry's a resourceful guy."

"Don't you miss arguing with him? You used to love that."

"If I really wanted to argue about politics, I could argue with you."

"You could, David, but I would crush you."

As they continued west toward the Rabbit Warren, David wondered if he had killed Barry Strongman. There was a good chance he had broken the homeless man's heart. It happened in the movies often enough, though it was usually in a romantic context. Yet David had always understood he was special; people developed strong attachments to him, on account of his rugged handsomeness, his charisma, and his political eloquence. These attachments could be perilous.

Abby walked ahead of David. She knocked on the door and Shirley, with a shabby baseball cap on, let her in. David and Garith followed, and sat on the wicker bench where they always sat during their visits. Abby hurried behind the counter beside Shirley, and put her hands over a heating vent.

"Before I forget," said Shirley, "here are my keys."

Abby took the keys and jingled them. "Instead of letting the appraiser in, we should stab her with these babies. Right in the neck."

It was the day they had been dreading, the day of evaluation. A real-estate expert retained by the university would visit all five houses in the Garneau Block to prepare a detailed market-value assessment. David and Abby and Madison had been up until two in the morning cleaning and rearranging in order to create the highest charm factor. By the look of Shirley Wong, she had gone to bed even later.

"Raymond called me last night and I answered. It was from a pay phone, so I didn't know to avoid it."

Abby turned and rubbed Shirley's arm.

"He said we don't have to worry about the appraisal. He said we're going to get the cultural designation because he has this plan. I hung up on him before he could explain."

David sipped his caramel mochaccino, which had cooled to a perfect temperature. He stared out the window at Barry Strongman's vacant corner. "Putting a bunch of teepees and bearskin rugs in 10 Garneau is a waste of time. He's going to humiliate us all with this stupidity."

Shirley shook her head. "Raymond Terletsky is a lot of things but he isn't stupid."

The heater powered off and the store went quiet. David unhooked Garith's leash so he could explore a bit. "How are your boarders?"

Shirley shook her head again and Abby rubbed her arm some more. In the past, Shirley had been so happy and positive that David suspected she was faking. Now he was certain. Her upbeat exterior was no stronger than the crust of a crème brûlée.

"Can't you just kick them out?" he said.

"No. I can't."

"Did you sign a contract?"

"I can't because I can't."

"Is it still the big guy?"

Shirley nodded. "Patch. He was up all night with some other juvenile delinquents, partying in the living room."

"Patch," said Abby, with a sneer.

"I have to say Steamer, the Mormon boy, is growing on me. I speak to him more than I ever spoke to my own kids. He's so . . . Mormony. But Patch, I don't know. If he's the future of hockey, it's in bigger trouble than I ever thought."

"I oughta march right on over there and punch his lights out." Abby attacked the air in front of her with a right and a left.

"Sweetie, how many times have I told you to keep your thumbs *outside* the fist?"

"Maybe I'll punch the appraiser too, and the mayor."

"That's my elementary schoolteacher, my gentle pacifist."

"Whoever said I was a pacifist? People are trying to take my house. Sometimes, in a revolution, blood must be shed."

"Oh boy." David patted his jeans to summon Garith. "Listen, you girls catch up. I'm off to run some errands."

Abby threw the keys to David. "The appraiser's coming to our place at 12:30 and then she's doing Shirley's. I'm going to stay here."

"Are you sure?" said Shirley.

"Absolutely." Abby put her arm around her. "You can help me think up names for my grandchild."

David walked out of the Rabbit Warren with Garith bounding into the cool air. On the corner, Barry Strongman's corner, David looked around and shook his head. Heartbreak was a terrible way to die.

56

the m-bomb

Business was light at Sparkle Vacations, so Madison put on a fleece jacket and sat outside with a cup of herbal tea. Morning traffic down Whyte Avenue had slowed enough that exhaust fumes were scarce. Students in their scarves and early-season toques with sardonic logos – I Love the World Bank – passed with name-brand coffee cups in one hand and cellular phones in the other.

The air of prosperity in Alberta seemed thickened with each penny added to the price of oil. Madison noticed it in designer jeans and shoes and jackets, and in the trucks the students drove to school. Of course, few young Albertans owned energy stock. They had just absorbed a sense of entitlement from their leaders. It was a conceit, a feeling that the future had migrated west from Upper and Lower Canada to the eastern slope of the Rocky Mountains. Students were confident that a foothill of cash waited for them on the other side of that degree so they were saying yes, yes, and yes to the credit card offers that arrived in the mail.

She didn't make a commission, so Madison hadn't enjoyed a cent of Alberta's largesse. When she graduated, the country had been coming out of a recession. She had spent what should have been the best years of her life under fluorescent lights in a travel agency with bad ventilation.

The cool morning air, heavy with the scent of decomposing

leaves, couldn't chill her. Though she and Rajinder had not yet kissed or re-booked their first date, they had spent hours of informal time together. Two rollerblades through the river valley, a bike ride up and down the Mill Creek Ravine, and an impromptu luncheon at Roots Organic around the corner from Sparkle Vacations.

And there he was, right on time, crossing the street from Corbett Hall in a deep-brown suit and tan overcoat. This morning, he had attended a meeting with the university's board of governors, hoping for a reprieve. Madison got up and rolled her chair back into the agency.

She knew it was ludicrous but each time she saw Rajinder she had to suppress an urge to say, "I love you." It was not possible to love someone after a non-date, two rollerblades, a bike ride, and an impromptu luncheon, so Madison knew she was misinterpreting hormonal outbursts for something else. When a woman declares her love too early, a fist of fear hits a man's major muscle groups. When a woman declares her love too early and announces, shortly thereafter, she also happens to be pregnant by a man who *may* be called Jean-something, the fist threatens to squeeze the blood from his heart.

The door opened, Rajinder appeared, and Madison pressed the word *love* down into her duodenum. "How did it go?"

Rajinder looked down at his polished brown Oxfords. "I failed."

"No, you didn't fail. You knew they'd say no."

Rajinder walked across the room, pulled Tammy "Sparkle" Davidson's chair out from behind her desk and sat. "I was hoping we would not have to rely on plan B."

"How do you mean?"

"I cannot fault Raymond for his enthusiasm. He is working twelve hours a day on the project, conducting interviews and phoning museum experts around the world for their advice. Consulting elders. But —"

"He wants to build a museum?"

"I was hoping to organize another community meeting tonight. Raymond can present his plan to the residents of the block. And yes. He wants to transform 10 Garneau into a museum."

"What sort of museum?"

"We shall learn tonight, I hope."

Madison looked at her watch. "What time is the appraiser coming to your house?"

"Later this afternoon." Rajinder got up to leave. "I suppose I should get home and tidy up, leave messages for everyone about tonight. It has been peculiar, the change from no contact with my neighbours to near constant contact with them."

Though she risked showing off her belly, Madison walked with Rajinder to the door. She had a strong desire to lick his neck, but, along with the urge to declare her love, Madison buried it. At the door, Rajinder put his hand on her shoulder and managed to smile. "I shall see you later."

"The black under your eyes is almost gone."

"At my meeting this morning, the university administrators asked if I had started kickboxing. I told them yes, daily lessons. I had hoped to physically intimidate them into placing a five-year moratorium on development. But even in this I failed."

"Next time just haul off and plow one of them in the stomach."

"Next time." Rajinder started out the door.

Madison waited alone in Sparkle Vacations for a moment. The fluorescent lights buzzed. She opened the door. "Hey!"

Rajinder turned around.

"Are you busy tomorrow night?"

"I do not think so."

"You still want to have a first date?"

"Very much." He took a step forward. "I was waiting until my face healed."

"Well this time it's a surprise. I'm going to take *you* on a date."

"Truly?"

"Yep."

"So you are asking me out on a date."

"Yep."

Rajinder took another step forward. "I should not say this, Madison, but I have been thinking: if my parents were still alive, they would disapprove."

"They wanted you to marry an Indian girl?"

"Absolutely."

"Not that we're getting married."

Rajinder opened his mouth to speak but did not speak. Madison's face went hot and she considered putting her head through the pane of glass on her immediate left.

"Nang," she said, through her teeth.

"I am looking forward to it, Madison. To our first date."

She waved and closed the door to Sparkle Vacations, slapping herself on the forehead for dropping the M-bomb, an even more destructive piece of ordinance than the L-cluster. When the phone rang and a man with a smoker's voice asked about honeymoon cruises in February, Madison pined for the desolation of February.

57

a real talent

David made his way to the fourth downtown homeless shelter. He didn't have much time before he had to get back and meet the appraiser, so David hurried up the cobblestone streets of the improvement district, past men and women in doorways and on the sidewalk, swivelling in their wretchedness. They asked him for money and cigarettes. If, as he expected, Barry Strongman was not at the fourth downtown homeless shelter, David would return to the Garneau Block satisfied that he had done everything, and more, to find the man.

Bruised by the slow savagery of self-destruction he had witnessed at the first three shelters, David found himself repeating, like a mantra, that these people had made a choice.

Several men and women were gathered at the entrance of the fourth shelter, passing a bottle wrapped in brown paper.

"How's it goin'?" one of the men asked, as David started up the concrete stairs to press the door buzzer.

"Very well, thanks. And you?"

The man looked down at himself, his layers of grey clothing and the mass of toilet paper and Superstore bags that served as his left shoe. "I haven't had a shower in a week and a half. Doin' brilliant, partner, A-number-one. I appreciate your asking."

David pulled his right sleeve over his hand, so he wouldn't have to touch the black buzzer. The intercom looked and smelled as though someone had seen fit to urinate on it.

"Yes?"

"My name is David Weiss. I'm looking for a fellow called Barry Strongman. I'm sure he isn't here. I was just . . ."

The heavy door hummed and David opened it. At the bottom of the steps, the man with the toilet-paper shoe said, "Liars told me they were *full*. Got half a mind to burn the place down."

Inside, pods of the unfortunate filled a vast room of chipped white tile. There was a pool table in one corner, several old couches in another, and what appeared to be a healing circle in a third. On David's right was a bulletin board. Five sheets, each a different colour, advertised a daily Let's Fix It meeting.

A woman with a big mess of dyed blonde hair, in red overalls, approached David with a wide smile. "You're here for the meeting?"

"Agh."

The woman shook David's hand, looked him over, and tilted her head. "I'm Jane, the assistant director. You're not . . . what are you doing here?"

"I'm a friend of Barry's. A few weeks ago I lost track of him."

"Well, he's in the middle of a session. Feel free to join in but don't interrupt until he asks for questions. Before question period, he gets a little testy." Jane led David to a door in the back of the room, not far from the pool table.

David recognized Barry Strongman's muffled voice coming through the thin wall. Jane opened the door and David entered. It was a classroom with only two empty chairs in the back, so David quickly settled into one and looked up. Barry Strongman, who had briefly stopped talking, stared at David and continued.

"There's top-down power and then there's bottom-up power. They're both important."

Near the front of the room, a few of the pupils grumbled in opposition.

"If you can't listen quietly, you can leave."

One of the pupils put up his hand. "But I think you're wrong."

"Really? Get out!"

"But."

"Out!"

The pupil, in a soiled lumberjack coat and CAT Diesel hat, shuffled out of the classroom with a mumble. Once he was gone, and the door was slammed, Barry Strongman paced the front of the room.

"Anyone else think I'm wrong?"

A few of the pupils said no.

"I can't hear you."

"No."

"Louder."

"No!" said the pupils.

Barry Strongman clapped his hands. "Do you know why all the trees in this neighbourhood are so skinny? It ain't from folks pissing on them so don't say it, Lou. They're skinny because no one's dreaming around them. No one's looking ahead and thinking, 'Dang, I'm gonna make something spectacular out of myself,' which is the vibe a tree needs if it's expected to grow. Anyone think I'm wrong about that?"

The pupils looked around at one another. It was close to noon and David was satisfied that Barry Strongman was safe and alive and, apparently, happy. So he made for the door.

"Where you going, David?"

He stopped and gripped the door handle. "Back home."

"Back home to do what? To *fix it*? We're fixing it right here, brother, where it counts. Let me tell you something, my people. This man kicked me out of a PC Riding Association meeting because I was homeless."

"Barry, that is a private matter."

"You see, we can dream past this place, hope ourselves into the future. But then we hit barriers like this man, David Weiss, who wants to keep us down because we threaten him."

"He is a top-down man," said one of the pupils.

Barry Strongman pointed at the pupil. "Shut up or get out!"

With that, David opened the door and rushed across the main hall. Jane jogged to intercept him. "So what did you think?"

David took a breath, to calm himself. "He's certainly a confident public speaker."

"A little bit too commanding, I'd say. But a real talent. Next thing you know, he could be pulling big bucks on the business-lunch motivational speakers' circuit. Don't you think?"

David walked out of the shelter and down the street, past the growing crowds and withering trees on the boulevard, with his finger on the Yukon Denali's panic button.

58

appraisals

David Weiss planned to charm the appraiser and to inform her, in an aside, that he was highly placed in the party. As much as everyone on the block dreaded and disliked this process, a pleasant experience for the university appraiser could mean thousands of extra dollars. So David turned on some Brahms and threw a Safeway pie in the oven just before she arrived.

The appraiser ignored David. She walked through the house with a clipboard in hand, humming and making notes. Both her shirt and slacks were fortified by multiple pockets.

David found he couldn't focus on his plan. Barry Strongman's petulance lingered in his mouth like a spoonful of old yogurt. How dare Barry Strongman, a *homeless person*, mock the president of the Strathcona PC Riding Association – in public?

Even if that public was a collection of thirty mumbling fools?

What lingered in David's ear was the idea that Barry Strongman had become "a real talent." If his story appeared in the newspaper, there might be a word or two about the evil David Weiss. David had been involved in politics long enough to know what to do: deny the rank accusation and call a lawyer.

"It's a beautiful house," said the appraiser, when she finished. "Pity what happened next door."

This was David's opportunity to convince the appraiser that no one gave the Perlitz tragedy much thought. Tragedy? What tragedy? Instead, he accompanied the appraiser to the front door and slipped into his Velcro dog-walking shoes. Garith hopped and barked and spun in anticipation.

As David led the appraiser down the front porch steps toward the sidewalk, he wondered if Barry Strongman might go on a drug-fuelled bender and die soon. It would be sad and happy all at once.

They started toward 11 Garneau and met Raymond Terletsky in the middle of the street. It was lunchtime. The brown-and-grey beard Raymond had been growing for a week was coming in thick and uneven, like much of the facial hair David had observed in the shelters that morning.

"There's going to be a meeting tonight," said Raymond. "The plan is flourishing. Who's this?"

"This is Ms. Jacobson, Raymond. She has been hired by the university to appraise our houses."

The woman held her hand out. "Chloe Jacobson."

Raymond looked down at her hand. He backed away and made a show of tossing his leather briefcase into the front yard of 10 Garneau. "Come not between the dragon and his wrath!"

"What?" The appraiser turned to David. "Who is this man?"

"Dr. Raymond Terletsky."

The professor backed further away from them and knelt on the lawn of 10 Garneau. He stroked his natty beard and howled. Garith began barking at him. "Thou whoreson zed! Thou unnecessary letter!"

David turned to the appraiser. "I'm really sorry about this. The university fired him for sexual harassment and then his wife kicked him out. He lives in my spare room."

"Thou art a boil, a plague sore, an embossed carbuncle in my corrupted blood."

"Do you think I should come back later?" The appraiser stared at Raymond, who continued to kneel and spout on the brown October grass. "Is he dangerous?"

"Tough to say."

Jonas had come out of his house in a sweater and toque to watch the spectacle. He ambled onto the sidewalk. The actor put his finger to his lips, shushed Garith, and approached David and the appraiser. "What's up with the big guy? Why's he screaming in Elizabethan English?"

Raymond snarled, "From the extremest upward of thy head to the descent and dust beneath thy foot, a most toad-spotted traitor."

Jonas picked at the goop in his eyes. It was clear to David that Jonas had just woken up.

David made the introductions and together the three of them watched Raymond and Garith. Man and dog had made a kind of peace. Garith licked the professor's ankle and growled. "Here I stand your slave," said the professor, to the dog. "A poor, infirm, weak, and despised old man."

"Jonas, can you take Raymond to my place? Get him a cup of hot chocolate or something? I'm taking Ms. Jacobson to his house and I don't want him going orangutan on her."

The appraiser interrupted them. "You know, I'll come back later in the week. What's a good time?" She pointed her toe in Raymond's direction. He remained kneeling, but had gone silent. "A good time to avoid this sort of thing?"

"Mid-morning or mid-afternoon," said David. "He works downtown."

"I thought you said he was fired for harassment."

"There's a labour shortage, Ms. Jacobson. We can't allow our best people, even if they are menaces, to wallow in un-employment."

They arrived at the point where Chloe Jacobson might have shaken their hands, but she didn't shake their hands. She just got in her car, a beige Toyota Camry, and drove away.

The block now clear of strangers, Raymond Terletsky approached David and Jonas on the street. David raised his eyebrows. "You know, pal, I don't think I've ever seen any-thing like that."

Raymond ignored him and regarded 10 Garneau.

From the south, Rajinder Chana arrived. With only a small wave for greeting, he joined the other three men of the Garneau Block. Rajinder glanced at the professor, who had recovered slightly but still appeared to be panting, and addressed David and Jonas. "Are you available this evening, for another meeting? Raymond would like to unveil his preliminary plans for making 10 Garneau into a cultural institution."

"A friend's coming over," said Jonas. "We were planning to sit by the fire pit in the back. We'll make it a party."

David shook his head. "This is ridiculous. We should just let that appraiser do her job."

"Thou shalt join us." Raymond lowered his voice. "And behold, thou shalt bring refreshments."

Even if David had possessed the energy to argue with Raymond, he wasn't sure he knew the vocabulary.

59

a fire in october

Madison spooned roasted eggplant into a bowl for baba ghanouj while Abby blended chickpeas for hummus. To Madison's consternation, they listened to her mother's favourite album: the Gipsy Kings' *Greatest Hits*. Shirley was not attending the Garneau Block meeting so it only seemed fair that someone else make the baba ghanouj.

"I'm not as good at this as Shirley. It's going to taste like boiled crap."

Abby slammed her fist on the counter. "If I hear one more negative comment from you . . ."

"What? What are you going to do?"

For a time, Abby seemed to be thinking of a punishment for Madison. Then she began chopping garlic.

Since Rajinder had left Sparkle Vacations that morning, Madison had grown increasingly anxious about their future together. And it wasn't just the baby.

Rajinder was not only handsome and intelligent; he was also rich. And rich people were obliged to honour their wealth by choosing partners who exuded a certain level of sophistication. Madison had one dress, a white dress from Jacob with a red wine stain.

If he were thinking about objections his parents might have had, perhaps he was also thinking about his own.

"Is it Rajinder again?"

"No." Madison smelled the collection of eggplant in her large blue bowl. It smelled of soil. "Yes."

Abby dropped a handful of minced garlic into each bowl and poured another splash of Chardonnay into her glass. "Have you told him yet?"

"No."

Abby took a long sip and smiled. "We're so alike."

"No, we aren't."

"When are you going to tell him?"

"I was planning to tell him tomorrow night, during our second first date."

"How do you think he'll react?"

"Like any sane man. He'll say congratulations. And then he'll think of the classiest way to extricate himself from the relationship. Which is really only a relationship in my mind anyway." Madison squeezed lemon juice into the bowl of egg-plant mush and twisted some kosher salt over it all.

Abby leaned against the fridge, which was covered in magnets and fifteen years of family photographs. "You're my favourite person in the world and I think it reflects poorly on Edmonton and society in general that you're still single, but in Rajinder's case, you're probably right."

"You're supposed to say Rajinder has to love me because I'm your beautiful daughter and who *wouldn't* love me."

"I'm taking a step back here, from the fuzz of overwhelmingly warm regard I have for you. And I'm looking." Abby looked down at Madison's belly for a moment. "Darling, you don't know your baby's father. You work at a travel agency, and, sorry to be blunt, you're kind of lazy."

"I feel like a princess. A wonderful princess."

"But you're beautiful. And smart and caring. What you are is a late bloomer, and I hope Rajinder sees that. You're a small mountain of potential."

Madison pulled two tablespoons of gooey tahini out of a jar and transferred them to the blue bowl. Then she plugged in the mixing wand and went to work on the mush. She couldn't hear Abby over the tiny engine inside the mixing wand, but she had heard enough from her mother. When the baba ghanouj had the right consistency, she unplugged the wand and heard the conclusion of Abby's speech.

". . . and I told him I wouldn't sacrifice my principles, no way. But we've made it work, haven't we? Haven't we, darling? Aren't we a social, political, and romantic model for the future? For harmony itself?"

"Can we go now?"

Madison and Abby put on their jackets and hats, and carried their dips, pitas, and vegetables through the alley. The voice of Raymond was audible, in the short burst of stuttering that prefaced one of his pronouncements.

"I've been thinking big," he said. "Bigger than I was raised to think. Big!"

The men spotted them and both Rajinder and David hurried over to help. Jonas threw a couple of new birch logs on the fire, causing the flames to leap up and the smoke to rise a deep black. The dips and plates of bread and vegetables were arranged on the picnic table, and a small line formed.

Carlos stood next to Jonas in a Stormrider jean jacket and an Eskimos cap. He removed the cap and replaced it several times, nervously. Jonas pulled Carlos out of the dip line and led him to Madison.

"I know you met briefly at the Next Act lo those many days ago, but this is my friend Madison. Madison, this is Carlos."

"Hello again."

Carlos smiled and tipped his cap. "Great to see you."

"So Jonas tells me you took him *hunting*. With a bow and arrow."

"That I did. That I did."

"I don't think I told you this, Maddy, but Carlos made me take a picture of him with the antelope he killed. And he propped the poor animal's head up, as though it were alive."

"Buck scored 81." Carlos turned his head and waved his pride away, as though it smelled badly. "I got lucky."

"Now I get to take him to *Bluebeard's Castle* and *Erwartung*."

"Gosh," said Madison, because she didn't know what else to say. On the other side of the fire, Rajinder stood with a paper plate full of dips and a Big Rock. She wanted to go over and talk to him but she was trapped by the spectacle of Jonas and Carlos, which beckoned like a highway accident. "That's just . . . gosh."

Raymond interrupted. "Does everyone have a drink and some snacks? Everyone? Then get comfortable. Sit at the picnic table or on one of the stumps. This meeting shall come to order forthwith, before it gets any colder and before anyone drinks too much beer."

In the commotion, Madison was able to extricate herself from Carlos and Jonas to sit on a stump next to Rajinder. He smiled at her. "This is splendid baba ghanouj. You need not have worried. It is clear you have a talent for Mediterranean classics."

"You think so?"

"I do, I do."

Raymond stood on a stump. The fire uplit his bearded face, hiding his eyes. He rubbed his hands together like a seller of fake Rolexes, or souls. As Raymond spoke of the future, of his plan to liberate the Garneau Block from the failure and death of Benjamin Perlitz and from the greedy clutches of the university, Madison grew afraid. Afraid to shift in her seat, afraid to reach back and scratch the itchy spot on her left shoulder. In only a few weeks, Raymond had changed from dirty professor to awkward prophet.

He prefaced his plan with glittering generalities, and then Raymond quoted Ralph Waldo Emerson. "A man should learn to detect and watch that gleam of light which flashes across his mind from within, more than the lustre of the firmament of bards and sages."

"What about a woman?" Abby lifted her glass of wine over the fire.

"A woman, too. Yes, yes, a woman." Raymond paused and pulled at his little beard. "I forget what comes next."

"Sorry," said Abby.

Raymond said shhh, and whispered to himself, trying to find the next line. He sighed. "Anyway, we shouldn't listen to other people, even so-called experts, so much as we should listen to the genius of our own hearts. All right?"

"All right!" said Jonas.

"What it comes down to is that 'God will not have his work made manifest by cowards.'"

A rumble of recognition travelled through the circle. Raymond was interrupted by footsteps crunching leaves in the grass behind him. A voice out of the darkness said, "Good evening."

Raymond attempted to see who it was and turned too far. His stump tipped and he landed with a thud on the grass. Winded, he gasped and honked for air. Rajinder was closest, so he turned Raymond on his side and said, "Relax, my friend, relax."

While her husband convalesced on the lawn, Shirley Wong smiled and introduced the young man who accompanied her. With his hockey jacket, perfectly parted hair, and gleaming white running shoes, Steamer looked to Madison as though he were visiting not from southern Alberta but from 1957.

"Why Steamer?" said David, who stood up so Shirley could sit next to Abby.

"It's a long story." Steamer took a seat on the picnic table.

"The professor's going to be twitching down there a while, I figure. We've got time."

Steamer looked at Shirley and said, "I have what a guy might call a nervous excretory system. Before a game I like to . . . I got to . . . Well, I need to go ahead and . . ."

"That's enough, Steamer," said Abby. "I think we understand."

"Thank you, Mrs. Weiss."

Rajinder helped Raymond to his feet. Still coughing, Raymond slouched back to his stump. This time he only put a foot on it, and leaned on his knee. "Shirley, my love, I'm delighted that you've come. It does my heart so much good to see you. You're like a balm to my soul, my everything. I wish for . . ."

"Shut *up*," said Shirley.

Rajinder flared his nostrils. "Perhaps, Raymond, you could outline your plans now."

"Yes. Yes, terrific, Rajinder. A round of applause for Rajinder, everyone, who's agreed to bankroll this project."

A round of applause ensued. Over the applause, Rajinder tried to protest. "I am uncomfortable with the word bankroll."

When silence returned, and when Raymond was finished staring at Steamer, his professorial voice returned. "The site of 10 Garneau will be a locus of Edmonton's mythic power."

"So a museum?" said David. "Big whoop."

"Not a conventional museum, no. Forget everything you know about museums. There will be no artifacts of recent history with explanations in both of Canada's official languages. I'm thinking of a more magical place. A labyrinth of our collective dream. A funhouse. Truth and energy, murder and heroism. Hockey. Immigration. Theatre."

"You mentioned a buffalo," said Jonas.

"I want input from all of you, of course, but, yes, I think we should have a herd of buffalo."

"Won't that make an awful mess?" said Abby. "And what will they eat?"

"No, fake ones."

"Maybe the fake buffalo should be flying out of the house, like ghosts, since our ancestors killed them all," said Jonas.

Shirley raised her hand. "Speak for yourself."

"So flying buffalo?" David opened a new beer. "Professor, I think you must have been smoking *The Magic Flute* instead of listening to it." No one laughed so David elbowed Steamer in the ribs. "You know what I mean, partner? As in wacky tabacky?"

"I don't do drugs," said Steamer.

"No. No, you don't. I'm not insinuating that. I was just letting you in on the joke there, Steamer." David elbowed Steamer again.

"Please don't do that."

David hopped up off the picnic table and Garith hopped off with him. "You're all lunatics. This neighbourhood's a goner." He walked out of the yard and into the alley, with Garith's collar bell tinking behind him.

"Should I go talk to him?" Rajinder whispered in Madison's ear.

She leaned back and placed her hand on Rajinder's neck, hot from the fire. She pressed her cheek softly against his and whispered, in his ear, "No."

"I think this is brilliant," said Abby. "But I don't know what you're talking about. What does a locus of mythic power look like?"

Raymond turned to Rajinder for a moment, and then back to Abby. "We need to brainstorm about exactly that, right now. And tomorrow I'll write something up, our vision, and fax it to some brave architects. At the top of the page I'll put an Emerson quote and maybe something about *King Lear*. We give them a few days to come up with something, we put a shortlist together, and we meet with them on the thirty-eighth floor."

"A few days?" said Jonas. "Artists don't work like that."

"If I hadn't chased the appraiser away today, the reprobates at the university would be writing cheques for us right now. My friends, we don't have six months or even two months."

Fatigue hung over them, along with confusion and alarm. For the moment, however, no one seemed willing to give up. So Raymond took out his African cave art notepad and pen, and they began to design the labyrinth of their collective dream.

60

the second first date

He didn't complain, but it was clear Rajinder did not enjoy being blindfolded. Thanks to Madison's poor leading skills, he had already grazed a tree with his shoulder. And only at the last second did she avoid slamming his fingers in the door of the Yukon Denali.

The closest parking spot at the Muttart Conservatory – three linked glass pyramids in the river valley – was far from the entrance. In her haste Madison had forgotten to put a coat on Rajinder after she had blindfolded him. By the time they reached the glass pyramids, he was shivering in his suit.

Madison opened the door and led him into the entrance corridor.

"Where are we?" he said. "Let me guess."

The central courtyard was decorated with curtains and flowers, and lit with candles. Madison led Rajinder to the right, into the tropical pyramid.

The automatic doors opened and a heavy blast of warm, moist air enveloped them. "The Malabar Coast," said Rajinder, with a smile. "You have taken me to India."

"Bingo."

Madison had wondered about the ethical ramifications of maxing her VISA to book their second first date, a private dinner in the centre courtyard of the Muttart Conservatory. Was it indecent, given the situation in sub-Saharan Africa, to spend hundreds of dollars on one night? Was it a thick move, given her salary and the hungry little being in her uterus?

She removed Rajinder's blindfold and he rubbed his eyes. "I have driven by this place one thousand times but I have never been inside." He took Madison's hands. "What a lovely surprise."

Together they walked up the concrete path, among the variegated snakeplant and pineapple flower. The lighting inside the pyramid was soft. Outside, in the valley, the sun had set and a few stars twinkled in the darkening sky.

Rajinder stopped under the Chinese fan palm, next to a pond with a trickling fountain. He looked down at the white and orange and gold fishes, their mouths opening and closing at the water surface as if to say, "Oh?"

And without much in the way of preparation, Rajinder put his arms around Madison and kissed her. While the fishes continued with their "Oh?" routine, Madison and Rajinder kissed and paused to smile at one another and almost speak, and then they kissed some more.

Madison had waited so long for a kiss that, in the midst of it, she was nearly overcome with the need to shove Rajinder into the bromeliads and devour him. Time passed, five or fifty minutes, enough for Madison to explore every square millimetre of Rajinder's face and neck, and the soft vicinities of both ears.

"We only have the conservatory for two hours. We should probably eat."

"There is food as well? I thought *this* was our date."

"We still have a prime rib dinner, and three more pyramids to investigate."

"Tell me one has cactus. I have a special affinity for cactus."

"Rajinder, one has cactus."

"May God refrain from striking me."

Madison licked the salt off her lips and swallowed. "I didn't have much choice. It was Cornish game hen or prime rib. I figured . . ."

"Every Alberta boy loves the prime rib."

They started back around the concrete path, strolling past the red powderpuff and the strange crown of the queen sago palm. Ginger and gardenia and a sausage tree, the collection of orchids. It was, Madison decided, the closest she had ever come to being in a Dr. Seuss book.

Near the doors, Rajinder stopped her. "I have a secret to tell."

"Yes?"

"On the night of our last first date, I looked into your suite and saw you dancing and becoming intimate with a monkey toy."

Madison jumped behind a frond. "I knew it! I knew you saw."

"It filled my heart with . . . I do not know the word."

"Fear? Disgust? Confusion? Balsamic vinegar?"

"You know that part in a romantic concerto when the music slowly rises and rises and finally reaches a culmination?"

Madison did not know, not really, but she emerged from behind the frond and nodded.

"That is what filled my heart."

"So it was good stuff."

"Much better than the best balsamic vinegar."

A man in a black suit and a woman in a black dress stood waiting for them in the central courtyard. Behind them lay food on heating trays and a bottle of red wine. As they approached the table, the gentleman server hurried over to pull Madison's chair away from the table.

They sat, and the woman brought each of them a small bowl of mixed greens in vinaigrette. Rajinder said, in a whisper, "Are we allowed to talk?"

"I think so," said Madison.

"This whole complex is ours? All four pyramids?"

"For two hours, yes. Even the washrooms."

Madison hadn't been able to shake the heavy feeling in her legs since Rajinder used the word secret. Now that they had kissed, now that it was clear they were on an actual date with romantic connotations, now that Madison was certain she wasn't imagining all of this, she would have to tell Rajinder about her situation.

"This is perfect," he said, between forkfuls of salad. "This is the sort of night you look back on, from the distant future, when you are old man, and say: 'I was very happy then.'"

Since the truth about her situation had waited this long, Madison decided to set it aside for another couple of hours. Tomorrow, or the next day. Or maybe the day after that.

61

northlands

The Jesters were down 4–1 in the final minutes of the third period. Thanks to a wily left-winger who seemed destined for the NHL millionaire's club, the Bonnyville Pontiacs went ahead early in the game. Shirley Wong was not the type to abandon her team, but the Jesters couldn't possibly penetrate the Pontiacs' ultra-conservative defence. Even so, she blew her horn and rang her bell, and cheered every time Steamer's stick touched the puck.

In the final minute of play, most of the remaining fans began to stand and stretch, grab their jackets and programs, and start up the tinny stairs of the Agricom. At the buzzer Shirley clapped, blew her horn, and rang her bell. Then she flopped back in her seat.

Exhausted.

Steamer had asked Shirley to wait for him. Since the guys would be going out to get wasted and pick fights, Steamer had hoped they could get a pizza and rent a movie or something.

Now that Shirley knew all there was to know about the Church of Jesus Christ of Latter-day Saints, and now that Steamer knew all there was to know about Raymond's flirtation with infidelity, they had become something like friends. Two days earlier, Shirley had baked a triple chocolate cake to celebrate Steamer's eighteenth birthday. Neither Patch nor any of the other players showed up for the party so they ate half a cake together and Steamer got about as drunk as a devout Mormon can get: on cocoa.

But this curiously satisfying relationship with an eighteen-year-old boy had only heightened Shirley's general sense of loss and fatigue. It was sad and strange and probably wrong to look forward to pizza and a movie, maybe a walk in the river valley, with Steamer from Cardston.

Shirley picked herself up and started walking to the LRT station near Rexall Place. The Oilers were also playing tonight, so the parking lots were jammed with cars and trucks. Even though she had vowed to punish professional hockey players with her indifference – Raymond and the Oilers had both abandoned her – Shirley read the sports columns as though they were pornographic essays. She had a few minutes so she walked around to the Gretzky statue, felt wistful, and returned to the LRT station to see Steamer waving.

"Sorry you had to witness that, Shirley."

"Nah, you did great."

"That number twenty-seven they got. He's the real thing."

"I saw Patch line him up a couple of times."

Steamer started into the LRT station and down the stairs. "That boy's way too fast for Patch."

They reached the bottom of the stairs and passed the busker, an elderly woman with an accordion. Steamer placed a couple of toonies in the woman's hat.

"Really enjoyable music, ma'am. Thanks."

The woman nodded and played a little faster as Shirley and Steamer continued through the turnstiles and toward the escalator. On the platform, a group of teenage boys in sweat-suits and early attempts at facial hair smoked and cackled. Loser kids, thought Shirley, and then she was disappointed with herself for thinking so.

Steamer dropped his bag. "Hey, we heard you up there in the stands. Coach even said so. He said you're our number-one fan and that we need to get some T-shirts printed up."

"Number-one fan." This too made Shirley sad. She turned and looked south, to the autumnal concrete wretchedness of Northlands Park, and sighed. What was sadder? She imagined a small, elderly man in thick glasses, wearing a bow tie, and standing with his hands clasped in front of an empty restaurant at 7:30 p.m., candles lit on each table, waiting for customers who will never arrive.

"You all right, Shirley?"

"Of course."

"I sure like your jacket." Steamer touched her arm. "I never saw pink suede before. It goes good with jeans."

Shirley smiled. "You don't have to cheer me up, Steamer. It's just one of those times. You know."

"I think you're lonesome. Is it bad to say that?"

The train arrived from the north, and the teenagers in their sweatsuits stood over the safety line so the recorded announcement woman would warn them to stay back.

The Oilers game was still on, so there was plenty of room on the train. Steamer and Shirley sat on a south-facing bench together, with the hockey bag under their feet.

"I hope it ain't bad to say it, Shirley. And I just notice because I'm lonesome too. Takes one to know one, you know?"

Shirley nodded. Somehow, she couldn't summon the energy to tell Steamer to stop talking.

"Have you seen *Napoleon Dynamite*?"

Shirley shook her head.

"We should rent that. It's my favourite movie because it's awesome even though there's no sex or swears or gunplay. Would that be all right?"

"Okay."

"What's your favourite pizza? If we get my favourite movie, we'll get your favourite pizza."

On the train, confronted with the question of her favourite pizza, Shirley understood what was wrong. She was depressed. On the night Benjamin Perlitz died, weakened by the NHL players' strike and hints of her husband's adulterousness, Shirley had been wounded.

Finding it too difficult to open your mouth when someone asks a question like "What's your favourite pizza?" was probably the textbook definition of depression.

"Thin-crust veggie."

Steamer slapped his leg. "Thin-crust veggie it is, then."

The train stopped at Commonwealth Stadium and the kids in sweatsuits got off. Shirley wondered if they were planning to steal a car or abuse a cat. It had to be one of the two. Shirley also wondered if it was possible to pull oneself out of a depression without resorting to pharmaceuticals.

"Shirley, can I tell you something?"

"Of course."

"I know, in my heart, that I won't make it to the show."

"Don't say that, Steamer."

"When you see a kid like number twenty-seven and you know you could never catch him, not in a million years, you better pay attention to that message God is sending."

Shirley nodded as gently as she could manage.

"So I decided what I'm gonna do. Do you like feet?"

"I suppose. As much as the next person."

"I like them a lot, so I'm going to be a doctor of the feet. What's that called again?"

"A podiatrist."

"I'm gonna be a podiatrist."

"That's terrific, Steamer."

"So I was wondering if, after our pizza is done tonight, I could examine you."

"Well . . ."

"I know I'm not a podiatrist yet, but it might be good for me to know what I'm getting into."

The train pulled into Churchill Station and the last man on their car disembarked. Avoiding eye contact with Steamer, Shirley looked down and considered her feet.

62

amigo, amiga

No matter how many times Madison showed him how to hold it, and to use his wrist instead of his arm, and shift his weight on to his right leg, Jonas could not throw a Frisbee.

He gave the Frisbee thing one final try and watched it sail high up in the air, turn sharply to the right, and fall at the base of a barbecue pit near the Hawrelak Park washrooms. Then he began making a giant pile of leaves under a nearby grove of balsam poplars.

Jonas worked quickly. The hill was of an admirable size when Madison returned with the Frisbee.

"What are you doing?"

"We must accept that I simply cannot throw a Frisbee. Next time let's make it a Nerf football, yes? Yes. Good. Now, back up a few paces and run and jump and land in these leaves. It'll be a gas."

"Jonas."

"What?"

"I'm a pregnant girl. I can't do that sort of thing."

"Pish posh. These are pillowy leaves."

"You go first."

Jonas was never a *go first* kind of guy. When he was a child, growing up in Beverly, he had made an art out of convincing the other boys to go first. This was a particularly important skill between grades eight and eleven, in the summertime, when the boys in his neighbourhood took the bus to Borden Park pool, waited until dark, and hopped the fence. His powers of persuasion, which he came to think of as Jonas Mind Tricks, allowed him to see nearly every boy from M. E. LaZerte High School in wet underwear. His own "chlorine allergy" kept him safe and dry in the lifeguard throne, flashlight in hand.

The pillowiness of the leaf pile was potent. Jonas was certain. So, contrary to his nature, he zipped his windbreaker and backed up. "Ready?"

Madison dished a thumbs-up. "Give 'er."

It wasn't until Jonas reached the foot of the pile that he realized running was unnecessary. Even though his brain understood that jumping, at this point, was foolish, Jonas jumped. He turned in the air, and went horizontal. In the air, flying backwards, Jonas had time to scold himself for going first. Jonas had time to think this was the last image he would see of the world: forests leading up to the deliciously expensive homes in Windsor Park.

He landed, with a thud, on his back, only his legs cushioned by the leaves. Once Jonas got his breath, and once Madison stopped laughing and assured him he hadn't fractured his coccyx, they lay together in the bed of leaves looking up at the purple bank of late afternoon cloud that had installed itself over the city.

"What are you going to be for Halloween?"

"Carlos and I are going to be Butch Cassidy and the Sundance Kid."

"Who's who?"

"I'm Sundance, obviously. Why don't you think for a second before you ask such moronic questions?"

"Has Carlos come to terms with his gayness yet?"

"When we're alone, in a house or in the middle of a deserted expanse of grassland, sure. It's Freddie Mercury time. Around other human beings, no. According to *that* Carlos, we're brothers. He actually refers to me as bro."

"I cannot imagine you as a bro."

"You know what he bought me last weekend?"

"A promise ring?"

"A snowmobiling suit. For snowmobiling. He has two snowmobiles, and calls them sleds. When the snow falls, and Carlos *can't wait*, we're going to go sleddin'."

"'Things fall apart; the centre cannot hold.'"

"Have you told Rajinder about the bun in ye olde oven yet?"

Madison pounded the leaves on either side of her. "I was going to. About fifty times. But I always chicken out."

"Don't you think he's going to figure it out soon, when you start wearing maternity pants?"

Madison buried her face in the leaves. "I'm a coward."

"What are you going to be for Halloween?"

"A big fat lady who hates herself."

"Be Buddha."

"No."

"Santa? President Ulysses S. Grant? Late-career Elvis? Aretha Franklin? You better hurry up and decide, girl."

Madison got up, extended a hand to Jonas, then tossed the Frisbee into the wind, and caught it herself. "Rajinder and I are going to see Jeanne and Katie tomorrow morning."

Jonas cleaned the bits of leaves and earth off Madison's face. He wondered how she didn't worry about pimples, putting all those tiny pore-clogging grains of dirt directly on her cheeks. "Can I come?"

"I don't think so."

"I thought we were going to be three *amigos*. Three best chums."

"I'm an *amiga*, aren't I?"

"If there's even one boy in the crowd, it's *amigos*. Sexist? Maybe. But you've completely excluded me."

"You've got Carlos."

Jonas turned and marched toward the stairs leading up and out of Hawrelak Park. The notion that Carlos, an *ur*-redneck from Leduc, could compare with her sophisticated Indian millionaire with the cute nose was preposterous. Insulting. Behind him, he could hear Madison talking to herself and jogging to catch up. He took the stairs slowly and waited on the sidewalk at the top, the traffic rumbling by.

Madison caught her breath. "We could go on double dates."

"You don't understand. A little while ago it was just you and me. Now there's this baby coming, and Rajinder and my pretends-he's-not-gay boyfriend, the whole save-the-neighbourhood thing. If it doesn't work, and it probably won't, we'll move away from each other and meet for soft drinks once a week. Then the baby'll come and there'll be less time, and all your friends'll be baby obsessed like you, and we'll just talk on the phone. About your baby. Then we'll begin to forget. Other priorities, breeder birthday parties, et cetera. Then we'll see each other from afar in Save On Foods and quietly agree to avoid meeting so we won't hold each other up. Then –"

"Come on."

"I really feel this way. It happens to people. We're losing each other."

They hugged and Madison reached up and slapped Jonas in the back of the head. "Let's not."

"Deal." Jonas held out his hand for a shake.

Madison took it. "Deal."

"So can I come with you tomorrow, to see the Perlitz girls?"

"I don't know. It took a long time to get Jeanne to say yes at all, and it isn't exactly a social visit. We have to get her to say no to the university and yes to our plan."

"That's exactly why I should come. Jeanne loved me. Everyone loves me so much, you know, because I'm exceedingly funny and striking to behold. It's sick and pitiless to deprive them of my company." Jonas dropped to his knees, which smarted, and took the Frisbee out of Madison's hand. He lifted the Frisbee to the purple sky and threatened to toss it down the hill. "Please?"

Madison sighed. "It's a sombre occasion. No shenanigans."

"None."

63

the power dinner

In all his time as president of the riding association, the party's executive director had never summoned David Weiss for a private meeting. Though he was not the nervous sort, David found himself trying on different shirt-and-tie combinations following his late-afternoon, post-leaf-raking shower. White shirt and blue tie? White shirt and red tie? Open collar?

David found the right complement for his black suit — white shirt and grey tie — and asked Abby for her opinion. She was at the dining room table with a glass of wine, listening to a Pavarotti greatest hits CD and fussing over the *New York Times* crossword. "Spin."

David spun.

"You're a stud, honey. What's 'baseball's Garciaparra'?"

"Nomar."

"Nomar? How's anyone supposed to know that?"

"Cubs shortstop. Can you take Garith for a walk in an hour?"

The dog heard his name and *walk* and hopped up from his bed in the back porch. David picked him up. "Daddy's going to meet the executive director for dinner at Culina tonight. By this time tomorrow, Daddy could be interim vice-president, Northern Alberta. Or, *or*, maybe he's going to tell me the annexation is off. Either way, Garith my boy, this is a big night for Daddy. Yes it is. *Yes it is.*"

"Stop that." Abby pointed menacingly with her pencil. "Right now."

David pulled into the tiny parking lot behind Culina as a fellow traveller in a Ford Expedition pulled out of a spot. The man manoeuvred his giant Expedition back onto the street and they nodded at one another; two level-headed men who knew, deep in the pragmatic cores of their hearts, that oil would never run out.

Inside the restaurant, the hostess led him to a table for four. David was a few minutes early and the first to arrive. Culina was such a small restaurant that the large table seemed an ungainly mistake. "How many are in our party?"

"Four," said the hostess.

David bobbed his head in time with the Indian pop music and attempted to figure out the red art on the walls. The lights were so dim in the little restaurant he had to hold his menu over the candle-in-a-bag to read it. He wondered who the third and fourth people might be. The premier and his wife? He sat back and closed his eyes. These moments of beatific anticipation were rare. This nervous buzz was natural, for he had entered a new and exciting phase of his retirement. Grandfatherhood, leadership, influence, and respect.

Woman Terry Ashton walked into the restaurant first, followed by Wayne Wernicke, the executive director. Immediately, something went sour in the back of David's throat. The fourth person he didn't recognize at first. He knew the man but there was something . . . no.

David greeted Woman Terry with a malignant smile and handshake. He whispered quickly in her ear, before Wayne Wernicke and Barry Strongman had manoeuvred around the table in the centre of the room. "You betrayed me."

"Oh, grow up, David," she said, a little too loud, in her British accent.

"My friend." Not only did Wayne Wernicke shake David's hand, the executive director of the PC Association of Alberta cupped the meeting of flesh with his left. "It's tremendous you were able to come tonight. Of course you know Mr. Barry Strongman."

During all of their morning social and political arguments on Whyte Avenue, David had appreciated Barry's candour. His authenticity. Most of David's other friends and acquaintances were double-dealers and cynics and strivers, so he had grown addicted to Barryness. The homeless man spoke what he saw as the truth. He was shamelessly self-reliant, an outsider, a genuine individual. If Barry had been a cartoon character he would have been Bugs Bunny, David's all-time favourite.

So in the weeks and months and years ahead, when David remembered the dinner at Culina, nothing echoed in his mind as powerfully as Barry's affected smile, head tilt, and handshake. It signalled the end of something profound in the belief system of David Weiss. Not his political belief system, but that other, deeper, more inaccessible one. "Great to see you again," said Barry. "You're looking well."

They sat, and David noticed Barry's teeth had been bleached. His hands were scrubbed clean, the fingernails shone. Wayne Wernicke warmed up the table with a few anecdotes about Liberals and the weather, but David could not stop staring at Barry Strongman. The haircut, the contact lenses, the trimmed eyebrows and glistening chin. Cologne. A phoney chuckle. Feigned warmth.

At the end of Wayne Wernicke's story, which concluded with a Liberal Party strategist attempting to fish with his bare hands in a mountain-fed lake, Barry Strongman shook his head as he laughed. "Hilarious, Wayne. Hilarious."

In no time, in a week, Barry Strongman had become a politician. He looked and smelled and gestured like a politician, repeated names, winked. When the server, a gorgeous young woman with severe black hair, took their drink orders, Barry ordered a San Pellegrino.

"Does anyone want wine?" said Wayne Wernicke.

Barry Strongman shook his head. No. Not for Barry.

"I'll take some wine." David looked at the list. He knew Woman Terry was already the new president of the Strathcona PC Riding Association. This would be his final dinner on the Progressive Conservative American Express, so David took the initiative and ordered the second-most expensive bottle of red, a Canadian, something called a Sumac Ridge "Black Sage" Vineyard Meritage.

Since the server had already written it down, and since she had already praised David, and the table, for their excellent choice, Wayne Wernicke was powerless. David smiled across the table with his coffee-stained teeth.

He knew it would be his only victory.

64

non-psychotic desires

Abby was asleep when David returned home not quite drunk. The Friday newspapers were stacked on the dining room table, so David poured himself a nightcap and searched through them.

Wayne Wernicke had referenced a profile of Barry Strongman that appeared that day, and somehow David had missed it. The story wasn't prominent but there it was, in the CityPlus section: Barry, in the same suit he had worn at Culina, standing up on a podium at an Edmonton Chamber of Commerce breakfast.

A man transformed.

Three sentences before the end of the article, David tossed the paper. It fluttered into the living room and knocked two vanilla candles off the coffee table. Garith hopped out of his bed and growled.

"David?" called Abby, from upstairs.

The softness of the final D in his name, almost lisped in his wife's sleepy voice, caused David to melt out of his chair and on to the wood floor. All that he had planned for the final twenty-five years of his life had been wiped away over a plate of pork tenderloin steaks with chimichurri sauce and couscous.

"David?" she said again.

With pawsteps like whispers, Garith moved across the floor to stare at his master. David lifted him up and accepted a few kisses, but lacked the energy for more. Inspired by the kisses, Garith sprinted across the room to retrieve his inside-the-house toy, a squeaky chipmunk, but David didn't throw it. Garith nudged the chipmunk near David's right hand, but David left it there.

A slobber stain glistened on the chipmunk's haunch.

Abby walked down the stairs and into the living room, where she stood over her husband in the lamplight. She wiped her eyes and put on her glasses. "What happened to you?"

Before he could answer, Abby dropped to her knees and embraced him on the dining room floor. Her left knee squished a yeep out of the chipmunk. For close to a minute they held each other, and Abby scratched the top of his head the way he liked.

"I'm out."

"What do you mean, you're out?"

David helped his wife up. Garith ran in a circle and hopped at David's leg, to no avail. "Woman Terry Ashton is the interim president, until they vote a new one in. They said I could still be in the party, and in the association, but only as a member. A non-voting member, for one year. I'm being *disciplined*."

"For what?"

"For kicking the rising star of the PC party out of a meeting. Barry Strongman is going to be the next candidate for Edmonton-Strathcona."

"Your homeless friend?"

"Let's go to bed."

"No, let's have some chamomile and talk about this."

"You were asleep."

"I *was* asleep."

David walked into the living room and picked up the newspaper. He set the smelly candles back up on their stainless steel foundations and plopped into his club chair. "All I really want to do is move away. Let's go to Victoria with all the other old people."

"No."

"All my friends are . . . I'm ruined. My life in Alberta is finished."

Abby shook her head. "For one night and only one night I'm not going to say I told you so. I'm not going to say you deserve this."

"Good."

"Let's pretend, husband, for the next hour, that we can do anything. Be anyone."

"We don't have any money."

Abby laughed and walked into the kitchen.

"I fail to see the humour in that." David listened to her drawing water into the kettle, a comforting sound. A winter sound. When she returned, Abby sat on the chesterfield across from David with a notepad and a pen. "What do you *really* want to do?"

"Lop off Wayne Wernicke's head."

Abby didn't make a note. "Only non-psychotic desires are allowed."

The squeaks and honks of the chipmunk interrupted David's machete fantasy. Garith dropped the toy on David's foot, so he lured the dog up onto his lap for a noisy game of pull-the-chipmunk. "I want to be a good dad and granddad."

"Very sane, very sane." Abby made a note. "What else? More selfish now."

"Maybe we could travel a little."

Abby made another note and nodded. "Southeast Asia, before it gets too expensive. Andalusia. Maybe Israel, if things quiet down. Next."

"I'm going to miss the party, especially the conventions."

Abby closed her eyes tight for a second, put the notepad down, and got up from the chesterfield. She transferred Garith to an arm of the chair and sat on David's lap. "Let's take a sabbatical from politics, me and you. Let's concentrate, for a year, on what we have in common."

"But —"

"Maybe we'll live a little longer if we stop talking so much about public policy."

"What about all your Ghandi quotations? Is that even possible?"

Abby bit her bottom lip and nodded.

"You should have seen Barry Strongman tonight. Everything I liked about him, they varnished over it. Now he's like this *doll*. I could have shaved in front of his teeth."

"I'm only going to admit this tonight, okay?"

"Admit what?"

"Left-wingers are just as feckless and goofy. Sometimes they're even more annoying than conservatives. I listen to the speeches, written and delivered by people without a sliver of talent. They know they're lying and I know they're lying and everyone else in the room knows they're lying, and lazy, and stupid as a salad bar, but we clap anyway. We cheer. We give standing-Os."

"Why do we do that, Abby?"

She kissed her husband. The water was boiling. "You know why we do it. Because we don't want to feel powerless and ineffectual and retired. By aligning ourselves with something that seems important and bigger than we are, something that might outlast us, we don't seem as –"

"Old?"

The kettle whistled. "It's time to refocus."

If his wife was talking about shuffleboard and bridge tour-naments, David wasn't sure he wanted to refocus. Three hours ago, before Barry Strongman walked into Culina, he was feeling about as good as he had ever felt. If by refocus his wife meant giving up, he definitely wasn't in. The kettle continued to whistle, and Abby continued to wait for his response, so he mumbled something that she wouldn't hear. A false positive.

65

complete honesty

Rajinder paced in slow motion, from the stereo system in his living room to the kitchen compost bucket. Every few minutes he looked at his watch and murmured to himself. Tango music from Argentina played at low volume and outside a light rain shower threatened to transform into snow.

Apart from work and a Frisbee toss with Jonas, Madison had been spending most of her free time with Rajinder. Her excuses for not staying overnight were becoming more and more ridiculous, but Rajinder was too polite to question them. While he paced, she sat on the chesterfield pretending to read a fat paperback novel about a crippled boy in New Delhi. In an hour, they were due to arrive in Summerside for a visit with Jeanne and Katie Perlitz.

Madison took a sip of her hot chocolate and smiled up at Rajinder. "Why're you so nervous?"

"Me?" Rajinder looked behind him. "I am not nervous."

"Why don't you sit down?"

"I have an aching knee. It helps to walk."

Madison nodded.

"Yes, to be sure, yes. You have me." Rajinder sat across from Madison, in a brown wing chair. He pulled a pillow out from under him, dropped it on the floor and allowed his head to droop. "I am extremely anxious."

"Is it because you lent Benjamin that money? I don't under-stand. Does Jeanne not know?"

Rajinder drooped some more. "For many of the past weeks, as you and I were seeing one another, I have dreaded saying this. But there is more."

"More what?" Madison's feet tingled as though they had been asleep.

"I am afraid I have not been completely honest with you."

Madison's first instinct was to cross the room, squeeze Rajinder's hand, and suggest they outlaw complete honestly. Who needs it, really? The past days of breakfasts and dinners and evening strolls, kissing and Patrice Leconte films, had been nearly perfect. Perfect but for the secret pregnancy growing between them, which so far had kept them out of the bedroom. Madison understood every new moment she didn't confess was another wound in their future.

"Good," she said.

"Good?"

"You don't have to be completely honest with me, if you don't want to be."

Rajinder leaned forward. "Admittedly, I am not an expert in affairs of the heart, but that does not seem right."

"Is it something about your past? Something about your life before we got together?"

"Yes."

"Well, don't feel guilty about keeping it a secret." Madison snorted. "It's none of my business, really."

Rajinder sat back in his wing chair. He looked toward the

stereo system, the unsettling hum of Astor Piazzolla's ban-
doneón. "I disagree."

"Okeedokee. I'm pregnant."

Rajinder made a squeaking sound.

"Four months' pregnant. Haven't you noticed I'm, you
know, expanding outward?"

The tango music seemed to be too much for Rajinder. He
walked to the stereo system and put in another CD, pressed
play, and walked out of the room. A Willie Nelson song filled
the room in his absence.

Madison's lips were dry so she licked them. Two competing
forces in her body, the need to cry and the need to scream,
crashed up against one another and caused a sort of emotional
paralysis. Instead of thinking of Rajinder and the bedroom
door he had just slammed – three times – Madison considered
Willie Nelson's long, braided pigtails. She wondered if Willie
Nelson had paid those back taxes he owed the American
government, and if his marijuana possession charges made
touring difficult.

The doorbell rang. Madison stood in front of the chesterfield, thinking about Willie Nelson. It rang again. On the third
ring, Rajinder plodded through the living room to the front
door without looking at Madison.

"Hey, lovebirds!" said Jonas.

When Willie Nelson wore his American flag bandana, was he
being sincere or ironic or both? Even though Madison had never
really liked Willie Nelson's voice, she felt a certain kinship with
him: the red hair, the aura of lost hope and disappointment.

Rajinder took Jonas's flowers, bottle of wine, and pony-shaped bundle.

"They're for Jeanne and Katie." Jonas took a couple of steps and slid on the hardwood in his socks. "You have the slipperiest floor, Raj."

Rajinder stood near the dining room table clutching the wine, flowers, and pony. Madison could only see Jonas with the rightmost edge of her peripheral vision.

Jonas stopped sliding. "I haven't been listening to the news. Is Earth gonna be hit by a meteor?"

All at once, the spell of Willie Nelson broke. "I told Rajinder I'm pregnant."

"Oh," said Jonas. "Oh."

"Good Hearted Woman" began to play. Jonas began stomping his feet and singing along. He clapped and hopped around in his thick black socks. Then he stopped singing. "Maybe I'll go home and drink a bottle of cheap vodka."

Rajinder turned to Madison. "I am having trouble deciding how to express the way I feel."

Madison bit the insides of her cheek so she wouldn't cry.

"This is not ideal."

"No, Rajinder, it isn't, and I'm sorry for that."

He walked across the living room and stood in front of Madison for a moment. Then he hugged her. Madison reached around him, and it felt as though he were flexing every muscle in his body. "Congratulations," he said. "What a tremendous blessing." Then he fetched her jacket and helped her into it.

According to his shoulders, which were up around his ears, Rajinder didn't want Jonas's company right now. Neither did

Madison. But the core of politeness in Rajinder was too strong and Madison didn't feel capable of speaking. In desperate silence, and cold rain, they walked out the back door to Rajinder's garage. Madison sat in the passenger seat and Jonas got in the back. Even though it required going the wrong way on a one-way, Rajinder drove through the alley to reach the Garneau Theatre parking lot and turned south.

Madison waited. She waited some more. Then she said, "So, Rajinder. What's *your* secret?"

66

suburbia

Rajinder Chana gripped the steering wheel with both hands, his jaw clenched. Next to him, Madison dabbed at her eyes with a red handkerchief.

In the back, Jonas slouched and the leather squeaked. Was it a character flaw, Jonas wondered, to *enjoy* romantic tension? It was tangible, chewy even; he wanted the ride to go on forever.

Driving south, with the smell of cut lumber in the air, Rajinder sneezed. Then he took in a long breath and said, "On the night Benjamin Perlitz was killed, I was at a Fringe play about the addictive nature of pornography."

Jonas remembered sitting in the beer tent that night with Madison and a few actors. At one point in the evening, during someone's drunken soliloquy, he had seen Rajinder – the young Indian man from across the street – pass with a program. "I saw you there."

"Benjamin had not planned to enter his own house. He had planned to enter mine."

"What do you mean?" Madison turned to him.

"Benjamin Perlitz had planned to shoot *me* that night. When he crossed the street to his own house, he had only meant to wait and watch through the front window until I returned. Of course, he wasn't blameless. Benjamin was verbally abusive with Jeanne and threatened to shoot her if she tried to escape with Katie. The police arrived after she sneaked a call with her cellular phone. Shortly thereafter, he went berserk."

Jonas slid to the middle of the back seat and leaned in between Rajinder and Madison. "Because you stopped lending him gambling money?"

"A couple of months after Jeanne sent Benjamin away, I became . . . a comfort to her. Somehow he discovered this. Through Katie, I believe."

"You were sleeping with Jeanne?" Madison's voice registered somewhere between fascination and horror.

Rajinder didn't answer for several blocks. In a small but sure voice, passing some strip malls, he said, "For a time."

"When did it end?"

"Long before Benjamin arrived with his rifle."

Madison shook her head. "How on earth did you keep it out of the newspaper?"

"Police discretion."

This inspired another long silence. In almost any other circumstance, Jonas would have slapped Rajinder on the arm and called him a dog. Nay, a dawg. But it didn't seem appropriate. The Mercedes motor was quiet, even when Rajinder accelerated, which added to the gloom. They passed the retail giants and fast-food outlets of South Edmonton Common, and Jonas realized he had forgotten to eat that morning. A nasty mood and low-level catatonic state of hypoglycemia could hit at any time, despite his present state of glee. "Hey, you guys think Jeanne'll serve snacks?"

Neither of them offered a thought.

"Potato chips? Watermelon?"

In the deep south of the city, the Summerside neighbourhood sat under several shades of grey. The wind galloped across the prairie and lashed the left side of the car as they waited at the stoplight. When the lights changed, Rajinder turned past the old country cemetery and into the flat subdivision of massive wooden houses.

"Those baby carrots, even? It's my own fault, I guess, for sleeping in. Not that I have anything to eat at my place. There's cereal but no milk. Well, actually, there is some milk. Do you guys have this problem? I have expired milk, way expired, and I know I should pour it down the sink but something – some mystifying inner force – tells me to leave it in the fridge. Leave it till next time."

No response.

"Hello?"

Madison pulled the sun visor down and inspected herself in the mirror. With the handkerchief, she dabbed underneath her eyes, then looked out the passenger window. A pink foam had formed along the banks of the artificial lake. Leaves, Tim Hortons cups, and refuse from Kentucky Fried Chicken bobbed on the small waves.

"Listen, you two. If it'll cheer you up, I'll jump in that smelly lake right now. *Right now.* I heard from a guy that a poodle swam in there last fall and it died. Even if that's true, I don't care. It means nothing to me, nothing. Because I love you guys. I love yez. You're my favourites and I hate to see this sorrow. I just hate to see it."

Rajinder pulled up in front of Jeanne's sister's house, a three-storey cream-coloured Cape Cod with two tiny birch trees planted in front. The trees looked so thin and forlorn, Jonas figured they needed hugs. He hopped out of the back seat and proceeded to embrace the first one. It was small so he had to bend low to get under the pokey branches. To his distress, both Rajinder and Madison ignored him.

The front door opened and Katie, in a winter jacket and rubber boots, ran out. Madison went down on both knees to hug the girl, who launched into a stream-of-consciousness speech about Halloween, her new school, fingerpainting, a kitten named Chris, and the distinct possibility that by this time next year she would have a trampoline.

Katie finished her speech, said hello to Jonas and Rajinder, and yanked Madison by the hand. Jeanne stood in the doorway, wearing a pair of jeans and a black sweater, her blonde hair tied up in a bun. Makeup did not hide the dark shadows under her eyes.

Jeanne and Madison hugged. Jonas insisted Rajinder go next because he wanted to study the interplay between the former lovers. They hugged as well, but not warmly. It was as though they were both worried about the other's hands being sticky.

"You look *amazing*," said Jonas, as he hurried in for his own hug. He picked Jeanne up into the air for a moment and as she went limp with discomfort he placed her back down on the entrance rug.

67

the wild things

Jeanne invited Rajinder and Madison to sit on the puffy leather couch facing the fireplace and Katie's overflowing toy box. Her new My Little Pony lay on the laminate floor, next to a pile of wrapping paper. They listened to Katie describe the situation at her Montessori kindergarten while wearing a Darth Vader voice-changing mask.

"We play with wood mostly," said Katie, in the voice of James Earl Jones.

Even though this ranked in the top-five most uncomfortable moments of her life, Madison couldn't stop smiling at Katie. For the first time in her four months of pregnancy, Madison felt thrilled to be having a child. A girl, hopefully, with red hair and brown eyes.

And if Rajinder wasn't comfortable with that, she just had to stop caring about him. Now or as soon as possible.

It helped that he had slept with Jeanne. It helped that he had been disingenuous about the Let's Fix It project. He wanted to Fix It because he had, from a certain point of view, caused It.

"We did a pond study last week." Katie nodded her Vader head. "My teacher's name is Mrs. Allen. Lots of the bugs we saw were dead."

Jeanne stood up from her own puffy chair and held a hand out for Katie. "That's great, honey. Now it's time for you to go upstairs and play."

"No." Still in the Darth Vader mask, Katie ran around the coffee table and hopped up on the couch next to Madison.

"*Yes*, Katie."

She took Madison's hand and squeezed it in hers. "No!"

"Once the adults are finished talking, Madison will come up and play with you."

Katie turned and looked for confirmation with her Vader eyes. "Really?"

"I absolutely promise," said Madison.

The four-year-old pulled off the mask, took her My Little Pony and a copy of *Where the Wild Things Are*, and started up the stairs. She stopped halfway and looked down. "You better not take forever."

Madison shook her head. "I won't be long."

The door closed upstairs and Jeanne sighed. "Can I get anyone a drink? Beer, wine, tea, juice?"

There was a plate of California rolls on the granite countertop. Jonas sat on a stool and dipped one into a mixture of wasabi and soy. "Your sister got any Scotch?"

Jeanne started around to the open kitchen. "She does, in fact, and no one ever drinks it. Want some?"

"Do I!"

Madison wanted to take this opportunity to say something to Rajinder. Yet she wasn't sure she could articulate it. So instead of speaking, Madison turned and punched Rajinder in the shoulder. Then she wound up and punched him again. "I am sorry, Madison," he said, rubbing the spot.

Jeanne returned to the living room with her own glass of Scotch. No doubt she had heard and perhaps seen the blows Madison had delivered. Smelling of imitation crabmeat, Jonas plopped down beside Madison on the couch and took a long sip of Scotch.

"So," said Jonas. "It's been ages. How are things, Jeanne?"

She took a long time to answer, which pointed to the absurdity of Jonas's question. "Shitty, all things considered. You?"

"Can't complain, can't complain."

Madison slid forward on the couch. "Katie seems to be doing all right."

"She still has the nightmares, but yeah. She's doing pretty well."

"Was she in the bedroom when . . ."

Jeanne nodded.

"I'm so sorry. We all are. It's probably an obvious and annoying thing to say."

Jeanne nodded again.

"Did you receive the letter from the university?" said Rajinder.

"I did. Thanks for forwarding it on."

Rajinder looked at Madison and at Jonas, and used his hands to indicate this was a team effort. "As a community, we have been searching for ways to save the Garneau Block from annexation and ultimate destruction. After some research and a lot of creative thinking on the part of Raymond Terletsky, we have decided to aim for a cultural designation."

"What does that mean?"

"We're not positive yet. Raymond Terletsky and I met with some local architects, a museum consultant, and the guest composer at the Edmonton Symphony Orchestra. As a matter of fact, Jeanne," Rajinder leaned back in the couch, as though he were seeking shelter, "we are here to discuss an important matter with you, something we hope you will agree is the best solution for everyone. I would like to buy your house. *We* would like to buy your house, and transform it into a sort of . . . a very special place."

Jeanne shook her head and took a sip of Scotch. "I don't get it."

"A museum but not a museum," said Jonas. "A site of Edmonton's mythic power."

"I still don't get it."

"There's probably gonna be some buffalo." Jonas made a sweeping gesture with his glass of Scotch, and the ice tinkled. "Right, gang?"

"Yes, buffalo," said Rajinder, with a faint scowl.

At that moment, Madison understood that 10 Garneau would never be anything special. This plan was boyish and egotistical and silly. Jeanne looked at Madison and lifted an eyebrow. "Is this a joke?"

Madison shook her head.

"I'm not selling my house to you, Rajinder. Not ever. I'm selling my house to the university so they can level it."

"Wait a moment, Jeanne. Let us explain."

"You want me to agree to something that is good for you, not me. I don't want Katie growing up with a big *something* on the site of her father's death. How will she ever forget if the house is a big monument to . . . to what did you say? Mystic power? Buffaloes?"

"Yeah, *mythic* power," said Jonas.

"The best thing for us is to forget that life and forget that house."

"It will not work, Jeanne," said Rajinder. "Believe me. You will never forget. You must not try to forget."

Jeanne finished her glass of Scotch in one gulp. "Get out, all of you."

There were no buts. Neither Rajinder nor Jonas tried to convince her. On their way out the door, Jeanne hugged Madison again and gave her the phone number so they could get together another time, with Katie.

As Rajinder backed the car out of the driveway, Jeanne Perlitz stood in the doorway. Madison turned in the passenger seat and watched her as they drove away.

68

the screening room

Raymond Terletsky had read through the proposals from the architects and consultants several times, searching for a perfect distillation of the city's mythic power. He wasn't disappointed or deterred, but none of the proposals quite did the job. Raymond didn't know exactly what he wanted, but he would not compromise or proceed with a mediocre museum. The future of 10 Garneau was there, somewhere, flickering on the edge of the professor's vision.

As the prairie sky blackened outside the thirty-eighth-floor windows, Raymond likened the sensation to that name you can almost remember. That taste you can almost recognize. The smell in the wind that takes you back to . . . where?

Raymond understood and heard and even tasted the future of 10 Garneau, but he couldn't yet see it. The architects' and consultants' proposals swirled through his mind as he walked on the treadmill behind his desk. A tower of goodness. The pyramid of northern urbanity. An underground system of caves with a portal on the Garneau Block, leading to five hundred small rooms – the room of immigration, the room of skateboarding, the room of dead-language scholarship.

And the "haunted" house, stacked with scurvy and speakeasies, the recent horrors of sprawl, unregulated exhaust pipes, chamber opera, homoerotic paintings of shirtless Germans, grizzly bears and dinosaurs and local flowers, the Triads, black gold, rhubarb jam, Wop May and Lois Hole and Joe Shoctor, native rebellions and agricultural mishaps.

Raymond was not worried about Jeanne's refusal to sell. Soon Jeanne Perlitz and all other skeptics would kneel before the majesty of 10 Garneau.

The performance poet stood in Raymond's doorway. She had shaved her head bald, and carried a transparent garbage bag full of white feathers. "You're not going to a Halloween party tonight?"

Raymond stepped off the treadmill. "I'm not big on parties at the moment."

"Neither is the boss."

"Is he still here?"

"In the screening room. He's been watching sad French movies and eating ice-cream sandwiches all day. When I checked on him this afternoon, he'd already been through *Les Enfants du paradis* twice and he was putting *Un Coeur en hiver* into the projector. I think I saw that Juliette Binoche film, *Bleu*, on the floor."

"Yipes." Raymond turned off the treadmill. "I know what it's like to have one's heart ripped out of one's chest, chewed and stomped and soiled with refuse and, ultimately, forgotten in a ditch."

"Right. Maybe you should talk to him."

"Maybe so."

The performance poet lifted her bag of white feathers and started down the hall toward the elevators. "Happy Halloween."

Raymond wiped the thin layer of perspiration from his forehead and walked to the screening room. In the hallway, he could hear the echoes of symphonic music from *Bleu*. Inside, Rajinder Chana sat in the middle chair. The performance poet had been right about the ice-cream sandwiches. Wrappers littered the adjacent seats.

Instead of standing in front of Rajinder, Raymond sneaked up behind him. On the screen, Juliette Binoche was alone in a Paris apartment. Her husband and child were dead. Raymond wanted to comfort his friend but it had to be perfect. He considered various options and then, satisfied he had discovered the right one, proceeded to mess up Rajinder's hair and say, "You old scamp, eh? Scamp!"

The professional arts philanthropist did not respond.

So Raymond spoke.

"I'm a loser. Really, the definition of a loser in the industrialized world. But I've managed to crawl a few feet out of loser-dom to do something noble. Thanks to you, Rajinder. Of all people, I'm shocked that you – you – would allow the word 'No' to deter you from saving the Garneau Block. That you would allow a secret pregnancy to ruin your relationship with Madison Weiss."

Raymond raised his voice. He felt a conclusive sentence coming on. "I want you to turn off the movie and come outside with me, so we can scheme our dazzling futures with the women we love. Let's go! *Allons-y!*"

There was a small cooler next to Rajinder. He reached over, opened the lid, and pulled out a fresh ice-cream sandwich. With both hands, Rajinder unwrapped the ice-cream sandwich and began eating it without a word, a nod, or any other acknowledgement of Raymond's presence.

Raymond retraced his steps to the door of the screening room. He turned and waited for a moment of cinematic silence. It seemed important that he say something memorable. So he said, "Remember, Rajinder. Halloween is a time for . . . feeling better than . . . you feel now."

On Jasper Avenue, in the chill air, goblins and zombies and Dick Cheneys stood in front of the New City nightclub smoking cigarettes. Raymond didn't want to go back to his tiny bedroom at the Weisses' so he walked south to the crest of the river valley.

A light snow began to fall. In an instant, the snow transformed from light to heavy and the wind whipped around him. He could no longer see across the valley, and the glow of the street lights turned pale and dim.

Raymond laughed, and climbed on a sidewalk bench. Soon, a full-scale Halloween blizzard had blown in over the valley. For a million people, Raymond knew, this would be unwelcome. "Cowards!" he said. "Self-deniers. This is the north!" He danced on the bench and clapped his hands and screamed wildly into the wind. The wet snow blew into his mouth.

In an old suit and a tweed overcoat, without a hat or gloves, Raymond recognized he would not last long in the blizzard. He walked to the steep edge of the valley for a last look at the city before the sky fell upon it. Raymond lifted his hands and conducted the wind and the snow, sang aloud in German, bounced and addressed the sky. Then, as the tops of his ears began to sting, Raymond slipped on a new patch of wet snow. He reached out for something to brace himself but there was nothing. Raymond slid, fell back, and tumbled down the hill.

69

groove is in the heart

Steamer stood at the living room window of 11 Garneau, staring out at the blizzard and sighing. While he stared and sighed, Shirley attempted to finish an article about Christianity and Canadian politics in *The Walrus*. She really wanted a glass of red wine but she had grown to feel the sting of judgment from Steamer every time she partook.

Again he sighed, and Shirley closed the magazine with a slap. "What is it, Steamer?"

"Oh, nothing."

"Go ahead."

Steamer turned around. "Do you promise you won't, I don't know, *judge* me?"

"Of course."

Steamer walked over and knelt before Shirley in his jeans and tank top. There was a thick scar on his right shoulder, from a baling accident when he was thirteen, and Shirley couldn't help but focus on it. She wanted to run a finger along the scar, perhaps when Steamer was asleep some night.

Slowly and tenderly, Steamer pulled off Shirley's socks and investigated her feet. She lifted the magazine so he would not look at her and read any pleasure in her face. His hands were soft, for a hockey player who grew up on a farm, and they quivered slightly. Shirley closed her eyes as Steamer drew his thumbs along the top of her foot and said, to himself, as though he were chanting, "Navicular, medial cuneiform, intermediate cuneiform, lateral cuneiform, cuboid." He took her toes in his fingers and Shirley worked hard to cloak a soft gasp. "Phalanges," he whispered.

Steamer slowly replaced her socks and lay on the floor. "So?"

Shirley swallowed. "So what?"

"Did I get them right?"

Steamer had given her a cheat sheet, and Shirley was supposed to have been keeping track. "One hundred per cent," she said.

"I'm sure glad you don't mind being my dummy. Before I start at Brigham Young, I want to know every bone and tendon and muscle by heart."

This pleased Shirley.

Steamer looked up at the ceiling. "You know, I never trick-or-treated. My parents wouldn't let me. They figured it was devilry, Halloween."

"What do you think?"

"I don't know. Maybe it *is* just about crops and pumpkin harvests."

"Did you ever dress up?"

"Never."

Shirley looked at her watch. "Because it's still Halloween for another three hours."

"I guess my parents wouldn't need to know."

Shirley invited Steamer into the spare bedroom upstairs, where her daughter kept all the clothes she refused to wear any more. Since her daughter had inherited Raymond's height and thickness, her high-school graduation dress, for example, was giant-sized. A perfect fit for Steamer, if he was interested.

"I can't dress up like a fairy."

Shirley held the pink dress up in front of him. "Why not?"

"One of the guys'll see me."

"It's Halloween."

"Are you sure about this, Ms. Wong?"

Shirley left Steamer alone in the spare room to try on the pink graduation dress. She heard the chiffon rustling before he opened the door. "Can you zip me up?"

There was an old Green Giant costume downstairs, so Shirley modified it into Peter Pan. Steamer could be Tinkerbell.

The lights were dim and the DJ had just started spinning a smash teen hip-hop hit from 1992 when they arrived at the Old Strathcona Business Association Halloween party. A crowd of monsters were gathered on the makeshift dance floor.

Shirley went to the bar and bought a glass of wine for herself. Tinkerbell trailed close behind. "Can I get you anything, Steamer? A pop? Water?"

After a few moments of deliberation in front of the cooler, Steamer said, "A beer."

"What?"

"I want to try a cold one."

Shirley bought Steamer a Grasshopper and they sat at one of the only empty tables. They touched plastic glasses and drank. "If you become an alcoholic, remember, I had nothing to do with it."

"I've been watching you, Ms. Wong. You have good morals,

your own business, a nice house. The Lord hasn't destroyed you for drinking liquor."

"The Lord hasn't destroyed me yet, but he's dallied with the idea."

Steamer's first few sips were painful to behold. But as he reached the middle of the glass, he stopped puckering. A thin film appeared in front of his eyes, and he smiled. "I get it. I *get it.*"

"Just take it easy, Steamer. Moderation is key."

"I'm not allowed to dance. But you know what, Ms. Wong? I want to dance."

Shirley nodded. "I bet even Jesus –"

"Now," he said, and pulled Shirley to the square in front of the DJ table. "Groove Is in the Heart" became "Love Hurts." At first, they danced apart. But when everyone else moved in and embraced, Steamer looked around and stepped in to Shirley. "Is it all right?"

"Of course."

Shirley placed Steamer's hands on her waist, and she put her hands on his shoulders. The graduation dress had thin straps, thin enough that his scar was bare. She could feel that Steamer was shivering with fright or a related emotion. One of the Sugarbowl owners danced next to Shirley with his wife, and he dished her a naughty look.

"Damn, Shirley," said the co-owner of the Sugarbowl, just loud enough for her to hear.

Without acknowledging the remark, Shirley led Steamer to the corner of the dance floor. She dragged her thumb along the scar on his shoulder. And then she did it again.

70

revolver

Butch "Carlos" Cassidy leaned against the bar and yawned. Jonas, the Sundance Kid, waved at Butch from the dance floor and Butch made like he was shooting the Sundance Kid between the eyes.

For the eighth or ninth time, a man – this one dressed up like a CIA agent – tried to pick up Carlos. Jonas could not read lips but he imagined Carlos saying, "No, no thank you. At the moment I'm marvellously in love."

For years, Jonas had questioned the motives of his friends who went to the Roost as a couple. A room filled with hundreds of inebriated and available men is designed to make attached people feel badly. You've either settled for an inferior partner or *you're* the inferior partner.

Somehow, Jonas felt neither inferior nor jealous. As he swayed to "Monster Mash," he tried to will Carlos onto the dance floor. Then he realized it was dumb to stand four metres away from Carlos and gesture at him. Jonas quit the dance floor.

"Is it always like this here?"

Jonas looked around. The drinking, the dancing, the smooching. "Apart from the Halloween costumes, yes."

"I never liked nightclubs. Even when I was a kid."

"How come?"

Carlos shrugged. "I prefer pubs. Or my house. Or just about anywhere, really."

"You're a senior citizen."

"My dad says that."

A surf rock tune started up and Jonas wanted to shake his tight blue jeans. But a strange thing was happening to him. He was beginning to understand his partner's discomfort. "You're sure it isn't a gay nightclub thing?"

"Well . . ."

"Would you like to leave?"

Carlos shrugged again.

"Be honest."

"I want to leave real bad, Jonas. *Real* bad."

Jonas crouched a little and performed his Paul Newman squint. "Kid, the next time I say, 'Let's go someplace like Bolivia,' let's go someplace like Bolivia."

"That's from the movie!"

"Good boy."

Carlos walked out of the Roost and into the blizzard.

A giant black truck emerged from the storm. Jonas grabbed the back of Carlos's shirt. "Butch has all the good lines but the Sundance Kid is better looking. Where should we go?"

At the Mustang, Carlos insisted Jonas sit in the car while he wiped off the snow and scraped the windows. Jonas reached over to start the engine and eject the Limp Bizkit CD. He found the case inside the glovebox and slipped the album under his seat.

Carlos got in and cranked up the defrost. It remained almost impossible to see. Jonas wiped the condensation from his window. "Should we maybe just call a taxi?"

"If we do, it'll take two hours." Carlos put the Mustang in gear and proceeded slowly. South of Jasper Avenue, in complete whiteout, Carlos shook his head and turned into the Chateau Lacombe where he eased into the underground parking lot.

Carlos removed a black bag from the trunk and led Jonas to the hotel lobby and elevator. In La Ronde, the revolving restaurant, the host bowed to them and apologized. The room was nearly empty. Food service had been cut off but they were welcome to have a drink.

Jonas ordered an old-fashioned and Carlos asked for a coffee. They sat near the window and Carlos pulled a thin laptop computer out of his bag. "Are you checking e-mail? That's awful, Butch."

"Can you speak Spanish?" Carlos peeked around from his computer. His face shone white and faintly blue.

"*Por supuesto*," said Jonas.

"Yes or no?"

Jonas didn't want to lie or explain about the limitations of level-two Spanish so he pointed at the laptop. "The only thing more tactless than talking on a cellular phone on a date is opening up a computer."

"When do rehearsals for *A Christmas Carol* begin?"

"Why, Carlos?"

"Just when?"

"The twelfth of November." Jonas would be Bob Cratchit in this year's Citadel production. The role didn't bring out his best qualities but the money was good and he would be downtown, within walking distance of Chinatown restaurants, for almost two months.

The server arrived with their drinks and it struck Jonas that he was beginning to favour comfort over adventure. Here he was, sipping a quiet drink in a revolving hotel restaurant on one of the wildest nights of the year. Later on, at his place or in Leduc, he and Carlos would romance one another like a married couple. Instead of starring in an experimental show at the Roxy, he was choosing to play off Scrooge. And he was thinking seriously about auditioning for a three-month dinner-theatre gig in January.

"What's happening to me, Carlos?"

Carlos was lost behind the computer screen.

"I'm becoming everything I thought I'd never be: a fussy bourgeois without the regular paycheque. I might as well start wearing khakis and subscribing to *Martha Stewart Living*." Jonas rested his head in his arms. "At approximately 10:15 p.m., Halloween night, on the dance floor of the Roost, Jonas Pond became his father."

Carlos closed the computer with a click. "It's done."

"I know. But you should have seen me fifteen years ago, baby. I was a star."

"No, I mean it's *done*. Our trip is booked, but I left the hotels open. You can negotiate in Spanish so it'll be cheaper. We leave for La Paz at 6:41 in the morning, November second."

Jonas leaned across the table and kissed Carlos on the cheek.

"Don't!" Carlos shoved Jonas away. He scanned the room to make sure no one saw, just as he always did when Jonas attempted a public acknowledgement of their relationship. The snow had dissipated somewhat and, through the window, the eastern half of the city revealed itself. Carlos pressed his forehead against the window. "Hey, someone's trying to crawl up the slope of the valley."

The Sundance Kid took his old-fashioned standing up, in one gulp. Then, without alerting Butch Cassidy, he walked to the elevator and pressed the call button.

71

quietude

In her favourite chair, surrounded by lit candles, Madison attempted to think. Not think while watching rap music videos or reading *Les Misérables*. Just think, in silence.

It was torture.

Does any woman, really, know herself well enough to enjoy the cacophony of her own thoughts? Piano teachers, maybe, and evangelical Christian housewives who volunteer a lot, but who else?

Madison wanted to pick up the phone and call someone, anyone, in Montreal. She wanted to go upstairs and steal Garith for an hour, or browse the Web for strollers from Italy. Since finger-chewing was the only distractive indulgence she allowed herself, the skin around her nails was pink and peeled. Ravaged.

A spot at the back of her skull grew hot. She reached back and touched the spot, and realized the silence was ruining her psychological equilibrium. By this time tomorrow she would be on antidepressants with the rest of her generation.

Yet this aversion to quietude was not her fault. Since self-awareness had first crept in at twelve or thirteen, she had been bombarded by a socially sanctioned media blitz. Shutting it off, all at once, was like trying to kick a lifelong amphetamine habit.

Twice in the past week Rajinder had knocked on her door, flowers in hand. And twice she had huddled in her favourite chair, unwilling to speak to him.

The candles flickered as warm air blew through the ceiling vent, and Madison leaned forward. Would one of the candles go out? No. There would be no drama for her tonight. She rose, intending to walk across the street in her pajamas, knock on Rajinder's door, and tackle him with kisses. Then she sat down again, picked up *Les Misérables*, and tossed it behind her chair.

Madison blew out the candles and watched the afterglow. When it was gone, and darkness was complete, she regretted blowing out the candles. Now what?

She was about to give up on thinking in silence, since it only inspired thinking in silence about thinking in silence, when there was a knock on her door. She hopped up out of her favourite chair, tripped on the ottoman, and fell into a wood-panelled wall. The light switch was easy to find, as she had rammed her cheek into it.

"Maddy, let me in."

She sighed. It was Jonas, not Rajinder. "Coming."

At the top of the stairs, his cowboy poncho covered in wet snow, Jonas hugged her. "I'm so glad to see you."

"Where's Carlos?"

Jonas pulled back and leaned against the door. "Don't ask. Just don't ask about Carlos tonight, please."

"All right."

Jonas started downstairs. "The stupid hick. How *dare* he?"

"Can I get you a drink?"

"An old-fashioned, no ice."

"Beer, white wine, or vodka with some cranberry juice?"

"Wine, then. Wine!" Jonas pulled off his poncho and tossed it in the corner. "You know, we were having such a nice night. I was worried about turning into white-picket-fence boy and then, then, he books us a trip to Bolivia. Wonderful, right? Wrong. He still thinks he's straight."

As usual, Madison broke the cork while trying to extract it. So she pushed it into the bottle and strained the wine into Jonas's glass through a J-cloth. "You're sleeping together. Who cares if he . . ."

"Hey. Hey, Madison. Didn't I say no talking about Carlos?"

"Actually, you said –"

"Stop. And get dressed. We're going back to the Roost."

Madison brought the wine and a glass of cranberry juice, and sat in the adjacent chair. "I'm not going to the Roost."

"I need you, Maddy. I'm distraught."

"So I go with you to the Roost."

Jonas took a sip and leaned across the arm of the chair toward her. "Yes, yes."

"And you blow me off instantly, and run on to the dance floor."

"Sure, yep."

"Ten minutes later, you're gone with some moustache."

Jonas crossed his fingers and closed his eyes tightly, clicked his heels together.

"So why do you need me there?"

"If I'm alone it looks like I'm just there to cruise. What kind of pathetic local celebrity do you take me for?"

Madison swiped the remote control from the coffee table between the two chairs and turned on the music videos. Jonas began making sarcastic remarks about them and Madison realized – with another pulse of heat in the back of her head – she had been here before. In her silk pajama bottoms, velour housecoat, and bunny slippers. Jonas blabbing about male pattern baldness and the genetic errors who controlled the film industry.

The heat intensified, itched, throbbed. Madison had been here before, so many times she could not remember specific instances. And she would be here again, eternally.

If she didn't do something now, on the cusp of her thirtieth birthday, Madison Weiss would leave this room but she would *never leave this room.*

72

a vision in the blizzard

Raymond Terletsky reached out to Death. Death huffed and mist eased down out of his nose. His head was the head of a buffalo. It looked like Death wore blue jeans, a bandana, and cowboy boots, but Raymond couldn't be sure. The snow had stopped falling but it was dark.

Though Death did not speak, Raymond understood.

If the professor stood up straight, he would fall back. If he tried to crawl forward he would slip again. His only hope was the hand of Death, a hand whiter than snow. "I guess you don't have much in the way of blood. Do you, Death?"

As he reached, and Death reached, Raymond received a vision of 10 Garneau. All of the architects and consultants had been wrong. He knew what the house would look and sound like. It was so simple, so obvious, so clear. He laughed and thanked Death, even though it was too late; like learning lottery numbers after the draw.

Death's hand was warm and calloused and strong. Climbing up the slope, a layer of wet snow over icy grass, Raymond slipped twice. But Death did not let him go. Death dragged him up. When he reached the sidewalk, on his hands and knees, Raymond said, "Thank you."

"I saw you from up there, Dr. Terletsky."

Raymond looked up at Death, but it wasn't Death. The young man from Jonas's backyard was pointing to the top of the Chateau Lacombe. "We better get you to a hospital."

Carlos led Raymond into the hotel, and the parking elevator. The heat made his ears and fingers and nose burn and itch, and he called out in the elevator and laughed some more. In all his years at the university, when it might have been handy to meet Death, nothing. What an interview subject. What a guest lecturer. What a contact.

"I never imagined he'd have a buffalo head." Raymond sat in the low passenger seat of the Mustang. Melting snow clung to the tweed of his overcoat. He shrugged as Carlos backed out of his parking spot. "I never thought he was a he. Or an it, even. What's your name again?"

"Carlos."

"Why aren't you out trick-or-treating, Carlos?"

They rose out of the parking lot and turned down into the valley. "Me and Jonas went out dancing. Then we went up to the spinning restaurant for drinks."

"That's nice. Did you see Death down there, before you saved me?"

"I don't know what you're talking about." Carlos ran his finger under his nose a few times, and sniffed. "Dr. Terletsky, when I was a kid, my dog Champ got hit by a truck."

"I'm sorry to hear that."

"The vet said he was too busted up to live, and brain damaged, but my mom refused to put Champ down. For six months Champ'd lay there twitching and crapping himself. One day he died natural. You know why my mom wanted him alive?"

Raymond shook his head. The heater was blowing hot air in the Mustang now, and his cheeks hurt. As the snow on his jacket turned to water, Raymond realized he was thawing out. The clouds cleared. With the pain in his ears came clarity.

"Because she was waiting for a miracle. She figured Jesus had nothing better to do with his time than fix Champ."

Carlos turned on to the High Level Bridge. Raymond touched the tips of his ears with his sore fingers, and wiggled his toes. "Thanks for coming down for me, Carlos. I think I would have died if you hadn't. I doubt Jesus would have had much time for *me* either."

"Did you grow up going to church, Dr. Terletsky?"

"I'm not of the Christian persuasion. Which explains certain things. Fear of an unpleasant afterlife might have come in handy as I made some of my more memorable decisions."

"If I'm gay, Dr. Terletsky, I don't have a mom. Or a dad. Basically life is over. The life I know."

Raymond lifted a finger to stall for time. He waited for the perfect words. They didn't arrive, so he improvised. "Carlos, a lot of people thrive without parents. Mine died when I was quite young, right around your age I guess, and I miss them. I think about my parents. I talk to them in dreams. There are times, especially recent times, when I might have profited from some guidance. But it's best to think of ourselves as free beings, rooted yet free. You're free to be your mother's son and a gay man both, an Edmontonian and a person of the greater world, a –"

"I'm from Leduc, actually."

"Do you want to be a gay man?"

"No, Dr. Terletsky, I don't."

"Are you a gay man?"

Carlos nodded. "Jonas says I can't be a homo and a homophobe at the same time."

"Are you a homophobe?"

"No. But my mom, and Champ, remember? I'm an oil-and-gas guy. I can't be a Creamsicle, everything to everyone. I can't be this gay guy and a straight guy, a Roost guy and a –"

"You can be a Creamsicle, if that's what you want. This is the best time in human history to have identity problems. Even a profitable time, if you know how to write grant applications. I'm sure it looks bad but you're lucky as hell, Carlos." In an instant, Raymond was overwhelmed with fatigue. "I have frostbite."

"You sure do, Dr. Terletsky, on your ears. How long were you out there, slippin' around?"

Raymond closed his eyes and Death stood there, huffing, with that buffalo head. "Jesus!"

"Exactly."

73

a rediscovery of hands

How long had it been since David and Abby walked down the street together, dogless and daughterless and coffeeless, holding hands? Over twenty-five years, David thought. Stacked up against careers, Madison, and a succession of dog leashes, holding hands had slowly become uncomfortable and embarrassing, like the silence after a racial joke.

They walked along Jasper Avenue, through thin puddles of melted snow. To enjoy the surprising warm air, they had exited the LRT one stop early. There was another Garneau Block meeting on the thirty-eighth floor of Manulife Place. On the way, without politics or Garith between them, David was rediscovering the muscles and veins and soft skin of his wife's left hand.

"Do you put moisturizer on these babies?" David stopped his wife in front of the Paramount Theatre and inspected her hands. "This doesn't just *happen*, does it?"

"I wish it did."

David took both his wife's hands and squeezed them. "I'm really, weirdly delighted."

"Me too."

A couple of men in navy-blue suits, talking on cellular phones, passed with vacant stares. David watched the men as though they were cheerless ghosts of his former self. "Today I skipped the federal election stories in the paper. I didn't even look."

"I'm so proud of you." Abby kissed her husband on the ear.

They started out across Jasper Avenue. It would be another half-hour before the sun set, and as it peeked out from a bank of clouds over the west side of the city, Abby's face went soft orange. David touched her cheek.

Abby stopped him in the middle of the avenue. "Oh, my God, I want to slap you, I love you so much."

"Go ahead. Please."

"Really?"

"If it'll make you feel good."

Abby slapped David below the eye, just hard enough to make a sound. A Mini Cooper waiting at the now-green light honked and so they hurried to the north side of the avenue.

Inside Commerce Place, on the escalator to the mezzanine level, David was stricken once again with his scheme. That morning, lying in bed, listening to the melting snow drop off the roof of his house, he had devised a plan to save Madison. Busy with the newspaper, making lunch, taking Garith to Canadian Tire to buy a new shovel, and partaking of a mid-afternoon nap, he had forgotten to tell Abby. At the top of the escalator, he turned to her.

"So, suppose you're a mother."

"I *am* a mother."

"So suppose you're a *new* mother and you have friends who are also new mothers."

"Am I pretending to be a new mother?"

"Yes. Shhh." David held both sets of doors for Abby so she could pass into Manulife Place. "You're a new mother and you want to stay fit, but you don't have anyone to look after Baby. Daddy's working."

"Or he's a *maudit franco* . . ."

"And the grandparents are busy. What are you going to do?"

"Cry? Get fat? Hire a babysitter?"

"You'll go to the affordable gym, spa, and playschool that has an ample parking lot and brain-enhancing Beethoven piped through the public address system."

"Is there such a thing?"

"No. But there ought to be. First in Edmonton and then we'll expand to Cowtown. You and I will cash in our RRSPs and get a bank loan. We can use the university money as collateral and rent an apartment for a year or two, until the revenue starts coming in. Madison can manage it with us for the first few years and when we want to retire she'll buy us out."

Abby pressed the up button at the Manulife elevators. "But we're retired now, David. Don't you think we should stay retired?"

"That's the only real flaw in the scheme. It means we start a new career together."

The elevator doors opened. "But running a business? What sort of a capitalist would I be? If a mom came in and said she really needed to work out but she couldn't pay, what would I do then?"

"You'll be in the back, teaching twenty-two four-year-olds how to count in Italian."

"I will?" Abby chewed the tip of her index finger for a moment, then smiled. "That sounds nice, actually. So *you'll* tell the poor mom to go away?"

"You bet, honey."

The doors opened to the thirty-eighth floor and French piano music welcomed them instead of Angela, the tall blonde. It sounded to David as though the singer had smoked far too many cigarettes before he recorded the song.

Rajinder approached, his tie crooked. "Did Madison come with you?"

Abby stepped forward and placed a hand on Rajinder's back, walked with him. "No, sweetheart. She didn't have it in her."

Rajinder sighed and slouched. David turned into the boardroom, leaving Abby to comfort Rajinder in the hall. Love can destroy even a rich Indian man.

Shirley and Jonas were already seated across the table from each other with coffees. At the far end of the long table, cleanly shaven for the first time in a month, Raymond stood in a new suit. His ears were angry pink and almost twice their usual size. On the table before him, a white sheet was draped over what appeared to be a soccer ball. David walked around to lift a corner of the sheet and Shirley slapped his hand.

"Manners!"

74

the future of 10 garneau

Once everyone was seated, Raymond Terletsky closed the boardroom door. He twitched the sheet so it draped in perfect symmetry. Shirley smiled, recognizing – even missing – his obsessive-compulsive behaviour. He looked up.

"Is everyone ready?"

Shirley observed Jonas and Rajinder across the table. They both looked heavily medicated. Neither turned to respond to Raymond, so she waved and gestured at her estranged husband. She was pleased to see he had shaved the beard and that he had acquired a modern black suit, two developments that nearly overwhelmed the cotton-candy pink of his giant ears.

Raymond wiped a few flakes of dandruff from his lapels. "It's no coincidence that I chose the Day of the Dead, *el Día de los Muertos*, to reveal this vision of our collective future. When I was on sabbatical for a semester in the late 1980s, I travelled to Cuilapan in Oaxaca, Mexico, to understand both the Aztec and Christian influences in *el Día de los Muertos*, this

complex interpretation of what it means to be alive, surrounded by death, in a world of multiple –"

"Enough with the lecture, Dumbo." Jonas sipped his
coffee. "Just pull the sheet."

Shirley wanted to crawl over the polished mahogany table
and pluck the actor's eyes out.

Raymond touched his left ear. "Does everyone just want me
to pull it?"

"Yes," said Jonas. "Yes and yes."

"A show of hands?"

All but Shirley raised their hands.

"Thank you, my darling, a thousand times, for your
patience. But this is a democracy. I'll pull the sheet now as long
as you will let me explain for a minute before you ask any questions or dismiss my vision. Say, where's Madison?"

Rajinder reached out with both hands and scratched the
table. Abby made a throat-slitting gesture.

"Onward then." Raymond gripped the white sheet with
both hands, leaned forward over the conference table so that
the lump remained hidden for another few moments, made a
drum roll sound with his mouth, and pulled the sheet away
with a flourish. Displaced air moved through the room.

The chipped grey mannequin head, inconsistently pasted
with curly black hair and yellow hard-candy eyes, with a couple
of children's birthday-party hats on top, fell over. Raymond
stood it up again, but a clump of hair had fallen off.

"Son of a!" Raymond licked the clump of hair and made a
sour face of instant regret. He attempted to stick the hair back
on the mannequin cheek, but off it fell again.

Given the high-thread count of the white sheet, Shirley had expected a more impressive model.

"Oh, that is shit." Jonas laughed, and took another sip of coffee. "You're a *real* genius, professor. The Garneau Block is saved. Hallelujah."

David pointed. "Where did you get all that hair?"

"A barber's floor, but that's not important. The important thing is . . ."

Abby raised her hand. "You did a terrific job of it, Raymond, but I can't tell if it's a gorilla or a sasquatch. It's a sasquatch, yes?"

"Shut up," said Shirley, "all of you. Please."

The French music on the loudspeaker began to skip. *Mademoiselle*, went the song, *je reste à Paris*, again and again. After several repetitions, Rajinder stood on his chair, climbed on to the table, and pounded the ceiling.

The song resumed and Rajinder returned to his seat.

"All my gratitude, Shirley. Raj." Raymond recovered his earlier composure. "On Halloween night, on the verge of hypothermia, I received a vision. It was Death, in blue jeans and cowboy boots, with the head of a buffalo."

Jonas laughed again and stood up. "I'm going to go get drunk on rye whisky and play the VLTs."

"Sit," said Shirley.

"Come with me, baby."

"Sit."

Jonas flopped back in his chair.

"This is an admittedly crude model of a buffalo head, the future of 10 Garneau."

But for the French music and the gentle creaking of David's chair, as he rocked back and forth, the boardroom was silent.

Shirley raised her hand.

"Yes?"

"Raymond, are you saying you want to turn 10 Garneau into a . . . buffalo head?"

"That's precisely what I'm saying. We will do some renovations to the current house and cover it in a buffalo head shell."

"Rye whisky going once," said Jonas. "Rye whisky going twice."

"You see, the buffalo is the great martyred god of Edmonton. Sixty million of them wiped from the plains in ninety years, and for what? For the short-term —"

David raised his hand. "Won't the hair rot?"

"A terrific question, David. I have taken the liberty of contacting the DuPont company in Wilmington, Delaware, and they have just the product. It can freeze in the winter and bake in the summer. Moisture runs right off."

Jonas raised his hand. "You're a knob."

"I don't agree."

Despite the crudeness of the buffalo head model, Shirley didn't agree either. The tone of Raymond's voice reminded her of the student she had met thirty-five years ago. Back then, he was on his way to Yale and Oxford; he was going to be the leading philosopher of his generation. Marriage, fatherhood, lack of regular exercise, poor eating habits, and a long succession of career failures had erased all of that. Suddenly Raymond was back and she tilted her head at him. "What will go inside?"

315

"Another good question, and a difficult one. The new composer-in-residence of the Edmonton Symphony Orchestra was here this afternoon and we discussed that very thing. If we all agree that a buffalo head affords the highest possible degree of mythic power – and I think we can – the sights and smells and sounds *inside* that buffalo head are of supreme importance. I was thinking –"

"Will the buffalo head house have a mouth, Raymond?" Abby approached the model. "Because this thing doesn't really have a mouth."

He sighed and raised his arms. "Maybe it would be better if I *drew* the model."

Across from Shirley, Rajinder grunted. "Are there any objections or alternate solutions?"

"I hate it," said Jonas. "I'm humiliated for us all."

David nodded. "Yes, it's quite ridiculous. And I must say, Rajinder, a considerable waste of resources."

"Thank you," said Rajinder, flatly. He sighed. "A show of hands, please. Who would like to proceed with the head-of-a-buffalo house on the site of 10 Garneau? If we agree, I will hire architects and Raymond will organize a publicity campaign to shame the university."

Slowly, all but Jonas and David raised their hands. Abby approached her husband and whispered in his ear until he smiled naughtily and raised his right arm.

"Jonas," said Shirley. "Raise your hand, you big tit."

It took several minutes worth of sarcastic remarks, and Shirley's promise that she would indeed take a rye whisky with him after the meeting, but Jonas finally lifted a finger in support of the buffalo head.

75

the crying men

Shirley and Jonas took their rye whiskies at Earl's on Campus, where they also ordered a plate of calamari and some spinach-artichoke dip. For half an hour Jonas mocked the idea of a museum shaped like a buffalo head until, that particular engine of mockery running out of fuel, he concentrated on littering, politics, architecture, and weather.

"What are you really talking about, Jonas?"

He sprawled in his chair and finished his whisky. "I hope the university destroys the block with a bomb."

"Jonas."

"I'm feeling quite hateful, Shirley."

"Don't say that."

"I hate everything right now." Jonas looked out the window at the intersection, where a black sports car rumbled before a red light. "How much you want to bet that guy lets his car idle all the time? When it's cold and when it's hot. For hours. Hours! And then he complains about high oil prices, the stupid inbreeding gaybasher. I bet Carlos does that too. The barbarian coward son of a zealot."

"Jonas."

"I'm a fool for living here and so are you, Shirley Wong." Jonas turned around and addressed the drinkers and diners. "Only idiots live in Alberta! You're all redneck idiots and I hate you!"

A man in a camouflage jacket and a collection of rings in his lip and eyebrows waved. "I hate you too, buddy."

Jonas and the man met halfway across the room, shook hands and introduced themselves. For a couple of minutes they complained about urban sprawl, gun control, herbicide use, and the sorry state of contemporary literature. While this went on, Shirley dipped the last few deep-fried squid in tzatziki and gave her credit card to the passing server.

Jonas returned. "That man's nickname is The Goo. He introduces himself to strangers as The Goo."

"You see? Edmonton's not so bad. The Goo lives here."

"It'll take a lot more than The Goo to make me love this city again. I'm gonna need to win the lottery or something. Something drastic."

Shirley signed the bill and took her jacket from the nearby tree. Before it got too late she wanted to get back home to Steamer, who was probably reading that podiatry textbook she had bought for him. Jonas followed her out of the restaurant, laying some skin on The Goo as he passed.

"Hate on, brother," said The Goo.

They crossed the avenue and passed the university theatre, where men and women in suits and dresses sipped drinks and nodded at one another and laughed. Jonas stopped. Shirley thought he was going to make a spiteful remark about the student actors. Instead, his eyes filled with tears. "I'm forty-something and I'm lonely."

In September, Raymond had been fired. Then, a day ago, regretful about his roguish behaviour on Halloween night, Steamer had cried twice about breaking his parents' hearts and sinning himself straight to hell. Now, Shirley comforted her third crying man the way she always comforted a crying man, by rubbing her hand down the back of his head and saying, "Shhh."

She walked Jonas to his door and waited in the kitchen while he completed his bedtime washing, flossing, and brushing regimen. It was stuffy in his house, a marriage of unwashed dishes, cologne, and marijuana smoke, so she opened a window. When Jonas was finished in the bathroom, she drew a glass of water and tucked him into bed.

"Am I going to be okay?" said Jonas, as Shirley walked out of his dark bedroom.

"Of course you are."

Walking home, Shirley studied her neighbours' houses. Madison's lights were dim. Upstairs at the Weisses, there was life in the kitchen and in the spare bedroom, where Raymond lived. Through his picture window she could see Rajinder reading a hardcover book on the white couch, his legs crossed daintily.

She entered her front door and a blast of wind sucked her in. This meant the back door was open, which was not an energy-efficient idea in November. She called out to Steamer, and Patch answered from downstairs, "He's taking his last load out!"

Downstairs, Patch was watching a show about swimsuit models.

"Taking a load out to where?"

"To the truck. I gotta drive him to the bus station."

"Why?"

"Search me. Says he's movin' out."

"But why?"

Patch ignored her, so Shirley climbed the stairs and went out the open door. On the parking pad in the alley, Steamer was arranging his bags and two boxes in the back of Patch's big red truck, a thin flashlight between his teeth.

Shirley watched him for a moment. He hopped into the truckbed and pretended not to see her, even when the flashlight stopped on her face. For several minutes, Steamer packed the truck in silence. Then he kicked a box and jumped down onto the concrete in front of Shirley. "This morning I woke up and decided it has to be one way or the other."

"It."

"Me and you." Steamer turned away and started back to the house. He opened the back door. "Let's go, Patch!"

The motion sensor attached to the back door splashed 200 watts of light on Shirley. "You're making too much of this. It was just some dancing and foot massages."

"Ms. Wong, don't play-act here."

"Why does it have to be this way?" Shirley waited a moment, and then forced out: "Instead of . . ."

Steamer didn't answer. They stood together in the backyard light, until the sensor couldn't read them and it went dark again. When Patch appeared on the porch, with his hand inside two opened buttons on his shirt, scratching his hairy chest, Shirley understood immediately what she had to do. "You might as well load up too, Patch."

"What? Why?"

Steamer's honesty had inspired her. "You're a yob and I don't want you in my house."

"A yob?" Patch turned to his teammate with his mouth opened. "But I'm Patch."

Steamer led Patch into 11 Garneau and down the stairs, to start packing.

76

the press conference

Raymond Terletsky spent a sunny November morning in the Garneau Theatre, thinking about dry ice. It had fascinated him as a child. Was it still awesome? Was it too late to get some? The architects, Mr. Bradley from Calgary and Ms. Florette from Edmonton, positioned themselves behind a long table on stage and tested their microphones. Two sweating pitchers of water sat before them. Lynn, a very expensive public relations consultant, inspected the cinema for garbage and chewed gum.

"We're clean," said Lynn, from the final row. "I'm going to open the doors."

Instead of looking through the Yellow Pages for a dry ice manufacturer, Raymond approached his boss. Rajinder sat in one of the first-row seats, rocking back and forth and lazily chewing a tuna sandwich. In his other hand, Rajinder held a small

Styrofoam plate of strawberries plucked from the caterer's table.

"Are you ready?"

Rajinder lifted his tuna salad sandwich in triumph. Then he said, "No. I really do not know, professor. It is difficult to focus and summon energy, and for that I apologize."

Voices and laughter echoed into the auditorium as Raymond sat next to Rajinder. Since he himself had been feeling this low or lower just a couple of months previous, Raymond understood. "Is there anything I can do? I know a couple of Ukrainian jokes."

With a sigh, Rajinder shook his head and pulled the lint off a strawberry.

"Why don't you just call her up?"

"She does not answer the phone. I visited several times and she refused to come to the door. I bought flowers, sent candygrams, hired circus children to do backflips before her as she walked home from the travel agency."

"And nothing?"

"I admit, certainly, that I had imagined Madison to be without child when we began dating. I cannot deny I would have preferred to see *my* child in her belly than . . . the child of whomsoever. Yet . . ."

Rajinder allowed the *yet* to float there, a helium balloon with a slow leak.

"Figure out what you want and grab it, Raj." Raymond mimed snatching something from an invisible shrubbery. "Take it!"

A few chews of his tuna salad sandwich later, Rajinder sang, "*Les feuilles mortes se ramassent à la pelle, les souvenirs et les regrets aussi . . .*" and then bit into a strawberry.

"I'm sorry to have to say this, Raj, because I really admire you. But you gotta learn to fight past this. Maybe she's gone and, sure, that's sad. But you're a *millionaire*."

Rajinder helped Raymond up. "Very wise analysis, professor. Shall we attend to the lobby, shake some hands?"

Lynn, the public relations consultant, was worth her fee. Among the milling people, several officials from the university stood near the food tables. Two television cameramen had arrived, and the theatre manager was leading them into the auditorium. Abby and David Weiss walked in, hand in hand. A few minutes later, Jonas walked through the door in jeans and a blazer. The mayor, a personal friend of Lynn's, and his assistant followed Jonas inside.

The mayor put his arm around Jonas and complimented him on the one-man show he had performed at the Roxy last March. "I'm just a business guy so I don't always know art. But sometimes I know art and that was *art*."

"Thanks, Your Worship."

"What's next for you?"

"I was thinking of selling Saabs."

The mayor laughed. "Come on, I mean it."

"Your Worship, I've been acting professionally twenty-five years and I can't even get a decent credit card."

As Jonas walked up the stairs, a look of genuine disappointment passed over the mayor's face. Before the mayor or his assistant could chase Jonas, Raymond moved in.

"Mr. Mayor, hi. Sporting of you to come." Raymond put his hands on the mayor's shoulders. "Listen, you can't let this happen. You can't. If we lose the Garneau Block, the city loses everything. Everything. It's the first brick in a collapsing building, really, the sign of cultural decay, a strike at the heart of –"

"I look forward to hearing the presentation," said the mayor, and his assistant led him to the food table, abandoning Raymond on the carpeted entrance steps of the theatre. He told himself to calm down, to control his enthusiasm before he "harassed" a politician or attractive television reporter.

Raymond scanned the lobby, where the guests sipped wine and munched on spicy beef samosas. Almost everyone from the block was here now, save Rajinder, who had apparently returned to his seat in the auditorium, and Madison.

Alone next to the popcorn machine, Raymond wondered if somehow everyone knew about his drives up and down 95th Street, his trouble with the masseuse, his lurid fantasies. Was he on an Internet watch list of Alberta perverts and harassers?

The confidence drained out of Raymond, and he leaned against the wall. To his left, a poster advertised a movie about the day Wayne Gretzky announced he was leaving Edmonton to play for the Los Angeles Kings.

Madison came in the main door and nodded. "Professor."

"Hello."

"I'm looking forward to your speech."

"You are?"

"Of course, Raymond. Everyone is. You're our last hope."

77

the science of snubbing

Madison was in the mood for neither samosas nor spanako-
pitas, watercress dip nor truffled goat cheese crudités. She had
a hard time listening to her mother, Raymond Terletsky, the
mayor, or anyone else who spoke to her over the food tables in
the Garneau Theatre. Though she could not see him in the
lobby, Madison knew Rajinder was in the building. The rumble
in her stomach was stamped with his name, the smell of his
cologne, the hair between his eyebrows.

When the other guests filed into the auditorium, Madison
lingered in the lobby. Jonas hovered next to her. "Want me to
save you a seat?"

She nodded.

"Where do you want to sit?"

She shook her head.

"Come on, Maddy. Close to the stage or far away? On the
sides, the second level? You know how I am about choosing
seats. You might as well ask me which finger I should have
chopped off."

The smell of last night's buttered popcorn was wreaking
havoc on her empty stomach. All morning and the night before
she had been anxious about seeing Rajinder again. She had
practised resonant phrases, drawn from haikus, in case he

approached. Instead of answering Jonas, she waved him away and proceeded to the washroom.

Over the gentle, echoing drip in the toilet, Madison could hear the professor's amplified voice as the press conference began. "We decimated the buffalo in the name of progress and civilization yet we long for the beast's return with *every neutron in every cell in our bodies.*"

Madison felt the professor was overstating things a bit. How could he account for all the neutrons committed to the holiday shopping season, which had begun in earnest? Or the popularity of Latin American literature? She did appreciate the rising orchestral background; the string music was slow and delicate, with a hint of Eastern European failure about it.

The nausea passed and Madison emerged from the bathroom to take the least offensive item on the food tables – an egg sandwich on rye. She crept into the auditorium and leaned on the carpeted baffle behind the floor seats.

Rajinder sat on stage next to a young man and woman. According to the signs in front of them, these were architects. All three of them were turned to Raymond, who shook his fist behind the podium as he spoke of the need in our hearts for *stories about ourselves.* Not stories about young sorcerers from the United Kingdom and divorced New Yorkers who only think about shoes.

"Handsome man, isn't he?"

Madison didn't know if the woman next to her was referring to Raymond, Rajinder, or the young architect. "Yes."

"I understand he's very wealthy. His parents owned half of Mumbai, I heard."

"Really?"

The woman nodded. The sticker on the front of her blazer said LYNN. "Single too, they say. But he's super quiet. I was here all morning with him and I didn't hear a peep."

Usually, food pushed the nausea away. But at the moment, nothing would help. Madison sniffed the egg sandwich, regretted sniffing the sandwich, and dropped it in the garbage can next to Lynn. The architects took the podium, the lights went down, and the curtain opened. On the screen, a digital image of an enhanced 10 Garneau, covered in a shell shaped like a buffalo head. Some guests laughed, others gasped, and still others howled and applauded. "Yes," one man said, "finally!"

Back in the lobby, two women in uniform poured champagne into small disposable glasses. Madison walked to a side door that led to a concrete fire escape. For some time she stood there, watching the children run and scream in the playground of Garneau School. She resigned herself to moving out of her parents' basement and into affordable housing somewhere on the LRT line.

The blend of exhaust and wet mulch and pizza dough on the avenue was surprisingly pleasant. Madison took several long breaths and imagined herself back in the auditorium, laughing and applauding with all the normal people. *Yes, he is handsome. Handsome indeed, Lynn, yes. Touch him and you fricken* die.

Madison sat in the lobby during the explanations and the question-and-answer session. The mayor and his assistant left the auditorium laughing. Twenty minutes later, the rest of the crowd followed. Almost everyone continued straight out the front doors except Lynn's closest friends in politics and the media, some university officials, and the Garneau residents. They stood near the unveiled plastic model of the future block, complete with a buffalo head on the site of 10 Garneau. They pored over possible exhibits and interior designs. Some openly mocked it. Others openly mocked the mockers.

Two camera lights shone on the tanned face of a public affairs official from the university. The gentleman understood the magnitude of the tragedy that occurred this summer in the neighbourhood, and the historic integrity of Garneau, and he applauded this creative, community-based plan.

"But this land is ultimately under university control," said the official. "We must find a site for a new veterinary research centre. Now, of course, we're eager to work with anyone on cultural projects. For goodness' sake, we've been trying to build our own museum for years."

Raymond hovered close to the cameras. Then, provoked by something, the professor bolted across the lobby to Rajinder, where he whispered and gestured wildly. Rajinder looked past him and met Madison's eye. Slowly he lifted his hand. Unsure whether to continue torturing herself, Madison waved back.

Just for a moment.

Rajinder smiled and Madison didn't want to smile but she smiled anyway. Her cheeks went hot and she bit her lips to banish the smile until Abby stepped between them.

"Did you see that model? We could actually live next door to a buffalo head."

"Even if the university agrees, Jeanne won't sell. She'll hate it."

Abby snapped her fingers. "We could bring her a tray of carrot muffins. Who could say no to that?"

"It's best to leave her alone."

"Your father's trying to snub the PCs." Abby turned toward David, who stood near some men with suits, his chin raised. "But these people won't be snubbed."

Madison turned away from the ineffective snubbing to stare at Rajinder, to try not to smile at him some more, but he was gone from his corner. She stepped into the middle of the lobby and spotted him, from behind, leaving the theatre with Raymond Terletsky.

78

american or japanese

Abby Weiss sat behind the steering wheel of a hybrid SUV. "I liked the Toyota better."

"Listen sweetheart, you're just saying that because this one's an SUV. What I'm trying to get across is it's a good SUV." David summoned all of his energy and prepared himself for a long afternoon. "Now sit back in that tasty leather and give this one a chance. Put your hands on the wheel. Think about how this will blend with the giant buffalo head next door."

Abby pretended to drive. "We don't need all this space, and

the little cars are cheaper. Think of all the cows that had to die for these seats."

"They were going to die anyway, Abby. We barbecued them in August, remember?" David hopped out of the passenger door and walked around the vehicle. A salesman with fake hair had been hovering since they walked into the showroom. For ten minutes, David had done his best to avoid eye contact. But the salesman intercepted him by the opened hood before he could reach the driver's side window, and Abby.

"She's a beauty, ain't she?"

"What's your name?"

The salesman shot his hand out so fast David thought he was about to receive a blow to the solar plexus. "Greg McPhee."

David kept his voice quiet, so Abby wouldn't hear. "Listen, Greg McPhee, go grab a donut or something. We're buying a hybrid and I want one of yours." He turned around to see Abby leaning her head out the driver's-side window. "My wife wants a little foreign number."

"No, no, no." Greg McPhee shook his head. "That'd be a *huge* mistake, sir."

"I know, I know. But my wife's easily infuriated by a certain kind of consumerism. She won't like you at all. So how about this, Greg McPhee? If we want one of these, I'll find you."

"If you have any questions –"

"I don't. Now beat it."

David pretended to inspect the engine for a minute, as though he knew what was going on in there.

"Nice," he said, "real nice," as he sidled up to the window and Abby. "You know, I was thinking. This vehicle proves you wrong about North America being a gas-addicted monstrosity hypnotized by multinationals. Unionized workers built this thing in Michigan."

"Kansas, actually!" Greg McPhee handed David a brochure with a big smile. He winked at Abby. "How you doing today?"

David slapped the side of the SUV. "What did I just tell you?"

"I'm beating, I'm beating." Greg McPhee hurried away to a cluster of pickups.

"Sweetheart, if we buy a Japanese car we'll just make elitists of ourselves, alienate our own people, drive them to Hemis."

"David, please, we don't have a *people*. We're Canadians."

"You know what I mean."

Abby opened the truck door. "This company, all these companies, have reprehensible environmental records. Every other vehicle in this showroom is a crime against humanity."

"But sweetheart, you have to admit . . ."

"I'll admit nothing." Abby pulled the brochure out of his hands and flipped through it. She pointed at the green-power logo on the front and shook her head. "Criminals. *Criminals.*"

David leaned against a shiny pickup truck and pondered his next move. A few metres away, Greg McPhee smiled and shuffled like a nervous ballet dancer waiting for his big demi-plié. David bared his teeth.

There were a few weapons in David's arsenal that he could always pull out to soften Abby. He could sing one of four songs from Joni Mitchell's *Blue*, an album that held magical sway over his wife. Its relevance in this situation, unfortunately, was wanting.

It came to him like a jolt of caffeine.

"Sweetheart," he said, and put his hand on Abby's waist. "If we start that business together, we'll need a vehicle. The little SUV will carry children *and* the toys and bags and giant strollers children of this generation always seem to have."

"So will the little cars."

"What about poor Maddy? When she borrows the hybrid and has to carry her little bambino into the house, are we going to make her bend down? Bend down and strain those precious muscles? She's already doing this all by herself. If we're going to make her bend down like that, we might as well push her against a wall later this afternoon and punch her in the lower back."

"You're veering into ridiculousness."

"Let's at least take it for a test drive."

Abby sighed and rolled her eyes. "This is stupid, David. It doesn't pass the need test. For me, it doesn't even pass the want test."

"Greg McPhee!"

The salesman came running over, his shoes squeaking on the shiny floor. "Yes, sir?"

"Can we take one of these for a test drive?"

"You bet, sir. Ma'am. If you'll just follow me into my office here."

David and Abby followed Greg McPhee, who walked with his toes pointed way out, to his office door. "You're gonna love 'er," he said, as Abby signed a couple of insurance forms. "She's a real beaut."

Aware of Abby's growing irritation, David put his index finger in front of his lips.

Greg McPhee winked and nodded.

On their way out to the car, David said into his ear, "If you say *beaut* one more time, all this is finished. We'll be driving right back to the Toyota dealership."

"No beauts. Gotcha."

In the lot, Greg gave Abby the keys and explained the particularities of the engine. As he did, the salesman referred to the hybrid SUV as a daisy, a sweetheart, a baby girl, and a little lady. Right after *little lady*, Abby dropped the keys on the concrete and walked to the Yukon.

79

the god of all that is good

Raymond squeezed his bottle of Dutch beer so hard he thought it might break. Fearing humiliation, he opened his eyes and closed them again as Rajinder switched back and forth between two local television news programs. At the end of an item on obesity, the Garneau Block story began.

"In the nineteenth century," said Raymond, next to the model in the lobby of the theatre, "the great European cities were defined by language, war, history, the industrial revolution. Edmonton is defined by singular forces today, however more subtle they may be. The boom cycle, immigration, triumph and murder and gambling and theatre, the ghosts of recent wilderness, a powerful river."

Jonas laughed. "What a pile of bullshit, professor."

The shot switched to a slow pan of the Garneau Block. The reporter made a lot of the fact that Raymond didn't know what actual *stuff* would go inside the buffalo head. Rajinder pointed at the television. "There is Madison. Her shiny legs in that red Japanese skirt."

Raymond was pleased that Madison had smiled at Rajinder in the theatre. Suddenly, the patron had some enthusiasm for his project. However, Raymond was not pleased to see they had cut out the most resonant parts of his interview, when he expanded on the mythic power of buffalo and the mystery and beauty of the North Saskatchewan River. He had even quoted Gwendolyn MacEwan. After a short bout of disappointment, Raymond was stricken with the certainty that the boobs in the editing suite had laughed at him.

The university public affairs official provided his counter-argument. Jonas opened a new beer. "Liar. Dirty liar. Stinking whoring greasy . . . do you guys think they're really planning on building a veterinary medicine centre here?"

Rajinder, in his seat again, shrugged. "Raymond and I rushed to see my friend on the board of governors this afternoon, and he confirmed it. Yes."

"May Dean Kesterman burn, burn, burn." Raymond imagined the burning for an instant, with a stake and some kindling underneath, the flames licking up teasingly at first and then, as the Dean screams, *inferno!* He sat back and lifted his bottle of beer. "Don't be discouraged, fellows. We'll get that cultural designation. We can convince the people of Edmonton that art and mythic power are more important than beef."

Rajinder and Jonas looked at one another, and then at Raymond. "Fat chance," said Jonas.

"We must argue there are better places in the city for a veterinary centre. The buffalo head house must be here." Rajinder pointed out the window at 10 Garneau. "In this neighbourhood."

Raymond walked to the window and looked out over the falling snow, illuminated by the street lamps. "It needs a better name than the buffalo head house."

"I met a guy the other night called The Goo," said Jonas.

"We can't call it The Goo." Raymond turned and regarded his two friends in their chairs. "It needs to sound inevitable. It needs to sound as though it has existed for all time."

"It's only a buffalo head house with a bunch of we-don't-know-yet inside," said Jonas. "So it needs a cool name."

"At one time, this area was a rolling sea of buffalo." Raymond tapped his bottom lip with the neck of his beer bottle. "To have killed them all: this is the very essence of us. We are capable of philosophy and love and science yet . . . yet we rape and destroy. The end of buffalo, the life of Benjamin Perlitz, this is us."

Rajinder paced the room with Raymond. "What do the Aboriginal people call their chief deity?"

"Manitou?" said Jonas. "But we can't call it Manitou, the god of all that is good. The guy who plays Manitou in the soaps is an illiterate little dope fiend. After a show he smells like the plastic wrap wieners come in. You know, that wiener juice?"

"The great spirit." Raymond put his hand on Rajinder's shoulder. "We can call it The Great Spirit. That way it's native-y and not-native-y all at once, urban and rural, churchy and secular. The Great Spirit says everything."

"Yes," said Rajinder.

They turned to Jonas. He paced a bit himself, and joined the other two men in the centre of the room. "The Great Spirit." A truck commercial featuring splashed mud and busty young women in cut-off jeans blasted country music on the television. Jonas watched the commercial for a moment, scowled, and turned to Raymond and Rajinder. "I hate everything, and I don't hate it."

Raymond pulled a small notepad out of his pocket and wrote:

THE GREAT SPIRIT
10 GARNEAU
EDMONTON, ALBERTA
CANADA

80

carlos's last stand

Jonas and Rajinder and Raymond celebrated their revelation. After drinking several beers each, it seemed important they retire to Rajinder's backyard and frolic in the new snow. Jonas could not remember who suggested it, but at some point they drew a squared circle and engaged in a wrestling tournament with no hitting or kicking.

Fifteen seconds into the opening bout between Raymond and Rajinder, the professor called uncle and proceeded to his bedroom at the Weisses' with what he called "a severely kinked neck."

Before he left, Raymond kissed both men on the mouth.

Raymond's sloppy kiss reminded Jonas that he was a failure with no romantic prospects. So instead of burdening Rajinder with a weepy tale of misfortune, he wiped the snow off the young Indian man and took the long way home.

Snow was romantic in a different way than rain. On a windless night with the temperature hovering around zero, after seven to nine bottles of Dutch beer, light snow and mature trees helped Jonas feel bigger than himself. In his twenties, he had often felt this way, humming, with an irresistible sort of energy.

At his best, on stage, he knew the audience plugged into this energy. Jonas also recognized, in moments of pure honesty, that his transistor was fading. New kids coming out of the university and Grant MacEwan were upstaging him. Even when the audience didn't feel it, Jonas did. And if he did not act now to get out of acting, his reliance on diminishing energy would eventually destroy him.

The long way home, from Rajinder's house, was through the alley and past the closed diner, bike shop, lounge, and travel agency. A block west to Emily Murphy's house and north to Saskatchewan Drive. The cool dampness in the air, after a warm day, brought a particular kind of fragrance to the air. A smell that would soon hibernate until its stinky cousin arrived in March.

Jonas walked into campus and past the Arts Building where, as always, he stopped to admire the classical details and wonder why the cheap fools who built this city didn't follow its model everywhere else. His careerlessness hit him like a snort of amyl nitrate and he considered going back to school for a law degree or an MBA. That way, sometime before his death, Jonas might actually be able to afford one of the 1905 American Foursquare houses he passed on his way back to the Garneau Block.

In the alley, Jonas greeted two cats. One of them flopped on its back, in the snow, to receive a belly rub. He entered his backyard and noticed another, much larger creature slumped on its back in front of his door. It was convenient and soulful to live in the inner city but there were compromises, including close relations with the homeless and destitute.

As long as the man wasn't trying to ruin or steal anything, Jonas would be kind. This wasn't the first time an uninvited visitor had taken advantage of his covered back patio. The man wore a parka and lay in the fetal position, his back to Jonas.

"Okay, time to get up." Jonas walked on to the concrete patio. "*Levántate.*"

Carlos rolled over and sat up and rubbed his eyes. "What time is it?"

"Late." Jonas sighed and leaned on a white plastic deck chair. "Why are you sleeping in front of my door?"

"I was gonna sleep in the 'stang but then you wouldn't find me." Carlos sniffed and hugged himself. "Were you out at the Roost tonight?"

Jonas sensed a species of jealousy in Carlos's tone. "No."

"Where were you?"

"None of your business. Now get up. I'll make you some coffee and you can drive home."

"You're drunk, Jonas. I can hear it in your voice."

"Of course I'm drunk." Jonas held his hand out.

Carlos took his hand and pulled Jonas in for an awkward embrace. It didn't last long. Jonas wanted to shake Carlos and shout at him, and he wanted to tell Carlos how miserable he had been since Halloween night. Most of all, Jonas just wanted to ask Carlos to stay with him.

Instead, Jonas said nothing.

"You don't miss me?"

"I can't."

Carlos stepped away from Jonas. "You can't miss me or you can't be with me?"

"I just can't."

"Why? Because I'm not gay enough?"

Jonas wanted to lift one of the terra cotta tomato planters and smash it on the concrete. If he opened his mouth, he knew what he would say. So again, despite his drunkenness, he stayed quiet.

"I love you."

"No you don't."

Carlos made two fists and growled. "Why do all you people have to be like this? Why does it have to be politics? Why can't it just *be*?"

"It's dishonest."

"My feelings aren't dishonest." Carlos pushed a plastic deck chair over. "Isn't *that* what's important?"

The saliva in Jonas's mouth had gone rancid. His heart was beating too fast and when he looked down he saw his hands were shaking.

"I'm not a bad person." Carlos backed out from the patio into the snow. "You know I'm not."

At that moment, Jonas teetered between kissing Carlos and shouting at him. In what he felt might be his last great performance, Jonas pretended he didn't care. Without a word, Jonas turned, opened his back door, and went inside, where he was bombarded by the mournful smell of his kitchen – two old banana peels, coffee grounds, and an unwashed fried egg pan.

81

drunk on risk

Madison sat in the backseat of the Toyota Prius with Garith. The dog panted madly and paced from one tinted window to the other, hopping over Madison's lap and slamming into her expanding belly. On Whyte Avenue, they passed a dog walker with a golden retriever, two dachshunds, and a standard poodle. Garith hopped and howled, slamming his wet nose into the window.

"Are those the puppies?" David's voice rose to a squeak at the end of the sentence. "Where's the puppies, Garith?"

Madison and her parents were on their way back from ATB Financial, where David and Abby had applied for a $750,000 business loan. In their smart black and grey suits, they were so giddy, so touchy, so drunk on their own financial risk that Madison worried their recent personal and political transformations were the results of a shared psychological disorder. That, or a lot of cocaine. To her immense discomfort, Madison had even heard moans coming from their bedroom in recent days.

Why had her parents dragged her to the bank? Certainly not for aesthetic reasons, as she had grown rapidly in the last couple of weeks and didn't have any proper maternity clothes. All Madison could wear at the moment were Hawaiian-print muumuus from her mother's pre-aerobics period in the early 1980s, so she probably didn't do much to impress the commercial banking manager, a tiny-nosed man of her generation named Trent, to whom David, in the midst of an attack of inappropriateness, offered a meagre dowry if he'd "join the Weiss team."

For this reason, and because they had ignored her earnest desire to stay out of the fitness business, Madison was not speaking to her parents.

"Come on, darling." Abby turned and reached for Madison's hand. "Why so glum? You've got to take the world by the nuts. Embrace change, make it your own."

"That Trent was a good-lookin' fella if you ask me," said David.

In the alley, as David stopped to press the garage opener,

Madison escaped with the dog. Before she slammed the door closed, both her parents called out to her. But their spirits were unassailable. They exited the garage holding hands, talking to Madison and Garith as though they were both dogs.

Madison already had her key in the lock when she turned and spotted Carol the Courier. Carol dropped her bicycle on the sidewalk in front of her parents' house and approached the mailbox.

"Dad, the university courier is here again."

David stopped kicking snow in Garith's face, one of the dog's favourite games, and hurried to the front of the house. Abby and Madison followed him.

"What is this?"

Carol the Courier shrugged.

The brown envelope from the university appeared thin. David shook the envelope before he ripped it. He peered inside and then suggested they go in the house, on account of the unpleasant wind.

Abby put some water on the stove to boil and they sat in the living room, Madison across from her parents. David pulled out two pages. "A media advisory."

"We're not the media." Abby took the pages and scanned them while David stuck his hand into the envelope looking for anything else. She scooched in close to her husband on the chesterfield. "Uh-oh."

Madison shook her head. "What?"

"They're making an announcement tomorrow afternoon at the Faculty Club and we're invited."

David took the pages back. "What are they announcing?"

"A decision on the Garneau Block."

Madison looked across the street, at Rajinder's house. He would be downtown at this hour, 10:50 in the morning. The artists-in-residence would be arriving right about now with giant coffees, walking into their studios as though they were about to attend their own funerals. Raymond would be manic.

And Rajinder? Planning lunch with the gorgeous twenty-five-year-old daughter of a wealthy Edmonton family? Interviewing gorgeous twenty-five-year-old candidates for the next artist-in-residence cycle? Watching French movies starring gorgeous twenty-five-year-olds who could speak proper French?

Merde alors.

Behind her, David and Abby speculated on whether the announcement would be positive or negative.

"They wouldn't have a press conference on a Thursday if it was negative," said David. "I mean, in politics that's a disaster. You always release bad news on Friday at 4:30 in the afternoon, even later."

Abby stood up to tend to the boiling water in the kitchen. "Now we'll have two things to celebrate, the loan and the block."

"And our grandchild." David joined Madison at the window and rubbed her hair. "We can't celebrate that enough, can we, Maddy?"

"I guess not."

David kissed his daughter on the cheek. "I'm sorry we won't be here for your ultrasound."

"I'd rather be in London myself than have an ultrasound."

"It's a *business* trip, remember? We're checking out a couple of spas that offer math and science tutoring. Very innovative."

David seemed to grow tired of hearing himself talk. Madison felt her father staring at her left cheek, and eventually he poked her arm. "Sorry I embarrassed you with Trent."

"Didn't you see his ring? Or my muumuu?"

David looked at his watch and put his jacket back on. "I better flee, Bruce Lee. A couple of federal Liberals want to meet me for coffee."

"What are you talking to Liberals for?"

"Maybe they want to know how to have a somewhat less crappy political party."

David hurried into the kitchen to kiss Abby, bent down to wrestle Garith for a minute, and opened the front door. "Can you believe your dear old dad's driving a Toyota Prius?"

Then he whispered so Abby wouldn't hear. "Inbred SUV salesman queered the deal by calling it girl names. Next thing you know I'll be eating tofu." He shoved his index finger down his throat a couple of times, produced a convincing gag, and bounded out the door.

82

higher education

Raymond strode into the Faculty Club a conquering hero. They had fired him, yes, but he had risen from darkness to smite them all. His dismissal had inspired the most creative period of his professional career, and as he walked through the doors, in one of his new suits, with his chest puffed out the way his father had taught him, Raymond smelled roast beef, mashed potatoes, horseradish, fresh bread, and victory.

Hands to shake? Eyes to meet with stern defiance? Bruschetta to devour? He scanned the room, but he discovered no one from the Arts Faculty. Where was Dean Kesterman, the wimp? After the announcement that the Garneau Block would live forever, and a few modest comments to the media, two bruschetta, and perhaps a devilled egg, Raymond planned to knee Dean Kesterman in the testicles. In fact, any of his former colleagues would do. His knee, covered in black Italian wool, was itching to knee some wimp's testicles. Whose would it be?

Most of his neighbours were already seated in the front row, with nametag stickers on their chests. The woman at the door, whom he recognized from the public affairs department, smiled and attempted to give him a nametag. But he would not have it. If you do not know Dr. Raymond Terletsky now, you will. Oh yes. *When The Great Spirit is unleashed, you shall know me.*

Raymond took a seat behind Shirley and greeted his neighbours. He winked at Rajinder. "We did it, pal. We did it."

"I hope so, Raymond."

The smell of his wife's perfume briefly inflamed him. He leaned forward. "Shirley Wong," he said, in her ear, "you are one of the world's great beauties. I was a fool to forget it. A damn fool. Let's go to Machu Picchu."

Shirley Wong reached back and pushed his head away. "Shush it."

At the front of the room, with large windows behind him, the chair of the university's board of governors tapped the microphone. Behind the man, wind moved the boughs of tall spruce trees on Saskatchewan Drive. It was a romantic scene. Perhaps there would be a tall spruce tree in the direct middle of The Great Spirit, Raymond thought, and pulled his African cave art notepad from his jacket pocket.

Spruce tree. Fake wind. Romance.

The man introduced the university president, stuttering slightly and fumbling words. He said "um" several times, and Raymond shook his head. Who writes these speeches? Why is rhetoric a lost art? "I'm already bored," he wanted to say, out loud.

The new president, a woman from Seattle, acknowledged the dignitaries and spoke in detail about Edmonton and Alberta being vigorous and diverse and powerful and progressive, not just a rich oil region but a centre of academic excellence with real tentacles out into the local community, the country, and the world.

"We've heard this one before, Madame President," said Raymond, into Shirley's ear.

The president looked down at her notes. A camera flashed. "Cultural excellence is just as important as scientific, mathematic, and critical excellence. And we recognize the Garneau Block Foundation's splendidly creative efforts to build a . . . bison head on property under the university's control."

There was a sudden pain in Raymond's abdomen. This boring speech was not so boring anymore. He wanted the president to pause, to change her tone. He wanted her to start over, give it another try.

"However, since the plan is still in its initial stages, and since we are not convinced the geographical location of the museum – is it a museum? – is essential to its success, the University of Alberta, in concert with the City of Edmonton, has decided not to grant cultural status to the property on 10 Garneau."

Raymond had to get to the microphone, deliver a counter-argument. Without excusing himself he started out from the seats, crashing into his neighbours' legs and stepping on their feet. Raymond careened out from the audience while the president continued.

"For several years, the university has been planning to build its own museum. And, as you all know, we received a generous donation of ancient and exotic textiles from Asia this spring. Therefore, we extend a hand to the Garneau Block Foundation even as we move forward in our plans to build a centre for veterinary research on the land. We . . ."

Raymond tripped on the small pile of black cords handling the public address system. In the process of falling, he didn't just tackle the president of the University of Alberta, he also knocked the podium to the floor with his forehead, which sent a piercing squeal through the room. On top of the president, who writhed and shrieked on the floor of the Faculty Club, Raymond couldn't recall what he had intended to say. His head hurt. It wasn't crucial, as the president didn't seem prepared to debate at the moment.

"Madman! Madman!"

Several men pulled him off the president and pinned him to the floor. As they did, Raymond found himself looking around for a madman. How did a madman get past the public affairs representative? And really, what *is* a madman? One woman's madman is another woman's husband or father.

The new black suit was in danger of sustaining a rip in the underarm, so Raymond stopped squirming. The president righted herself and throughout the room people exclaimed, moaned, laughed. The laughter sounded as though it belonged to Jonas Pond.

"Jonas," he said, "where are you?"

"We're with you, professor! You crazy son of a bitch!"

The president stood over Raymond and fixed her dress. She turned to one of her assistants. "Who is this Frankenstein's monster?"

Raymond clenched his teeth and closed his eyes.

83

the documentary

Jonas found the balance between talking too little and talking too much, being too jokey and too serious, supergay and super-straight. He enunciated, but not so much that he sounded like Cary Grant.

In short, he was perfect.

"Where do you want us to go?" Madison stood in the middle of the Garneau Block. They were already rolling and she had already been warned not to address the camera directly. But that's exactly what Madison did, again.

So Jonas sighed, took her arm, and led the way. "In Edmonton, you can either live downtown or in Old Strathcona. A lot of people say downtown is the way to go but there just aren't quite enough restaurants yet. Oh, and by the way, why can't the university build its veterinary thing somewhere else? Huh? Like in *Leduc*."

"Um," said Madison.

The producer, a tall woman from Toronto in a tiny jean jacket and scarf that weren't nearly warm enough, asked the cameraman to stop rolling. Jonas had delivered several clever lines, and he worried they would be lost. "Focus, Maddy, focus."

"Just be natural, you guys," said the producer. "Please, no speeches. Just talk to each other, not to the camera, the way you normally would while strolling through your neighbourhood. Pretend we aren't here."

"I'm not good at pretending." Madison pointed at Jonas. "And he isn't being himself."

"There is no self in acting."

The producer drooped slightly. "Remember, this isn't acting."

"Sweetheart, *everything* is acting."

"So act like you're not acting. Act like you're Jonas, the guy who's getting kicked out of his neighbourhood. The guy who needs to find a new apartment."

Jonas engaged in some mouth exercises, as it was around zero and his lips could freeze up at any time. Drooling on *The National* was not ideal. "Map of Indonesia. Look, looters. In

Paris, people portent pantaloons." He shadow-boxed for a few seconds. "All right, I'm ready."

"Action," said the producer.

Jonas led Madison toward the eastern edge of the block. "You have to be a few blocks north of Whyte, or the kids'll get drunk on the weekends and throw up on your peonies."

Madison smiled and shook her head. "I'm not so worried about that."

"I am, because stupid people irk me."

"Jonas."

"All right, compromising irks me. The Garneau Block is *perfect*, which is why all this is so tragic. You're close to the university, close to Whyte, close to downtown, yet far from vomit."

"That isn't true, Jonas. In September, at the frat houses? When it's hot out, all you can smell is puke."

"Either way, I don't want to move away."

Madison paused and looked around. "It won't be home."

"Home, which is something we have for another . . ." Jonas looked at his watch. "Twenty-nine days."

"They said we could take an extra week in January, on account of the holidays."

Jonas broke the rule and addressed the camera. "If only every university were as compassionate as ours."

The producer allowed a moment to pass and clapped her hands. "Now, please, if you guys could just back up to the corner again and do the same walk."

"You said you wanted natural," said Madison.

"No talking this time. We just want to shoot you from behind. Then you're done."

The cameraman set up and Jonas and Madison walked, gesturing with their hands while they imitated themselves talking. After two takes, the producer released them and walked deeper into Garneau to find B-roll.

Alone with Madison, Jonas had trouble easing out of character. In front of 10 Garneau, he remembered what he had meant to ask her. "Why does David want to take me out for a drink?"

"I don't know."

"Maybe he's confused after that hug in Manulife Place when we were drunk."

"My dad's not really the confused type."

Jonas had to agree. David Weiss seemed rather staunch about his heterosexuality. "I've been taking St. John's Wort, for the career-related depression. So far it hasn't done sweet jack nuts. There's an ad in the paper every day for call centre jobs, with benefits and holidays, and I dream about the ad. The ad is an emotional prison."

"Emotional prison."

"You're getting fat, hey?"

"I can't fit into anything. My top button is always undone." Madison looked down. "Maybe it's the hormones, but I really, really don't want to move. Where's my baby supposed to –"

"Can you not? The St. John's Wort hasn't really kicked in."

Rajinder Chana came out his front door, wearing an old brown business suit and work gloves. He waved and addressed himself to a pile of sunflower carcasses. Madison began to veer home so Jonas took her hand and dragged her toward 13 Garneau.

"Hello, Indian neighbour!"

Rajinder turned and smiled. "Hello. You two."

Madison had stopped squirming so Jonas released her. "Damn. That is a fine outfit, Raj."

"I understand it is ridiculous." Rajinder looked down at himself. The brown suit seemed two sizes too big. "It was my father's favourite and I could not throw it away. So it is my work suit."

"And the shirt and tie?"

Rajinder pulled at his blue silk tie and concentrated on it for a few moments.

An airplane passed overhead, and all three of them looked up to watch it pass. Jonas wanted to be on it, wherever it was going. When Rajinder stopped looking at the sky, his eyes went directly to Madison's swollen belly. Her swallow was audible.

"I am tired of this." Rajinder pulled his gloves off and dropped his shovel. "I waited too long and now the ground is frozen. It was only a cure for boredom. Can I invite you in for a piece of wild blueberry pie? Last night I made the pie to cure insomnia. All these cures. It is not an abominable pie."

Before she could bolt, Jonas took a handful of Madison's jacket. "We'd be delighted," he said.

84

surrounded by bizet

Rajinder Chana's wild blueberry pie was better than *not abominable*, but not much better. A couple of the blueberries were still frozen, most were sour, and the crust was chewy. If Rajinder asked for her opinion, Madison vowed to be honest. But she doubted she would get the chance to speak.

Jonas was running his mouth about the university, same-sex marriage, the PC leadership race, Raymond Terletsky's assault charge, the overall smelliness of live buffalo, the healing powers of a nice glass of Scotch, and the inevitability of his career as a phone solicitor.

This went on for some time, and Jonas seemed prepared to talk all day long. He allowed comments but Madison didn't feel inspired or provoked by anything Jonas said. In Rajinder's house, in the earthy smell of Rajinder's house, all she really wanted to do was throw a couple of pillows around and bawl.

Rajinder didn't seem to have much to say either. Every few minutes, he would offer more Scotch for Jonas and more chamomile tea for Madison. The Garneau Block, once his chief passion, seemed lost to him. When Jonas asked about Jeanne Perlitz, how she took the news of the university's plan, Rajinder just shrugged.

"My mouth is getting dry, you assholes," Jonas said, finally, after a monologue about melting polar ice caps. "Please. Please say something."

"Global warming is a concern of mine as well." Rajinder looked into his tea.

Madison nodded. "Eco . . . systems."

"Oh Jesus, you two." Jonas approached the stereo. He inspected a Bizet jewel case, opened the slot, and put the disk inside. The music began far too loudly, so Jonas turned it down. "If you don't stop this I'm going to urinate on the coffee table."

"Oh," said Rajinder.

Madison wanted to clang both men over the head with the stone Krishna and Radha statue. Yes, she wanted to be with Rajinder. Of course she did. But not if he was the sort of man who threw temper tantrums simply because, for example, he discovered his girlfriend had been impregnated by a smelly Québécois hiker. Then again, in the past couple of weeks Madison had wondered whether it was Rajinder's reaction or her own shame that had kept her from answering the door when he arrived with flowers. Like him, she wished they could enjoy a traditional courtship, without a remnant of the past growing inside her. But her shame had diminished. Madison no longer wished the baby would go away. The little thing was all hers now. Jean-something became more and more remote every day. If Rajinder couldn't accept it, she didn't want him.

But she did want him.

Madison understood she was being stubborn, immature, and self-destructive. Yet there was comfort in allowing herself to be the cloistered victim.

Surrounded by the earthy smell and Georges Bizet, she decided not to clang anyone over the head with a statue.

"Can you leave us alone please?" said Madison.

Jonas pointed to himself and Rajinder. "Me or him?"

"You, Jonas."

"I'm not done my Scotch. Why do I have to go? There aren't any secrets here."

"Please."

Rajinder nodded. "It would be simpatico."

"This is a rip-off. I didn't mean you had to have a talk right *now*. Wait until tomorrow, when I'm out looking for a call centre job or maybe something in used mattress sales. At the moment I'm really digging this Scotch."

Madison clapped her hands together in prayer. "Jonas?"

"Take the Scotch, my friend."

"I don't drink alone. What do you take me for?" Jonas downed his Scotch, put on his jacket, and slipped into his shoes. "I'll be across the street. If you guys decide you need a mediator or just a friend, give me a ring."

Rajinder met him at the door and shook his hand. "Thank you for your understanding. Madison and I really must —"

"I know, I know." Jonas opened the door and left, his footsteps on the porch and down the stairs. His head bobbing in front of the picture window. Madison watched him, and used him as a reason to remain silent as long as she could.

Bizet was a veil over the room. Weeks ago, when they had been alone, conversations had been easy. They were a couple of chatty introverts, unfolding their lives. Now it felt as though a CBC producer stood at the end of the hall, begging them to be authentic.

Madison had only been this uncomfortable once before, on the night of her sixteenth birthday. She returned from a roller-coaster party at West Edmonton Mall to encounter her parents at the dining room table with a small paperback called *Talk Sex* by Dr. Sue Johanson. David and Abby wouldn't accept Madison's assurances that she already knew everything from health class and movies, and they proceeded to deliver a speech – based on handwritten notes – about masturbation, heavy petting, oral sex, and . . . *it*.

"Jonas is a comical man," said Rajinder.

"He is."

"You have known him a long time."

"Ten years or so. He's a good guy."

"Yes. Yes."

"And a complete ass, too."

"It is difficult to be funny. One is born with it, I think. Like eye colour."

"I'm not funny."

"Yes, you are funny at times." Rajinder coughed and shook his head. "But I am not. When I try to be funny, I merely confuse people."

"Some books are funny. There's this one book –"

"I am beyond sorry," said Rajinder. "I behaved poorly."

Madison had wanted to be tough, but her tear glands did not co-operate. "No, no it was all my fault. I was scared to tell you because I thought you wouldn't like me any more, and then when I did tell you I –"

"Like you?" Rajinder hurried over to her chair and lifted her out. "I love you."

"You do not."

"No, I really actually do."

Madison sobbed violently. Snot gushed out of her nose and on to Rajinder's father's favourite suit. It took fifteen minutes for her to say she loved him too.

85

the edmonton remand centre

Due to the ferocity of his attack on the university president, the special testimony of Claudia Santino, and his own snooty behaviour the following morning at the bail hearing, Raymond spent a few days in jail. When Shirley Wong refused to pay for his release, and forbade his friends to do it, Raymond spent two more.

On the fifth day, Shirley asked Abby to look after the Rabbit Warren and she took the LRT downtown. Since Raymond wasn't a risk to the Crown, the police allowed them to meet in a small conference room in the Remand Centre.

In the conference room, his beard patchy and uneven, Raymond cradled his left arm in his right hand. Before Shirley had a chance to ask him what had happened, he showed her his new tattoo. The word BEEYATCH spanned three inches just below his elbow.

"You want to know how they made my tattoo?"

Shirley was horrified. It was a bloody mess.

"They cut me with a sewing needle and used the ink from a Bic pen. A Bic pen! And guess what would have happened if I had complained or cried out?"

Raymond lifted his hand to stop her before she could speak. "*Other* forms of initiation."

When she had endeavoured to teach Raymond a lesson, this was not what she had imagined. Shirley had assumed prison was sort of like *M.A.S.H.*, without the doctoring, and not in Korea.

"I hope these past weeks have been gratifying to you." Raymond slouched in his chair. "With your little hockey players."

"On the contrary."

"You hate me."

"I don't hate you."

"Well, it's some lunatic sicko kind of love, letting me spend a week with a collection of addicts and mental defectives. My bunkmate, a charming drug dealer and chronic masturbator from Saskatoon, gave me a nickname. You want to know what it is?"

Shirley pursed her lips. She wanted to wait a few minutes before telling Raymond he was free.

"The pink lady."

"The pink lady?"

"They call me the pink lady."

"Why?"

Raymond pounded the table and slouched again. "I'm not telling."

"The kids are coming home for Christmas."

"Both of them?" Raymond's tone changed, and he smiled. He shook his head. "I can't believe it. How long has it been?"

"Six years."

"Am I allowed to come? I mean, at least to dinner?"

Shirley held out her hand. After a moment of confusion, Raymond took it and followed her out of the interview room.

"Did you bail me out?"

"I did."

Raymond's favourite guard, Yolande, a squat women with thick glasses and a Portuguese accent, dished him a thumbs-up. "It's been great having you, Dr. Terletsky."

"Thank you for everything, Yolande. For your protection and the chocolate-chip cookie yesterday. It was a hint of civilization."

Raymond gathered his clothes and completed all of the sign-out procedures, and they started out of the building southwest toward Winston Churchill Square. It was a cloudy day and almost dark even though it was not yet four in the afternoon. Light snow fell. Shirley did not speak until they reached the art gallery.

"If you agree to a couple of rules, I'll let you move back in."

They entered the square. Raymond did not respond. A group of boys sat and silently smoked at the cenotaph in front of the giant glass pyramid of City Hall. To Shirley, they didn't look older than ten or eleven. But an air of adult failure and desperation surrounded them already. Considering the boys, in their puffy parkas and obnoxious logos, Shirley was satisfied that despite all of her regrets and Raymond's lapses in sanity the family had never sunk so low.

At the southwest corner of the square, Raymond paused. "When?"

"Today. Tonight, after the game. I know you don't like hockey games but you're coming. What do you have at Abby and David's, apart from clothes?"

"Books. A mini-stereo and my *Magic Flute* CD."

Shirley started ahead but Raymond remained.

"You won't regret this. I'm going to be a good husband again, a good friend. A good man, really, and I'll follow all of your rules."

Raymond tried to kiss Shirley's hand but she pulled it away. "The first rule is no touching until at least Christmas. Now let's go. You'll need a shower and shave before the game."

By the end of the first period, the Oilers were leading the Boston Bruins 4–1. Merriment filled Rexall Place. The wave had passed three times and Shirley and Raymond had joined several refrains of "Here we go, Oilers, here we go." A group of twentysomethings in the nosebleeds had even sang the *na na na na, hey hey hey, goodbye* song.

In the opening minutes of the second period, Boston tied the game. The blues overtook the middle blue seats in Rexall Place. According to his custom, Raymond detached himself from the action at the most crucial point and began reading the program for the third time. He went for hot dogs and pop, and by the time he returned, Boston was ahead 5–4.

"Prison food is for real criminals," he said, two bites into his dog. "So what's the plan? It feels like we should get the neighbourhood together for one last effort. Physical attacks are out, I promise, but there's got to be something."

Shirley watched Ethan Moreau cross the Boston blue line and skate right into a giant Bruin defenceman. "Keep your head up, Ethan!" she said, and turned to Raymond. "We're going to do nothing."

"What do you mean?"

"I mean, Raymond, that's the second rule. We do nothing."

"So we're just going to let the heartless university bulldoze the Garneau Block and –"

"Yes."

"You can't be serious, Shirley."

"Those are my rules. My only rules. I mean, aside from the trawling for prostitutes business, which goes without saying."

Raymond clenched and released his fists. The Oilers iced the puck. A whistle blew. A commercial for snowmobiles exploded on the Jumbotron. "Should we stay in Old Strathcona? Or try Oliver?"

86

the political life

A bowl of popcorn with coarse black pepper sat on the small table between David Weiss and Jonas Pond. Though it was fluffy enough, and glistening with oil in the candlelight, neither man had taken a piece. A bottle of red wine also sat between them, so far unpoured.

While David related what he had read in the *Farmers' Almanac* about the weather this coming winter, Jonas considered escape routes. The scenario felt like either a prank or a trap. Though Jonas couldn't remember doing anything illegal in the past few months, his memory wasn't as elastic and reliable as it once was. Maybe David was working for the police, eager to have him arrested for . . . what? Looking at men in diapers on the Internet?

"It was a rainy summer, sure, but it isn't nearly as cold as it used to be around here. Not that I'm looking to blame anyone. Industry or whatever. It is what it is."

Jonas poured the wine. "I know what you mean."

"What? What do I mean?"

Since he hadn't been paying attention, Jonas just said, "The weather."

"Right, yes." David cracked his knuckles. "For all we know, Madison's child could be living in a desert in fifty years. If the oil peaks soon, maybe we'll all have to live closer to the equator. Unless, of course, the earth twists on its axis and we all die instantly. Making all of this moot." David lifted his glass and touched Jonas's glass. "Moot or not, we got the hybrid now. We're doing our part. Right? In a world of declining oil supplies, that's all a guy can do, right?"

"Moot." Jonas started to sip his wine and, instead, finished it in a couple of gulps. "David?"

"Yeah."

"What are we doing here?"

David placed an elbow on the table and squeezed his bottom lip between two fingers. He looked around the Sugarbowl. "I've become a Liberal."

"No."

"Yes, my homosexual comrade. A Liberal."

"How did it happen?"

"Peak oil, various treacheries that aren't your concern. Your concern is the upcoming federal election, and our common need for a credible candidate in this riding. The current nominee is polling badly and she's poised to drop out. In her place, we need someone with name recognition, a way with words, no criminal record, and a passion for public service."

"Uh-huh."

"Someone like you, Jonas."

Jonas finished laughing and filled his glass again. He imagined himself in the House of Commons, wearing a blue pinstriped suit. The so-cons would *love* a gay, quasi-trilingual man from a riding in Alberta. A quiver of warmth went through him. "Before I say anything, David, are we on camera?"

"No."

Jonas took a piece of popcorn and listened to the people around them, having their own insane conversations. His constituents.

"Listen, I know I haven't always been good to you, Jonas, but I grew up in a different era, when people like yourself were —"

"Stop talking. What would I have to do?"

"Come to our meeting tomorrow and get yourself nominated. You'll need twenty-five signatures, which shouldn't be too difficult."

The trouble with being a Liberal in Alberta, thought Jonas, is everyone hates Liberals. Jonas saw himself knocking on a door and smiling artificially, like a figure skater on his way down to the ice, while a woman tossed a cup of hot chocolate into his face. "*Thief! Boondoggler! Pedophile!*"

Besides, the Liberals didn't exactly throw a parade of unanimity over the same-sex marriage bill. "I don't know, David. Maybe I'm more of a New Democrat kind of guy."

David made a fist. "In federal politics, in Alberta, if you're anywhere left of the Conservative Party you have to be a Liberal. It doesn't matter if you're a Marxist-Leninist, a Green, or a member of the Marijuana Party. On paper, you have to be a Liberal. No matter how much it might hurt."

"What's a federal politician's salary? Ballpark?"

"With the tax advantages, we're talking six-figures. Any Liberal from Alberta who isn't a pinhead will also end up with a cabinet position. There's a lot more money in that, and travel."

"I'm not a pinhead."

"No, you aren't, Jonas. But you do get into the sauce a bit too often." David gestured at the wine glass. "It's something to think about."

"I still get hangovers so I'm not an alcoholic."

David leaned over the table. "If you decide to run, you'll have to be more discreet."

"Discreet. I can be discreet." Jonas finished his glass of wine and gestured at David to do the same. He slipped the server two twenty-dollar bills. "Let's get some air."

Jonas led David on his long way home, down Saskatchewan Drive and through campus. At a break in the trees, they spotted a couple in the valley playing golf in the snow with headlamps on.

As they walked, Jonas learned a thing or two about Liberal policy and the strict ethical guidelines that would govern politicians of his generation. With each crunchy step, Jonas felt more comfortable with the idea. It was better money than he would make as a hot tub salesman or a telephone solicitor, and he would still be performing. There might even be billboards!

It sounded lovely. Jonas wondered why he hadn't considered it before. "Why don't you run?"

"For most of my adult life I was a Liberal-hater, so they could nail me as a flip-flopper. Plus, certain political enemies of mine could make a pretty good case that I have racist views toward Aboriginals."

"Do you?"

"Absolutely not. But I did a bad thing to a homeless man."

Jonas put his arm around David. "Do you think I'll get to hang out with any Trudeaus?"

"Almost assuredly."

"Which ones? They're all so adorable."

"I can't say at this time, Jonas."

"I think I'd make a top-shelf Minister of Fisheries and Oceans. Don't you?"

David stopped at 110th Street and held out his hand for Jonas to shake. "Let's just get you elected."

Together they walked through the Garneau Block. There was a new feeling of loss and resignation around the five houses. Chimneys and skylights and address numbers and strips of crown moulding would be smashed and carted off to the landfill. The old trees would be firewood by spring. Jonas and David stopped in front of 12 Garneau for another hand-shake and Jonas pulled him in for a hug.

"Easy, fella." David extracted himself from the hug. "I'm sober."

Jonas put his hands on his hips. "What'll we do without this place?"

David Weiss sighed and shrugged and walked up his front steps. He pulled out his keys but didn't need them. The door was unlocked.

87

the national

A WELCOME HOME RAYMOND banner hung on the wall behind Shirley Wong's television. Each letter was printed on a separate piece of white paper and the words were held together with packing tape.

"The professor made it himself," said Jonas, in Madison's ear. "I love him so much."

Madison had just arrived with her parents, and she was already settled into the best spot: between Rajinder and Jonas on the chesterfield. She wanted to hear more about the banner, and the details of his homecoming, but Raymond Terletsky appeared in front of them in a red smoking jacket. He kissed

Madison's hand. "I don't think I've congratulated you yet, have I?"

"Not yet."

"Congratulations!"

"Thanks, Raymond."

"What can I get you from the bar?"

"A water'd be nice."

Raymond bounded away into the kitchen and the senior Weisses followed him. "Coming right up! Icy clean!"

Rajinder leaned forward. "I am no psychologist but . . ."

Jonas swirled his temple. "He's unzipped."

They were all distracted by the start of *The National*'s introductory music. Lines and photographs zipped across the screen. Abby clapped and perched on one of the dining room chairs next to the chesterfield. Shirley and David and Raymond filled the others.

Peter Mansbridge, in that million-dollar voice, introduced tonight's top stories. "And in our magazine . . ."

The residents of the Garneau Block screamed. There it was, the buffalo head. The neighbourhood. Jonas and Madison walking and talking on the block. The university president, a public relations official, the mayor.

Raymond Terletsky stood on Saskatchewan Drive with the gleaming late-afternoon city skyline behind him. At the end of her voice-over, a quick shot of the Toronto producer. "This is a story of tragedy, architecture, animal husbandry, and an historic neighbourhood in one of the most beguiling cities in Canada."

The residents applauded.

"Did you hear that?" said Jonas. "She called us beguiling. She's from Toronto and she didn't patronize us once, even gently."

"That was just the teaser." David looked around. "She has plenty of time to patronize us during the documentary."

The first half of the program concentrated on a federal poll, oil prices, Iran, and Newfoundland, allowing the residents to gather around the dining room table and eat dips and salty snacks. Jonas announced his candidacy for the Liberal Party, which inspired another round of applause. Then Madison dropped her Royal Chinette plate when her father announced he would be the campaign manager.

"What, are you a Liberal now?"

"Really, sweetheart, a Conservative who lives in the city *is* a Liberal." David Weiss seemed to notice all eyes in the room on him. He lifted a triangle of pita and waved it about. "Can't I just be a *man*, without a label?"

In the few minutes remaining before the documentary began, Raymond cajoled them all downstairs to look at the Garneau Block model. He had acquired several toy people to represent his neighbours. "It's not to scale, of course, because Garith is bigger than the cars."

"He's also a zebra," said David.

"So it isn't perfect. But take a good look at the model. Tonight, on *The National*, I have a feeling the university is going to make an announcement. A wonderful announcement."

Shirley shook her head. "What did I tell you about plans and projects?"

"But . . ." Raymond looked down at his hands.

"Did you hear something, Raymond?" Abby picked up the toy Abby, who stood on the lawn of 12 Garneau in a bikini. "Did the university call?"

"I had another *vision* last night." Raymond started back up the stairs.

The rest of the Garneau Block residents cast a final look at the model before following him. Madison was a Strawberry Shortcake with a baby frog glued on to her stomach and Rajinder was a Ken doll who had been shaded with a brown felt pen.

Abby started up the stairs and stopped and turned. "Isn't that a hate crime, the little Rajinder?"

"It may be," said Shirley. "It worries me more that he was playing with the toy people earlier, making them talk."

"It's on! Get up here!"

Everyone hurried upstairs and settled into their seats. The story began with a montage of Edmonton, and a few words about the debt-free provincial government. The surplus, the university, the new mayor, the sprawl, the centennial year, the Garneau Block.

Next came file footage of August 28th, from the site of the Fringe Festival to Benjamin Perlitz leaning out the upstairs window of 10 Garneau. Screams and demands. Nightfall and, eventually, the single shot echoing through the neighbourhood.

String music played.

"I forgot to invite Jeanne," said Shirley. "Damn it."

Following the gunshot, the documentary veered into the past. In 1906, Premier Alexander Rutherford chose river lot five, Isaac Simpson's farm, on the south shore of the North Saskatchewan, to be the site of Alberta's university. Over the course of the twentieth century, the university grew until it overshadowed the adjacent Garneau neighbourhood, named after the fiery, Riel-supporting Métis who first homesteaded the land.

The producer walked through the block at night, lit eerily by the street lanterns, and said, "Some will tell you the ghost of Laurent Garneau still haunts these streets."

Jonas laughed. "Laurent Garneau. That's a made-up name."

"Who told her the ghost stuff?" said Abby.

Raymond raised his hand. "I might have."

Madison was having trouble concentrating on the documentary, which was wholly sympathetic to the Garneau Block. Though she was moved by her father, who became teary-eyed during his interview, when the producer asked what it was like to raise a child around here.

"God damn it, they said they weren't going to use that part," he said, crushing his plastic wine glass.

Madison was having trouble concentrating on the documentary, and on her father's protests, because the baby inside her was executing its first somersault.

88

an alliance of book clubs

Contrary to Raymond's vision, nothing revealed in the CBC documentary about the Garneau Block saved the neighbourhood. University officials stated that if the buffalo head were already on the site, they would reconsider. As there was currently nothing on the land that warranted cultural status, either by the city's or the university's criteria, the Garneau Block would become the Ernie Isley Centre for Veterinary Research by fall 2007.

Which was, by the way, quite a wonderful thing for the city, the province of Alberta, and for meat lovers around the world.

Friends called from all over the country to tell David Weiss they had seen him bawl. The newspaper put him on the front page. Both national papers interviewed him and all the local television outfits came to do their own stories.

During his morning walk with Garith down Whyte Avenue, strangers recognized David. An elderly woman stopped him in front of the Granite Curling Club and told him he was a "real cutie."

One of the men who slouched near Second Cup with a girl who looked to be about twelve, next to a KICK A PUNK FOR A BUCK sign, pointed at him. "Hey, are you the weather guy?"

All of this irritated David. Not only had he been forced to become a Liberal and buy a Toyota, now he was a crybaby. So far he hadn't told any of the media that he didn't mind moving nearly as much as his wife and neighbours.

While Abby and Madison scouted properties in North Glenora and Mill Creek with the real-estate agent, David hid out at home to pack. There was so much to do, as they had to get out of the house and prepare the parents-and-kids spa business for a grand opening in mid-April, but he was frozen. Not bored, but something.

In two hours of packing he filled precisely half a box of paperbacks.

In the office upstairs, underneath shelves of books, was a collection of photo albums. Instead of stacking Saul Bellow next to Margaret Atwood, he flipped through pictures he hadn't looked at in ten years or longer. The first classes he taught at Harry Ainley, with his beard. Family picnics at Emily Murphy Park before his own mother and father died, trips to the mountains, Madison's firsts – birthday, poop in the potty, bathing suit, kitten, tooth, playschool, concussion. Hidden in the drawer of an old armoire, David even found a few suggestive photographs of Abby, taken in the late 1970s.

David was pleased to be alone, as the photographs inspired his second crying fit in a week. His father's straw hat, stained by his father's sweat, made him cry. Two-year-old Madison, with her sand bucket and tiny plastic shovel, made him cry harder. He lay on his back on the upstairs carpet and looked up at the moulded ceiling that would soon twist into rubble and he didn't even bother to wipe the tears.

There was a knock at the door. David hopped up and snuck behind the office door.

Another knock.

Due to an overhang that protected the front porch, David couldn't see who was at the door. So he crept down the stairs and crawled across the living room floor. The wood hurt his knees so he travelled, instead, by modified slither.

Twenty women stood in front of the house, marching to keep warm in the snow.

David went into the bathroom to splash water on his face and pat his eyes dry. Then he straightened his shoulders, cleared his

throat, and opened the front door to a stirring of the crowd. The
moment he appeared before them, the women began to applaud.
They shook their heads and smiled. "We love you!" said one.

"Do you have the right house?"

An attractive black-haired woman nearest him on the
porch, wearing a long purple jacket and a fluffy purple hat,
nodded. "We have the right house, Mr. Weiss."

David noticed each of the women carried an item in her
gloved hands. There was a bucking horse carving, an antique
camera, a woven blanket, a stuffed Richardson's ground squirrel, a tiny rocking chair, a framed map of Edmonton. "Can I
help you?"

"We're an alliance of five book clubs," said the woman in
purple.

"That's great."

"Independent of each other, we were struck by the story on
CBC the other night. And then the newspaper."

"They weren't supposed to show the crying part. I could
take legal action."

"Mr. Weiss, we were all so touched." The woman in purple
adjusted the old teddy bear in her arm and placed her right
hand upon her heart. "Thank you."

Before him, the women applauded again.

"But they weren't supposed to –"

"We decided, in our small way, we had to help you poor
people."

"Actually, the university's giving us ten per cent above
market value for the house and prices are already at a historic
high, so I don't know if poor is the right . . ."

A camera flashed. And another. While he was speaking to the woman in purple, the crowd had grown. Men had arrived. The photographers seemed like professionals, with khaki vests and bland looks on their faces.

Across the street, Rajinder stood on his porch in bare feet. David shrugged at him and said to the woman in purple, "What are you doing here?"

89

mob rule

Madison was making her thirteenth batch of mulled wine when Jeanne Perlitz arrived with flowers. The CBC story had outed Madison as pregnant, and Jeanne wanted to congratulate her. She also wanted to understand what was happening to the neighbourhood and why Rajinder had left nine messages on her answering machine that afternoon. Strangers were packed into the four inhabited houses of the Garneau Block, their collected voices a roar within the walls, and more arrived every minute.

"Who are all these people?" Jeanne had to scream. "What is this?"

Abby took over at the stove so Madison could lead Jeanne into the only empty part of the house – her suite downstairs. Edmontonians in parkas high-fived them on the way. Next door, in Jonas's backyard, upwards of fifty people gathered around the fire. The local urban radio station had set up speakers in the alley, and played a slow R&B song about rumps, a ruckus, and, of course, *making love to you, girl.*

In her tiny living room, Madison caught her breath. "Where's Katie?"

"With my sister. What's going on?"

"They watched the documentary and read the paper. They're here to help."

"Looks and smells to me like they're here to get hammered."

Madison had to sit. In three hours she had cooked ten litres of mulled wine and accepted over two hundred congratulations. Folksy wisdom and clichés abounded. Strangers assured Madison she would be a terrific mom, and smiled coyly as they said having a child would "totally change her life."

The house creaked. On the old couch, Madison wondered if the floors could give out. Jeanne looked up and bit the tip of her pinky finger, evidently wondering the same thing.

"The university says your house doesn't count as a cultural site."

Jeanne sipped the plastic cup of mulled wine Abby had forced upon her. "They're right about that. It's the house where a man died, and that's about all it is."

Madison lay on her side, with a pillow between her legs. "Sorry. I'm just really sore from standing."

"I understand, believe me. Katie was over nine pounds."

"*Vive la France!*"

"Don't buy it when people tell you it's magical. Get the epidural early." Jeanne inspected the photos on Madison's mantel. Two were of Katie. Something happened upstairs that inspired applause. "This is all quite nice but I don't see what any of it has to do with my house."

"A small group of women, in a book club, bought the professor's argument about mythic power."

"Uh-huh."

"So they decided to bring over things that, to them, held mythic power."

"I don't understand what that means."

Jeanne picked up a piece of petrified wood Madison had found on the shore of the North Saskatchewan River when she was a kid. Madison pointed at it. "Like that."

"Wood."

"Wood's just an example."

"I still don't understand."

"The university says they'd build the Ernie Isley Centre somewhere else if the buffalo head was already on your property. There's no time for that, so these people want to make your house into a cultural site now. Today. So that the university might reconsider."

Upstairs, someone started singing "Jingle Bells." Soon it was thunderously loud, and not only in the Weiss house. The entire block reverberated with "Jingle Bells," and when the song stopped it started again.

"All these people brought something?"

"Yep."

"How did they know?"

"Word spread. It was on the six-o'clock news, every channel."

Jeanne sat down again and sighed. "So what am I supposed to do?"

"I don't know. You can either open your house and let these people leave their . . ."

"Wood."

"Or you can say, 'forget it,' and go back home. Take the university's money, move to Buenos Aires, and forget this ever happened."

"I *can't* forget this ever happened. That's my problem, Madison."

"So stop trying. Let the rest of the city help you. Let your house be, I don't know, something."

"It's a bad place."

"Make it a good place again. I remember when it was a good place."

Jeanne slapped her glass of wine on the coffee table. "This is insane." She started up the stairs. "I've told you people I won't do it. And I won't do it!"

The door slammed at the top of the stairs and Madison eased herself up. If she hadn't been pregnant and somewhat queasy from the mulling of wine, she might have chased Jeanne. She might have begged or enlisted her father to squeak out a few tears.

She drew a glass of cold water and peeled a banana. Through every one of her windows, all she could see were feet and legs. Hiking and snow boots. Madison finished her banana and started upstairs to find her father. Outside her door, bodies flowed down the icy concrete walking pad toward the street. Madison stood behind her door, unable to open it.

Finally, as the crowd thinned, she snuck outside. There was Jeanne, on her front porch, surrounded by people, opening the door. Jeanne turned and saw Madison over the sea of heads and she paused. On the verge of a smile, Jeanne turned the key and walked inside. The people followed.

A teenage girl, in a knit toque and puffy down jacket, started past Madison. As she did, the girl opened the lid on her white wooden music box. A tiny ballerina spun to The Blue Danube Waltz.

90

mythic furniture

Rajinder piloted the rented moving truck into a strip mall on Gateway Boulevard. It was an unusually warm December day, with a sweet-smelling wind blowing in from the distant western hills, so Jonas had the window open in the passenger seat. High in the cab of the truck, which came with a CB labelled "Don't Touch," Jonas pretended his can of root beer wasn't diet. He pretended he cussed regularly and had trouble with his little lady back home. *Darlene.*

When Rajinder pulled the key out of the ignition, Jonas hopped out and pretended he was pot-bellied and bowlegged. He cussed quietly about Darlene, who never did the damn dishes.

"Did you hurt yourself?" Rajinder stopped at the entrance to Shangri-La Exotic Home Decor. "And who are you speaking with?"

Jonas walked normally. "It's a political exercise I've invented. Over the course of the election campaign, I want to *inhabit* the voters."

"What does that mean?"

"I've never been a handyman, a mover, a roofer, a digger, a roughneck. I've never been a secretary or an accountant or a housewife. But I have to appeal to all of them."

Rajinder did not seem to know how to respond. He opened the door to Shangri-La and allowed Jonas to lead him to the bookshelves and cabinets. To fully express Edmonton's diversity, they wanted to display the small objects of mythic power on furnishings from around the world. Nordic, yes, but African and Indonesian, too.

This was their fourth trip in the rented moving truck in as many days, as 10 Garneau was to be completed by the weekend. Rajinder and Jonas had moved the Perlitz belongings into storage. Then they had bought lumber, paint, and other building supplies for the volunteer carpenters and designers. Now, Rajinder and Jonas were driving all over the city to buy tables, counters, shelves, and hanging baskets.

The owner of Shangri-La offered them tea, coffee, or hot chocolate while they browsed. But they didn't have time to browse. Jonas chose two cabinets and Rajinder picked two matching bookshelves. They parked at the back of the strip mall and stuffed new items in with other shelves, tables, 1930s stereo boxes, and extended glass display cases.

Back in the van, Rajinder reached out and squeezed Jonas's arm. "Are you Jonas or are you inhabiting a garbage man or somesuch? At this moment?"

"At this moment, Jonas."

"Good. Now, since you are Madison's best friend, this may feel like an imposition or a betrayal of her trust. But please. Tell me. How does she feel about traditions like marriage?"

Rajinder turned out on to the street. Jonas leaned into the passenger door and smiled. "You're blushing, Raj."

"No, I am not."

"You are."

"Remember, I am brown. If I were to blush, it would be invisible to the eyes of a white man. Please, do me the favour of answering the question without drawing undue attention to it."

Jonas crossed his legs and said, "Hmm." It pleased him to torture Rajinder. "Let me see now. Madison, Madison. Marriage, marriage. I know she wanted *me* to get married after the bill passed in the summer, but of course I had no one to marry. Still don't. Never will, most likely. It's hard for someone like me because I'm picky. I don't want to be with a funboy or a homophobe or a German. I can't explain why, but I have an aversion to Germans. And the town of Blackfalds. It's not a word I like to say: Blackfalds. Now Granum, however, is another thing altogether. I like saying Granum. Say it with me, Raj: Granum."

"No. Answer my question."

"Granum, Raj."

"We have a saying in Punjabi: *thusi kalay kuthay kahn.*"

"No. Granum."

"Here you go then: Granum. Please enjoy it."

The sun broke through the clouds and reflected off puddles, concrete, cars and trucks, old hotels, discarded Tim Hortons cups. Both men gasped and reached for sunglasses. "Madison is all for marriage. If the right person asked, she would even convert to Sikhism."

Rajinder smiled. Driving north on 109th Street, past the big church on the right, he shook his head. "That would be unnecessary."

"How are you feeling, Raj, about the pregnant thing? She's getting *huge*. Every time I see her now, all I can think is, Wow. Girl, you definitely had sex."

"The physicality of it is extraordinary. I cannot imagine going through this myself. Men are so very lucky. Our burdens are light."

"Unless you're born fruity."

"Indeed, fruitiness is a heavy thing to carry."

Rajinder pulled into the Garneau Block and, to Jonas's delight, backed on to the sidewalk in front of the Perlitz house. "Beep, beep, beep," said Jonas, in time with the truck. Workers stripping the vinyl siding from the house and donors standing in line with small objects of mythic power parted to make room.

"Hello, good-looking people," said Jonas, to the crowd in front of 10 Garneau.

The good-looking people greeted him. A small group of men hurried across the yard to help carry the furniture inside. Jonas didn't want to lift another heavy item as he had to go door-to-door in the morning with his new red pamphlets. A strained lower back would make him one grumpy Liberal.

Instead of lifting half a table or a bookshelf, Jonas jumped inside the back of the truck and pretended to be a manager. He furrowed his eyebrows and looked at his watch, said, "God damn it," and made disdainful remarks about the volunteers.

To the bald man who prepared to lift one of the Shangri-La cabinets with Rajinder, he said, "Come on, come on. I'm not paying you to pick your nose here."

The man opened his mouth in apparent horror. "Pick my . . . pardon?"

"Please ignore him," said Rajinder. "He is pretending to be a nuisance."

"Oh."

Jonas followed Rajinder down the ramp. "So are you gonna ask Madison to – you know – have a monsoon wedding?"

"Go get a table."

"Well, answer this. Do you know how to build IKEA things?"

Rajinder opened his nostrils.

"It looks easy, Raj, but it's really hard."

"Stop *inhabiting* an imbecile and help us."

Jonas left Rajinder and the bald stranger near the front door of 10 Garneau and returned to the truck, where he accused some volunteers of wasting company time.

91

small objects

In the living room of 10 Garneau, Abby and Madison sat behind two computers. They catalogued each small object of mythic power according to a number, a description, the owner's name, and a sentence about its resonant properties. Raymond Terletsky, who discovered he was born to be a curator, greeted each donor at a small desk in between the kitchen and living room.

"It's a bird," said a tiny, elderly woman. She held the ornamental blue jay in her quivering hands as though it would fly away if given the chance. "A local bird."

Raymond had already written her name – Gladys Poon – and a description of the object. What he had to extract from her was its meaning. "Why is it important to you, and Edmonton?"

"Well," said Gladys Poon. "You see, I feel for it."

He pretended to write that down. "Where did you get the small bird?"

"My husband bought it for me sixty-two years ago. Every year at this time we would put it on top of our Christmas tree."

"Instead of a star?"

"Yes."

"Does Christmas mean a lot to you?"

"I'm Buddhist but I love the lights, giving presents, sharing time with friends and family."

"So the bird . . ."

"The bird has soaked up sixty-two Christmases in our house. My husband has passed now, and the children have their own families, their own children and grandchildren. The bird is not lovely enough for any of their Christmas trees."

Raymond lifted his pen in triumph. "Soaked up sixty-two Buddhist Christmases in the house of Gladys Poon."

"Arthur and Gladys Poon, if you please."

Raymond made the adjustment and took the bird. He

shook the tiny hand of Gladys Poon and guided her to the door. "I thank you, Mrs. Poon, and the entire city thanks you."

"You're very welcome."

Abby and Madison looked up from their computer monitors to say, in tandem, "Thank you, Mrs. Poon!"

As the volunteer greeter helped Mrs. Poon out of 10 Garneau, Raymond tore the sheet out of his ninth notepad and placed it in the in-tray of the Weiss women. He took the blue jay's sticky number, 9012, and pasted the number to its underside. The bird would either sit on one of the shelves with its sentence of resonant properties or wait in the storage area downstairs for its two weeks on display.

Raymond's job as curator was becoming increasingly difficult. More and more Edmontonians were lining up with their objects of mythic power, and the house was beginning to feel small. The university president and her entourage would arrive for a tour of 10 Garneau on the eighteenth of December, so between now and then Raymond had to decide on an opening exhibit. The collection of items had to represent the whole of Edmonton, its history and its contemporary social and political culture, the peculiarities of its people. The Great Spirit had to be perfect, even though it would lack the buffalo head – for now.

The bird would stay upstairs.

Screaming electric saws and twenty hammers, multiple footsteps on the second floor, the echoing voices of men and women, filled the house. Each room had to be transformed into a gallery space. Due to an odd confluence of noise just as the next donor entered, Raymond had to introduce himself with a scream. He was so accustomed to this ritual that he hardly noticed the man before him, with a copy of Henry Kreisel's *The Betrayal* in a gloved hand, was Dean Kesterman.

Dean Kesterman removed his right glove and offered forth the novel. "Signed first edition," he said.

"Do you have a moment to sit down, Dean?" Raymond pointed at the chair. "We have a bit of a formal process here. How long were you waiting?"

"An hour and a half, two hours. But there's a musician out there singing and playing guitar, and a woman gave us coffee and puffed wheat squares. I'm a little bit jumpy."

Raymond numbered the book and wrote the Dean's name. He tried his best not to appear nervous or shameful. "You think we have a chance here?"

"Not a hope in hell."

"You're wrong."

"Between you and me, certain people are whispering there are better places for the Isley Centre. But they aren't the right people."

Raymond enunciated. "I need a sentence from you that explains the resonance of your object."

"I hardly need to defend a Henry Kreisel first edition."

"It's part of what we're doing here."

The Dean removed his hat and scratched his temple. "Let's see. Expert use of the North Saskatchewan River as symbol. An urban Edmonton novel with elements of the immigrant experience, which is really the Canadian experience. The death camps —"

"Sorry, Dean, Not good enough."

Dean Kesterman sat up in his chair. "Well. Well, I didn't know I was going to be *judged.*"

"How about a quotation?"

"That's what I'm trying to give you, Raymond."

"No, a quotation from the novel. Do you remember what it's about?"

"Of course I do!"

Raymond assured the Dean he would take care of it, and escorted him to the door. In tandem, Abby and Madison looked up from their computer monitors to say, "Thank you, Dr. Kesterman!"

The volunteers led two tubby and nervous adolescent boys into the house. Raymond stood in front of the picture window and surveyed the scene before him. Workers putting a new facade on 10 Garneau. A seemingly endless line of donors. Three women and a man behind a table borrowed from the community hall, brewing coffee and singing along with the guitarist. Beyond them all, his house across the street, *his house again*, the warmest place in the world.

92

fitfamily

The floor of the abandoned health club was strewn with dust, glass, Molson Canadian cans, Burger King detritus, nails and screws, and smashed fluorescent light tubes. It looked to David as though a coil of human feces had been left on the boot mat in the entrance.

"What is that?" Abby looked down at the coiler.

"Just keep walking, honey."

"It didn't look like the Hell's Angels clubhouse a month ago."

David found the rest of the lights and the health club, 20,000 square feet in a strip mall south of Bonnie Doon, buzzed alive. The white tile floor threatened to burn David's retinas. "Do you have the equipment list? We better make sure when they cleaned up they didn't *clean up*."

Still dazed by the sight of the coiler, Abby waved a faxed sheet of paper and approached a stairclimber. She plugged the machine into the wall and began stepping. The machine whirred. "Hooray."

David plugged in a bank of stationary bicycles and elliptical trainers. "These work too."

They inspected the machines, counted the barbells, and met in the middle of the room. Abby buried her face in David's shirt. "Can we hire people to clean this place?"

"Absolutely not."

For the next hour they explored the club and strategized. They drew crude plans and, finally, swept the floor. Abby unplugged the machines and David turned out the lights. In the Prius, fear struck David like a bout of food poisoning. "What if we've done the wrong thing?"

"We haven't."

"How can we move out of our house and build FitFamily at the same time?"

"We'll find a way." Abby reached over and scratched the back of David's head. Her voice took on that authoritative yet reasonable tone, that new tone. "Flabby locals, with their under-stimulated children, need us so badly. The engines of capitalism must be stoked."

David shook his head and parroted her: The engines of capitalism must be stoked. As much as he understood the professor's oddly chaste dalliances with younger women, at least once every day David Weiss congratulated himself for marrying Abby and never needing younger, dumber, less beautiful women to satisfy . . . what?

They crossed the Whyte Avenue bridge over the Mill Creek Ravine and snaked through the east Strathcona neighbourhoods. The houses for sale were the same houses for sale a week previous, $350,000 dumps rented out to stoners who didn't shovel the snow off their sidewalks. David was about to criticize the prices, the houses, and the stoners who lived in them when Abby did it for him.

"Vancouver East."

David waited to turn back on to Whyte. The street lamp glow highlighted his wife's pretty face. "I am so lucky."

"And don't you forget it."

"Is the Perlitz house going to be ready?"

Abby smiled. "Even if the whole block has to work all night on Friday."

"I'm not letting Madison stay up a moment after midnight." David was curious about his daughter and Rajinder, as they were spending time together again, but he was afraid to ask Madison. Since she became an adult, David had taken a *let her tell me if she wants to tell me* approach to parenting. "Has she said anything about Rajinder?"

"Not a thing."

"Are they?"

"I don't know, David."

"She'll tell us when she's ready. She'll do that, right? Tell us?"

"The girl's six months pregnant. It would certainly be a bizarre courtship. I just hope she doesn't get her hopes up and, you know."

David started north toward the block. "It's not so bad, getting your hopes up. What's the alternative?"

Every night for five nights it had been the same; they accepted objects of mythic power until 10:00 p.m. and then sent everyone away with a goody bag of puffed wheat squares and a tiny plastic container of hummus. Few, if any, people complained.

Environment Canada was saying a genuine blast of winter weather was on the way, but David couldn't feel it. Neither could the dancing crowds in front of 10 Garneau. One of the Sugarbowl DJs had set up on the newly painted porch, designed to look straight out of 1905, and played music that sounded to David like it ought to be a cartoon soundtrack.

Abby had already gone inside 10 Garneau so David pulled his hood over his head and walked and danced among the Edmontonians in the lineup, hoping to learn a thing or two about voter sentiment. To his disappointment, no one talked about politics.

Near the front of the line David almost walked right into Barry Strongman. Barry held a small medicine pouch in his hand

and stared straight ahead with a satisfied smile. An assistant was on a little silver cellular phone, waving his arms and frowning.

In his suit and wool overcoat, Barry Strongman looked calm and confident. He held the medicine pouch with great care. Standing in soft snow in the middle of the lawn, David's next instinct – to hide behind a spruce tree and whip a snowball at the back of Barry Strongman's head – faded into something like pride.

93

the symphony orchestra

The violins rose, danced with one another, and then, after a dramatic silence and a mournful plea by the concert master, faded into an echo. It had been so good, so pure and perfect and insightful, Madison couldn't help herself. She clapped. Even when it was clear she was the only person in the Winspear Centre clapping, it took a few stern messages from her brain to stop her hands.

Rajinder spoke into her ear. "Most people do not clap between movements."

"Why?"

He paused for a moment. "I do not know. It is an old European tradition I suppose. You save all clapping for the end." Rajinder opened the program and showed Madison the Mozart concerto was split into three parts – Allegro aperto, Adagio, and Tempo di Menuetto.

"Whoops."

The conductor and musicians prepared to begin again. "How could you have known? This is your first time." Rajinder leaned close and said into her ear again, "So, do you like the symphony?"

"I've wasted so many nights watching TV when I could have been here."

The violins started anew. Someone nearby in the VIP seats said, "Shush," so they shushed.

Madison had not looked forward to her night at the symphony. She wasn't permitted by her mother or by Rajinder to say this aloud, but she felt like a rhinoceros in her stretchy black dress. Since she was always tired, she also worried about falling asleep. But this was a special night for Rajinder, as he was surrendering his anonymous status and becoming a named patron of the arts. Madison knew it made him anxious and she didn't want him to be alone.

Now that she understood, Madison saw it would be impossible to fall asleep at the symphony. This was not like sitting at home with the newspaper or cleaning the kitchen while listening to the Kronos Quartet. While the musicians played, Madison dreamed with her eyes open. And her dreams were so vivid she wondered if it was all a hormonal fluke or if someone in the lobby had slipped a tab of acid into her Perrier.

At the end of the Tempo di Menuetto, Madison joined the rest of the Winspear Centre in clapping. Someone in the floor seats even said, "Woo!"

The public "Woo!" had always vexed Madison. Was the woo designed to make the artists feel good about themselves and their performance, or was it really all about the woo-er drawing attention to him or herself? It vexed Madison further that she thought up all her best Psychology 101 essay topics fourteen years after taking the course.

The conductor left the stage while the musicians prepared for the final concerto. For the twentieth time that evening, Rajinder leaned over and asked Madison if she was feeling all right. His eyes flashed down at her belly, just as everyone's eyes flashed down at her belly.

What did Rajinder think when he considered her belly? Madison hoped he saw *her baby*, not the baby of Jean-something. With her brain properly stimulated by Mozart, she hoped Rajinder would one day see it as *their baby*. If humans can design violins and write concertos and build halls like this, surely they can forget about Jean-something. She took Rajinder's hand. "How are you feeling?"

"Apprehensive," he said.

The composer-in-residence of the orchestra, a sinewy middle-aged woman in a shiny blue dress, stepped out. The loud *clack* of her heels on the stage seemed to embarrass her, so she hurried.

At the podium, the composer introduced herself. Nancy Barislawski. From Philadelphia, originally. She looked to her right, to the box where Rajinder and Madison sat, and talked about being summoned to the thirty-eighth floor of Manulife Place. She talked about 10 Garneau and Rajinder Chana's impossible request. To design a concerto that said everything there was to say about the mythic power of Edmonton. In a month!

Nancy shrank from Rajinder in mock-terror and went on to say how much she enjoyed the impossible project, and how she hoped it would help restore the neighbourhood to its true owners. The audience applauded politely and Nancy introduced Rajinder. She asked him to stand and then she asked his fiancée and Garneau Block neighbour Madison Weiss to stand as well.

Fiancée? The word, its French threat, hung before Madison like a flock of red bats. Rajinder turned and gripped her hand. "I am sorry."

"No. It's . . ." Madison sat down, her cheeks on fire.

"A mistake. A mistake. I will fix it." Rajinder, still standing, waved at Nancy Barislawski. She stopped talking about the music everyone was about to hear and turned to Rajinder. "Excuse me," he said. "But Madison is not my fiancée."

Nancy Barislawski opened her mouth and squinted.

"She is only my girlfriend thus far."

"Oh, I apologize," said Nancy.

She seemed prepared to continue discussing the concerto of mythic power when someone below them, perhaps the woo-er, said, "Thus far? What does that mean?"

Rajinder didn't seem to know if he should respond. "I mean she is my girlfriend currently. But someday, perhaps, if she feels like we can maybe . . ."

"Are you waiting for a full moon or something?"

Madison wanted to crawl under her seat. On stage, Nancy Barislawski shifted her weight from one high-heeled shoe to the other. Someone in the balcony yelled, "Go on, ask her, already."

"That girl looks ready to me," said a gentleman with a Slavic accent.

"Woo!" said the woo-er.

Rajinder shook his head. Madison pulled on his arm, wanting him to sit down and save himself from this, but he appeared to feel obliged. He addressed the crowd: "What if we would prefer to do it alone?"

A woman called out, "You got a ring, kid?"

"I do happen to have a ring, yes."

The audience erupted in applause. Several woo-ers joined in. Rajinder looked down at Madison again and shook his head. "This must be horribly awkward for you."

It was and wasn't. Aside from the afternoon talk-show spectacle of the thing, Madison was comforted by members of the audience saying what she herself felt. Ask her, propose, woo. Rajinder went down on one knee, pulled out a small jewellery box and said, "Will you?"

"Will I what?" Madison bit her finger.

"Marry?"

The orchestra broke out in a quick, impromptu "Here Comes the Bride" as Madison nodded.

Once Madison and Rajinder were in their seats holding hands, their hearts unified in dangerous velocity, and everyone had stopped clapping and laughing, Nancy lifted the microphone again. "Upstage city. Sheesh. I only wrote a *concerto* here."

94

the terletsky-wongs

At four in the morning, Raymond Terletsky and Shirley Wong locked 10 Garneau. The winter storm was finally blowing in. Raymond's lower back was so sore from bending and standing he leaned on his wife as they crossed the street.

"Get off."

Raymond took a step away and slipped on the new sidewalk ice. He landed hard on his tailbone and sat there as Shirley continued to the front door. She opened it and turned.

"You coming?"

Instead of rolling on to his hands and knees and standing, Raymond lay back to watch the snow fall in whorls above his head. From his spot on the sidewalk, Raymond heard a sigh. Shirley started back down the steps and through the snow. She held a hand out for Raymond and helped him up. "You look like hell."

"I feel like hell."

After almost two weeks of cataloguing and curating the rotating exhibit that would be the modified Great Spirit, Raymond felt as though he ought to sleep until Christmas. The president and the mayor would come by in just a few hours, at noon, and Raymond might have done more – touched up the paint, polished the wood floors – but in his fatigue he was in danger of ruining something.

He followed Shirley toward his front door. On the porch Raymond turned and looked back at 10 Garneau. In the front yard, lit by the street lamps but obscured by the snow, stood the man with the buffalo head. Raymond had not seen Death since Halloween night, and had certainly wondered what had become of him. Unless the man with the buffalo head wasn't Death at all. Raymond waved to the man with the buffalo head.

As he stepped inside, Shirley handed Raymond a snifter of cognac. He cradled it. "Thank you, darling."

"Get your shoes off and sit down. When's the last time you really sat down?"

"In prison, I suppose." Raymond flopped on the couch.

Shirley turned out all the lights except those on the Christmas tree. She sat next to Raymond on the couch. "We're going to have to figure out what to do when the kids show up."

"What do you mean?"

"I mean the bedroom situation. The 'no touching' rule."

Raymond sipped the cognac. It was difficult to form words. "Your choice, darling. I wait anxiously for permission to touch you again."

"I pushed all the houses off the model downstairs the other day when I was mad at you. It's a ping-pong table. All it needs is a net."

"Ping-pong," said Raymond.

"It's difficult for me to say this but I'm proud of you. The house really does look like a museum, or something. It speaks."

The man with the buffalo head stood in the living room now, next to the Christmas tree. The sight of him did not startle

Raymond but he didn't want Shirley to see the man with the buffalo head and get the wrong idea.

"You can go now," he said, barely above a whisper. "I don't need you."

Shirley turned to Raymond. "What?"

"Talking to myself."

Raymond ignored the man with the buffalo head and, after a snort or two, the man turned and disappeared. Then Raymond reached down, took his wife's feet, and lifted them on to his lap; he didn't know why there were three bottles of peppermint foot rub underneath various coffee tables, and he didn't think he wanted to know why. But he reached for one and opened the top.

"You're breaking rule number one," said Shirley.

He removed his wife's socks and warmed the cream in his hands. From his own massages, Raymond knew a thing or two. He started with long strokes and gentle yet concentrated circles. He separated her toes and massaged between them. After a while he sneaked up her ankles, but not too far.

"What am I going to do with you, Raymond?" Shirley's voice wasn't much more than breath. She lay back on the couch with her eyes closed.

Raymond turned to see if the man with the buffalo head was gone for good, and he was. "Maybe we could go on dates once in a while. See a few more Oilers games, go watch *A Christmas Carol*."

"You're bored at hockey games and you hate Charles Dickens."

"That was the old Raymond."

Shirley smiled. "That's the way gamblers and addicts talk."

Even though he risked falling asleep on the floor, Raymond lowered himself on to his knees and crawled so he could rest his head on his wife's chest. "How many times can I say I'm sorry? You have to let me prove myself. These rules . . . they'll drive us both crazy."

"That foot massage was nice. I like foot massages."

"It's a risk, right? If you trust me again and I'm good, the last thirty years of our lives together can be romantic and exciting. If you treat me like a mentally handicapped roommate, well, I don't see much of a future for us."

His wife's eyes were closed.

In a few days, their children would arrive at home and he would be Dad again, in his sweater and slippers. The man who carves the turkey and fills up everyone's glass of wine and stuffs the stockings hanging on the fireplace. For hours he would sit with them and listen to their new stories of social triumph because his son and daughter were the sorts of people who were unembarrassed to tell stories of social triumph. Maybe his children were boors. Maybe he was a boor and they were boors by default.

There was nothing he could do about it now but love them. Let them see their own ghosts. Of course, he could always take the boy aside and warn him about propositioning massage therapists.

Shirley was asleep. With his head rising and falling with her chest he listened to the soft breaths of the fragile being that was his wife and hoped she would live forever. Then he carried her to bed.

95

the last jog

Rajinder was so adorable in his black tights Madison wanted to get down on her knees and take a bite out of his thigh. "Like this?" he said, as he stretched his calves against the mountain ash tree in front of her parents' house.

"Perfect."

A clean new blanket of snow covered the block. It hung heavily on the trees and roofs, and hid gutter sand. It was two hours before the mayor and the university president were due to arrive and, in the sunshine, 10 Garneau looked like an advertisement for northern living. Madison had gone to bed early the night before so she hadn't seen the finished project. But she didn't want to spoil the new snow for a peek into the window.

"Remember, we must talk the whole time." Rajinder jogged on the spot and pointed at her. In the four days since their engagement, Madison had been moving everything important out of her parents' basement and into his house across the street. Before they went to sleep every night, Rajinder flipped through her pregnancy books and one of his own: *The Expectant Father.* "If you cannot speak normally, you are exercising too hard."

"Yes, sir."

Madison was too far along to jog, really, so she planned to walk quickly while Rajinder ran. It was difficult to stretch. Her parents' front door opened and Jonas Pond and David Weiss walked out on to the porch in black suits. Garith was with them, in his white knitted jacket and hat.

Jonas hurried down to Madison and Rajinder and pulled one of his pamphlets out of the satchel. "You know where we're going right now? Door-knocking."

"Best of luck to you, my friend." Rajinder shook his hand. "You have my vote."

"That's one," said David Weiss.

"You look nice, Dad."

"I know. Not nearly as nice as my future son-in-law, though, in his superhero tights. The Stinking Rich Hornet."

A shudder went through Madison. Now that they were engaged, soon to be married, it was perfectly acceptable to mock Rajinder. Once in a while, she knew, her father would say something inappropriate. Later this afternoon, after the mayor and university president visited 10 Garneau, she vowed to take her father aside and talk to him about that.

Across the street, Raymond Terletsky appeared in a snow-mobile suit and a giant Russian fur hat. He held a shovel over his head. "If they say no today, one of these," he said, and swung the giant aluminum shovel through the air. "Just joking!"

It was not funny. It was so not funny that Madison started her quick-walk out of the block. Rajinder trailed behind, and turned to wish Jonas good luck.

The men of the Garneau Block cheered like football players. As she turned right toward Saskatchewan Drive, Madison amused herself by imagining them in a huddle.

At the top of the stairs leading down to the river valley trails, Madison paused. "What happens if they say no?"

Rajinder, already out of breath, shook his head. "We move somewhere else."

"They won't say no, will they?"

"The business case for saying no is very strong."

Madison started down the stairs. The extra twenty-two pounds were most noticeable on stairs. "You should be very proud, for everything you did. Tried to do."

Fifteen or twenty stairs later, Rajinder whispered thanks. Then he stopped Madison and kissed her. "I am unconditionally happy. For the first time since my parents died."

"I'm happy too."

"Well. What else is there?"

Down the remainder of the stairs and on to the snowy path, Madison answered the question in silence. Money, air quality, Down syndrome, drinking and driving, nuclear proliferation, global poverty, new country music, climate change, semi-automatic weapons, fundamentalism, declining oil reserves, cancer, crime, crack cocaine, reality television, being forced out of your house, veterinary medicine.

Yet there was also the soft skin at the back of Rajinder's neck. The way he ate breakfast and read the newspaper wearing slippers with his suit. Two mornings ago, on her birthday, her millionaire fiancé did not buy her a present; instead, he sat at his piano and sang an Edith Piaf song. There was the modest altar to his parents upstairs, with photographs and his father's turban, his mother's favourite sari. How about the new pregnancy yoga DVD he bought and followed with her in his basement? How about crisp winter days leading to the gush of spring? Abby and

David and haiku, mythic power, hummingbirds, the promise of travel? A baby?

Twice Rajinder had to stop. He was not a jogger. On the east side of the Kinsmen Centre, he bent over to catch his breath.

As she watched him, Madison worried, for a moment, about losing all of this. She worried their happiness would not last. They would get old and their feelings for one another would change. The cool wind on a Saturday in December would carry no pleasures, no simple mysteries.

Rajinder stood up straight and surveyed the path before them. Then he took her hand and kissed it. "What?"

Madison smiled. "Nothing," she said, and they walked deeper into the valley.

Acknowledgements

Thank you to my extraordinarily smart editor, Jennifer Lambert. Thank you to Ellen Seligman and all the other fine people at McClelland and Stewart.

Thank you to my brave and supportive patrons at the *Edmonton Journal*, where this book had its first life as a daily serial – Linda Hughes, Allan Mayer, Barb Wilkinson, Peter Maser, Roy Wood, and my other extraordinarily smart editor, Shawn Ohler.

Thank you to Edmonton. My original plan was to thank the small army of e-mail correspondents who followed *The Garneau Block* in the newspaper. People like Pete Gasper, Darka Tarnawsky, Dean McKenzie, and Annie Dugan. But the list was becoming very, very listy. Thank you, all of you, just the same.

Thank you to David Robinson at *The Scotsman*, and to the great Alexander McCall Smith for reading, and liking, an early draft.

Thank you to Gina Loewen, Avia Babiak, and all my other informal researchers: Shirley Schipper for the medical advice, Duncan Purvis and Tami Friesen for legal concerns, Karine Germann-Gibbings for *les corrections*, Kirk Babiak for information about hunting pronghorn, Nola Babiak for tips on mothering.

Thank you to Anne McDermid and Martha Magor for seeing the potential in this, and in me.